SURVIVING JOE TASKERMAN

DAVID GOLDING

DAVID GOLDING

First published in Great Britain in 2022 by Riverhead

A CIP catalogue record for this book is
available from the British Library

ISBN 978-1-9164294-7-5

Design and Production by Riverhead, Hull
Telephone: 07890 170063
email: mike.riverheadbooks@gmail.com

Printed by: Fisk Printers, Hull

FRONT COVER PHOTOGRAPH:
Downstream by Val Walker

CONTENTS

FRIDAY

1

TRAVELLING LIGHT

As the week staggered through Friday afternoon towards the holiday weekend, Ivan K Driver had no idea that he was about to kill Joe Taskerman. And no idea that with him would be buried the myth of great leaders upon which history is based and the future foretold.

'That's me she's talking about. She's telling the story because I couldn't do it myself. Is she reliable? We shall see. For now let's just say that she's right, I didn't know. I couldn't have known. I wouldn't have wanted to know. At that moment I wanted only to turn my back on the window that looked out onto the main gates.'

Turning from the window, Ivan shivered and clenched his shoulders. He had seen a large brown rat. It had run along the channel at the edge of the yard and disappeared into the finishing bay. He was puzzled. The gates were open but there was no one in sight, and this was supposed to be the busiest time of the week.

With a shrug he strode across the room towards the desk. In his haste he caught the edge of a folder sending it spinning through the air. He threw out a hand instinctively, but he was too late to prevent the contents from scattering across the floor. Leaving the folder and its contents where they lay, he allowed his legs to collapse from under him and sat down more heavily than intended.

Easing his position on the chair, he once more began checking the figures on the papers in front of him against those on the screen to his right. But he lost his place as his eyes overran the speed at which he could take in the information.

'Not so fast,' said a voice in his ear, reminding him that although hurrying may hasten his arrival it wouldn't tell him where he was going.

'If I knew where I was going, I wouldn't go,' he said.

'If you knew where you were going you wouldn't want to,' said the voice in his ear.

Ivan knew he was subject to a chain of command and would have to live with pressure from above. He knew that increasing targets were to be expected when output became the agent of progress. And he knew the imposition of those targets would make for uncomfortable times. More recently there had been questions as why it had to be so, but for now he could think only of how each tick of the fingers on his white-faced watch took him closer to a release from all that.

Biting heavily on the pencil that had strayed between the rows of grinding teeth dissipating his frustration, there was a crunch as a mixture of graphite and splinters ran around the edges of his tongue. He spat the disgusting cocktail across the papers on the desk and slowly wiped the back of his hand along his chin.

For the ninth time in a minute and a half he looked at his watch without noting the time. Then hauling himself from the chair he went across to the window, from where he could see that loading had resumed. With a sigh of relief, he went back to complete another line of figures, looking to his right for confirmation from the screen before checking once more the papers on the desk. Whilst the fingers of his watch ticked on, heedless of the task and oblivious to his condition.

Manufacturing may have been in decline, but Ivan knew it was still the engine of the economy. He knew too that there was always a sense of urgency on the day before a long weekend and this had been one of the busiest days he could remember. Having been running at full speed all week there was little he could do but chew on his pencil and wait for the final figures to arrive, before he could sign them off and say goodbye to another week of rushing around at the beck and call of a man who thought that being in charge meant you had to beat and bore the brains out of everyone who crossed your path.

The demand for high-tech components in a competitive market meant that a reliable supply chain was vital, but just-in-time had a different meaning for Joe Taskerman. His sole concern was to ensure that everything in sight was despatched. It would enhance his figures at the end of the week and returning a good set of figures was the one thing that mattered to him.

Ivan knew Joe Taskerman wasn't the only problem. He just happened to be the one irritating piece in the jigsaw he had to live with every day. Of course, he could leave, as anyone could. But where would he go? To another Joe Taskerman or woman doing their best to produce higher returns from less and less, whilst inflicting misery on everyone else. And since more and more people were forced into as many part time jobs as they could get, he had to be grateful for having a full time job, which at least didn't require him to work in a call centre.

His screen went blank for a moment, but the relief was short lived as a touch on the space bar restored a picture of the afternoon's progress. Which was less than he'd thought. Seeking a change of subject, he stared at the poster above Heather's desk. Hair of that colour in a man always made him smile. If he'd been of a later generation, perhaps he too would have had a ring in his nose by now, although at that moment it wasn't the piercing of his own body he was contemplating.

He wondered when the weekend was going to get a move on and put an end to his misery. If only he could be somewhere else. He knew the only thing preventing him from leaving, was his responsibility to the figures on the screen. His dependability was one of his finest qualities. That was why Joe Taskerman was able to take advantage of him, such that flying out of the window whilst awaiting screen updates had become a means of escape.

'Right now I'm with Rowena on a beach ordering drinks… now I'm with my Grandfather picking strawberries in his garden… and now I'm back, without any contribution to global warming and no carbon off-set required. I went and I returned in the blinking of an eye, and you didn't even notice that I'd gone.'

It was true that once you'd realised how easy it was to transport yourself to another place and time there were few limitations. Open or closed you could fly out of a window any time you liked… to a place where weekends began as soon as you began to think about them. It didn't require knowledge of quantum theory to be attuned to the possibility of being in two places at once. And it was more fun than social networking no matter how great your friends were. There was no need for anyone to be a passive receiver. Even the most hesitant could absent themselves and fly off to wherever their fancy took them… to the hills or the sea, where the heat of the sun and the cool of the breeze were in harmony.

'Unlike ourselves and Joe Taskerman,' he muttered.

The question of what to do about Joe Taskerman had been on everyone's mind. Ivan had often threatened to strangle him. Many people had. It was how they retained their sanity. Joe Taskerman had been sent to his grave in a kaleidoscope of colourful endings. And yet there he still was. At the top of the pyramid. Or so he thought, for the strange thing about pyramids was that no matter how high you climbed there was always someone above you.

Someone above him or not, Ivan looked forward to spending a whole three days without having to think about Joe Taskerman. Were it not that one of the downsides of being in two places at once meant that browbeaters could come in through your window just as easily as you were able to fly out. Still, the appearance of an ogre like Joe Taskerman at your window might be regrettable, but there was still a lot to be said for flying through windows; travelling incognito; flying off here; dropping in there; mapping the future; revisiting the past. Getting away was easy. Staying put was the difficult thing to do once you'd realised you could go anywhere you liked in the blinking of an eye.

A telephone rang and picking up the receiver he waited for a voice to tell him he'd won the weekly prize draw. But it was an enquiry as to whether he'd heard the news. Archie's wife had died.

'Oh no.' Archie, who had been ill for some time, had himself died only a month ago. Many were convinced that given the nature of his illness it must have been the plant that had made Archie ill, but the company had said they had no proof, and the health and safety inspector had been interested only in approving the size of his bacon sandwich. The results of the screening were due on Wednesday and there might then be more evidence. In the meantime, awaiting the results, most people's attention was upon hoping it wouldn't be their turn next. As for Archie's wife, Ivan had seen Dorothy only last weekend. She had looked so well he'd thought she was beginning to recover from the shock. Now that was not to be. Poor Trevor. Trevor was their son, and he would be devastated.

Stretching his legs beneath the desk, Ivan winced as his ankle caught the edge of the filing cabinet beyond. The filing cabinet was unmoved. The filing cabinet had been there longer than either Ivan or Joe Taskerman, and it would be there when they'd gone. It had been a witness to so much and would see a great deal more. Perhaps that was why it squealed when you opened a drawer.

Screwing up a sheet of paper from the desk he tossed it into the air and fired an elastic band in its direction, missing the target by yards. But then with an admirable sense of timing a mug of tea arrived, brought by Nigel from the floor below. Thank goodness someone looked after him when Heather was away. It had been quiet without Heather today. She would be in Sicily by now.

'I brought you some cake,' said Nigel. 'It's Gordon's birthday today. Thought you might like a piece. Sad about Archie's wife.'

Ivan devoured the cake and swilled down the tea. Then he went over to the window where he saw that another load was on its way. Returning to check the screen he uttered an expletive as he stood on a pencil that had fallen from the desk. Now he really did need to be somewhere else but any thoughts of that were interrupted when again a telephone rang. This time it was his mobile, which he chose to ignore. He guessed it would have been Rowena wondering what was keeping him... or Roland asking whether he would be joining them in the pub later... or Joanna enquiring as to what time they would be arriving on Sunday. None of those were questions he would have been able to answer.

By the time the last of the figures had appeared on the screen there had been so many journeys to and from the window and so many broken and re-sharpened pencils, that all he could do was slump in the chair having exhausted his capacity for enjoyment of the release he'd been anticipating all afternoon.

It was a cruel twist of fate that left him sitting there once it was no longer necessary, but it didn't last, and he soon summoned the strength to raise his body from the chair. Now he could turn his back on the scene of the week's torments and walk away... away from the lines of figures on the screen; away from the papers on the desk; away from the folder and its contents still lying on the floor; and away, away, away from the window that had been a reminder of his misery for so long. Pausing only to confirm the letter he'd been handed was still lying unopened on the desk, he raised a scurrilous but triumphant finger in the air, and with one quick movement made his exit from the room.

His elation was short lived, because within a few minutes he was in a queue waiting to enter the stream of traffic coming from the right. Someone muttered that it might have been quicker to walk, reminding him that he was not the only occupant of the car. Philosophers might question the use of the term occupant, but that is what philosophers are meant to do. Should the term occupant, or could the term occupant be said to reflect the nature of the three characters sharing his car? Ivan had no such questions. He knew they were sharing much more than his car.

'This car is noisy,' said a voice from the rear, being that of Owen, speaking with sufficient edge as to suggest it might not be a genuine complaint.

'Noisy?' said Bernard, taking the matter entirely at face value. 'This is one of the quietest cars on the road.'

'Perhaps he was referring to the fact that someone had started the engine,' said Henry.

'You have to start the engine,' said Bernard. 'Unless you only want to use the car as a conservatory.'

'The benefits of conservatories are overrated,' said Henry.

'I wouldn't have said the Moscow Conservatory was overrated,' said Bernard. 'Especially when you consider that Sergei Rachmaninov is still around... er if you see what I mean.'

'What is he talking about?' said Owen.

'You can't expect him to know that,' said Henry.

'Pillock,' yelled Ivan when a mud-stained van cut in front of him as he joined the traffic on the ring road. Owen suggested the roads would be a good deal safer if some vehicles were used only as conservatories.

Ivan had no difficulty in agreeing with that. He'd already become more agitated than he'd been at the start of the journey. And now he was hanging onto the steering wheel with a grip he'd not known since clinging to the underside of that bridge before falling into the river all those years ago. He cursed the dryness in his throat. He cursed the tightness in his chest. He cursed the fires that were threatening to burn through the lining of his stomach. Until no longer able to contain himself he began hammering his fists on the steering wheel.

From the corner of his eye, he saw that he was being observed now that the main stream of traffic had come to a standstill. He gave a taut smile to the man in the car beside him, which did little to curtail the burning within.

'Arrgh,' again he hammered his fists on the steering wheel without regard for its effect on the man to his right. Such was his anguish that he was in danger of yielding to the temptation to leap from the car, take off his clothes and run naked along the roofs of the vehicles in front of him. He shuddered to think of what Rowena would say to that.

('Exhibitionism doesn't become you?')

'*It wouldn't be the first time I'd taken my clothes off in front of strangers.*'

Sufficient reason there may have been, but Ivan had not been in the habit of taking off his clothes with an audience of more than one after exiting the school changing rooms for the last time.

He was saved from the ignominy of revealing his body to the world when the traffic began to move again, there having been no obvious explanation for the hold up; no road works; no lower speed restrictions; no damaged vehicles to be seen; the only sure thing being that the carriageway must have been designed with a lower volume of traffic in mind. And yet to everyone's relief this being a relief road they were on the move again, racing along the far from open road – in Ivan's case it being his mind rather than the car that was racing, to neither his relief nor his surprise.

'Has it not occurred to you that with or without good reason Joe Taskerman may have decided to make you redundant,' said a voice with which he was all too familiar. He'd been trying not to dwell on the subject, but he had to concede it was seldom far from his mind. As for having good reason, Joe Taskerman had never considered it necessary to justify anything he'd done. Ivan could think of no one more sure of themselves whilst being so far out of their depth. Perhaps the letter he'd left unopened on his desk had been informing him of his redundancy. But the subject of the letter would have to wait because now the traffic had slowed to a crawl again, leaving him with little to do but control his emotions by counting the number of fingers that were impatiently tapping the steering wheel. 'One-two-three-four-five...'

Flashing his lights at a brightly coloured motorcyclist, enabling him to enter the stream of traffic, he thought someone ought to quantify the amount of time that had been wasted before deciding to build a ring road around the town. Twenty years too late. Not least because so much additional traffic had been generated, that now the evening paper was full of letters demanding a by-pass to relieve pressure on the ring road. It seemed everyone was an expert in traffic management, though it seldom turned out that way. No one had been able to predict the effect of road improvements on volumes of traffic – just as no one had been able to solve the age-old puzzle of why the chicken had crossed the bleeding road in the first place. Unless it had been to avoid bumping into Joe Taskerman. He paused for a moment to consider who was going to answer these questions. Was anybody listening? Certainly not the lone policeman covering for the failed traffic lights at the junction where Ivan left the ring road, who could hardly hear anything above all the noise.

By the time Ivan turned into the High Street he'd begun to feel a little calmer. The traffic too was less, for by now most people were heading for the suburbs.

'Where are we?' Owen murmured sleepily.

'We're here,' said Bernard.

'As distinct from being where Sergei Rachmaninov is,' said Henry, eyes staying firmly closed.

Fortunately, the one with his hands on the wheel knew exactly where they were. Turning off the road at just the right moment and taking care to avoid the stone pillars guarding the narrow entrance, he pulled onto the drive and stopped the car. After listening to the noise levels of the stationary vehicle for longer than was necessary he switched off the engine, got out of the car, and walked stiffly towards the front door.

2

HAVE A GREAT WEEKEND

Ivan took the keys and phone from his pocket and placed them on the bedside table. Then peeling off his jacket and tie, he threw them on the bed with a flourish. Now at last he could savour the prospect of putting the week behind him. He had nothing but admiration for the weekend. Only a few short hours ago it had been edging its way forwards, seeming to be getting nowhere whilst advancing towards centre stage. From where it had begun to exert a calming influence on his pulse that was nothing short of miraculous. And now the weekend had arrived he was faced only with the question of where and how he was going to spend it. Have a great weekend is what they said, and that's what he was going to do.

'Your time starts now. Ivan K Driver your specialist subject is… forgetting-Joe Taskerman. At the end of that round, you have scored no points.'

'Which is about what I would have expected – failed again and not even making it to the televised rounds. How humiliating. I may never be able to watch the programme again. Nor take that long awaited trip to Iceland from where it all began.'

'If you could ever have faced the journey in an aeroplane with so little clean air to breathe that carbon emissions would have been the least of your problems with a deep vein thrombosis to worry about,' said a voice he'd never been able to prevent having its say.

Not relishing a journey of any kind, he sat down on the end of the bed and took a deep breath. No wonder armchair travel was appealing. An armchair gave you access to so many journeys you could enjoy without going anywhere. Those working on cyber tourism may have thought they were onto a good thing but the means had been there all the time…

read all about it, the new world traveller stays put.

'Oh no he doesn't.'

Then what was he going to do? It was a big question, and not one that he was able to answer because first he must ask Rowena what she would like to do... as though he hadn't been asking her all week. Still, by now she may have decided, and looking forward to a resolution he picked up a clean shirt, and went out onto the landing.

Glancing at the Hockney print at the top of the stairs he remembered how often the briefcase on the chair had made him want to fly off to somewhere exotic... before he'd begun to question his reason for doing so. With a memory of warm beaches and cool drinks he tore himself away from the picture of which he'd become so fond and went into the bathroom. Placing the clean shirt on the edge of the bath, he bent over the washbasin and swilled his face in cold water. He recoiled as the shock caused his skin to contract. Turning off the tap he reached for a towel and began rubbing his face with a vigour that could have removed the skin from his cheeks had not his arms begun to ache so that he had to quickly lower them.

He thought how nice it would be to carry out a simple task without feeling he was about to expire, and began to consider the attractions of redundancy. But that merely served to remind him of how stupid he was, because with no reason for his existence he would soon find other ways of exhausting himself. In the meantime, perhaps he ought to concentrate on the whirring cutters that were getting too close to his ear.

He supposed having no job would allow him to shave at any time of the day he chose. He did rather like the idea of shaving at three o'clock in the afternoon. It had a wonderful anarchic feel to it. Imagine being able to shave at three o'clock in the afternoon and Joe Taskerman could go and stuff marrows up his trousers, because at three o'clock in the afternoon, or for that matter whatever time it happened to be, he would be out of reach of Joe Taskerman for evermore. That cheered him up, and buttoning his shirt he waltzed out of the bathroom with a lighter step.

Pausing for a moment to look through the landing

window, he saw that two boys were playing cricket against a lamppost, where it was apparent the practice of holding the bat high in the air as the bowler came in to deliver had now reached street cricket. The only advantage Ivan could see in a stance like that was it might be an effective way of causing the wicket keeper to stand a little further back. Although it didn't seem to be having much effect on the wall behind the lamppost occupying that position at the moment. More to the point was how they were ever going to learn to play a fast in-swinging… 'BMW, Christ, look out.'

The speeding car swerved before registering its audible annoyance. But the protest was lost because the more serious issue of a disputed lbw decision had now to be resolved. And that, recalled Ivan, could take care of the rest of the evening. He remembered that traffic had been less of a hazard in his own days of road cricket. Six-and-out in the river had been more of a problem in the games he'd played as a boy, concerning the question of whether they would ever get the ball back.

'Ivan,' the voice of Rowena rang out from below, curtailing any further thoughts of flying through windows into times past but not forgotten.

'Coming,' he shouted as he ran down the stairs, knowing punctuality was required when it was Rowena's turn to prepare the evening meal.

'The old fool's off his pencil again,' he said commencing an assault upon the first of his lamb cutlets.

To anyone unfamiliar with Ivan's preoccupation with Joe Taskerman, it may have seemed an obsession akin to that found in a monumental love affair. Which in some respects it was, having begun like all great love affairs with an engagement – Ivan's engagement by Joe Taskerman. And whilst no one would have suggested it had been love at first sight, neither did it require an unobtrusive observer (sweet touchstone of the human soul) to see they'd become attached to one another. Indeed, it would have been evident to a strategically placed dead fly that Ivan was devoted to keeping Joe Taskerman at arms length, and Joe Taskerman liked to put Ivan in his place at least once on each and every day that had the temerity to raise its head above the horizon.

Ivan had often reproached himself for not recognising that the tunnel vision he'd identified even at that first meeting with Joe Taskerman, would sooner or later become intolerable. But like many a seasoned traveller on the highways and byways of daily survival, his attention had been upon how he was going to take the next step in front of him.

'Please have your boarding card ready.' He recalled how he'd been standing face to face with the necessity of earning a living, and that joining the one-song cheap flight to nowhere of Joe Taskerman had not been an option to which there were many alternatives. The cities of the plain were cluttered with pyramids. In which control of the many was exercised by the few. It was all so infuriating because even if you swallowed the line that structures were flatter nowadays, it still left you with the problem of centre and periphery. Ivan had understood this in principle but had continued to act as though skill, knowledge and understanding were more important than position even though he knew they were not.

He wondered why he was becoming angry with a lamb cutlet. After all, it wasn't as though the rules made by Joe Taskerman were rigid. On the contrary, the clown was always changing the rules. The problem being that changing a rule changed nothing. Apart from the rule. The whole purpose of changing a rule being to maintain a means of control whilst creating mental fatigue in those who had to suffer the changes made.

Stabbing a cutlet with his fork he cursed the fact that pyramids were held in such high regard. He mocked the emphasis placed on the need for great leaders who would be judged on results. Results arising from the efforts of others. He cut into the cutlet in dismay at the neglect of structures offering more efficient ways of harnessing knowledge and expertise. It was surely one of the ironies of progress that having known expertise came from experience, it had always been a matter of position.

'How are the cutlets?' said Rowena, not entirely from a desire for information.

Ivan unloaded another forkful of potatoes into his mouth, swallowing quickly when the heat burned his tongue. His eyes watered and he silently cursed as a lump caught in his throat. He remembered there was a whole evening in which to eat his meal and told himself that if taking more time resulted in his food going cold then it could only be to his advantage.

'Fine... fine love... fine,' he nodded.

'Tender aren't they?' said Rowena.

'Yes, tender... tender, they are tender.' He began to establish a second front on the third of his cutlets. 'What would you like to do this weekend?'

'What's the matter with him now?' Rowena displayed that strange masochistic feature of many a great listener. Having achieved a successful diversion, she immediately undermined it.

Ivan stole a glance at Rowena wondering how he was going to explain.

'Targets,' he said by way of an initial response.

'Targets?' said Rowena, her mind more occupied with what they were going to do about the shortfall on their endowment policy; whether their son Timothy would go from bad to worse now that Rebecca was no longer there; whether they ought to try and spend more time with their daughter Joanna and her family; and not least, how she was going to respond to the latest nonsense to come from the mouth of the insufferable little creep who occupied a similar position to that of Joe Taskerman in her own life.

'He wants to increase production to five thousand per week.' Ivan surprised himself by the manner in which he was able to convey the information without distributing a mouthful of potatoes across the surface of the table.

'Silly bugger,' he said having taken the precaution of emptying his mouth. 'Five thousand per week? We couldn't make five thousand in a month.' He knew that hot air and bluster were natural companions in an age of hype and hedonism, but he knew that if they were to have a future, they had to retain their reputation for high quality. That was the one market niche in which they might survive. If they were to make the mistake of going for quantity, they would be wiped out in a matter of weeks by one of the low cost economies, with which they could never compete.

'If we cut any more corners they won't last five minutes let alone the five years we guarantee,' he said before being distracted by an image of a man in a pale blue tee shirt and matching trousers reminding him that by the middle of next week he might himself be informed he was unlikely to last beyond the next five days, never mind the lifetime he was hoping for. The hospital was one place he had no desire to visit before the appointed hour. His next consultation might bring news that would cause him to make the fastest exit through a window in the history of medical science. In the meantime, he would prefer to look on the bright side, there being at least a chance the whole thing would come to nothing. Nothing? He should be so lucky. Lucky? He was unlucky to have been there in the first place. But earning a living was like that. You had only to look at Archie... except it wasn't possible to look at Archie any more. Nor his wife Dorothy. A shiver ran down his spine as he furiously tried to hang on to his knife and fork.

'More gravy love?' Rowena held the gravy boat above his plate.

'Hmph? What? No, no.' Few parts of anatomy are suitable for the containment of gravy and the back of the human hand is not one of them, as Ivan found to his cost when some of the gravy reached his plate.

'The man is mad, quite mad,' Ivan licked the back of his hand in confirmation.

'It's a good thing it wasn't hot,' Rowena stifled a laugh.

'Hot?' said Ivan, 'I'll say it was hot. When I muttered under my breath what he could do with his targets you could have roasted chestnuts in his armpits.'

'I'd like to do something interesting for a change,' said Rowena returning to the question of what to do with the weekend whilst contemplating the possibility of a serving hatch in the wall behind Ivan's left ear.

As they rose from the table the telephone rang, and Rowena was first into the hall.

'It's for you love,' she called towards the kitchen where she could see Ivan had begun stacking the dishes.

Ivan went out into the hall and picked up the telephone leaving Rowena fiercely repositioning appliances on the kitchen worktop.

'It was Bill,' said Ivan coming back into the kitchen. 'He's taking a party around the old brewery tonight. He's going to be a few people short. And so he's invited us to join him… with drinks on the house.'

'Aren't you going out?' Rowena was conscious of more than one level of incongruity in her question but sought to avoid expressing an outright rejection of the invitation by reminding Ivan of the long-standing commitments he had on Friday evenings, in spite of knowing he was frequently too exhausted to fulfil them.

'Oh I can go out anytime.' Ivan knew exactly what she meant. 'But this sounds too good to miss – don't you think?'

'No, no,' Rowena could think of nothing worse. 'I er, it sounds er, I'm too busy… er too tired love.'

She restored the kettle to its rightful place beside the toaster and dragged the food mixer to the other end of the worktop. Ivan watched her for a moment, trying to figure out why she was turning down such an opportunity, before resigning himself to the situation and going off in search of his jacket.

'I'll do the dishes when I get back,' he called as he ran up the stairs.

He found his jacket where he'd left it in the middle of the bed. Threading his arms into the sleeves, he hitched the shoulders into place and turned down the collar. Picking up his keys, he switched off his phone and deliberately left it where it was, feeling relieved that he wouldn't have to spend the weekend reading and answering text messages and emails. Now the weekend could really begin. Now he could put Joe Taskerman and the massaging of output figures behind him. Now all that remained was to decide what he was going to do with the rest of the weekend. Perhaps it would be better if he were to leave those decisions to others. An invitation to join a party visiting a brewery was certainly a better start to a weekend than he could have imagined for himself. Already the weekend had taken a promising turn and he hadn't been called on to do anything beyond taking a telephone call and putting on his jacket. He would have preferred Rowena to come along. She liked a glass or two now and again. She seemed at odds with herself and he wondered why.

As he went down the stairs, he could think of no good reason why a trip around a brewery should be undersubscribed but with a shrug and a sigh decided to feel immensely pleased that it was.

3

THE SCALE OF THINGS

His pleasure was intensified when less than an hour later Ivan found himself listening to a rib-tickling introduction to the art of brewing, the effect of which was enhanced by the delivery of the speaker, a short rotund man with the doleful expression of a sombre duck. The man was wearing a bow tie with a tweed jacket and a velvet waistcoat above Rupert Bear trousers. Almost anything he said was therefore bound to be funny and indeed a good deal of restraint was required so as not to laugh before he began to speak.

When he did speak it was with a voice pitched about an octave higher than expected. Yet it was a very cultured voice with a proud Reithian approach to pronunciation that would not have been out of place on an old recording had it been customary for such tapes to be run at twice their normal speed. The effect of the diction was further enhanced by the issuing of a loud wheezing sound each time the man paused to draw breath. This could have been distracting, but in the event Ivan found it provided a welcome opportunity for a periodic re-calibration of his ears.

Unaware of his afflictions, the man captured the attention of his audience with a story of passion that could only have come from one whose life has been dedicated to the achievement of perfection in brewing, although there was to be a sad side to the story. It seemed the brewery, one of the few independent large-scale producers left, would be closing in a couple of months time. There was a gasp of dismay when this was announced and in an effort to cheer everyone up the man became yet more animated. His commitment to the unfolding story of malt and hops had never been in doubt, but as he got more into his stride he revealed a further dimension of his talents in the shape of a series of perfectly timed asides and wheezing one liners worthy of the best of stand-up comedians. This might have had a greater impact on the audience had it not been that most of them were already in hysterics as a result of a man in the front row having remarked, not quite under his breath, that he hadn't expected to spend the evening being addressed by a bloody Punch and Judy man. Ivan bit his lip, thinking that giving the man his due he could have made a more than adequate living in one of the legal professions which had an undeniable affinity with a certain kind of beach theatre. But the true measure of his performance was still to come, for when the time came to move off and start the tour of the brewery the man's announcement to that effect was greeted with groans of disappointment.

Nevertheless, file obediently they did, one by one, through the tiny door at the end of the hopper room in which they'd been standing, to find themselves in the fermentation bay confronted by six enormous meringues of foaming wort.

'Ugh,' cried Owen dragging a finger through the foam of the nearest tank. 'That tastes awful.'

'You are supposed to smell it,' said Bernard.

'The man said we could taste it,' said Owen.

'The man has a sophisticated sense of humour,' said Bernard.

'That's true,' said Owen taking another sample in defiance of his taste buds. 'I can't argue with that.' He grimaced as the loaded finger reached his tongue.

'Come on,' said Bernard, heading for the door where some of the party had already passed through into the filtering room beyond.

'What's the hurry?' said Owen. 'It's not every day of the week we get an opportunity to inspect the inside of a brewery.'

'It isn't very interesting,' said Bernard.

Henry blinked at this suggestion with an incredulity he hadn't felt since hearing the voice of a former Prime Minister say he wanted to live in a classless society.

'They aren't showing us how it works,' said Bernard. 'You know, the chemistry, as distinct from the scale of things.'

'The scale of things is interesting enough,' said Owen, sticking his head into another tank. 'Here, smell this one.' He threw his head back in delight as the bouquet cleared any vestiges of nasal congestion he might have.

Ivan found his eyes following the lines of cables running up the wall beside him, until they disappeared at the point where the steel columns met the castellated beam roof structure. They emerged on the far side of the column he was standing beside, then ran along at high level before descending beside the next column, to where they terminated in a switchboard behind a gangway which ran along the length of the fermentation bay. His mind went back to the steelworks. The switchboard in front of him was smaller than those he'd known in the steelworks so many years ago and yet the impression was the same – of a silent functioning telling only a part of their story. He began to ponder the profundity of silence, reminding himself that switchboards were no different to anyone else, there being a price to pay for neglect, as they had occasionally been known to bring to the attention of anyone standing close enough at the time.

'Look at this,' cried Owen.

'Quick, grab him,' said Bernard, running to where Owen was hanging precariously over another of the open tanks of wort. 'Before he falls in.'

Reminding them the man had said the foam might be as much as three feet thick Owen scooped a sample from the tank and pronounced it to be one hell of a good head.

'I can't see why every decent pint shouldn't have a head like that,' he said, forgetting for a moment he was looking at the fermenting yeast, the extent of which was unrelated to the head on a glass of beer at the end of the brewing process.

'For the perfectly good reason,' said Bernard, 'that a barman pulling a pint with a head like that would soon have a riot on his hands.'

'Not to mention, a very wet shirt,' said Henry.

Ivan compared the tanks in front of him with the tanks in the plating shop he was trying to forget for three days. The fermentation tanks were smaller and there were fewer of them. They were also producing lower emissions. With every chemical process there were bound to be fumes created but there was no sign of a toxic cloud gathering in the fermentation bay. The annealing and plating tanks with their steaming acid were another matter. Seldom a day went by when you could see to the other end of the plating shop. Joe Taskerman had said robotics was the obvious answer, but that needed investment. In the meantime the new extraction system would be a big improvement, and until Archie had been taken ill, Ivan had been almost ready to believe there was little for them to worry about. Other than a worry that he was beginning to sound like Joe Taskerman.

'Pooh-pooh, nothing to worry about, everything is working as it should.'

'O yeah, then why is my hair turning green?'

It was true, people's hair used to turn green in there, and as Ahmed, the plant chemist, had been quick to point out, the far from laughing cavalier had done little to determine the lasting effects of the new acid they were using. Not for him an interest in anyone's long term survival. Speaking of which Ahmed had also taken a huge risk with his own survival in reminding everyone it was their own lives they were putting at risk the moment they set foot in there, and that since everyone had been left in no doubt they were responsible for their own lives in this life, they owed it to themselves to be sure at least of their own doubts.

Ivan wondered how often the brewery fermentation tanks would be emptied and cleaned, hoping it would be a good deal more often than those which came under the jurisdiction of Joe Taskerman, who no doubt would have something to say about the frequency of cleaning if he were in charge of the brewery. With a fluttering of an eyelid Ivan found himself back in the plating shop listening to Joe Taskerman.

'The cleaning of tanks is all very well, but in order to clean them we shall have to empty them, and in order to empty them we shall have to clear out the sediment, and if we clear out the sediment we shall have to dispose of it. Bury it? No, that'll cost money. I'll tell you what we'll do. We'll flush it out and let it find it's own way into the river. I don't care if it does upset the eco system, the river is not my concern. I'm not paid to stand around looking at rivers all day – that's somebody else's funeral.'

Ivan imagined that Joe Taskerman would conduct the service at his own funeral if it meant he could get one more load through the plant and out of the main gates before the next hymn. Ivan had been to more funerals than he cared to remember, but he had to admit the funeral of Joe Taskerman was one he wouldn't want to miss. That was one procession he was looking forward to marching in. Always providing it came before his own in the schedule of things – notwithstanding the difficulties of ensuring the chronology of that, at the very least requiring knowledge of when his own funeral would be, such speculation reminding him he might become party to that information sooner than he'd hoped.

The next thing he knew he was back in the hospital considering the prospect of what he might be told when he went back to see the man in the pale blue tee shirt and matching trousers. The man had merely said, can you come back next week, but he had delivered the question with such gravitas Ivan had not considered he was being given an option.

'Of course I shall be there. So long as I can still walk.' It occurred to him that by the middle of next week, far from walking around with a spring in his step he could be having difficulty dragging his feet across the floor. He might have been refused permission to put his feet back onto the floor. He might have to stay in there. In fact he might never come out. He might not even survive the day. To think that he may never again be able to put his arms around Rowena. Nor give a big hug to Joanna nor a timely rebuke to Timothy, and whilst everyone had to go one day, imagine not being able to cuddle his lovely granddaughter when she climbed upon his knee.

'Oh Molly my lovely, if only your grandpa had some idea of what was in store for him. Why do these things take so long? Next week doesn't seem to be getting any nearer. Today is still Friday and Wednesday might well be in the middle of the next century for all the good it is to me now, even knowing there are only one-two-three-four-five more days to go.'

For no apparent reason *('no apparent reason?')* he began counting the rivets along the lip of the fermentation tank he was standing beside. Moving in closer to the tank he leaned over and peered inside noticing how the foaming wort had turned a little brown at the edges just like the scum which often collected on the surface of the annealing tanks.

'This one is lager,' said Owen. 'You can tell it's lager because the thickness of the wort is less. The process of fermentation in a lager is different, the yeast acting from below rather than from above.' He relayed some of his recently acquired information wondering why he'd been the only one to glean anything useful from the man in Rupert Bear trousers. 'If you look closely it's a different colour. Here, taste it,' he said offering a finger of the stuff.

'Taste it yourself,' said Bernard.

'I will, I will,' said Owen, again in danger of losing his balance on the edge of the tank.

'There you are, I told you it was lager,' he said enjoying the verification if not the taste. What beats me though is why anyone would want to brew so much lager.

'Because they have a lot of customers who like to drink lager,' said Bernard.

'That's quite an assumption,' said Henry.

'You've never understood the mechanisms of a market economy, have you?' said Bernard.

'What's he talking about now?' said Owen.

'I'm not sure, but I fear we may be in for another attack upon the Frankfurt School,' said Henry.

'Well if that's the case,' said Owen, 'then I'm with him all the way. I fail to see how anyone can eat those appalling lengths of stuffed piping. They're named after the place you know, when they should have been named after the fingers in condoms they resemble. How anyone could speak of those things in the same breath as those wonderful creations we have come to know and love as saus…'

He found that he had no alternative but to stop in mid sentence having run out of his entire stock of saliva.

'When you have finished,' said Bernard, 'I was talking about customer choice.'

Henry suggested the supply of a product such as lager may have more to do with the marketing strategies of multi-national companies than with customer preference or need, causing Bernard to raise his eyes aloft and declare that any company which made a product their customers didn't want would soon be out of business.

Ivan noticed that by now most people had gone through the door at the end of the fermentation bay from where the man in Rupert Bear trousers was encouraging the remainder of the party to join him in the filtration room for an explanation of just how the head on a pint of beer was achieved. Ivan was less interested in the head on a pint of beer than in what he might do to the heads of the three characters doing their best to lower the tone of the visit. Submerging them one by one in a tank of foaming wort would be a good start. But he knew he was in no position to do anything about their frequent interruptions any more than he was able to banish all thoughts of Joe Taskerman from his mind. It vexed him to admit that even to himself, though no more than it bothered him to acknowledge he would miss the characters terribly were any of them to perish in a tank of foaming wort. They were after all the ones who kept him sane when irretrievable despair was the only other thing on offer.

Taking a deep breath he decided he could do with some fresh ideas. Whether he was likely to find them in a brewery was another matter. In the meantime it seemed sensible to allow anyone who could shine a light on the subject to air their opinion in any way they wished.

'The pressure to produce more from less is a familiar enough feature of modern life,' said a speaker from a platform which had appeared above the switchboard on the other side of the gangway.

'Not now,' said Ivan mopping his brow. The anxiety of waiting for the screening results was taking its toll. A shiver went through him at the reminder. And yet what else could he do. It seemed he ought to try to stop himself from getting so wound up. There wasn't really anything to worry about. He wasn't unhappy. Far from it, he and Rowena had a good life (*'Huh?'*)

Ivan and Rowena did have a good life. They were devoted to each other and over the years their love had grown. They had retained much of the excitement of their first meeting and that had given them the confidence to express their disagreements without compromising the belief they had in each other. Knowing they had such a bond of trust had given rise to a conviction their love was unshakable. They had continuity in their lives and had drawn strength from there being no need to renew their commitment to one another with trinkets. Just being together was confirmation enough.

'You mean you can have anything you like so long as it's lager,' spluttered Owen, wishing he hadn't taken to the sampling quite so enthusiastically now that his tongue had begun to congeal to the roof of his mouth.

'That's rubbish,' said Bernard, 'as you of all people should know, having spent so much time peering into the tanks of fermenting wort that prove you can have mild and bitter too if you wish.'

'Though not for much longer,' said Henry, reminding him that the brewery was about to close. 'What's more, if that's the basis of your confidence in freedom of choice, no wonder people are beginning to realise how little say they have in what they drink.'

'Then how do you explain the rise of so many breweries making real ale?' said Bernard.

'No explanation is necessary,' said Henry. 'They are a small segment in a huge market, and their existence only goes to prove my point.'

'A huge market in which you can have anything you like so long as it's wet,' said Owen, staring at his dripping hand before pretending to look the other way whilst wiping it dry on Bernard's trousers.

Henry and Owen were still laughing when they filed into the mock public house in the basement of the brewery at the conclusion of the tour. The yellow coach lamps dotted around the stucco brown walls and the leather seating along both sides of the room gave the effect of climbing into a stagecoach. And when, standing beside the door, the man in Rupert Bear trousers welcomed everyone aboard with the hope they'd had a pleasant trip, he created not a little confusion amongst his visitors as to whether the visit to the brewery was now over. But they needn't have worried, for once they were all assembled the most important thing the man had to say was drinks were on the house and that since this was a private party there would be no official closing time. Whereupon the lights on the bar at the end of the stagecoach came to life, sending out a glow in promise of a trip that was reassuringly only just beginning.

'Now we can really see how good that lager is,' said Bernard.

'Speak for yourself,' said Owen. 'I'm not drinking that stuff, not even when it's free. It's a pint of beer I'm looking forward to.'

'The shoddy euphoria brought on by the anticipation of a free drink is another fine example of the shallowness of critics of a market economy,' arched Bernard. 'One promise of a free drink, and you lose all sense of proportion.'

Ivan took his place in the queue at the bar, musing on the fact that Joe Taskerman must have lost his sense of proportion to have come up with a figure of five thousand per week. It was as though he'd come from another planet and perhaps he had, it being not entirely unreasonable to assume that a man who spoke a completely different language to any spoken on this planet must have come from another planet.

'God I'm hungry,' said Owen, the lamb cutlets having become a distant memory.

Henry said it didn't look as though he would get much to eat before he'd been tempted into having far too much to drink.

Looking around to ensure he hadn't missed any tell-tale signs of a buffet, Owen observed that successive agricultural policies seemed to be having a far from desired effect on food production, prompting Bernard to suggest that even a simpleton like Owen could see that the absence of food in an isolated context had nothing to do with agricultural policies.

'Then why haven't I been handed a menu,' said Owen.

'There you go, babbling on in that stupid way of yours such that any establishment falling short of a Michelin star is deemed unworthy of your custom,' said Bernard.

'A Michelin star eh? Now you're talking,' chuckled Owen.

'Correct me if I'm wrong Bernard, but if it was a Michelin star you were after, then rather than Habermas shouldn't we have been talking about Foucault and Lacan?' said Henry.

'And who in God's name are they?' said Owen.

'Oh,' said Henry, 'they're just a couple of wine merchants Bernard happens to know,' but his voice was lost in the throng as he was thrust against the bar by someone pushing heavily from behind at the sight of a mouth watering tray of pork pies that had just been produced.

4

A MEMORIAL FOR ARCHIE

The failing light from the courtyard window to his right, and the dim reflected glow of the angle lamp, were barely sufficient to distinguish the outline of the neck and the head bent low over the papers on the desk. The indifferent light coupled with his more than careful entry meant that his own presence had not been detected, and he had time to consider his position. He knew that no matter what the subject of the papers on the desk might be – an inconclusive report here, a line of unreliable figures there – they would soon have been raised to a plane of immense importance. That others might consider the content of the papers to be of little consequence would be of no interest to the head on that particular neck. Which seemed very still, there having been no movement of the head, neck or arms since he'd entered the room. Perhaps the bent figure had fallen asleep. He smiled when he remembered that here was a creature believing sleep to be an unnecessary function. There was no question of anyone falling asleep in this room. On the other hand, perhaps… yes perhaps the heart that beat in the breast below the neck which supported the head had ceased… that was too much to hope for. There may be little evidence of life at the moment but he must not allow himself to be distracted. He must concentrate on the neck and look for a point where he could… he noticed that there was a pulsing vein about an inch and a half below the left ear... that would be a good place – or perhaps there would be more chance of success if he focused on the point below the right ear. It was true that if he were to choose a point below the left ear it might raise suspicions. They might start looking for someone who was left-handed and immediately make him a suspect. Why should he worry about being a suspect? He was going to admit what he'd done. Admit what he'd done? He was going to proclaim it to the world.

The figure at the desk stirred, causing the intruder to momentarily cease breathing... only resuming when a hand picked up a pencil and began to scribble furiously across the papers on the desk. As the seated figure leaned further over the desk yet more of the neck became visible so that he could now contemplate the execution of one quick... but his train of thought was interrupted and he became full of misgivings about what he was planning to do. Sitting there with half of the body in the chair, half leaning over the desk, the figure looked so helpless, were it not that there was nothing helpless about this creature. This was a coiled rattlesnake and he was standing uncomfortably close to it. If he didn't finish the job with one blow the rattlesnake would bite him. The rattlesnake had been biting him for years. His mission was clear. All that he had to do was... and yet a moment ago, coming up the iron staircase with the stench of the annealing tanks in his nostrils... yes coming up the stairs there had been no thought of anything other than the reaction he might expect to the news of the latest figures. But then he'd entered the room and seen that neck. Whereupon his mind had become flooded with possibilities as to what he might do to the old... he supposed he could simply announce his presence, tell him to go to hell, and walk out of the place. That would be so much easier. Though it wouldn't be much of a payback for Archie. Nor Dorothy. Neither would it provide their son Trevor with a feeling that justice had been done. Nor give much reason for hope to anyone else. He must remember his responsibilities. He could relieve a lot of suffering with one quick... then suddenly he was wide awake, unsure of where he was and why there was an elbow digging into his ribs.

SATURDAY

5

THE BOUNDARIES OF NORMALITY

Ivan raised the three and a half ton lead ball that was attached to his neck, managing to lift the mass a full inch from the pillow before having to quickly lower it again in order to allay the next wave of nausea that came flooding over him. It seemed there was little he could do but lay still and try to remember what he could have eaten that had left him in such doubt as to whether he would ever again be able to relax those parts of his body concerned with ensuring that everything he'd consumed stayed exactly where it was.

He could see the prospects were not good as once more he had to tighten his grip in the face of another onslaught. He'd been trapped in a vicious circle for many hours alternately clenching and unclenching those muscles he could control, no sooner having convinced himself that he was recovering than finding quick preventative action was needed. In the course of this struggle he'd become weary, not least of the shifts between hope and despair that had been assailing him since he came wide awake in the early hours of the morning. Now more than ever he needed to be elsewhere, but how unlikely that seemed when his attention was so urgently required where he lay. It occurred to him that he may have unwittingly identified another of the problems of being in two places at once – you were least able to fly out of a window when you most needed to.

'I take it that you were allowed to taste some of the brew,' said Rowena.

Ivan tried to look up without moving his head, but the next wave was upon him and he had to keep his mouth closed so as to avoid giving the impression that it might present a means of escape for the turbulence below.

'It was good of Bill to invite you,' Rowena tried to sound cheerful.

Ivan supposed that some of the pork pies served at the brewery must have been beyond their use-by date, in which case he didn't think it was at all good of Bill to have invited him. With respect to his present condition it would have been better never to have known Bill. It would have been better if Bill had been endowed with the genetic foresight to strangle himself at birth. Then it wouldn't have been possible for him to so much as contemplate taking a single footstep into Ivan's life. On the other hand since Bill had been intent on surviving then would it have been too much to ask for him to have grown up to become someone else's acquaintance? Not to have known Bill would have been one step towards ensuring he would never encounter the possibility of making up the numbers on anybody's trip around a brewery.

He made another attempt to raise the lead ball that was attached to his neck, but succeeded only in creating a life and death struggle with the emptying mechanisms of that vessel which in better times he'd been happy to know as his stomach, saving Rowena the empirical evidence of how good the evening had been by creating what must have been close to a world record for swallowing – fifteen times in three and a half seconds.

'I'm pleased that I decided not to go,' Rowena reminded him there had been an element of choice in the matter.

'I... I...' he realised his throat had become taut and dangerous and so decided it would be in the interests of the duvet not to express an opinion. His neck seemed to be connected to his solar plexus by a steel bar and he curled himself into a ball so as to minimise stress on the bar.

'Did you get up much in the night?' Rowena enquired.

Did he spend much time in bed would have been an easier question to answer. He remembered sitting on the cold hard edge of the lavatory pan, having been in no condition to know the invention of lavatory seats had predated Bill's organised trip around a brewery. He'd found it difficult to recall what the precise function of a lavatory was, to say nothing of how it might differ from that of an abattoir. Yet he must have been in the bathroom balancing on that cold hard edge for the best part of an hour on one occasion. Although not to exaggerate, he supposed it could have been a particularly long minute for having lost all track of time there had been no way of knowing.

One thing about which he had been convinced had been the importance of the bucket between his knees. He'd wondered whether it had been a recent arrival or had been there on that fateful day when he'd first wished he'd never been born. If the floor had stayed still long enough he might have been able to solve the mystery, but of rather more concern was that if the floor were to come any higher he would have to lie down to prevent his head from banging on the ceiling.

Perhaps he should have accepted an invitation to exit through the door as it swung open each time the floor had moved in that direction. That would have been easier had his path not been blocked by the frog that kept appearing at the door and croaking… 'Have you finished yet?' If only he'd known where to start.

Sitting on the edge of the lavatory pan in the middle of the night he must have fallen asleep… or perhaps he'd been dreaming whilst still awake? He had no idea, but one thing he did remember was that in the early hours of the gathering nausea a man had started hammering nails into the soft part of his spine just below the base of his skull. His first hope had been that the man had come to install a tap to secure the upper exit from his stomach, but as with so many of these privatisations the amount of effort had been out of proportion to the end result. It had also been rather inconvenient since the man's arrival had coincided with that of a plumber attending to a serious malfunction in his alimentary canal. The plumber must have been on an excellent bonus given the speed with which he'd begun to remove what he had evidently decided were lengths of redundant piping, the reaction against which had resulted in a periodic lurch of Ivan's head causing the man working on the base of his skull to bend several nails.

Then unbelievably, with all that was going on, he must indeed have fallen asleep. He could think of no other explanation for how his feet had come to be jammed behind the pedestal of the wash basin; why his hand was exploring the darker regions of the lavatory pan; nor why his head was in the bucket. More worrying still had been that his other hand was telling him that he may have dislocated his hip causing him to wonder whether he would ever walk again.

He'd managed to extricate his feet from behind the pedestal of the wash basin easily enough, and his head from the bucket, though only to find his face lying against the stiff bristles of the discoloured lavatory brush which had also seen better days. As for his hip, well for once he'd been lucky – lucky enough to realise that far from his hip, it had been the radiator valve he'd been holding. And lucky enough too, to realise that when you lived your life believing that anything was possible there would be times when you were so unsure of yourself that you could see advantages after all in the kind of tunnel vision exhibited by Joe Taskerman. The kind of advantages which told you hips were attached to bodies, radiator valves to central heating systems.

'I didn't get much sleep,' said Rowena.

Ivan felt another wave beginning its journey and quickly marshalled his defences.

'I was disturbed by a great shaggy dog which kept rocking the bed,' said Rowena unaware of the more immediate danger accelerating upwards.

Ivan clung on as the crescendo came with the speed of a lift cage arriving at the top of a mine shaft after surfacing from the bowels of the earth too quickly. He was convinced that all was lost as his mouth opened involuntarily, but to his surprise all that came out was an explosive release of gas. He could hardly believe that the bridgehead had been contained and that the entire contents of his stomach hadn't followed. Yet they hadn't, and reasoning that the eruption would have led to a lowering of abdominal pressure, he hung onto the thought that the risk of a more substantial expulsion might have lessened.

Rowena was less convinced, as with a glare she slowly wiped the back of her hand across her cheek.

Ivan slid under the duvet and made one of those immediate yet ultimately transient vows, swearing by the almighty one great sculptor in the sky, that should he live beyond the next hour, having enjoyed his trip around the brewery or not, he would never again eat such questionable food whilst drinking more than was good for him, nor again, nor again, nor again, but have one for yourself landlord.

He wondered what his mother's reaction would have been if she'd seen him in this condition. She had always tried to instill a sense of responsibility in her only son and in return he had developed what he believed was a healthy suspicion of anything that could be called moderation let alone be raised to a position of the highest plane.

She of course would have ignored the possibility of dodgy food and homed in on the amount of alcohol he'd consumed, the subject of which had received a lot of attention in Ivan's teenage years.

His mother had never suggested he should be abstemious. She had merely laid out what she considered were the boundaries of normality. She had done so in that light amusing way she had, such that the purpose might have escaped the notice of anyone unfamiliar with her methods.

Ivan recalled his mother's reaction upon first suspecting he'd partaken of the ruinous beverage as she'd termed it. He'd been only seventeen at the time and had expected the retribution of a devil's disciple. Yet hardly anything had been said. Until allusions had begun to appear concerning the actions of other people's children who drank alcohol to excess. Being familiar with his mother's approach he should have known better, but he didn't and began slamming doors behind him. Only to see his behaviour treated as an adolescent response to a chastisement which had not occurred, thereby in its turn requiring only the merest of indignant sighs.

(*Thus conscience doth make cowards of us all?*)

Back in the heart of the weekend Ivan brought his head out from under the duvet and returned his attention to the possibility of not after all being sick. He decided it was still early days, the simple movement of his head having been enough to remind him there was still a long way to go.

Perhaps it would have been better if his mother had been

less determined to avoid losing her temper. Perhaps they might both have gained something if she'd indulged in a little screaming and shouting. Perhaps occasionally she should have expressed her misgivings more directly than through stories of terrible consequences for some other person's child. But she'd been unable to do so, and it had been against the transferred foreboding in the stories his mother told that Ivan had cut the teeth of his independence. Falling into the river whilst attempting to cross hand over hand on the underside of that bridge had been one result of his choosing to disregard the warnings his mother had given. He'd never for a moment thought he was being defiant and had known he wouldn't be punished – at least not in the ways in which some of his friends might, Ivan's mother believing it would be more effective to focus upon the new cricket bat he needed if he was ever to prove his father had been wrong to dismiss his abilities. It would have been unthinkable for a cricket bat to be seen as in any way conditional. Ivan knew he would be given a handsome contribution towards acquiring a new cricket bat as soon as his improving abilities warranted the need for one. It was just that parties to such transactions had to appreciate that the timing of rewards were closely related to the success they had in convincing others they were doing everything they could to realise their potential.

6

HOW'S THAT?

Finding himself able to move a little more easily in the bed, Ivan turned over so as to protect his eyes from the glare of the window. He wondered how anyone with his timidity could have acquired a reputation for being so worldly wise. He could only feel shame at his naivety when recalling the first fumbling explorations of what his teachers had called the distinguishing characteristics of gender. He recalled how unprepared he had been for embarking upon a study of the little differences – the little differences which gave rise to such excitement in adolescence and such anguish in later life. And he recalled too, how the extent of his discoveries had been limited by a fear of overstepping the mark – the mark of which he'd been made so aware, his mind being full of the fearful consequences which had been spun from the great spider of a storyteller in whose web he'd spent what now seemed so little time.

His mother on the other hand had felt rather pleased with herself. Until she'd realised his apparent lack of interest in matters quaintly referred to as the opposite sex had extended well beyond his schooldays. She had then begun to worry about sexual inclination, especially when it had dawned on her that she of all people was making little progress along the road to that most important of maternal responsibilities – the consideration of potential candidates for the bearer of one's grandchildren.

Ivan had been more intent on ensuring his mother had nothing to do with any such considerations. He'd experienced more than enough difficulties in the severance of what he'd known only too well was a secondary umbilical cord. He had consequently taken the one approach that would give him any say in the matter by ensuring there would be no contact between his mother and anyone who might be seen as a prospective candidate for anything in his life. He'd maintained this practice for many years and even upon leaving school and entering the steelworks had not taken any of his girlfriends, including some quite long standing ones, to meet his mother. But then following that magical day upon which he and Rowena had stolen their first kiss, he had taken her along to meet his mother that same night.

It appalled him now to realise how little consideration he'd given to the possibility of his mother reacting vengefully to his sudden change of heart. He had simply assumed she would be relieved. A chill went through him when he pondered the audacity of that assumption. But then he remembered the one thing he did know about his mother was that she would never have allowed her real feelings to be expressed. There had never been so much as a hint of a crack appearing in the cocoon she'd spun around herself, and from the moment he'd carried Rowena over his mother's threshold in jest, a connection had been made between them. It was as though two previous acquaintances were meeting again in another world. Ivan supposed this connection may have had something to do with Rowena's mother being French. Ivan's own mother had spent part of her early childhood in France. She had always been reluctant to talk about that part of her upbringing no matter how persistent the questioning. Neither had she shown any inclination to re-cross the channel, but meeting Rowena may have led to a sudden exposure of feelings that had been submerged for many years. Whatever the reason, from the day they met, his mother had never had anything but praise for his choice of Rowena, and Rowena had never, within earshot, been heard to say anything other than how lucky she was to have such a splendid mother-in-law.

Not surprisingly his mother had been intent on becoming a perfect grandmother, a supreme example of the species, giving maximum support, with minimum interference. After the death of Ivan's father, his mother had said there was nothing left for her except to enjoy her grandchildren and be of some use to Rowena. Ivan had registered no surprise at his own omission from that equation, knowing his mother would have been so eager to show her concern for others that his exclusion had been inevitable; he of course being still a part of herself.

His mother's determination not to become a burden to anyone, had resulted in her moving herself into a home for aged folks, as she'd called it, without any prior discussion of her intentions. Ivan and Rowena had worried that their inability to find a way in which that could have been avoided was an indication of how they'd failed in their responsibilities, no matter how many times Timothy and Joanna had assured them their grandmother had been perfectly happy where she'd chosen to be, and where she had insisted upon remaining right up until that thoroughly miserable day on which she'd died.

'I suppose it could be worse,' said Rowena.

Ivan's imagination had deserted him for once. He was unable to think of anything more awful than how he was feeling at that moment.

'At least you won't have to face Joe Taskerman today.'

It was as much as he could do to prevent a full blown shriek at the sound of the name, and so he quickly turned his attention back to the more tolerable headache that was merely threatening to burst open his skull. Yet he had to acknowledge things could be worse because he did feel in less danger of spilling the entire contents of his stomach upon the bed. And what was more, a feeling that the centre of turbulence was shifting towards the darker regions of his digestive system had increased that security. Now all he had to contend with, apart from a throbbing head and a mouth like the Kalahari desert, was an occasional shooting pain in his lower abdomen giving rise to the possibility that he might be about to give birth to a donkey.

He preferred to pursue the conviction that he was feeling better, and told himself a further improvement in his condition was more or less inevitable now that the day had become more strident in its claims over the weariness of the night. He even managed to drink a cup of the luke warm tea which Rowena had made on first awakening, and received yet more confirmation that there was a brighter side to things, his condition meaning it was now out of the question for him to leap out of bed, dash into the garden, and begin excavating the cracked drain that was in need of repair. On the contrary he had no alternative but to spend the rest of the day in bed getting up to date with news in the world at large.

'Or I could read the newspaper instead,' he muttered to himself, feeling pleased that at least his sense of humour hadn't deserted him.

Deciding he could risk a more comfortable sitting position he raised himself in the bed, being reassured by the fact that he didn't immediately have to lie down again. He congratulated himself once more on the progress he was making and picked up the newspaper from where Rowena had thrown it in disgust. He didn't get far however, because Rowena came in with a cup of rather warmer coffee than the tea had now become and he found his attention drawn to the matter of whether to accompany her to the supermarket.

Ivan could imagine nothing more appealing than going to the supermarket. It had to be an improvement upon what he was doing at that moment. There could hardly be a more promising way of escaping from his miserable condition. He became thrilled at the prospect of being surrounded by the rattle and clatter of baskets and trolleys as so many hungry bodies darted and weaved around in search of who-knows-what-but-we'll-try-one. He could think of nothing finer than to be in the midst of all that clinking and clanking of bottles and cans as one item was piled on top of another until trolleys could take no more, before being emptied as soon as they'd been filled, only to be reloaded on the other side of the check-outs. Oh yes the supermarket was the place to be. A trip to the supermarket was like – well yes it was like hunting. You were in a way stalking the prey, choosing the moment to go in for the kill... 'What do you fancy today, oh sorry, I do beg your, hey haven't I er, I mean er, seen you somewhere before... no, well I could swear, oh I guess it must have been someone else... there's a bright golden haze on the... quick get the trolley in front of these two pushy pain-in-the-neck, what, who, me, oh sorry, sorry (liar) well they were the ones driving like lunatics, shopping is so relaxing isn't it... look at that, what do they think they're doing, the boring self-indulgent bourgeoisie, isn't that typical, they're rehearsing a chat show in the middle of the canned foods gangway... oops, oh dear is it bleeding? It's bleeding wonderful,' thought Ivan. Until he himself was hit, first by the coffee and then by the reminder of how fragile he was, raising the question of a possible downside of any decision to go to the supermarket on this particular Saturday morning.

Rowena resolved the problem by taking her leave without so much as a smile or a wave, a short whoop being the only indication of her departure as she leapt down the stairs two at a time having decided it would be preferable on this occasion not to convey so much as a hint of a possibility of him accompanying her to the supermarket.

Ivan knew he was in no position to argue and issued only a half-hearted complaint under his breath as he picked up the sports section of the newspaper and turned to the county cricket scores.

'Defeat accomplished in style.' He surely couldn't have read that correctly. But he had. There were some situations which even rain was unable to save, despite being played in what for some were the noble wet lands of their cricketing fathers. It occurred to him that the introduction of acid rain was the only hope for some of those lost causes, whereupon they might not be able to start the game at all. He supposed that would be one way of attracting publicity. He could see the headline now – pollution stopped play. And with that thought he came up with a better idea than he'd had all morning.

'I suggest that we move the plating tanks to the edge of the square.'

'The authorities might not like that,' said a voice from inside his headache.

'We wouldn't be asking them to like it. We'd be asking them to notice it,' he produced his most extensive smile of the day at the thought of so many people being given a clear view of what Joe Taskerman was doing to them.

'We are not at fault. We are operating strictly according to regulations,' said the man with a silver tongue.

'And so say all of us,' echoed a chorus from the shop floor.

'At least those of us who want to keep our jobs in this caricature of a land of free speech,' said Ivan forgetting for a moment the delicate condition he was in.

'Look, free speech is all very well, but remember who pays your wages,' said a member of the remunerations committee.

'You mean we all have the freedom to speak, providing we speak with one voice, no matter that consistency is not our strongest suit?'

'How's that?' echoed a cordon of slip fielders.

'You won't get far appealing to the umpire on that one. He seems to have fallen asleep. Perhaps it's the plant that's put him to sleep. How's that indeed. The plant has been putting people to sleep for years.'

'Hey can you prove that?'

'Of course I can't. There isn't a chance of a rusty link in a chain gang of ever doing that. Not in a million years. Everyone who's ever worked here knows the only thing which matters in this travesty of a habeas corpus is that you are guilty even if you were somewhere else at the time.'

'Habeas corpus... guilty... is this some kind of court then?' said a puzzled newcomer to the proceedings.

'Oh it's a court all right. Although there's little justice to be had when you're faced with a judge who believes he has jurisdiction over everything,' said Ivan throwing the sports pages of the newspaper across the room as far as he could from his sitting position.

7

THE SLOWEST OF SLOW MOTIONS

Ivan lay propped on a pillow wondering whether he ought to stretch his legs. The throbbing vein in his temple seemed to suggest otherwise, reminding him that in order to walk you had first to be able to stand up.

'Well, there's only one way to find out,' he said as a voice within insisted it was time to put his improving condition to a more stringent test.

With an effort he pulled himself into a more upright position, and taking a deep breath discovered that his lungs had not collapsed. It was time to try something a little more ambitious and he swung his legs over the edge of the bed expecting terrible things to happen. But they didn't, and being careful to hold onto the edge of the bed, he turned himself around and began to stand up. Taking the one shirt that came to hand he slowly eased himself into it before reaching for the trousers that were lying across the chair beside the bed. He suspected that entering them would be a more difficult task yet found the opposite to be the case, and was so heartened that he decided it was time for the ultimate test of stability. Placing his feet in the slippers which must have landed right beside the bed when he'd kicked them off on the previous evening, he began to put one foot in front of the other.

There seemed little indication that he might be about to fall over, and so he picked up those sections of the newspaper within reach and set off as though embarking upon one of the great journeys of his life. He managed to get downstairs as far as the lounge, but instead of collapsing into the nearest armchair he dropped the newspapers onto the floor and made off for the kitchen, to be confronted by a pile of dishes still lying untouched on the draining board. He'd been in no condition to do anything about the dishes on the previous evening and even now had no idea how he was going to steel himself to approach them. But he knew that he must. Loading up a dishwasher was one thing, but washing them all by hand was entirely another matter. If only they'd bought a new dishwasher instead of trying to repair the old one. The tightness in his stomach and the heaviness of his arms told him that if he were to launch himself in his usual manner, concerned only with the completion of the task, there could be dire consequences for the crockery.

Then with a blinding flash he saw the solution was staring him in the face. Knowing how easy it would be to become thoroughly annoyed with the task, he must convince himself that washing the dishes would be an enjoyable thing to do. The impact of this discovery made his head spin. Yet it had been a dishevelled man in a cardboard box, who echoing the great Russian novelist, had suggested that questions about the meaning of life only made sense when you began to see the search for meaning as the meaning you were looking for. So long as you didn't expect to find it. And to think he'd given the man only a measly fifty pence, when here he was on the threshold of an important adjunct to that, whereby if he could focus on the process rather than upon completion of the task, then it should become relatively easy to enjoy washing the dishes.

He took the bowl from under the sink and began filling it with hot water. Perhaps he ought to give himself a little more credit for his achievements. Perhaps he ought to congratulate himself more often. Beginning with a huge pat on the back for never having so much as glanced at anything brought home from the sweathouses of the working world, knowing that in slaving for any Joe Taskerman you couldn't be seen leaving the premises before midnight unless you were struggling with a mountain of papers under your arm, whether or not you intended looking at any of them. Given his success in that sphere, it made no sense to approach household chores in a way which mirrored the striving for more output of which the prospect of making five thousand per week was merely the latest example.

Again his thoughts returned to whether the explanation for

the unpleasantness of Joe Taskerman may have had something to do with the letter he'd received. He wondered whether anyone else would have received a letter. He'd been determined not to open his own letter until after the weekend. Now he began to have second thoughts. The old fool might indeed have decided to make them all redundant, and with the scale of his incompetence he would probably have included himself in that. Ivan could find only joy at the prospect of Joe Taskerman being made redundant no matter who the initiator. Joe Taskerman had put his foot in his mouth so often he deserved everything that was coming to him.

'Did you hear that Footmouth? Even the rats are feeding on the knowledge that you've brought this upon yourself.'

He was rejuvenated by the idea of Joe Taskerman being given something to think about for a change – forgetting that Joe Taskerman had always refused to think about anything that couldn't be quantified. Now he could indeed feel quite different about washing the dishes. Of course it would be unreasonable to allow his accumulated frustrations to influence the way in which he approached the dishes. More than unreasonable, it would be insane. He must put an end to that kind of thinking. It was time to begin the second half of his life with a promise that it would be a lot less frantic than the first half. There was no need to rush headlong into this. He had plenty of time. There were no targets to be met. He could begin by pretending his feet had been glued to the floor. That ought to slow things down a bit. And it did. To the slowest of slow motions. He would have cursed himself for not trying this before, had he not tried it many times before. Yet this time it seemed to be working. He hadn't moved for three and a half seconds. Three and a half seconds. On the other hand, slow motion or not, three and a half seconds was a long time – long enough to conjure up an image of not being able to move at all, and so seeking reassurance he began to glide across the floor, raising his arms into the air and wondering why at a crucial point in his life he could not have met up with a man called Nureyev instead of one called Taskerman.

SURVIVING JOE TASKERMAN

Returning to the pile of dishes on the draining board, he wrapped his fingers around a cup and gently lowered it into the bowl. The water conveyed a warmth to his hands causing him to purr with delight. Until he found himself imagining that the cup he was holding was the neck of Joe Taskerman. His pace increased and his blood stirred in anticipation as he fought desperately to cast this image from his mind. But he succeeded only in despatching the innocent cup to the floor, where it now lay in considerably more pieces than it had been in a few moments ago.

He was saved from an urge to sweep the whole pile of dishes onto the floor by an image of his grandfather dissipating his anguish by counting up to ten after removing the end of his finger with an old band saw, which his grandmother had immediately confined to the dustbin... 'One–bloody finger; two–bloody saw; three–bloody sharp; four–bloody hell; five–arrgh...'

Ivan could get no further than five, but the memory of his grandfather's reaction gave him a huge surge of confidence. Of course you could change the way you did things. Of course you could convince yourself you had all the time in the world. Of course you could become your own foster child of silence and slow time – once you had realised that your movements were entirely within your own control.

Making the most of his new found confidence he took hold of a dinner plate and lowered it into the water, allowing his hands to linger in the water before removing the plate and transferring it to the draining board. How strange that this senuous pursuit should have been given such a bad press. But there again you could never trust a tabloid journalist. An ability to enlarge upon experience was one of the main requirements for the job. Every blind reporter worth a column inch knew how to produce a sensational report on anything under the sun moon and stars such that somebody or other ended up in hot water. If it was copy you were after they would provide you with copy all right, with a nod, and a wink, and a my word no, 'We never disclose our sources guv.'

The subject of enlarging upon experience reminded him too

that there was an even higher priority than one of making five thousand per week. For the most important storyline in any enterprise run by Joe Taskerman would always be one of demonstrating that a total of five thousand per week had been made. That was after all why Joe Taskerman kept telling them the security of their jobs was dependent upon showing results. You had to admire the simplicity of this. If all you had to do was show you'd been successful for the world to become your oyster then how could anyone complain? There wasn't much anyone could ask other than that it should be the results which counted, one-two-three-four-five, for there it was in sweet-sweet black and white, five thousand times, five thousand with not a bead of sweat in sight. Oh it was the results which counted all right. That was what had been drummed into them until they were sick of hearing him repeat it over and over again.

Ivan found it infuriating to think of the credit Joe Taskerman had been given for the figures he'd produced, although why was he talking about credit when debit was more the kind of thing he had in mind. Still, credit or debit he supposed it didn't make much difference in a world in which ambition was an asset and shareholders capital was a liability.

Ivan's father would have said that a reluctance to make up his mind about anything was about the extent of his son's abilities, and Ivan might have been prepared to agree had he not suffered more than enough from that kind of muddled thinking. He could smile now about the fight he'd put up when faced with making a choice between arts and sciences, but he hadn't found it so amusing at the time. Of course he'd lost and done sciences, the questioning of the need to make a choice having been the last thing his father had wanted to hear. Ivan had tried to reason that you could only be indecisive in a situation which required a decision to be made. But his pleas had fallen on deaf ears, his father having taken the view that in questioning the legitimacy of that choice you were denouncing the very basis of educational opportunity upon which matter there was nothing further to say.

SURVIVING JOE TASKERMAN

There had never been any question about the decisiveness of Ivan's father. He could point to any number of occasions upon which he'd been decisive. Beginning with his acceptance of the terms offered by the county cricket committee, where he'd been able to demonstrate his decisiveness to even larger audiences, never having been known to call for a run that couldn't be made, as he'd told Ivan on many occasions.

The cricketing fortunes of his father had been a source of both inspiration and disappointment to Ivan. His father would have been the first to admit that he'd never been close to selection for an England place, but he'd been in and out of the county side for a good number of years, being a member of that group of hard working professionals referred to by sport's commentators as bread and butter players.

On retiring from county cricket, Ivan's father had taken a full time job with the sportswear distributor with whom he'd worked during the winters in the years of his playing career. He'd risen to become area sales manager, and had taken the company from being a regional stockist for small shops to the position it now held as a supplier to some of the large nationals. Well, he and a few more people, there being no denying that from those early foundations, the company had gone ahead in leaps and bounds.

There had never been any likelihood of Ivan following in his father's footsteps. The possibility of him becoming a professional cricketer had been dismissed at an early age, Ivan's father having been quick to realise that his son lacked a good enough eye for the game. And as Ivan had discovered on more than one painful occasion there may have been an element of truth in that, although it hadn't prevented him from believing he would improve with practice and neither did it mean that cricket wasn't in his blood.

In his blood or not Ivan played cricket in the street, did science, and went to work in the steelworks. He would have been there to this day had it not been for the intervention of decisiveness in a bigger way than he could have imagined. What a strange business that had been – never mind the problem, what were you going to do about it had been the essence of that call to decisiveness. To this day, Ivan remained unclear as to what he'd been meant to do other than cultivate an ability to pretend he knew what he was doing in order to show the world he was decisive. In his own way he'd tried to make the best of working in the steelworks, which in turn had done its best to confirm his conclusion that decisiveness was an overrated virtue. Virtue? What was he saying? Decisiveness was a vice.

'There you are, we told you this pillock couldn't make his mind up about anything,' a voice from down the years rang out.

For once Ivan ignored the provocation as he carefully lowered another cup into the water, casting his mind back to those long summers before the arrival of decisions. The only results that had mattered in those days had been how many runs you could score before the end of the school holidays, or more likely before the river had claimed your last ball.

Ivan's father had spent most of those summers living away from home, returning only for an occasional visit, during which he would deliver a lecture on the sacrifices that had to be made in pursuit of his profession. Then his father would be on tour again and life would return to endless days in the woods and fields, with broken-down walls and muddy footpaths beside the river. On some of his visits home, Ivan's father would bring a new ball and cricket would be in season again. Until the river defeated their latest retrieval mechanism and sent them back to the World Pebble Skimming Championships; or to watching water voles along the eroded river bank; or occasionally to the more exciting prospect of potty-spotting for the knur and spell players in the field beside the railway embankment.

When his father left county cricket, summers had become less governed by fixture lists, making it possible for Ivan to be taken on a seaside holiday for the first time. He remembered the Monday morning of that first holiday by the sea. They'd gone to the tennis courts in the hope Ivan might possess an aptitude for what his father had called our other great summer game. But he'd been adjudged to be lacking the co-ordination required, and so his father had abandoned him to the beach and gone off to play golf.

Ivan had found the sea boring and had longed to be back by the river. But the holiday had been paid for in advance and he'd resigned himself to spending a whole week shivering at the edge of the water with no inclination to remove anything beyond his shoes and socks. At the end of the week he'd turned and walked away vowing never to go back to the sea, until he'd found himself many years later introducing Timothy and Joanna to that same water's edge. They of course had taken to the water like seals whilst he had been still trying to remember what they were doing there. He wondered why he hadn't been taught to swim by his father. His father was a strong swimmer... 'Well, you had to be able to swim in order to play cricket in England,' Ivan would say, although not whilst his father was within earshot. Which hadn't been very often he thought ruefully. He recalled too that he'd never seen his father play cricket, neither for the county nor for the second eleven. It had never been possible to arrange that, due to the long distances involved and the restrictions on players during county championship games. His father's parsimonious approach to the accumulation of runs meant that he'd never played in any of the white ball games.

Ivan had always looked forward to watching cricket with his father once his playing days had come to an end, but the demands of a second great career had prevented that. Looking back, Ivan could see that his father's sporting achievements having been less than his dreams, he'd become consumed by a need to demonstrate unbridled success in an alternative arena.

Ivan's boyhood passion for cricket had thus grown into an adult obsession with less influence from his father than might have been expected. In fact from the moment of his leaving the game he could hardly remember speaking to his father about the fortunes of the county side right up until that long and lonely night during which an umpire had raised his finger for the last time.

8

STRONG TEA

Ivan looked at the pile of dishes on the draining board. At this point he would have begun to dry them had he not read that drying-up cloths were full of bacteria and that providing you'd rinsed the dishes thoroughly it was better to allow them to dry naturally. With a sense of relief he filled the kettle and emptied the dregs from the teapot, pausing to hang onto the worktop for a moment when he felt a sudden dizziness in bending towards the waste bin under the sink.

'Take cover,' cried Owen, as he dived under the kitchen table, creating such turbulence that Bernard was forced to take evasive action by jumping onto the refrigerator.

'What the hell do you think you're doing?' said Bernard.

'I think he may finally have cracked,' said Henry.

'Cracked what?' Bernard sounded almost hopeful.

'Well,' said Henry, 'judging by the way he went down it's obviously something important.'

'Important to whom?' said Bernard.

'To you and I if he has to spend the next six weeks with a leg in plaster.'

'You're right,' said Bernard. 'We would never hear the end of it.'

Having washed everything in sight and some of the items twice, Ivan had decided to make a fresh pot of tea. He was standing beside the singing kettle, preparing to warm the pot, when his eyes were drawn to the window as a gust of wind whipped up a cloud of apple blossom still falling after the cold spring. Then just as suddenly the gust died, leaving the blossom to float in the air as though someone had opened up a feather mattress.

'Get down,' cried Owen, noticing that Henry was standing in front of the window.

'Not likely,' said Bernard, still courting the higher ground on top of the refrigerator.

'Not you….him,' Owen gestured towards Henry.

'What on earth for?' said Henry.

'Look, look… look out there. It's a nuclear winter,' said Owen.

(*'Oh please.'*)

'It's nigh on high summer, said Henry. The only thing wintry out there is due to the fact that it's snowing apple blossom.'

Ivan warmed the teapot and returned the kettle to the boil. Resting a hand on the handle of the teapot he yearned for the characters who were sharing much more than his car to be a little more helpful. He tried to recall an occasion when he'd been allowed to enjoy a quiet moment without interruption. They seemed to consider it a duty to invade his trains of thought. Did they really think he would fall for the trick of believing he needed them? He'd never needed anyone until meeting Rowena. He hadn't been a lonely child. He'd had many friends... friends with whom he'd climbed trees, played cricket, walked river banks, sailed boats, made rafts, ridden bikes, and had picnics on the moors. There was even a gang to which he'd belonged – a gang in which he'd learned most of what he knew about the opposite gender. He smiled when he recalled that hadn't been quite the description used in gang conversations.

He supposed that keeping him occupied with things he could do little about was all he could expect from the characters who were real enough to him. Whatever their origins, he knew they were far from indicators of abnormality. Their existence was a perfectly rational response to an alien world. It was sometimes said that inner voices were an expression of someone's unease. Well anyone would be uneasy after a week of banging their heads against a brick wall. His situation wasn't at all unusual. Of course he had a fragile identity. Many people had. That was one way of dealing with the awful daily reminders of how few choices you had, no matter how many times you changed your job; moved house; began a new life… uh uh, he had a feeling he knew where this was heading. He'd been through enough crises of the self doubting kind to last a lifetime. Questioning his reason for being, was second nature to him. He had no idea why he was here. Apart from putting whatever he encountered to his advantage, which was what he'd always been advised to do by those with his best interests at heart, as distinct from those with only their own interests in mind.

Turning to look out of the window with its view of the floating petals, Ivan was struck by how much the scene did bear a passing resemblance to one of those rose coloured January days when the setting sun has not quite been obliterated by the already falling snow.

'Come on, be honest,' said Owen, scrambling out from beneath the table with a grin stretching from one side of his face to the other. 'That made you stop and think didn't it?'

'It certainly made me think,' said Bernard, 'although I confess mainly about when you are going to cease making yourself an object of derision.'

'You should be grateful,' said Owen. 'It's the existence of characters like me that makes the world a safer place in which to live.' There was a worrying hint of conviction in his voice.

'It would be a misnomer to describe as safe any world in which you were an inhabitant,' said Bernard.

'Why can't you see that we only have ourselves to blame for making the world a more dangerous place?' said Owen.

'He's never been one for looking much below the surface of things,' said Henry.

Ivan poured himself a cup of tea wondering whether it was an extraordinary level of self confidence or simple stubbornness that had given rise to Joe Taskerman's refusal to look below the surface of anything, leaving him unable to distinguish between a difficulty to be overcome from a problem that was irresolvable.

'I take my responsibilities seriously,' said Bernard. 'It wasn't me who declined to vote in the last election.'

'That may be so,' said Henry. 'But having a right to vote is of limited use in the absence of alternatives upon which to cast your vote.'

'Exactly,' said Owen. 'And it's because those alternatives

are not being presented that we need to give them a higher profile.'

'No we don't,' said Bernard, finally climbing down from the refrigerator. 'What we need is a cup of tea.'

'Here you are then,' said Owen, handing him a cup.

'What on earth is this?' said Bernard, examining the liquid in his cup.

'It's the last of the washing up water,' said Owen, his lip curled not entirely humorously.

'Are we out of tea?' Bernard pursued the matter insensitively.

'I think he may have been under the impression that you didn't like strong tea,' said Henry.

'But I do have a preference for tea rather than hot water, said Bernard. 'As a matter of fact I have generally found the best way of making tea is to use those tiny pieces of what I believe in the sub-continent are called tea leaves.'

'Tea leaves?' said Owen. 'You wanted tealeaves did you? I must confess I normally throw those away.'

'Well there won't be many to throw away on this occasion,' said Bernard, returning his cup to the table with a force that was in danger of breaking a good deal more than the cup.

9

BEWARE THE YELLOW MONSTER

Wandering back into the lounge, Ivan fell into the nearest armchair where he sat staring at the television screen beaming out its pathetic cries for attention from the corner of the room. He had long ceased to regard this as a feature of residual phosphorescent dots. The invention of plasma and LCD screens had confined most of that technology to the dustbins of history. Although that had done little to prevent the demands from persisting long after the sets had been switched off. Why otherwise over the years would he have spent so many Saturday mornings engrossed in the matrix planning required to confirm there would be nothing worth watching on any of the five over-hyped channels over an entire evening's viewing – to say nothing of the dismal output from the additional channels made available by the digital switchover once you had decided whether to take the terrestrial or the satellite option. The easiest route had been to choose the terrestrial option, especially if the means of receiving additional channels had been included when you'd been persuaded to buy the new television you hadn't needed. The trouble was the included channels didn't give you much access to live cricket, and so in Ivan's case, swallowing hard, the satellite option it had been.

'Channel hopping is a manifestation of our essential disaffection,' said a man in a minority programme on a channel he'd never watched but had once seen through a shop window.

'Is that why we have to put up with you,' he recalled a man behind him having said on behalf of the silent majority.

Ivan had long ago decided that apart from cricket, he could have done without any of these channels endlessly plugging their own programmes. He needed something more substantial. Something to take his mind off his present condition. He consoled himself with the thought that Rowena would be back soon. Then he could have an intelligent conversation. In the meantime he turned over a page of the newspaper looking for the financial section, which immediately floated off on a journey of its own, scattering the soot which had gathered on the hearth. It seemed the ducting in the chimney may not have been been properly seated when the gas fire had been installed. Another job to join the list. Not wishing to dwell on how long that list had become his eyes fell on the travel section of the newspaper. But all that did was provide him with another reminder of how little it was possible to achieve in one lifetime – if in this case with respect only to how much of the newspaper would remain unread at the end of the day.

'Well, at least it's not raining,' said Henry.

'It's not Christmas Eve either,' said Bernard.

'Why would anyone imagine it was Christmas Eve?' said Henry.

'Why would anyone imagine Christmas began three months before its arrival?' said Bernard.

Ivan got up from his chair and wandered over to the bookcase. He went through the titles one by one, in each case deciding to leave the book exactly where it was. Then he moved over to the bay window, peering along the road first in one direction and then the other. His view was restricted by the overgrown hedge, so standing on his toes and stretching his neck he tried to get a better view from the higher panes of the window.

'I've come to warn you,' cried Owen, suddenly bursting on the scene.

'It's too late you're already here,' said Bernard glumly.

'And a good thing too,' said Owen. 'For I've come to warn you.'

'Oh go on then if you must,' said Bernard.

'I've just seen a huge yellow monster coming along the road,' said Owen.

('*Oh no.*')

'Would you believe it?' said Bernard.

'You must believe it… you must,' said Owen.

'There's a huge yellow monster coming along the road.'

'Maybe it has something to do with that nasty yellow bruise around your eye,' said Bernard.

Ivan considered the school of thought claiming that weekends were for relaxation. He supposed it would depend on what you did with the rest of your week because digging a tunnel under the river Thames might be a relaxing way to spend a weekend if it helped you to forget about Joe Taskerman. Unless your condition prevented you from doing so – a thought which in itself might cause you to heed the claim that lying down in a darkened room was the only effective way to deal with a morning after a night you'd rather not have had. He decided that an unmitigated outburst of hilarity was the best response to that kind of prescription, since the moment you lay down in a darkened room was likely to be the point at which your torment began. The only use for a darkened room he could think of would require him to lock up the three characters currently doing little for this particular morning after a night he unquestionably wished he'd never had.

He was reminded of a time when at the end of a day of laughing and fooling around with a bunch of friends in the woods, he'd gone home and realised there was no longer anyone with whom he could have an ordinary conversation. His father's absence and his mother's inability to say what she thought had meant there was nothing to compete with the wonders of an afternoon spent listening to the sexual exploits of the older boys, roguishly embellised or not. The resulting anticlimaxes had provided the characters who were sharing much more than his car with all the opportunities they needed. And here they were again taking advantage of the condition he was in.

'You don't understand,' said Owen. 'There's a huge yellow monster coming along the road… and it's eating houses.'

Henry gazed at Owen in awe. To be in the company of someone with such imagination was remarkable. No one could doubt Owen's flair for invention. Although in the light of this, Henry was more concerned about its effect on Bernard in his current state. But he needn't have worried for

Bernard had already prepared himself for a quick deflation of this latest flight of fancy.

'Oh I see... is this the card?' said Bernard, holding up an imaginary playing card to remind Owen of the magician in the holiday hotel the previous summer, who in demonstrating his skills with a pack of cards, had removed Owen's watch without him having any idea of what had been taking place right under his nose.

'This is not a trick... this is real,' said Owen.

'Well I have to admit it's an interesting idea,' said Bernard, 'but unfortunately we're right out of need for that kind of thing today. Thank you for thinking of us though. Good morning.' He made as if to show Owen the door.

'It's not an idea, it's true. There is a great yellow monster and it's heading in this direction.'

'So we have been led to believe,' said Bernard a little more tersely.

'It's true,' Owen persisted. 'It's heading this way and it's demolishing houses as it comes along the road.'

'It is funny you should say that,' said Bernard. 'We'd heard something like that was happening.'

'You don't understand? It's demolishing houses and it's coming this way,' cried Owen.

'Perhaps we shall catch sight of it then,' said Bernard.

'You can't stay here. It might pick on this house.'

'Well it is a nice house.'

'This is serious,' cried Owen.

'Of course it is,' said Bernard. 'Demolishing a building without planning consent is a serious offence.'

'Oh for God's sake... why don't you just shut up and listen,' said Owen.

'We were rather hoping you might be the one to do that,' said Bernard.

'Hey, just a minute,' said Henry, intent on disentangling perception from reality. 'I think Owen may have a point. There is something odd going on out there.'

'I can't see anything,' said Bernard.

'Perhaps you should take a turn at cleaning the windows,' said Owen.

Ivan was conscious of an ache in the back of his legs as he tried to raise himself ever higher on his toes. Afterwards he would wonder whether his appearance in the street had been a result of his inability to elevate himself further, or whether it had simply been a matter of momentum, the force which only rivers and politicians understood. Whether or not, it didn't entirely explain why he was treading so warily along what was after all a thoroughly suburban road, although he did have a feeling he might be about to find out.

'There it is,' cried Owen, pivoting on his heel, fearing they may have been surrounded.

His companions turned to see a huge yellow monster with a lunging neck thrusting its head into a hole in the road. The monster was twice the size of anything they'd seen before, and each attack was accompanied by a gurgling roar as it appeared to suck the very heart out of the road in what Henry would later describe as a compelling demonstration of the logarithmic basis of the Richter scale.

The huge yellow monster, which was not after all a function of anyone's imagination, seemed to be having an early lunch, and in response to the incredible noise Ivan found himself staggering backwards through a privet hedge. Crouching behind the hedge he was aware of how much the ground was shaking as the monster thrust its head down another hole in the road. Then just as quickly off it went, bellowing along, leaving its silent observer undetected, but feeling weak and watery as a stream of cold sweat ran down the inside of his shirt.

'Don't know what they'll bloody priv'tise next,' a voice boomed out from behind him.

Ivan felt his heart leap into his mouth and turned to see that he'd wandered into someone's garden. The voice was coming from an open space lying between a mud-stained black beret and an old tweed suit, the latter of which someone had left leaning against a lawn mower. There was little to suggest occupation of the suit other than the paint blistering noise coming from the space between the beret and the suit, but that was evidence enough.

'Bloody lib'ty,' screamed the voice. 'See that?'

Ivan wondered how anyone could have missed it. Perhaps whoever was inside the suit thought he was blind. He certainly seemed to be under the impression he was deaf. There was just time for him to recall that he'd never been so close to a foghorn when the onslaught resumed. It was almost as loud as the monster itself, but fear is relative and when you've just been through hell, high water is often not so intimidating. This time he only backed away along the line of the hedge a couple of paces.

'See that? Bloody coun-cil. Bloody stupid. What d'they think this is... the Suez Canal? Look 't bloody size o't. Bloody silly dahn a road like this? On a bloody Sat'day... aye, an' a bloody bank hol'day an' all. What d'they want t'priv'tise drain cleaning for? Bloody tu'pence cheaper that's why. Bloody loonies. Appen they'll priv'tise thee next. Appen they already have.'

'Quite,' said Ivan inadequately.

'Might as well be livin' at bloody Gatwick. Seen that house? Der'lict it is. It's der'lict nah... 'bin shaken to bloody bits ain't it?'

'Has it really?' said Ivan. 'Is that... er so?'

'What d'yer mean, is that so? O' course it is. I just bloody said so didn't I? Ere, yer don't work for t'bloody coun-cil do yer?'

'No no, I work for.. ' but Ivan never finished the sentence as with a soft groan he turned and emptied the contents of his stomach into the bottom of the privet hedge.

'Bloody hell,' cried the foghorn.

10

NOTHING IS PERFECT

'Oh there you are,' said Rowena putting her head around the door.' How do you feel?

'I have to admit I'm feeling a bit rough,' said Ivan.

Rowena agreed he didn't look well and added that perhaps it was a good thing he'd chosen not to go to the supermarket since it had been extraordinarily busy.

Ivan said it had been busy where he'd been too, and stretching his legs out in front of him began furiously rotating his ankles in demonstration.

'I feel as though I've just driven in a Grand Prix.'

Rowena said he looked as though he'd just been run over by one, and not entirely divorced from that went on to ask if he would like a sandwich.

'A sandwich... er, I'm not sure. I've er been sick actually and so perhaps I should give my stomach a rest.'

'Sick? You've been sick? What, you mean physically sick?'

It occurred to him that chemically sick would have been a more accurate description, but not wishing to encourage a repeat performance, he restricted himself to a simple confirmation of the fact that he'd been sick.

'Now I wonder what could have caused that?'

'I'll tell you what caused that,' said Ivan launching into a description of the circumstances that had led him to succumb to an accommodating privet hedge. Ignoring his fragile condition he gave a vivid account of the great yellow monster with the dinosaur neck as it had run amok along the street. Leaving little to the imagination in his portrayal of the ferocity with which it had attacked, he underlined his point with a reference to the earth shattering consequences for the derelict house.

Rowena said she'd noticed the derelict house had finally collapsed, and had assumed a demolition team had been at work. Indeed, thought Ivan as he continued his story of a far from restful morning by describing his meeting with another interesting character who'd entertained him with a convincing impression of a Foghorn. Rowena said Foghorn sounded a bit like Footmouth, a suggestion which Ivan scorned. The idea of any resemblance between Foghorn and Footmouth went no further than a cursory observation that they were both well-practised in the use of the loud pedal. Being a loudmouth was about the extent of Footmouth's repertoire, whereas in Foghorn's case at least he had something to shout about. Unlike Footmouth he knew that privatisation was not an answer to everything and that there were limits to economies of scale.

'Foghorn knows it's impossible to get blood out of a stone,' he said. 'Whereas Footmouth would never accept that – not even if it meant having to grow the stone himself.'

Rowena grimaced at the thought, before remembering that she too had something to shout about with respect to the question of lunch.

'Are you sure you don't want a sandwich love – I've got smoked salmon.'

'No, no, er I think er, a piece of, er dry toast, er that is er, if you don't mind dear.' He was unable to bear the thought of anything that might have been within a hundred miles of a fish coming near to his stomach at the moment.

Rowena managed to restrain herself from commenting on the self-inflicted cause of his rejection, choosing instead to make an unbecoming gesture to the figure in the hall mirror as she passed by on her way to the kitchen, leaving Ivan to wonder why she hadn't suggested opening a bottle of champagne to accompany the smoked salmon.

'I can always get an evening job,' he said in a voice calculated not to carry so far as Rowena.

'We've been strapped for cash all our lives struggling to pay for the bricks and mortar, so why should we expect things to be any easier now? Although, perhaps you're right. What on earth would be the point of getting ourselves into a position from which we might claim we were solvent?'

Experience had taught Ivan that when you worked for a

living the prospect of insolvency was never more than a couple of squares away on the monopoly board. He knew there was little chance of stability in his life. Even his own name was a confirmation of that. To the world he had always been known as Ivan K Driver no matter what his birth certificate said. Who was to know the mythical K had been an invention of his own? Imagine being called Ivan Driver. ('*Thank you mother.*') Yes, thanks were due to his mother, his lovely long lost mother, for a drollery she had always refused to concede no matter how many times he'd complained.

Ivan had been repeatedly told he was unlikely to achieve much in his life. Although most of that had come from the people least likely to know, witness their pronouncement that he would be unlikely to have reached the required standard in most of his subjects ('*yes, I only got nine O levels*'). Whilst of course they were the real failures. They were failing to provide much of an education for who knows – fifty, sixty, maybe as many as seventy per cent of the bums on seats in front of them. They'd certainly done their best to jeopardise his own future, precipitating his entry into the steelworks without so much as a gesture in the direction of an alternative.

'Another bucket of swill in the trough if you please, for the newcomer with nine O levels,' said a voice from the shop floor.

'Nine what?' queried Moses.

'I said nine O levels, but there's no need for you to worry your head about that Moses. We don't expect you to understand the significance of that. No-one else does. The important thing for him to learn is that now he will have to fill up the trough for himself. I doubt they'll have taught him much about that in his bucketful of nine O levels.'

Down the years Ivan knew he was sometimes seen as one of life's failures. Marginalised and disregarded. But was he really a failure? By whose standards? Things had changed of course. For one thing O levels had been replaced by GCSEs. Did that mean he'd been left behind? On the contrary he felt he was in front, because he understood, more so than those who thought modern disruption in classrooms was a consequence of kids no longer being taught to speak only when spoken to.

'Now then young Driver.' It didn't take much of a journey through a window, open or closed, for Ivan to be back in the steelworks. 'Your bucket's got a hole in it? Welcome to the world. Just be thankful that a little of the swill reached your trough in spite of the hole. And whilst we're on the subject of being thankful, remember you are a principal boy now. We know it's a drag, but that's what you are. A principal boy in a cast of what you are about to learn is a whole series of long running pantomimes, though don't expect to be applauded for your performance. You will learn soon enough which way the wind blows through the hole in the bucket of the trough that feeds you.

Ivan supposed that was where his education had really begun, although from the start he'd been left in no doubt that he was unlikely to find anyone willing to accept the label of teacher in that school.

'From now on it's up to you young Driver. Just keep out of the foreman's way that's all. You won't get any help in that direction. To hear him talk you'd think we did nothing but sit around on our arses all day. According to him, no-one had ever done anything useful. Useful? Not in a month of Sundays. Talking of which, from now on you'll be working on Sundays. You heard me. I said you'll be working on Sundays and what's more you'll be paid a good deal less than many of those who don't have to work on Sundays, the consolation being you'll have one thing they will never have and that's prospects.'

'Three cheers for the prospects,' cried a voice from the high bay gantry.

'Hey don't knock the prospects. The prospects are worth a lot more than anything else you'll find on offer in this place. Oh God, I'm beginning to believe my own bullshit. Prospects? You should try opening a bank account with prospects. Go and see how far you can pull the wool over their eyes with that one at the sign of the Griffin and the Black Horse.'

And so Ivan had taken his hopes and dreams into a

steelworks apprenticeship without having any idea of what an apprenticeship entailed. Other than that it seemed to dispose of alternatives for the next five years. He supposed five years would seem an age by today's standards. It had been a long time since five-year apprenticeships were the way of things.

Ivan would later have regrets about where his own apprenticeship had taken him, but at that point in his life he couldn't fail to have been impressed by those who'd told him what a good thing an apprenticeship was. And since for as long as he could remember people had been asking him what he planned to do when he grew up, he'd been proud to tell them in the manner of the perfect little gentleman he'd been brought up to be.

'Like yourselves, I expect I'll become a pain in the arse.'

'Now, now, enough of that young Driver. You know perfectly well what is being asked of you. The question concerns the opportunities you are being offered at the beginning of your working life.'

In a flash he was back in the classrooms of myopia…'er sorry Miss… to tell you the truth Miss, for years I've been fairly clueless Miss, but now it seems Miss that I'm about to become an apprentice, aren't I the lucky one. An apprentice what, did you say? Well knowing me I'll probably be an apprentice fart Miss, all wind and no ambition. Save that kind of talk for the playground? Thanks to you I don't go to school anymore if you remember.'

That was another thing about which he couldn't have been more wrong. For there was a detail in his indenture they'd omitted to bring to his attention. It was in the small print – the small print that no-one had been given time to read in the rush to get to the front of the queue that had led to the exciting prospect of spending the next five years in an apprenticeship which paid less than you'd earned on your paper round and the odd bob-a-jobbing you'd done in the street where you were born. Yes, it was there in the small print – the small print which required you to attend the local technical college, and told you that some of the attendance would be in your own time. Such that any thoughts you had about leaving school were wider of the mark than those you had about having any prospects.

Ivan shuddered as he remembered that attending night classes had led to the apprentices viewing their school-days in quite a different light, causing them to remember the happiest days of their lives with an affection that would have made old Froggy proud. Looking back, Ivan had to acknowledge that in one sense his schooldays had been quite an education – albeit not by way of a curriculum approved by a pontificating minister on any party political broadcast it had been his misfortune to hear.

'Hold it there young Driver. This is a school, a school, a school.' That was the one thing he could remember anyone saying in the schools he'd attended… ' along with, 'Have you got that well and truly imprinted on your forehead Driver?' He had sometimes thought they'd meant that literally.

'You are here to work young Driver.'

'But I thought you said this was a school sir.'

'Take a hundred lines Driver.'

'Er, where shall I take them to sir?'

'Take five hundred lines Driver.'

'What shall I write sir, I must not show that I have a mind of my own sir? Sir, how would you know whether I had a mind of my own? That's something no-one in this place will ever find out because all you've been trained to say is this is a school, a school, a school and that I'd better remember that.'

Would he ever forget? Still, giving credit where it was due, his apprenticeship had been a little more grown up than that. In those days apprenticeships had meant something. It was said they were your ticket. Ivan couldn't recall ever being given a ticket, but he supposed he must have claimed to possess one when approaching some of the doors he would later come to regret having passed through. Not least the one that would lead to him landing a starring role in Joe Taskerman's palace of varieties. But that was to come later. At the beginning of your working life it was the obtaining of an apprenticeship that was a cause for celebration.

'Oh Mrs Driver, is it true what they say about Ivan (does

your son really shine all the time) has that oh so beautiful baby of yours, that no-one ever wanted to grow up, has he got himself an apprenticeship? That's good news Mrs Driver. We knew young Ivan would do well (success around the corner) we knew he'd get a plum job (just like Johnny Horner) you must be very proud of that darling baby of yours Mrs Driver (pulling out his smelly thumb) and you must be proud of yourself too young Ivan (from the foreman's grotty bum) all those hours of homework were worth it you see (and sniff-sniffing what a good boy am I).'

'No I don't see. Perhaps I need those glasses after all dad.'

He'd discovered that he also needed a slide rule, a drawing board and a tee-square, and what was more, if he'd carried on acquiring everything he was told he would need, he would have needed a bank loan on his prospects before he'd had the security of knowing there was a pay packet waiting for him at the end of the week.

'When am I going to be taught something useful? That's what I want to know.'

'Come now young Driver. You are in no position to assess what you need to know. Your job is to remember you are an apprentice and that you're here to learn.'

'Learn? I don't remember much about that when I was at school. This is all new to me. Although it sounds as though it might be useful.' For only with hindsight did he realise that the one useful thing he would learn at night-school was how to avoid falling from a chair upon which he'd been anaesthetised by boredom.

'Oh Christ, er sorry sir, have I missed anything?'

'Not unless you still count on your fingers grammar-school-boy.'

'I do sir, I do so all the time sir, one-two-three-four-five, and what's more sir, I'm beginning to understand why you spend so much time telling us how lucky we are. You know a great deal about luck don't you sir, hanging onto your job whilst teaching us stuff that will be obsolete before we've left the room, not counting that which was out of date before we arrived.'

Was there any wonder so much emphasis had been placed

on keeping up to date in the steelworks. There were a lot of things you had to know. Such as the whereabouts of the foreman, on the well founded principle that you couldn't enjoy your cricket behind the tool room annexe if you had no idea of where the foreman was at the precise moment he decided to come and have a look at what you were doing.

'We were indeed playing cricket Mr Foreman sir, but it was in our lunch break. It was in our lunch break that we began our innings.'

That was the one aspect of keeping up to date in the steelworks for which Ivan was well equipped, and it would enable him to make a significant contribution to the really important decisions. Such as who was going to follow Boycott and Brearley as the first wicket down in the test team half way up the ladder to the Hollerith roof. My what a view there was from there. Bugger the test team hang on to your cap. No kidding you had to have a head for heights to go up there. Especially if you went with Moses.

'Makes no difference to me,' says Moses. 'I can't see the ground from up here. Tap-tap, blind as a bat. Bloody Moses. How many rungs can a blind man see? One-two-three-... Christ, look out Moses, I've only got two hands, I'm still an apprentice remember.'

Ivan recalled that no sooner had they arrived on the roof than it was time to make the tea. That was something he could do.

'What do you mean that's something I can't do? Why can't I make the tea? That's your job is it Moses? I'm here to learn a trade? I do know how to make tea, and what's more I'm happy to make it for you, big Joe, and anyone else who'd like some, including whoever should follow Boycott and Brearley at Lords, Headingley, Old Trafford and the whole winter tour of Australia.'

Down the years, in the confines of his armchair, Ivan shivered as he recalled there had once been another Joe in his life, although unlike Joe Taskerman, he had fond memories of big Joe.

'On second thoughts (he thought he'd thought, whilst thinking so again) you can make the tea yourself. I'm not sure

I do want to make big Joe's tea. Nor anyone else's if I have to climb up that ladder with a can full of boiling water. Why do you want to know where my snap tin is? It's in my... oh bugger I'm beginning to feel dizzy. Down the ladder... back up the ladder a step at a time, don't look down... phew. Where do I sit then? On the edge of that what? Bloody hell, come back Froggy all is forgiven.'

Ivan supposed that must have been where he'd first realised his means of survival was in his own hands. There was really no need to sit in terror eating his sandwiches hanging from the edge of a roof. In the blinking of an eye he could be anywhere he liked. In one sense there was nothing new in that. He'd been in the habit of dreaming he was somewhere else for as long as he could remember. Yet on that day on the roof of the Hollerith building, had come the realisation that he didn't have to feel guilty or embarrassed about doing so. After all, in absenting a part of yourself from a situation you were not avoiding your responsibilities. On the contrary, if you had a talent for something it was your duty to embrace and enhance it.

'Go to where did you say big Joe? Go to the stores? Hey Moses did you hear that, I'm being given something to do for a change. And so off I go and in no time at all, if I recall ('*I do*') I'm in the queue already. My turn now mister, please can I have the large feelers for big Joe? That's what I said, the large feelers... er why are you showing me your hands? Ha-ha, those are the largest feelers you have are they? They've felt everything there is to feel in the whole town have they? Well don't put them on my boiler suit then, Jimmy.'

Ivan remembered that even the dour storeman had raised a laugh at the sharp way in which he'd managed to extricate himself from that predicament, although he himself had been less sure. He knew he'd been lucky, and suspecting things would not always be so easy, his display of apparent nonchalance as he walked away had been short lived. To be supplanted by a desire to find a place in which to fret and curse and shed a tear for his inestimable naivety, a place where no-one and nothing but the rats could see or hear him. It had been good though because from that moment he ceased to have any doubts about whether the steelworks was an education. In its own way it was a school. A school in which there were many things to learn.

'Things of which you never told us Froggy, but to be fair how could you? Your knowledge of irregular verbs was unlikely to have done much to save you from a sharp-tongued storeman. On the other hand, a knowledge of irregular verbs might have had its uses in the steelworks. Although perhaps not Froggy, in a way that would have met with your approval.'

'Go to the tool room for an inspection bend did you say? And get on with it? Right away big Joe.' Ivan had suspected there may have been more to the request than was being revealed but he'd felt he'd better go. Or rather he'd better go but not go.

'You're learning young Driver,' said a voice from the past. 'You're getting the hang of things with your sense of fair play and the sharp tongue that one day will get you into more trouble than you could ever have imagined at that point in your apprenticeship. You're learning all right.'

From the comfort of his armchair approaching what he hoped would soon be the end of an almighty headache (itself a reminder that no matter how clever he thought he was, he'd learned very little) Ivan remembered that the tool room had produced its own evidence of how quickly you had to learn. He'd discovered this from a less fortunate apprentice who'd been subjected to a colourful initiation rite reserved for those who did not suspect there was more to an inspection bend than they might have imagined. The initiation was delivered by a group of women operators in the tool room polishing-bay who had their own way of celebrating the distinguishing characteristics of gender. These imaginative but by no means light-fingered operators were only too happy to oblige any apprentice who asked for an inspection bend. Quickly bending the naive apprentice over a bench, the lad (it had to be he) would unceremoniously be debagged and subjected to precisely what he had asked for, there being no guarantees that the inspection would be restricted to a mere visual examination of the parts. On completion of the visual inspection, a thick coat of machine oil would be applied and massaged into what in the less than euphemistic argot of the women in the tool room polishing-bay were referred to as, t'prentices' goolies. According to rumour it was at this point that the buffing machine came into play. Tradition had it that the machine was introduced as a joyful threat and had never been used for that purpose, but with the benefit of hindsight it was still enough to cause Ivan to shift his position in the chair at the memory of his narrow escape.

Oh there was no doubting that an apprenticeship placed you in a school where you had to learn. Whether it would have been an appropriate school for the education of the sons and daughters of gentlefolk was another matter.

'What did you learn at your brand new school for apprentices today Johnny? You learned how to put one on?' ('Oh Johnny how could you?')

'It's true. Ask big Joe. No don't ask big Joe, ask Moses. He's the one who's always telling us he knows how to put one on. He can do it from memory. Memory is the one thing he has left, but you wouldn't know that to hear him talk. The only loss of faculty Moses will admit to is having a reduced capacity. How many pints did you put away last night Moses? Really useful information that. Only six? Only have six nowadays do you? A bit regular i'nt it?'

'Reg'lar every morning an' all are yer,' said big Joe? 'No bloody wonder. Hey yer not the dead rat man are yer?'

Ivan could only shake his head. He'd done his best to introduce people to the idea of being somewhere other than on the rooftops of Hollerith buildings but no-one had wanted to know. Except for Moses. Moses could see the attraction of being in a bar with a foaming pint of beer in his hand at any time of the day or night.

'Christ look at that snow.' Easily distracted, big Joe's mind was already elsewhere. 'Bloody hell I could, I bloody could. Phew, if me missus heard me she'd have me ration book destroyed. Moses, Moses. Where the hell 'av yer been? Up Rose Lane 'av yer? Aye we've all heard that one. Even t'apprentice has heard that one. Ere don't tell me to piss off, you piss off, except you'd better not piss off whilst I'm hangin' from this bloody roof. Moses, Moses. Pass us t'driver will yer. Pass us bloody driver I said. Pass t'bloody screwdriver yer pillock. Moses, put t'apprentice dahn an' pass us t'bloody screwdriver for Christ's sake.'

'Ho-ho-ho, every one a winner,' cried big Joe.

'Ho-ho-ho, every one a winner,' echoed Moses.

'Ho-ho-ho everyone a sex maniac,' said Ivan not quite under his breath.

'Aye, Moses wer right. Yer wern't ready for this wer yer young Driver, if the truth wer known? If the truth wer known, apprentice, yer don't know what day it is. So bloody serious in yer crepe soled shoes and arse licking boiler suit. Don't lick the foreman's arse that's all. That's Noah's job and he gets jealous doesn't he Moses? Moses. For Christ's sake where's he gone now? Try telling t'sodding foreman yer only resting yer eyes. Yer'll have blisters on yer ears as well as on yer hands if he hears yer sayin' that. Try resting yer bloody 'mag'nation fer a change Moses.'

'And there you have it dearest Froggy of our long lost dreams and classroom farts. Can this be what you spent your life preparing us for? Probably not, but I haven't the the heart to tell you that they speak a language you will never know in this world of linguistic undertones. Undertones, and overtones and something-on-the-side tones. In-out, up-down, all around the town, the town. The whole town is at it if you believe everything you hear. Sing-sing-sing the music of the spheres is ringing in my ears. Who says the spheres are in my trousers and not in my ears? What do you mean it matters not that the spheres in my trousers are not spherical, and that I will find in this world, young Driver, nothing is perfect?'

11

YOUR COUNTRY NEEDS YOU

Ivan had been in no position to pursue perfection of any kind at that point in his apprenticeship, for the routines of his life had been interrupted with a message of your country needs you.

The letter had arrived like a bolt from the blue. It had landed on the mat one cold Saturday morning when by pure chance he'd been at home enjoying one of the few weekends on which he'd not been earning a little extra money whilst learning his trade. There was no contractual requirement for him to work weekends, but most of the apprentices did and since he wanted to be like everyone else the money came in useful. Now that was about to change.

The letter had announced that on Her Majesty's Service, his application to join the territorial army had been successful and that his presence would be required forthwith. The terms of his engagement would require him to contribute a good many evenings, several weekends and most of his annual holidays. What on earth could have possessed him… but alas, he didn't have the courage to say he'd changed his mind. What a fool that would make him look. Still, he supposed the school cadet force which had given him the idea hadn't been so bad and there was always a chance his flat feet would cause him to fail his medical such as it was.

With hindsight he wondered whether his next visit to the man in the pale blue tee shirt with matching trousers might have been a better option than the medicine man he'd been obliged to come face to face with before being admitted to the territorials. He recalled the doubts expressed by many as to the qualifications of the man who'd conducted that medical examination. He had shown little interest in the state of his feet no matter how many times Ivan had tried to direct his attention to them. Which seemed like only yesterday. But then he remembered yesterday, what had been a problem with his feet, had today become a question about the condition of his lungs, concerning whether there would be much left for the enjoyment of tomorrow. An awful lot of acid had gone through the plant and most of the fumes would have reached somebody's lungs by now. Life was so transient. And yet no matter how much he wished things would get a move on today, why oh why couldn't they yesterday have examined his feet more closely.

'Next… speak up laddie… speak up you 'orrible snotty nosed son of a professional… a professional… ere did you hear that corporal? This laddies father's a professional cricketer. Right then laddie artillery for you… next.'

It hadn't been quite like that Ivan chuckled, but you had to enlarge upon things a little as time went by, otherwise everyone would realise what an unutterably boring experience the whole thing had been. Moreover, there came a point when so much of your spare time was being wasted there wasn't much else you could do but laugh, and well, it hadn't been so bad once the great myths of purgatory and damnation had been laid to rest on the square.

'Up-two-three, down-two-three, knees up, knees up, this is not a cricket square laddie… squad, squad, squad will move to the right in threes, right, right, wait for it, wait for it…'

Ivan had been relieved that at least he hadn't been sent to a war zone for his two week annual holiday *('holiday?')* although successive years in Aldershot after spending the first one in Catterick was a bit of a disappointment even for an unambitious flat foot like himself, and yes it had been strange how his A1 grading had completely overlooked the condition of his feet.

Jimmy the Jaws had said he knew a man who'd known a man who'd become a reservist with only one hand. Would you believe it? Only one hand. Well as Jimmy the Jaws had said, someone had to keep moving the targets on the firing range. Jimmy had maintained the one thing you must have if you wanted to get on in the territorials was a large mouth; in fact he'd said that if you had one big enough (he was never very modest) and you knew how and when to use it (he had been very specific on that too) you could become a corporal in three and half months.

Ivan had got on well with Jimmy the Jaws, despite his uncanny knack of always having known someone who'd gone one better than the people in the stories anyone else told. Remembering Jimmy the Jaws, Ivan leaned forward in that conspiratorial way Jimmy had of making people feel they were his sole confident. Speaking in what he considered was a passable imitation of the infectious chuckle Jimmy had in his voice, Ivan bit his lip in an effort to prevent the chuckle from becoming the full blown guffaw which threatened to break out whenever he thought of Jimmy the Jaws.

I once knew a man,
who'd met a man
who'd lived twice, so he said.

I once knew a man,
who'd met a man
who'd met Christ, so he said.

'So he'd said,' laughed Ivan sinking back into his chair. On the other hand, as Jimmy had also said, if you didn't fancy what you were letting yourself in for, you had to remember that notwithstanding your feet, you might not be accepted. A testimony to that being the lad Jimmy had told them about. The lad's heart had been set on becoming a reservist but he'd failed his medical with bronchial trouble. He had then gone on to become northern counties cross country running champion three years in a row. Still, as Jimmy had maintained, the lad had no cause for complaint, a view with which Ivan had been quick to concur whilst again pondering why they had refused to examine his feet.

When he finally came to his senses and gave up on the territorials, Ivan went back to working weekends in the steelworks. By then he'd reached the age where he had to accept the same responsibilities as everyone else, no matter that he was still an apprentice. It seemed the wages department were the only ones not to recognise the anomoly. There were other changes too. Big Joe was promoted to foreman and Moses was moved to another department which meant that a lot of the fun had gone out of the job. A more instrumental approach was taken and the emphasis shifted to the necessity of carrying out that which had to be done in as painless a way as possible. That was when Ivan had first begun to realise how the idea of greatness had been devalued by the urge to produce more from less. Economic growth had become the deity of progress, relegating to the realms of idealism those who were trying to build on the generosity of the human spirit. The really great men and women.

Paradoxically, people had said those were the great years in the steelworks – years when a new hot mill was built, a new cold mill, a new rod mill, and even a new scrapyard (Jimmy the Jaws would have seen the funny side of that). The old machine shop was demolished, and the tool room, polishing-bay and all, was dismantled and rebuilt downstream from a new rolling mill. It seemed that almost nothing was left standing where it used to be, including Ivan remembered, several green fields and a birch wood where the main road was diverted to accommodate a new culvert over the river in order to get an extra three feet on the finishing line in the strip mill. At least this served to keep the water voles dry when it rained which it generally did whenever Ivan was on the Hollerith roof, until they knocked the Hollerith building down too.

'Oh no… what a memory.' Ivan snorted as he leapt from the chair and dashed across the room to switch on the television.

'So a fine start by these two,' said the voice of the late Jim Laker indicating that this was archive footage and that it must be raining at the one day international. He returned to his chair with a groan just in time to see the next delivery.

Here can you take this?' said Rowena standing over him with a delicately balanced tray containing a mug of tea and a plate of toast.

Huh, huh, oh yes… yes, thanks love.'

Ivan took the tray without looking up, whilst Rowena went back into the kitchen to return with a second tray, this one containing a cup and saucer in addition to a whole pot of tea, a jug of milk, and a plate of smoked salmon sandwiches.

'Must you watch that?' said Rowena deliberately choosing a chair near to the window from which she would be unable to see the screen. Without taking his eyes away from the speeding figure running in from mid-wicket, Ivan said that it was after all the second of the one-day internationals.

'Oh that's a magnificent stop,' said the voice of the late Jim Laker.

'It's the one day I have to relax,' said Rowena purposely excluding the remaining two days of the holiday weekend. Ivan responded by saying that he found cricket to be very relaxing. To which Rowena replied that in the right proportions she too found cricket to be relaxing, but that since the whole of Sunday afternoon had been earmarked for watching cricket then it seemed reasonable for her to ask to spend at least one day of her life having lunch with her husband.

'She's put him down,' Ivan could have sworn he heard Jim Laker say.

'Cricket-cricket-cricket,' muttered Rowena launching into the first mouthful of smoked salmon sandwich without noticing what she was eating, being more intent upon a condemnation of the very idea of watching television at lunchtime drawing as much satisfaction from the targeting of her comments as from the subject of her complaint. Whilst in return Ivan concentrated upon not listening to what Rowena was saying, deriving amusement from the knowledge that although she couldn't see the subtitles appearing on the screen, had she been listening to the soundtrack she would have recognised the voice of Jim Laker. Given her years of exposure to the game she would have known that Jim was sadly no longer with us and would have realised that Ivan was watching the recorded highlights of a one-day international from a previous era, rain having stopped play in the scheduled game.

Ivan's thoughts turned to a greater concern as he realised that recorded highlights or not there hadn't been a single run scored since he'd switched on the television. But then he reminded himself that England were batting, and as the late

Jim had said, it had been a fine start by these two for they hadn't yet lost a wicket.

Rowena was undeterred and continued to issue a stream of half muttered abuses towards the cricket, the television, the loss of sleep she'd suffered, and anything else that came to mind, the more specific purpose of which was only thinly disguised.

It was inevitable that some of her remarks would reach their target, and that when they did this would result in a build up of the kind of tension many generations of batsmen facing a hostile attack would have recognised. It was thus of no real surprise to anyone on that side of the room when Bernard threw down a half eaten round of toast sending one of Rowena's favourite china plates clattering onto the table. But fortunate that Henry, ever alert to the possibilities, was just in time to prevent Owen from throwing the mug of tea in pursuit by taking it from him and placing it very deliberately onto the table.

'He's taking a fresh guard,' said Jim Laker.

'He's lucky,' said Rowena having finally made contact with the soundtrack if not the identity of the speaker as she launched into a tirade about spending the night with a shaggy dog which had insisted upon kicking the end of her bed each time she'd been on the verge of falling asleep.

Ivan sprang to his feet and announced that he needed some fresh air. His terse invitation for Rowena to join him in a trip to the mere was greeted with a wave of exasperation resulting in his departure before he found himself trying to persuade her.

'He's gone,' Ivan just missed hearing Jim Laker say upon the fall of the first wicket before he was cut off in mid sentence.

12

A PAINFUL BUSINESS

Confirming the late commentator's pronouncement in less time than it would have taken a new batsman to reach the wicket, Ivan jumped into the car and with a quick glance to the right and left, reversed out onto the road. Pressing his foot down hard, the engine almost stalled in response to his attempt to set off in second gear, and when he subsequently changed from second straight into fourth, the gearbox too coughed roughly in objection to the treatment it was receiving.

The traffic was light however, and the car soon recovered its composure, enabling him to overtake a couple of unsteady cyclists and a vintage Ford Anglia impeding his progress. Then almost leaping out of his seat when he felt the first twinges of cramp in his right calf, he tried to steady the muscle by pressing his heel into the floor taking care not to alter the angle of his foot upon what he still maintained was the accelerator and not the gas pedal. But then he felt a twinge in his left calf, raising the possibility and the fear that he might be sickening for something. He raised his left foot from the floor with the aim of engaging it in a flexing motion hoping that might curtail the onset of cramp, but was a little too eager so that his knee came up higher than intended and hit the dashboard with a resounding crack. With a curse he returned his foot to the floor asking himself how it was possible with such frequency for him to do something he had sworn never to do again so long as he lived.

N O T I C E... the notice had been placed in the centre of the notice board from where it had been displaying its message for several days. No-one knew how many people had stopped to read it, but had anyone been monitoring such activities the impression gained would have been that the notice had not attracted much attention.

OPEN MEETING... it proclaimed. There will be a meeting in the works canteen at 12.00 on Friday at which a new round of career restructuring opportunities will be announced, was what those who had stopped to read the notice would have seen that it said.

The road ahead was clear and Ivan took full advantage of this, keeping his foot firmly on the pedal, easing off only as he went over the brow of the hill, from where his eyes picked up the familiar line of the road descending into the valley below. The bonnet of the car dipped as he went over a subsided section of carriageway where a stream taking the water away from the hill passed under the road. 'Another culvert about to give way,' he muttered, recalling the day the road by the steelworks, together with the end of the strip mill finishing bay, had fallen into the river.

The insularity of the car created a feeling of remoteness from the world outside, and realising he was beginning to feel sick again he lowered the window drawing in lungfulls of air which quickly brought him round. Though with mixed blessing for in no time he was back to thinking about Joe Taskerman. Bearing in mind the immense changes made in the steelworks during what had become known as the great years, it occurred to him that perhaps it was not so difficult to imagine how someone in Joe Taskerman's position could delude themselves into believing that anything was possible. Being able to convince yourself of your own invincibility was a prime requirement for anyone reckless enough to accept such a job. Not to mention the inflated self image you would need in order to step into a pair of shoes that were two sizes too big for you, but which you would need in order to maintain your position.

Ivan winced at the thought of position being everything. Alternative means of control had been tried, but the sad thing was that pyramids had been more resilient. Pyramids had their advantages but a lot of work was needed to mitigate their worst excesses and there were few who were prepared to undertake such work other than in a perfunctory way, there always being more important things to do.

He shook his head, and expelling the air from his lungs tried once more to discipline himself to the task of trying to forget about Joe Taskerman. His mind went back to the previous evening, and to the question of why food poisoning wasn't taken more seriously.

'Why do you keep saying it was food poisoning?'

'You were the one who suggested it was.'

'I was being allegorical.'

Food poisoning or not, Ivan had thought, it was evident the whole experience was designed to ensure people paid for their enjoyment, it being a well founded principle that nothing was for nothing. Even if it was free, he reminded himself that he hadn't parted with a penny for the privilege of the previous evening, which had already written off most of today. It had often been said pleasure was a painful business and the pleasure of the previous evening had certainly been a source of ensuing pain, such that he was beginning to wonder whether he would ever recover. He shivered as he realised that at this very moment a radiologist might be working on the details which by the middle of next week might in his own case provide an answer he wasn't looking for.

He decided he would rather consider the ravings of Joe Taskerman than those of the radiologist. Which was a measure of his confusion, for how could he believe anything Joe Taskerman said.

'There is nothing to worry about, we have taken the precautions necessary. The health and safety inspector has approved all of our procedures.'

Ivan remembered the health and safety inspector had been interested only in approving the size of his bacon sandwich. No-one had ever seen such a sandwich. He reminded himself that it hadn't done much for Archie's bacon, nor his wife, and that it wouldn't be much good telling their son Trevor there was nothing to worry about. Neither would it help to be told there was little anyone could do about having spent a whole lifetime in the wrong job. Selective omissions in your employment history would do nothing to save you from being in the wrong place at the wrong time. He realised this was far from serving to relax the muscles in his calves but was unable to prevent himself from lamenting the lack of evidence that had given rise to the situation in which so little was known about what was being done to so many by so few.

DO NOT DISTURB - was the sign which those attending the meeting would have seen had been hung on the door...

Company have examined operations... (productivity) (efficiencies) (incentives) (working practices)... were the kinds of things people would have registered in their preliminary scannings of the papers which had been placed around the table.

Ivan wondered how far the yellow monster with the dinosaur neck would have got to by now. He wondered how many attacks the monster could make in one day without completely shaking itself to pieces. He wondered who owned the derelict house. He wondered why Foghorn needed to shout so much. He wondered when Rowena would realise that cricket was not just a game. He wondered if anyone would ever understand why so many people were promoted into positions which were beyond their abilities. But then as he approached the wood beyond which lay the mere, his thoughts were once more interrupted when he realised that his grip on the steering wheel was causing his arms to go numb. He tried to reduce the tension by forcing his shoulders down from the position they'd adopted close to his ears but succeeded only in creating yet more tension in his legs as fifty years of exhaustion ran along his spinal column looking for alternative accommodation.

13

ECHOES IN THE WIND

As Ivan drove up to the mere the sun came out, lighting up the trees around the water. With a grin he gave thanks to the one who'd switched on the floodlights to announce his arrival and began to relish the couple of hours of undisturbed peace awaiting him.

'This is more like it,' he said, as he walked up to the five-bar gate that stood at the entrance to the mere. The tension in his legs had lessened a little but he was far from steady on his feet, and so hanging his arms over the upper rail he allowed the gate to take his weight.

The line of trees along the shoreline and the stillness of the water reminded him of how calming the countryside could be. There was a stark contrast between the scene in front of him and the place where he'd spent most of the preceding week. It was almost incomprehensible that the two could exist within such a short distance of each other. Equally bewildering was a thought that those figures on the screen and on the desk were now so far away. Although he knew that no matter how remote they may seem whilst leaning on a gate looking out over the mere, he must not allow himself to believe the cares of the week had been confined to the dustbins of history. Whilst experience told him that during any weekend there would be moments when weekday troubles seemed to have been laid to rest, he knew that was not the case. In the bright lights of Saturday night fever (hey ho says Rowley) those troubles may be no more than partial recollections of routine, hard to place and difficult to recall. Yet they would still be there – lodged in a remote corner of his mind, ready to undertake their own invasion when the time was right no matter how much he tried to circumvent them with a manic flexing of his imagination. As if to confirm the importance of the passage of time he found himself looking at his watch.

'Thanks for providing some ticks in my life,' he said with a widening of his eyes when he realised how awful his condition must be for him to be talking to a watch. Again he wondered what it would be like to feel comfortable inside his own skin, suspecting he was not about to find out as his head fell forwards onto his chest and instead of the ticking seconds he found himself counting the bars of the gate supporting his weight.

'One-two-three-four-five.' Then he found himself counting the fingers on his hand. 'One-two-three-four-including thumbs-five.' There was a coincidence. He felt his knees go weak, and he became aware of a tightening in the muscles of his neck, against which he fought, causing his head to come up like a horse on the rein. He tried to lower his shoulders in the hope it would release some of the tension, but this resulted in his head falling forwards so that once more he found himself counting the bars of the gate.

'One-two-three-four-five? One-two-three-four-including thumbs-five?' There was a coincidence all right. Which he found strangely reassuring as at last he felt able to relax parts of his body which had been held in check for longer than was good for them. The relief was short-lived however, for a flood of panic swept through him when he realised that his hands had begun to swell. The full flow of blood to veins which had for too long been starved meant that the swelling was spreading along his arms, across his shoulders and up into his neck, from where it was threatening to take over the whole of his body as though he'd suddenly become inflatable.

'My God I'm turning into a balloon,' he cried as the bizarre thought occurred to him that he might have to take a job as a sex toy in that shop at the end of the High Street.

'Oh Lord, Rowena will never speak to me again.'

He quickly dismissed such nonsense, knowing his connection with Rowena was stronger than that. Thinking of the marital tensions his son and daughter-in-law had been experiencing, he gave thanks that his own marriage had survived. It had survived because he and Rowena had never lost the excitement of waking up each day to find right there on a pillow beside them was a reminder of the love they had for one another. He knew it was the familiarity of their regard for each other that had enabled them to avoid the celebrity-age distortions of the meaning of love. People were often advised not to take their loved ones for granted. That was one of the modern world's great misunderstandings, for the very basis of being able to take a loved one for granted – the knowledge that unconditional love, care and support, being always there – was one of the foundations of a lasting relationship. He and Rowena had grown stronger in the knowledge they could take each other for granted.

He looked down at his hands and was amazed to see they were not so enormous as they felt. He put one of these hands out in front of him, expecting to touch the horizon yet found he could get no further than the end of his arm. The swelling in his throat meanwhile felt as though it might occupy the whole of his neck raising the prospect of imminent suffocation.

He began to fear he might be sickening for something worse than he'd thought. Perhaps he was about to fall victim to a previously unknown virus – a more than likely possibility if the number of times he'd been told so by his doctor was anything to go by.

'You have a virus, Mr Driver.'

'I do? Well I expect you're right doctor, but shouldn't you have waited until knowing why I've come to see you before offering a diagnosis? Shouldn't you have asked to see my throat and looked into my eyes – yes I have two of those, although it could be more, which is why I'm here doctor, because I already have the makings of what feels like two headaches and I was hoping you might know what to do about that. Lie down and drink plenty of water? But what if it's a water born virus doctor?'

He threw back his head and sought the kind of inspiration that would raise him from the confines of his body and allow him to fly off to a place where he could forget everything. But that was of little help, for no sooner had he entertained the thought of leaving his body than he was overcome by a fear his head might be flattened by a rapidly moving cloud now only about a foot and a half above his head.

Being unnerved at the prospect of being frightened by a cloud, he clung on to the security of the gate, deciding that five was more than a coincidence. Five was not an abstract number after all. In essence it was all quite logical. More to the point it was quite ontological. Hands begat gates and therefore five was bound to be significant. You could count on it. You could indeed, for hands came before gates, and gates came before pocket calculators. For a moment it seemed that everything had fallen into place. Just as he'd always thought, if you looked closely enough you could see the whole world in a grain of sand. Now he knew that was the case for here was the very heart of existence, hidden, nay enshrined in a five-bar gate.

'Well all that was required was a little imagination,' he said as though believing the gate deserved an explanation.

'And some of us have more than enough of that,' replied a mocking voice which no amount of imagination could attribute to the answering voice of a gate.

He looked out across the mere and willed his exhaustion to leave him. His sigh was echoed by the wind as a sudden gust disturbed the leaves on the trees by the side of the mere. The trees responded by ushering the gust away along the line of tufted grass beside the path where its energy was dissipated in the brambles on the wall by the gate.

He reminded himself of why he came here, especially in the spring and early summer when the blossoms gave rise to a new freshness in the air which took him back to happier times beside the river. The image of a gently flowing river encouraged him to make one last effort to put the cares of the week behind him, and so with a smile and a much lighter step he opened the gate, went back to the car, and began to unload the dinghy.

14

A RIPPLE ON THE SURFACE

Releasing the dinghy from the roof of the car and manoeuvring it through the gate, Ivan found himself poised on the edge of the water, from where with one heave and scarcely a touch of his toes in the water he launched himself, to land unceremoniously in the bottom of the dinghy as it came to rest six feet from the bank upon which he'd just been standing.

'It's a good thing the dinghy was there,' said Bernard.

'It was there because I put it there,' said Owen, picking himself up from the bottom of the boat. Seating himself in a more orthodox position facing astern he took up the oars and set about impelling the dinghy into the open waters.

'We're not moving,' said Henry.

'We may not be moving,' said Bernard, 'but Owen is.'

'Stop rocking the boat,' said Owen, wrestling with the oars.

'I told you the mere was polluted,' said Bernard. 'The oars have silted up.'

Pulling on the oars, Owen tried to remove any thought of canteen gravy from his mind. He knew that the resistance exerted by water upon a pair of oars was a perfectly natural occurrence and that you had to move water in order to – well, in order to leave it behind. And yet he also knew it was the case that a consignment of gravy salt had been reported missing from the works canteen.

Cook walked slowly along the line, examining each person for signs of guilt. She shook her head at the state of their green hair, scruffy overalls and filthy boots. There was no chance of picking out a suspect from this lot. She would do better to forget the theft of her gravy salt and serve them pie without gravy. They could always buy a second cup of tea with which to wash it down. That way she might even be able to balance the books.

'I think we're beginning to move,' said Bernard, more by way of encouragement than evidence.

'I do believe you're right,' said Henry, closing one eye and carefully lining up the bow of the dinghy with the branches of the third willow tree to the left of Owen's right shoulder.

It did seem that the dinghy was building up a little of what might have passed for forward motion had it not remained the case that Owen still seemed to be moving a good deal more than the boat, raising in Henry's mind a question of the efficiency of the operation at least with respect of the input-output equation as it might have been called by some of the more optimistic engineers he remembered having known. In Owen's case, Henry thought, the efficiency equation may be more akin to that of a nuclear power station – there was a lot of molecular activity, but you had to ask yourself whether it was worth the risk. And given the way in which Owen was putting his back into it, Henry feared there was a risk of him putting his back out of it – for the rest of the day at least.

'The water is a funny colour,' said Owen, peering into the dark expanse beside him as he paused to draw breath.

'You're not much better yourself,' said Bernard.

'Makes you wonder what William Morris would have made of this?' said Henry.

'One thing's for sure,' said Owen letting go of an oar and trailing a finger in the water. He wouldn't have found much inspiration for a lily pattern in this stuff.

'He might not have found inspiration for a lily pattern in anything if he hadn't been perceptive enough to realise that the pursuit of another five thousand per week would have disastrous effects on the environment,' said Henry.

'Oh come on,' said Bernard, 'it's rather stretching a point to equate the obsessions of a modern day lunatic with the designs of a previous century.'

'You don't imagine the designs were coincidental to the concerns of the designer do you?' said Henry.

'I wouldn't have said there was anything utopian in those designs,' said Bernard.

'What a sad reflection on our times,' said Henry. 'That we should cast as utopian someone who was prepared to draw attention to the damage being done to the environment.'

Bernard suggested the environment in which William Morris lived had been much worse and that he'd probably think we'd done remarkably well to clean things up since his time.

Henry said that was the kind of comment you might expect from someone who couldn't see the wood for the trees. The fact that we had replaced smoke which could be seen with invisibles which could not, and on a much larger scale, was obvious to anyone with half a brain, adding that if Bernard really believed things had improved then he should give serious consideration to becoming a politician where he would be paid for saying things were better when they were clearly a thousand times worse and a million times more dangerous.

Listening to this exchange, it occurred to Owen that there are moments in life when a sudden epiphany brings a heightened sense of awareness resulting in things being seen in quite a different light – but that this wasn't one of them.

'Oh shut… shut up… the pair… the pair of you,' he said as he began edging the dinghy further into open water.

'I don't suppose there'll be many fish in here,' said Henry in an effort to curtail his urge to launch into an exposition of the unthinking pursuit of material growth.

'Perhaps you should, should... should try, try… Harry Ramsden's,' spluttered Owen mischievously.

'Harry who?' said Bernard.

'Har… Harry… Harry Ramsden,' said Owen. 'P... pl, plenty, plenty of fish... fish in there.'

'It's a fish and chip shop. Or rather it's several fish and chip shops now, the original of which had the reputation of being the largest fish and chip shop in the world,' said Henry, gazing up into the sky imagining that he was a bird looking down upon the dinghy as each pull on Owen's oars sent a flurry of spray scattering across the mirror like surface of the water.

'See… see you... see you all… you all at Henley then,' said Owen, still finding it difficult to establish any co-ordination notwithstanding the ideal conditions.

'You won't see me within a hundred miles of that place,' said Henry.

'Nor me I suppose,' said Owen.

There was a sudden lurch of the boat as the port side oar missed the water completely, propelling Owen sideways with a wrench that resulted in the dinghy slowly drifting to a standstill with it's engine room in disarray.

'One-out,' cried Bernard.

'Two-out,' chimed Henry.

'All-out,' the voice of Ivan cut in causing several mallards and a water hen to take to the air as the three characters disappeared over the side of the boat, leaving Ivan to recover the offending oar before heading off for the line of willow trees peacefully absorbing the warmth of the afternoon.

15

SOURCES OF IRRITATION

Rowena turned off the television with a mixture of relief and annoyance. The relief from the resulting silence was welcome enough, but the pain of having had to drag herself from the chair in order to retrieve the remote buttons Ivan had thrown to the floor, made her less than conciliatory towards the door left open by the recent departee. Aiming a foot in the direction of the door she caught it more firmly than intended sending it crashing into the doorframe, which thanks to natural settlement and the effects of central heating was less than securely attached to the wall. She stormed across the room in fury, throwing herself back into the chair.

'Cricket, cricket, cricket,' she snarled.

Gripping the arms of the chair as though about to throw it through the window she glared at the remaining portion of smoked salmon sandwich and the empty cup. She had no inclination to pick up the sandwich a grave enough situation in itself, but neither could she bring herself to tilt the teapot in the direction of the cup, an altogether more serious matter. She attempted to short circuit the process by commanding more tea to enter the cup without lifting the teapot, suggesting that her annoyance might be in the ascendency rather more than was any feeling of relief.

The roses on the teapot were wilting, but the teapot was unmoved. Teapots were used to being taken for granted, although a little more consideration might have produced better results. The teapot may not have tilted its spout unaided but Rowena of all people should have known that allowing things to go cold was not the best way to encourage co-operation.

With a heavy heart she acknowledged there was little prospect of avoiding the cloud which had been threatening to descend on her all morning. She tried to console herself with the knowledge that she and Ivan had survived whilst many of their friends were separating and relinquishing control of their bank accounts to the serpents of divorce. There being such a sense of permanence in their lives had meant that Ivan and Rowena were able to accommodate their differences. They were regarded as unfashionable, idealistic, even pathetic by some of their friends, but that didn't matter because they knew it worked. Whether in fight or flight their love had made it possible for them to stand their ground, argue, become angry, walk away, sulk, all without prejudicing their regard for one another. They could shout, laugh, cry, joke, be both serious and ironic, poke fun at and ridicule each other, having learned the importance of being able to express their doubts and disagreements without recrimination.

Telling herself to be grateful for what she had, Rowena shook her head in an effort to be rid of her irritation, but succeeded only in creating a stabbing pain in her side and a tight feeling in her stomach giving rise to the confusing possibility that she may have eaten more than was good for her, despite one whole portion of smoked salmon sandwich remaining untouched.

'Cricket, cricket, cricket,' she cried again. 'Why do I have to get so worked up about absolutely nothing?' Unquestionably she had been annoyed with Ivan, not least for having had the audacity to leave the room before switching off the television, he having been the one who had occasioned the unwarranted intrusion into the enjoyment of their lunch. But she was also conscious of being rather less at peace with herself than was probably good for her health, notwithstanding anything Ivan may have said or done. She was troubled that her irritation should have been so spitefully expressed, since it should have been obvious that given his indiscretions on the previous evening Ivan would have been in no condition to respond other than in the way he had.

She was annoyed with herself too for having given the impression that cricket was the source of her irritation. She had no aversion to the greatest of all summer games. She liked watching cricket. There was no better way of relaxing than to snooze in a deck chair in the warmth of a summer's afternoon at the festival towards the end of a season in which there had been so much to look forward to. With such fond memories there was little chance of deceiving herself into believing that cricket had been the source of her irritation. She knew the problem was more serious than a game of cricket through the wonders of television or not.

Raising herself from the chair, she stood with hands on hips staring through the window just as her husband had done earlier. But it wasn't a strange creature in the street that caught her attention. Rather it seemed to be something in the house, and as though remembering what that was, she turned from the window and strode across the lounge towards the door.

Going out into the hall she caught sight of herself in the mirror, groaning at the heaviness around her eyes, before hurrying into the kitchen only to return into the hall a few moments later on her way to the dining room. Where noticing the computer on a table in the corner of the room, she declined to check whether there were any unsolicited emails awaiting the placing of a finger on the delete button. She was more concerned with putting a finger on why she was prowling around the house like a caged lioness, with no idea as to what was making her so irritable. Again she tried to tell herself that whatever it was, it couldn't amount to much. Nothing could be so bad. Nothing ever was. And especially not when you were at a point in your life where things were beginning to go so well. Why, even the realisation that your response to the cricket had been a displacement was a measure of how well you were doing. An ability to recognise such a displacement was not something you should underestimate however bad things were. Although to keep things in perspective, neither did it entitle you to imagine it would be easy to identify the cause of your irritation.

Experience had told Rowena that a difficulty worth having was unlikely to be an easy one to resolve, and therefore you had little choice but to pursue every idea that came into your head, no matter how improbable it seemed. The precipitate nature of her behaviour suggested she was used to being deflected from one thing to another, never having enough time to finish one job before being side-tracked into the next. She knew it was not a sensible way to conduct your affairs, but sometimes there was little you could do other than scold yourself for allowing those conditions to prevail. She reminded herself how easy it was to bring yourself to such a pitch of self denigration that you became convinced that a removal of yourself from the arena of your irritation was the only sensible course of action.

Rowena knew things were rarely that simple. She had always been able to see other ways of looking at things and was the last person to see anything unusual in having an argument with herself. She suspected the number of people who argued with themselves was exceeded only by the number of people who denied they did any such thing. Having been brought up under the eye of a more than watchful mother, she had been reminded often enough that not a moment went by in which you should not to be thinking a little more about what you were doing.

16

THE BEST LAID PLANS

Rowena stared at the dark pool of fluid on the hard shoulder as it gradually expanded.

'Oh God, not today,' she cried, thrusting her oily hands into the pockets of her white raincoat without a thought for the consequences. Lashing out a foot she sent a small stone flying across the road where it hit the kerb on the central reservation and sailed into the air directly into the path of traffic on the opposite carriageway. She put her head down and held her breath as she saw a Mercedes bearing down upon the flying stone. But the stone passed harmlessly beneath the car and with relief she began to breathe again. She decided it would be safer to address herself to the stricken vehicle beside her, and aiming a retaliatory shoe at the front wheel carefully timed the kick so that its kinetic energy was well and truly expended before her foot landed. Then taking out her phone to find that it's battery had no charge, she shook her fist at the vehicle and spat out a string of curses to the effect that this would have to happen today. There weren't many days in the year when you were in a position to take advantage of your good fortune. Not many occasions upon which you could look forward to forgetting entirely who you were. Not many opportunities for telling the world to sod off and take care of itself. Only for this to happen. It was so unreasonable.

Releasing the retaining arm, she took hold of the bonnet of the car and dropped it more heavily than intended. Turning her back on the whole miserable scene she strode off along the hard shoulder. After walking for a little way she stopped as though thinking better of it. Then, muttering an oath, she doggedly retraced her steps to the car, pointed the key at the lock, pressed the button, registered the double flash, and once more set off along the hard shoulder.

17
THE SYSTEMATIC APPROACH TO
PROBLEM SOLVING

Rowena retraced her steps to the bay window of the lounge. She was sweating profusely, and had she been asked would have said her face must have turned bright red, were it not that upon passing the mirror in the hall she'd noticed it was in fact quite pale. She reviewed the situation in the manner of a barrister attempting to build a sustainable advocacy from insufficient evidence. Was it a case of this? Was it a case of that? Was it a case of something else? Perhaps she ought to be a little more systematic in her approach. But where to begin? You had to begin at the beginning of course. Of course. And therefore she must first of all define her terms. That was an improvement upon what she had been doing for now at least she had a method. She was beginning to sound like Bodmas her old mathematics teacher in a former life. He would unquestionably have approved of her being more systematic in her approach... 'Brackets-Of-Division-Multiplication-Addition-and-Subtraction... recite after me.' It had been one of the best lines he'd had.

She wondered how anyone could be expected to define their terms when they knew so little about the problem they were facing – especially if the problem amounted to a difficulty in defining terms. In which case there wouldn't be much of a problem because if you'd been in a position to define the terms you would already have resolved the problem. Was there any wonder the systematic approach to problem solving had made so little progress?

She decided there were too many occasions on which she'd been obliged to respond to a situation without having time to define anything for that kind of approach to be of much use. When the gauntlet was thrown down you had to pick it up. The principle of reciprocity was so ingrained that even the retriever of an ordinary glove which had been dropped by accident was said to be in for a surprise. The surprise however, was seldom of the kind Rowena remembered, having received upon retrieving the garden glove from behind the tomato plants in the greenhouse on that stifling hot day last summer. Perversely she had gone into the greenhouse to cool off, having discovered that Ivan had removed a whole row of newly planted sweet peas in his efforts to rid the garden of anything that wasn't a rose. Yet there, leaning over the tomato plants, close to losing her balance, she'd been surprised by the ferocity with which she'd switched from suppressed anger to naked desire when Ivan had leapt upon her from behind.

Dismissing such thoughts from her mind, she contented herself with the reminder that at least she hadn't fallen into the trap of pretending she knew what was wrong with her. There was little point in engaging in that kind of pretence. Especially when living with a menagerie of ghost-like characters each one of which happened to be your husband whether he knew that you knew that or not. After all, who wasn't pretending they were not in the predicaments they were in? That was one reason why Rowena had no difficulty in understanding her husband when he said that pretence was the greatest temptation you faced once you became a card carrying member of the human race.

'What do you pretend?'

'I pretend that I'm not pretending.'

'You should be so lucky. I pretend that I don't know I'm pretending that I'm not pretending.'

The trouble was when you'd been brought up in a world which taught that if you were clever enough you could get away with anything providing you kept a straight face, the temptation was always there. Though what you would gain from pretending you were somewhere else at the time was another matter. If you happened to be the one standing behind the Queen's arras when the Prince of Denmark made his pass, you were the King whether you were pretending to be somewhere else or not.

Down the annals of time, pretending that you could

displace yourself from the source of your problem had never worked. And especially not whilst knowing you were displacing your feelings onto a mere game of cricket. The reminder of which raised the possibility of it being her husband she should have been thinking of displacing. She'd considered that many times but had always come to the conclusion that neither was there anything to be gained from that kind of displacement. The one thing to be thankful for in marrying into cricket was knowing it was precisely on those occasions when the grass did turn out to be greener that you were really in trouble.

She decided she needed some fresh air, and having wandered back into the kitchen continued walking straight out of the door into the garden. Where she began pacing up and down as though convinced vigorous exercise was the best antidote to the irritability consuming her. But it seemed even the garden was against allowing her to attain the peace she sought.

'Bugger off,' she cried taking a swing at a bee which persisted in trying to land in her hair.

She turned to pick up a hoe from the edge of the floribunda rose bed where it had been left by Ivan, and launching herself into a thick cluster of dandelions began to scatter them in all directions. The roots remained stubbornly in place however, and throwing down the hoe she stomped off towards the greenhouse. Stumbling against the edge of the paving surround she remembered the day Ivan had stood on her foot in the queue in the steelworks canteen. The memory of which made her wonder whether that might in itself have been the source of her problems.

Ivan had been nudging forwards in the queue, so engrossed in the details of the fare on offer that he'd failed to notice Rowena had stopped in front of him. He'd apologised immediately and had continued to do so for many days, expressing heartfelt regrets each time that he'd seen Rowena. He'd been unable to believe a single apology could be an adequate response to the calamity, and such had been his remorse that expecting Rowena to seek revenge, he'd taken to looking nervously around the canteen queue in the manner of someone expecting to find a grenade in his pudding. An unlikely event as the cook could have told him, the budget not even allowing for sugar in the custard.

'Budget cuts, budget cuts, budget cuts,' sang a chorus of cooks. From whom Ivan might have gained more information had he been listening to anyone other than Rowena upon whose every word he had been hanging.

Revenge had been the last thing on Rowena's mind but Ivan had not been in a position to know that, and eventually it had been his foreman, the very same Big Joe, who had taken the unknowing but decisive step by sending Ivan to undertake a repair in the office in which Rowena worked.

Initially, Ivan and Rowena had been intent on keeping their distances, she in order to protect her other foot, and he so that apologising to her did not occupy the whole of his working day. They'd been unable to sustain those precautions however, and had soon come to accept the inevitable, Rowena feeling there was so much about Ivan she wanted to know and Ivan knowing there was so much about Rowena he wanted to... well touch (not during working hours young man). As a result, they had fallen in love at a pace which had surprised Rowena every bit as much as it had terrified the crepe soled shoes and arse licking boiler suit off Ivan.

18

DUSTY OLD COBWEBS

... something seems to have caught Rowena's eye as she approaches the greenhouse which lies behind the remains of the old laburnum tree – a tree she remembers Ivan having cut down the moment Timothy had taken his first unassisted steps. Peering through the moss covered windows of the greenhouse she sees two figures in the midst of a crowd. Moving closer, she sees one of them is the tall figure of a youthful looking Ivan, and with him is a young woman she doesn't recognise as they walk hand in hand along a beach with the wind in their hair. She watches them as they kick off their shoes and run into the sea, high stepping and splashing around as though not having a care in the world. She recalls how the sea had been cold, and through the windows of the greenhouse she sees them retreat from the water's edge, rubbing their toes in the sand in an effort to get warm. She remembers the occasion and recalls them eating fish and chips watching the boats in the harbour bobbing to and fro on the incoming tide. The fish and chips had been followed by ice cream as they'd strolled along the promenade, pausing to look at the dodgem cars tearing around. Through the windows of the greenhouse she sees the couple have reached the point from where they will enter the penny arcade. She remembers them having won immediately and recalls how they'd torn themselves away before losing what they'd gained. Their high spirits had led them to venture onto the waltzer, neither of them wishing to admit they hated it. After which they'd retreated into the park to watch the ducks dipping and diving around on the lake... and now they are in London where it must be the occasion of the visit organised by the steelworks cricket club. They had been the first to book places and been so looking forward to the trip, their enthusiasm being dampened only on arrival. She sees that it's raining heavily and remembers that the rain had continued for most of the day. And she knows that two dripping figures will return to the coach at the end of the day without having noticed how wet they've become, their eyes being only for each other. For now though, she sees that Ivan and the young woman are walking in the rain towards St John's Wood, where she knows Ivan will want to see the W G Grace gates at the headquarters of what she remembers him telling her old Parky had referred to as the Marylebone Clodpoles Club. She knows too, the figures will visit the Victoria and Albert museum, where the young woman will spend what had seemed like an age in the Medieval tapestry exhibition. From the vantage point of her window into their future (which she shudders has all too quickly become their past) she recalls and anticipates how they will retire exhausted to the museum restaurant where they will eat chicken and apricot pie, before once more walking in the rain, arm in arm, pausing only to gaze into shop windows displaying things they couldn't possibly afford... when through the window of the greenhouse she sees that the Fair has come to town. Couples are out in large numbers, some walking hand in hand, some arm in arm, and some so close and entangled that there should be no mistaking who was pledging themselves to whom that year. She sees that the figures of the youthful Ivan and the young woman who is also called Rowena are no exception, clearly enjoying every minute of their time in the great annual confirmation of commitment to one another. The considerably older Rowena is reminded of how in the midst of all the hubbub she'd asked the figure of the youthful looking Ivan whether he would still be with her when the fair returned the following year. The scene in front of her having reached that point, she strains to hear his reply, anxious to discover whether it will be just as she remembers from all those years ago. And sure enough, with the words of Little Richard drumming in her ears, she feels a shiver along her spine as above the screaming, whirling cacophony of fairground noise she hears the youthful Ivan say Good Golly Miss Molly, I hope to be with you on the day that I die.

Which makes the years fly by... for now Spring has arrived and the couple are walking through a bluebell wood... followed by a leisurely stroll across a meadow, their lighter clothing suggesting it is already high summer with its stifling heat... until the sun is driven away by the rain which again seems to have set in for the day now that Autumn has appeared and the couple are picking blackberries which Ivan's mother will make into his favourite jam to be eaten when winter sets in... where the couple are rubbing their hands to keep warm and walking more briskly along the road beside the river... but then, the now older Rowena feels an increase in her pulse as she sees and recalls the figures approaching the point where the consequences of their growing love for one another will have to be faced. She remembers and experiences again the excitement, straining to see what they will do as the unspoken need to establish the limits of their intimacy increases. She remembers the mounting tension as they made and remade the decision as to whether the time was right, and recalls how this had been fuelled by memories of the warnings delivered by the great matriarchs in their lives concerned to establish in each of them an awareness of the dangers of the path they were treading. The warnings had been so severe that once more she feels and recalls the fear that had remained with them long after the need for caution had passed. She sees they are even now edging closer to the precipice and she bites her lip as though having no recollection of how the resolution will come... but the figures edge back from the brink, and she is surprised how little passes between them. She recalls the strength of their unspoken agreement and with a mop of her brow reminds herself how they had become victims of the age in which they'd lived, the realisation bringing home to her the absurdly repressive nature of their times.

'Talk about the murder of innocence,' she cries out aloud. 'Little wonder we should have talked - or not talked - ourselves into such confusion.' She shakes her head in dismay.

'The oppressive zeitgeist of all our yesterdays,' she jeers. 'How could we do anything but screw ourselves up – other than in the way we desired?' She is trembling and becomes aware that she is holding onto the frame of the greenhouse too fiercely... but relaxes when through the window she sees they are now in the Lake District. She remembers with fondness their holiday together, and how youth hostels with their separate dormitories had been a means of saving them from sacrificing everything. She sees the couple holding hands beside lake Ullswater and remembers how from there they'd begun the mammoth trek which had taken them along the Grisedale valley, joining the route upwards (upwards ever upwards she remembers) to emerge onto the spectacular high level ridge of Striding Edge. From where she watches them even now proceeding with care as they pick their way along the precipitous route, culminating in what she recalls the guidebooks had described as a final scramble onto the summit of Helvellyn, before traversing the windswept path skirting the fearsome Nethermost Cove towards Dollywagon Pike. She recalls it having been at this point their lack of fitness for such an expedition had begun to take its toll. She can only watch helplessly knowing their knees will begin to weaken on the descent to Grisedale Tarn as they struggle to reach the village of Grasmere before dark... she feels a stiffness in her limbs as though having undertaken the trek only yesterday. She leans heavily into the frame of the greenhouse and becomes aware of an ache in her shoulders, spreading upwards into her throat and making her feel nauseous. Placing a hand over her eyes she worries that she might be about to faint. But then the aching and the nausea subside, leaving her to wonder whether her excellent head for heights may no longer be what it was... she opens her eyes and peers through the window once more to see only the dusty old cobwebs left clinging to the glass, following Ivan's halfhearted attempt to clean the greenhouse... with a sigh she turns and walks back along the lawn towards the kitchen full of regrets that memories have now become the means of realising their dreams from so long ago.

19

FOOD FOR THOUGHT

Rowena recalled the changes made following their holiday in the Lake District. The holiday that had done so much to confirm their love for one another. Returning to the kitchen from the garden she remembered the speed at which events had begun to move. There had been no time to consider the enormity of the decisions they'd taken until it was too late. Informed opinion had been united in urging them to make an entry into the housing market whilst they could still afford to do so. Those were the days they'd said (and you can have them today) well just about if you were lucky, thought Rowena, wondering what the property market would be like when her one and only granddaughter came of age.

'From hell and the bloody Building Society,' she recalled her once and future husband having cried in response to their momentous decision. As things had turned out the state of the housing market had been the least of their problems, but they hadn't known that at the time. So determined had they been to act before it was too late that the possibility of a single person taking out a mortgage for house purchase hadn't occurred to them. There had never been a requirement to have two signatures on the downside of a mortgage, and yet thought Rowena, such had been the banana-skin basis of their decision-making that this had never entered what she was now more inclined to refer to as their tiny little minds. And so a partnership it had been, and if other subsidiary contracts had come along in consequence of that decision, then Good Golly Miss Molly or not, that was how it had to be. No matter that nothing and no one could have convinced them how much it would turn their worlds upside down.

They'd been married in a small church and had gone away for a quiet honeymoon in what by then was well on its

107

way to becoming the tatty old Queen of the English Riviera. They'd then gone back to the steelworks. The only change being the direction from which they came and went each day, Ivan having insisted he was perfectly happy to move away from the river for the first time in his life, and Rowena being too preoccupied to notice.

And so with their heads full of dreams, they'd set out to build a life together whilst continuing to hold down two demanding jobs. Not to mention the hundred and one other jobs for which their parents, had they possessed the merest understanding of their offspring, could have prepared them, other than in terms of they themselves having for too long been taken for granted. Ivan had discovered it took a good deal more to start a day than blackberry jam, and that jam or marmalade it required a regular supply of bread in order to make toast. He had been on the verge of saying so when he'd realised to whom he would have been addressing his remarks, and he did not mean Rowena. For her part, Rowena had discovered she had no taste for blackberry jam and neither did she care much for cups of cold tea with her morning crispbreads, although she too had refrained from expressing that sentiment, no matter how captive the audience.

'Work, work, work,' Rowena recalled having cried each morning upon waking. 'It's one damn thing after another.' This was supposed to bring us closer together but it's driving us further apart. 'What are we to do, do, do, my love?'

'I resign,' she recalled her husband having replied forever intent upon being helpful.

But their debt to the arm and a leg Building Society had ensured that relinquishing either of their incomes was not a course of action open to them, and so what a charade what a façade, what a pan full of empty promises was more the kind of thing she herself remembered having cried.

'Ivan where are you? The idea of buying a house together was to spend more time in each others arms, but I sometimes feel whole days go by without so much as a sight of you. We've been married for three years and I still feel I hardly know you. You know how much I love you. Oh Ivan I do love you, wherever you are.'

('And I love you too my darling even when I'm not there to say so.')

'I know you've continued to spend these nights trying to improve your prospects even though attendance is no longer a condition of your employment. And I do know you work, work, work, so hard, but please hurry home, please please hurry home to your darling Rowena who's waiting, waiting, waiting beside your own front door.'

But work had continued to rule their lives. Morning afternoon and evening. Until the day they'd put the infernal Building Society to the back of their minds and resolved the problem in the time honoured way by having children. Thereby creating a whole new list of things that had to be done, in the course of which the young woman called Rowena, so recently dancing her way through the scenes of a greenhouse window, would sooner than she'd ever anticipated, become a considerably older woman. And being an older and wiser woman struggling to get to the bottom of whatever was troubling her meant that she would solve the problem exactly as she'd always done. Which was why, when Ivan came whistling merrily along the hall from his afternoon at the mere, he opened the door into the kitchen to be greeted by the sight of Rowena surrounded by an array of buns, cakes, quiches, flans and tarts in every combination of flour and butter imaginable.

'Good Lord I'm in the wrong cafe,' he said.

'Oh hello love,' Rowena almost sang in celebration of her irritation having been banished in the face of a couple of hours of hyperactivity of the kind she rarely had time for, nor entirely approved of nowadays.

'Did you have a good time?' She seemed genuinely interested.

'Wonderful,' said Ivan inspecting an egg custard rather too closely for the end of his nose.

'You're supposed to eat them not inhale them,' said Rowena taking another tray of jam tarts from the oven.

It was customary for Saturday tea to be taken in the kitchen, although seldom involving such a flagrant disregard of their low fat diets. Yet the temptation to taste everything from the results of Rowena's manic afternoon was irrisistable, and not least in celebration of suspended hostilities, they ate far more than was good for them. When an hour later they emerged from the kitchen they were in more than a little discomfort. Rowena staggered into the lounge and collapsed into her favourite armchair. Ivan followed her, pausing at the door when he heard the old grandfather clock stifle a titter at the sight of two heavily bowed figures dragging themselves across the hall. He turned to stare at the clock, and smiled enigmatically, before entering the lounge and lowering himself gently into a chair so as not to disturb Rowena who had already fallen asleep.

Unable to follow her example, Ivan began fidgeting with the cushions, but realising he was in danger of awakening Rowena, decided a little light reading might be good for his digestion. He managed to reach some of the newspaper without getting out of his chair, but since he couldn't possibly risk turning the pages without disturbing her, he abandoned the idea. Trying once more to imagine what it would be like to have not a single thought in his head he acknowledged that he would probably never know. On impulse he rose from the chair, and carefully making his exit from the room left the softly murmuring figure lying prone in the chair beside the window.

20

THANKS FOR THE GAME

Deciding that a walk in the evening air would do him good, Ivan left the car on the drive and set off at a brisk pace. With the result that in not much more than half an hour in a somewhat more boisterous environment he found that he'd already amassed a break of five. This had been achieved by fluking a red, and then by miraculously potting the brown ball which had been balanced on the lip of the centre pocket, at the same time managing to prevent the cueball from following the coloured ball by the skin of its teeth.

A break of five meant a club record was possible and Owen was beginning to believe there might be a chance of achieving this when with the kind of immediacy a soccer commentator might convey when describing a striker's entry into the box, he became aware that Bernard had arrived.

'Go for the blue,' hissed Bernard.

Owen's feet all but left the ground as he swung round narrowly missing the glass of beer on the table behind him. He froze when he saw how close to disaster he'd been, and taking time to collect himself eyed Bernard with a look of disdain the likes of which a contributer to prime minister's question time would have been proud. For having just potted the brown ball in what was unquestionably a skilful shot, Bernard should have known another red was required. That was a simple rule of the game. All over the world, from the frost bitten tables of Siberia to the heat of the Crucible in May, a red must follow a colour. Everyone knew that was how it worked, and so what on earth could Bernard be thinking of?

'Take the red by the pink and come back up the table for the blue.' Bernard filled in the missing details of the break he'd been planning, whilst Henry, who had now appeared beside Bernard nodded approvingly.

Owen looked first at Bernard and then at Henry, before turning his eyes back to the table where the evidence awaited him. How stupid of me he thought, before quickly recovering his composure and deciding it would be better to pretend he'd known the details of Bernard's plan all along. He walked around to the other side of the table so as to give the impression of making sure a less obvious alternative hadn't been overlooked. From where he saw there was no question of any other shot, the blue ball being the only logical progression following the one red which could be potted from his current position.

It could have been a lack of experience that had led Owen to disregard the significance of the blue. Or perhaps it had been the euphoria of having already potted two balls in succession which had told him that by the law of averages he couldn't hope to repeat such a sequence until the middle of next year. Whatever the reason for his oversight, Owen knew that the essence of success in any sport was to proceed to the next stage removing from your mind any thought of whatever fluke, mistake or misjudgment might have occurred. And so he dutifully applied chalk to the tip, tapped the cue against his shoe, and swung it into position to prepare for the most important shot of his life.

Lining up the shot he took the cue so far back as to cause his audience to retreat a couple of paces. From where they stood helplessly by as Owen contrived to miss the easy red. Bernard would no doubt have said missing the red was hardly an adequate description since it may have created an impression of the red ball having narrowly missed the pocket, whereas a fuller account would have included the information that the cue ball had not even reached the red ball, there being no danger of anything going into the pocket.

'Incredible,' said Bernard.

The embarrassment of the occasion enveloped Owen for a moment as he staggered from the table banging his cue on the parquet floor in a struggle to come to terms with his ineptitude. His opponent, a stoney faced man with grey eyes came forward preparing to take advantage of the position he'd been left, whilst Owen sat down looking thoroughly miserable with himself. His depression was short lived however, for he was back at the table in less time than it had taken him to sit down. To find he'd acquired a further six points, more than off-setting the four he'd just given away, as his opponent had inadvertently clipped the pink ball on its way to the red that was still sitting on the edge of the pocket.

Owen took up the battle once more, trying to close his mind to the advice being given by Bernard who clearly had no conception of what was required. Otherwise why would he be pressing him to take his time, when it should have been obvious that the more time he took the more uncertain he became? Bernard seemed to be suggesting he should think about where the cueball would come to rest. Owen was more concerned with striking the cueball cleanly enough to prevent his cue from spinning off into orbit than he was about any consideration of where the ball might go.

He proceeded to miss the now easy red into the centre pocket, although on this occasion the cueball having made contact with the red ball he could take some satisfaction from the shot.

Bernard turned away from the table in anguish, whilst Henry shrugged his shoulders in a gesture of impassivity developed over many years of listening to the England cricket score.

Ivan sat down telling himself he ought to be a little straighter in his cuing action. But that would have to wait for another day because the timekeeper had signalled the end of the game and called the next group of players to the table. Ivan's opponent headed off in the direction of the door to the clubroom without so much as a word of thanks for the game old sport, leaving Ivan with little to do but try and forget how badly he'd played.

21

FOUL PLAY

Left to himself at last, Ivan supposed that if satisfied about nothing else in the world he should be thankful his mother hadn't married a man called Taskerman.

'I should say so,' he said forgetting for a moment his indiscretions of the previous evening as he pulled on the contents of the glass in front of him.

He wondered what might have caused the swelling sensations in his arms at the mere. Perhaps it was an indication of something more serious... and yet that didn't seem very likely. The invasive process of which everyone was fearful was less immediate than that. Although it was a good deal more subversive. Which was why it was so dangerous, having developed the means of creeping up on you with such stealth it could arrive before you had any idea it was there. And they had asked him to come back next week. Forgetting for a moment that everyone else had been asked to return for the results of the screening too, he wondered what they were expecting to find. Would they uncover the cause of the swelling sensations in his arms? He tried to think of alternative explanations for the swelling, but could get no further than conjecture as to how his flesh could have summoned up the energy to perform anything but the most essential of movements... such as that of raising a glass to his lips, which this time he did a little more circumspectly.

Any further thoughts on what might be wrong with him would have to wait, for now he was joined by Bernard and Henry, followed by a more hesitant looking Owen still embarrassed by his performance on the snooker table.

Ivan could only groan at the prospect of quite another invasive process in the shape of meanderings that would get him nowhere. Looking for a retreat he found himself once more taking refuge in the labyrinths of his dim and distant past, even though he knew there was little chance of an escape in that direction. He had learned from experience that sudden plunges into the frozen layers of memory, from which the storylines of history are made, frequently resulted in would-be travellers not having the faintest idea of where they were. Familiarity with the territory was of little help in finding your way around in that place. The shelves were piled high with recorded moments from each ticking second which had ever told its tale, all of them taped, stored, never to be forgotten, but alas unclassified and therefore difficult to recall. There were no clues on the cutting room floor in there. It had never been anyone's job to mark up and file the rolling tapes of screenplays that were stored. The one thing you could be sure about once you stepped inside the creative hot-bed of the next thought that came into your head was that you were likely to remain a long way from knowing where you were. Though you had to acknowledge the lightening pace at which business was conducted. That was a fast lane enterprise by any standard. If you stood around too long wondering which way to go, you would be on your way again, doing something for somebody, whether you had any idea of what you were doing or not.

Ivan had a good idea of what he would like to do at that moment, and that was fly away as far as possible from the three characters about to disturb one of the few moments in the weekend when he'd found time to be alone with a quiet drink. He tried to recall when he'd first become aware of the characters. It seemed they'd been with him forever. They'd been there when Margaret Thatcher became prime minister because he remembered Henry saying he'd never seen anyone in such a responsible position demonstrate how far out of their depth they were. He was sure they'd been there during the three-day week too, for he'd often laughed when recalling Owen putting the remains of a burnt out candle on the forehead of Bernard who had fallen asleep in the gloom. They'd been there when England had won the World Cup, and they had been absorbed in the coverage of the assassination of Jack Kennedy because he could remember Henry pointing to the importance of the grassy knoll, to the disquiet of Bernard.

And yet their interventions had left him with little idea of who they were. They could hardly be imaginary friends when there had been so many occasions on which he'd strangely enough become one of them. Or so he feared, judging by the reactions of Rowena. Which raised the unedifying prospect of not only being in the midst of a life in which he had no idea who he was… but one in which he was also devoid of any clue as to when he was whom.

'I must say this place is more pleasant than that pub we keep ending up in,' said Owen. 'I can't believe anyone's thirst would be enough to justify going in there.' He was doing his best to pretend nothing untoward had happened.

'What's more, the beer is cheaper here and I can also play snooker.'

'That's a matter of opinion,' said Bernard.

'You're right, it is a bit quieter in here,' said Henry, anxious to head off a review of events on the snooker table.

The effort of walking backwards and forwards around a snooker table for three-quarters of an hour no matter how few balls had been potted had taken a lot out of Ivan. It was time to concentrate on the more rewarding task of wrapping his fingers around his glass, raising it to his lips, and notwithstanding the after-effects of the previous evening, gently squeezing the contents into his mouth before once more returning the glass to the table.

'Look, you can get fifty pounds off your summer holiday,' said Owen, pointing to the beer mat he was holding.

'I've always thought holidays were overrated,' said Bernard without regard for the consequences of what he was saying.

Ivan yawned and attributing his condition to a sedentary life, decided it was time for a stretch. Clasping his hands behind his head, he sought to steady himself by placing his feet against the table. But the table responded by moving away, forcing him to roll sideways to prevent his lower vertebrae from taking the whole weight of his body as he pivoted across the edge of the seat.

'Being on holiday is a state of mind. You can be on holiday any day you like if you choose to think of it as a holiday.'

Ivan shivered in response to the falsetto voice that rang out from a figure, which had he not known such things were impossible was tripping in far from light footsteps across the top of his head, making him feel dizzy and rendering him unable to prevent the voice from having its say.

'You are on holiday.' The voice jangled every nerve in his body and believing he was a Cartesian of sorts, a few he would have sworn were not in his body, including one that resulted in a response from a voice he recognised only too well.

'He does have a point you know. You never do a stroke of what could be called real work.'

'I...' Ivan realised that he was in danger of speaking aloud and in his determination to curtail this nonsense, responded by scuffing the flat of his hand rather too heavily across the top of his head sending his hair flying in all directions.

He decided to take control of the situation and order another drink. But then a reminder of his condition made him wonder whether it might be a good idea to restrict himself to just the one drink this evening. On the other hand, having walked to the club this was the one evening on which he could have another drink without worrying about going over the limit. If only he could remember what the limit was. And if you couldn't remember what the limit was, how were you to know when you'd exceeded it? Was the effect of your intake in relation to the limit governed by your condition and therefore your body's rate of metabolic recovery? Would it be lower now than it might be on a Sunday evening when you were a little more relaxed? And would that matter if you were to end up dead in a ditch, it being of little concern to you then how much alcohol you'd consumed, even if alcohol had not been responsible for causing you to run off the road? But unless they'd been with you all evening, the people who found you wouldn't know either, and so would be bound to jump to their own conclusions, whether or not you, or they, knew what the limit was. It was clear that the only sensible course of action was to drink no alcohol at all. The trouble was he'd already had one drink and ought not to drive until the effects had worn off, having for a moment forgotten that he'd walked to the club and didn't have to drive. He could after all order another drink. But then the previous evening's indiscretions came flooding back to remind him there was a further reason for not knowing whether to order another drink. He put his head in his hands and was about to tell himself that he could do with a holiday when he realised those were the very words he'd been trying to avoid.

It was time to change the subject, but alas to one that was no better because now it was the clear retentive image of the man in the pale blue tee shirt and matching trousers speaking.

'We'd like you to come back next Wednesday,' Mr Driver.

'Next Wednesday? But that's not until the middle of next week.' He shuddered as once more the agonies of the fading week were overtaken by the anxieties of the week to come. It was unbearable, as was the realisation that his pulse was racing, and so he closed his eyes and tried to dismiss all thoughts of pale blue tee shirts and doctors who preferred to be known as mister, from his mind. Unsuccessfully.

It would be a routine procedure they'd said, and that had been his hope when agreeing to take part in the screening. Now it had become anything but a routine procedure. It had taken on a life of its own. Causing his mind to suddenly move up a gear as his thoughts were consumed by uncertainty, the uncertainty that gives rise to fear, the fear that is fuelled by necessity, the awesome daily necessity of putting one foot in front of the other.

A voice from within cried out something incomprehensible and with that his pulse began to return to normal. Though not for long because he had to stifle a cheer when it then occurred to him that Joe Taskerman might be one of those whose results meant he was heading for a sticky end. A cheer wasn't too unkind a reaction because a sticky end was where they were all heading – no small thanks to the double-dealing banker who had given them their starters for ten in what most of them had failed to realise was a target game in which they were themselves the sitting ducks. It wasn't surprising they should have become confused. If they couldn't trust a double-dealing banker whom could they trust?

Again he had no idea, but he knew his pulse was once more racing and that it could only be made worse by putting a question to the silent majority who supported Joe Taskerman – yet he would do so nevertheless. And so why did the gang of shrugging shoulders in the contest of our times feel it their duty to piss on the ball whenever someone so much as thought of drawing attention to the rules of the game. Of course he knew why, yet still he winced at how many blind mice were prepared to swallow everything Joe Taskerman said, without a thought for the possibility of it catching in their throats.

He reminded himself of the responsibility he had for pausing to draw breath, and tried to steady himself by accepting that one day he might have to dance to the tired old tune that echoed in the ears of everyone who had ever been born to work for a living... noses to the grindstone, think about your holidays...

His thoughts were interrupted as a bald headed man in an orange jacket approached.

'What'll you have?' Ivan greeted the newcomer.

'No no, my shout,' the man with the orange jacket insisted, going off to order drinks and returning with two pints of the creamy topped lubricant that once more reminded Ivan of how badly he'd played in the previous evening's rather different game of clear the table. He had a sudden recollection of a privet hedge and emitted an audible groan.

'What's up... you not feeling well?' asked the orange jacket.

'I was thinking of the game I've just played,' Ivan lied.

'How did you get on?'

'I won,' said Ivan unable to hide his embarrassment.

'Oh... cheers then,' the orange jacket with the bald head raised his glass in celebration.

'Seventeen-eight,' said Ivan, declining to say most of those had been giveaways.

Ivan wondered how he would explain that score to those with wider experience in the game of snooker since a score of seventeen-eight might suggest the circumstances of an incomplete game. How would they ever understand that in the halls frequented by Ivan K Driver a clearance of all the balls from the table was acknowledged as merely one way to play the game? It lacked the delightful operation of the guillotine occasioned by the apportioning of time slots, in which it was possible to record a result without the necessity of potting any balls. In that way a frame could be declared complete no matter how many balls remained on the table. Whereas if play were to continue until the table had been cleared, no one else would ever get a game. As for the idea that clearances might lead to more proficient play in the long run, in the short run things could only get worse for if some of them were to stop missing balls, then with no giveaways no one would make any score at all.

'Foul… four away,' a mocking voice amid laughter came in confirmation as the cue ball of the next group of players on the table rolled past Ivan's feet and hit the side of the bar.

Ivan slapped his thigh and joined in the merriment, which was suddenly curtailed as the beer he'd just swallowed hit the pastry he'd eaten earlier, reminding him that his recovery still had some way to go.

'One-two-three-four-colours to the blue-five,' he mumbled as he closed his eyes and once more tried to think of rolling hills and lush green meadows.

He supposed he ought to explain to the bald jacket with the orange head that he'd closed his eyes to gain a moments relief, but before having time to say anything his arms fell across his thighs, his head sank onto his chest, and his breathing became noisy and irregular.

A pall of green smoke rose in the air and Ivan took a step backwards when he saw the smoke was coming from a plating tank immediately in front of him. He wondered what a plating tank was doing in a snooker hall and began looking for evidence of foul play. Which he found in the shape of a figure concealed by the smoke, where a sudden bout of coughing revealed it was none other than Joe Taskerman who seemed to be inhaling the stuff as though he was on a promenade filling his lungs with sea air.

'You see, I told you this stuff was harmless,' Joe Taskerman called out. 'We should be bottling and selling this as a by-product. Look how well I can sing with this in my lungs.' He began to sing the Marseillaise.

'You'll bloody sing if I get my hands on your throat,' cried Ivan, quickly changing his mind as he recoiled from the thought of putting his hands on any part of Joe Taskerman's anatomy. He dismissed the ridiculous figure from his thoughts and was just in time to see that the tank had become a snooker table on which all the balls had been cleared leaving a pristine surface of green baize. This was a sight he'd seldom seen and therefore a cause for celebration. Although celebrations were short lived when his eyes fell on the three characters who were sharing much more than his car.

His heart sank but he needn't have worried for they too seemed more interested in the sight of an empty table, and he soon discovered why. The accumulation of smoke in the room made it difficult to be sure but he could have sworn he saw the table move. How could that be? It was supposed to be balls not tables that moved. Yet sure enough, the table was slowly rising into the air. He pinched himself as Owen, closely followed by Bernard and Henry, came rushing past with cries of wait, wait... but to no avail for the table went sailing away into the dark night air with the three figures in hot smoky pursuit.

Ivan turned to the bald orange with the jacket head. But it seemed he had gone too, leaving just a wispy lining on his empty glass.

'Here now, pull yourself together. We don't do bed and breakfast here.' The steward shook Ivan by the shoulder waking him with a start.

SUNDAY

22

WHOSE TRUTH?

Disturbed from an anxious sleep, Ivan opened his eyes wondering why he was walking through a plating shop in his pyjamas.

'I know if I can be in two places at once there is nothing to stop Joe Taskerman from doing the same, but do I have to listen to him before I'm awake?'

'Your call cannot be taken at the moment please try later.'

With the realisation there would be no hiding from Joe Taskerman even in a parallel universe Ivan leapt out of bed convinced he must be running late. No sooner had his feet touched the ground than he remembered what day it was and with a groan climbed back into bed pulling the duvet over his head. He was unable to settle however, and after a spell of fretful tossing and turning decided it was time to begin the day afresh, this time with a leisurely stretch and a yawn making at least for a pretence of a more sedate entry into the heart of the weekend.

Rowena was still sound asleep, her deep breathing and peaceful expression suggesting there was little likelihood of an early awakening. Ivan began to dress slowly and carefully so as not to disturb her. In the silence he found his attention drawn to the vexed question of how much of his life was governed by things outside of his own control. On the face of it he supposed that wasn't too surprising in view of how few challenges were made to what had always been taken for granted. There was little point in trying to change that. To raise the merest possibility of there being an alternative would cast you as a rebel, an outsider, open to ridicule, and unable to convince anyone of anything that really mattered.

He need go no further than the first example that came to mind, which was opportune because the one thing he hated about equivocation was the constant searching for examples when what you were engaged in at the time was a perfectly adequate case in point.

And so why was he getting up on the one day he could stay in bed? Because... there he was again, about to react in the same old way. That was the way things were, that was the way they'd always been, since time had begun on a Sunday morning you... he stopped to ask who had decreed that to be the case and in so doing put his finger on the pulse of an aspect that was rarely questioned – viz the elevation of Sundays, religious or secular, to a position that was unassailable. He was as guilty as anyone, the inordinate focus upon Sundays being a preoccupation of those who had to work for a living, despite a higher proportion than ever of those lucky enough to have a job, now having to work on Sundays.

It was amazing that Sundays should have maintained their standing, considering how often they'd failed to deliver. It was to counteract such disappointment that Ivan had so frequently told himself Sunday would be the day upon which he could escape the futility of the week's exertions, concentrate his efforts, and achieve something really useful. But of course that drove him further into the horns of the dilemma since Sundays were all too often the days on which his exhaustion caught up with him, meaning there was little hope of achieving anything beyond a confirmation of how stupid he'd been to imagine there was.

Leaving the bedroom satisfied he hadn't disturbed Rowena, he moved across the landing into the bathroom and in a commanding voice began to address an assortment of toothbrushes, soaps and deodorants.

'We would do well to remind ourselves that Sundays are merely structural components of the Gregorian calendar,' he proclaimed grandly. 'Conveying little other than their position in relation to the days with which they have come to be surrounded.' Relishing a captive audience for once he went on.

'And yet who could deny the effect of our own anxieties in this veneration – indication enough of our insatiable desire to resist the passing of time.' He threw a handful of cold water over his face and picked up a towel from the rail beside him.

'We must not delude ourselves,' he continued rubbing the back of his neck with the towel. 'For the exaltation is not a cerebral phenomenon.' He turned to face the empty toilet roll holder perched high above his old friend the lavatory brush. 'It is an immensely physical experience, which whether or not of our own making, is nonetheless a tragic confirmation of our place in the scheme of things.'

Placing the towel back on the rail, he supposed being upwind of Monday year after year, holding off the chill blowing in from another week, was an onerous task for any day to undertake. Not surprising therefore that on a bank holiday when responsibility was passed down the line to Monday, Sunday would be set free. To leave Monday keeping guard over the rushing in of Tuesday, making Wednesday the second day of the week, bringing what the man in the pale blue tee shirt and matching trousers might have to say a little nearer... he hoped that particular man would have more on his mind than what was on his own at the moment, but had to interrupt his train of thought as the mere contemplation of what might lay in store for him at the hospital began to turn his legs to jelly, reminding him of how much he would have liked to be going somewhere else for a few days.

He decided to take comfort from the fact that he didn't have to spend the day which had just dawned making numbers in hard copy tally with those on a screen. On the other hand the thought of what he was about to do instead was enough to remind him of how easily it was to respond to any space you had in your life, by filling it. He supposed the one thing you learned about space when you joined the human race, was that it was there to be filled. That may have been one explanation of why within not much more than an hour of first waking he found himself filling it for all he was worth, despite giving the impression he was emptying it given the size of the hole in which he was standing.

In the bottom of the hole was a huge slab of concrete reminiscent of the old wartime sea defences. His efforts didn't seem to be having much effect on the slab however, as

124

he violently swung a sledgehammer against it. There was no sign of the slab yielding, and for a moment he thought it might be fighting back. He told himself not to be deceived by the evidence of his own eyes, and blinking hard reassured himself he was witnessing minute vibrations as the slab struggled to absorb the energy of the hammer.

'Ooosh,' he swung the sledgehammer high above his head.

'Arrrgh,' the hammer descended and hit the concrete slab causing a stream of sweat to spray from the end of his nose.

'Ooosh,' again the hammer was raised in the air.

'Arrrgh,' the energy was released, the only thing looking as though it might break being Ivan's arm as the impact caused a bone-crunching shudder from his shoulder to his wrist.

'Ooosh,' the physical exertion had the effect of sharpening his concentration and he picked out a nodule of the slab imagining that it was Joe Taskerman's left ear.

'Arrrgh,' he brought down the hammer with renewed vigour. The descending blow had little effect on the concrete slab but it seemed to make the wielder of the hammer feel better. He wondered how Joe Taskerman could have come up with a figure of five thousand per week. Everyone with a part to play in the proceedings knew it was impossible to produce five thousand in a month, within the required tolerances, and since Joe Taskerman would never risk a situation in which there was a chance of any mistake of his being exposed, it didn't make sense. He surely didn't believe that if he repeated it often enough it would by some magical process come to pass. It wasn't as though he was a complete fool. Rumour had it that he was a graduate and that he'd got a 'first'. In which case you would have thought he would have some idea of how things worked.

With sweat dripping from the end of his nose, Ivan wondered how Joe Taskerman could have attained that qualification whilst having such an absence of common sense. Still, he supposed that common sense would have had little to do with how he'd been able to talk himself into the job he had now. An ability to tell those who mattered what they wanted to hear was more likely the kind of thing they would have been looking for, and he would have been well able to satisfy them on that score, his education having perfectly equipped him for a life of repeat after me.

'Ooosh,' the hammer swung high above his head.

'You must be more than a little deluded Footmouth to believe that output is dependent on everyone doing exactly as you say. We may appear to be hanging onto your every word, but we're a long way from being deceived by that snoot-snoot way of talking down your nose at the poor sods polishing your ego.'

'Arrrgh.' The concrete slab was unmoved.

Ivan thought it a pity the high and mighty hadn't been in the steelworks where he could have had his balls polished, and without doing a stroke of work for it too. With his own near escape in mind he wondered what the brand new hood and gown man had done after completing his education *('education is never completed')*. He remembered Heather telling him that as a new graduate Joe Taskerman had joined the forces.

'The forces of darkness?'

'He didn't need to join. He was already a fully paid up member.'

'Ooosh.' Paid up member or not, Ivan wondered whether that may have been why he'd become a graduate entrant into old aunt Elizabeth's private army (begging your Majesty's pardon, nothing personal in that you understand Ma'am. We were referring of course to your quasi-monarchic sovereignty). You had to admire the consistency. Imagine having the foresight to follow an education that had done so little to deflate your pomposity by entering a career which was devoted to the polishing of egos.

'Longest way up, shortest way down, two-three…' He was beginning to see how all this acclaimed expertise was honed into shape – looking after the fine back trouser crease of the commanding officer, the only Colonel in history to wear his trousers on the end of Footmouth's nose.

'Arrrgh,' the hammer descended with little effect on the slab causing Ivan to wonder what other sleights of hand Joe Taskerman had learned in the army. It was a good thing indeed that no one had sent him for an inspection bend.

Bending would have been the last thing to be caught doing on the firing ranges where he'd learned everything he needed to know about targets. Although the army had at least taught him how to wipe his arse on nettles. A really useful skill that. When the going got tough, the tough got nettled. He'd been nettling people for years and there was nothing Ivan would have liked better than to see Joe Taskerman on the buffing machine with his trousers down, unable to imagine what a cluster of five thousand eager fingers could do in the hanging gardens of Babylon which lay beside the hole in the pocket of his childhood dreams.

'Ooosh,' the sledgehammer swung high in the air.

'Arrrgh,' its energy was dissipated against the slab. Ivan supposed it wasn't too surprising Joe Taskerman's military training had turned out to be a waste of time. He'd been so intent on pushing out his chest that he'd failed to spot they were sending him up. The great Joe Taskerman who knew everything there was to know about putting people down, didn't know they were sending him up. And that was how in the midst of having his pisser pulled, the miracle of five thousand per week was born. What the army should have taught him was that everyone had to walk before they could run and that even then you couldn't rely on it because as anyone with an ounce of grey matter knew, you couldn't march an army on roller skates. Sooner or later someone would fall flat on their face and before you knew it you were all a bunch of dominoes.

'Ooosh.'

Ivan tried to avoid thinking about falling flat on his face whilst the hammer was at the top of its arc. Telling himself to press on regardless, he nearly had a seizure when he remembered that was the kind of thing Joe Taskerman would say when facing a difficulty. Although in his case it was a matter of pressing on regardless of the fact that he was a passenger. No one had fallen for his trick of believing he was the driver... the driver... now there was an unsuspecting irony you hoped never to find lurking beneath the surface of anybody's Cherry Orchard. Not that Joe Taskerman would recognise the fruits of a cherry orchard before giving the order to start cutting the trees down. The only new order he ever had in mind involved making more than could possibly be produced in a month of working round the clock and twice on Sundays. Whilst the new order everyone else had in mind was the one that would see Joe Taskerman escorted off the premises.

'Now that would improve the quality of our working lives. Oh what a lovely way to spend a lifetime without facing an unrealistic target of anywhere near five thousand per week.' The mere thought of him leaving would be an improvement. 'Output up.' Even a rumour that Joe Taskerman might be on his way would be enough. 'Output up-up.' Joe Taskerman? Who was Joe Taskerman? 'Output up-up-up.' Think of the boost that would give everyone if he were to grease his arse and slide down some other poor bugger's rainbow for a change.

'Arrrgh.'

One thing Ivan did remember Footmouth claiming, was that on leaving the army he'd been put on the fast track. The fast track to greatness. A pity they hadn't put him on a slow boat to reality. Imagine falling into the trap of believing everyone was pulling in the same direction. He should be so lucky. With all his so called education it didn't seem to have occurred to him that the foot soldiers too were working to maximise their returns. In their case on the sweat and tears they'd had to shed for the benefit of people like him. Was it too much to expect a would-be great man to know that in order to have everyone pulling in the same direction, you were dependent on the efforts of others.

'Too much, too much,' sang the chorus of a work gang in the plating shop.

'Ooosh.' Ivan's efforts were having such little effect that he began to wonder whether he was wasting his time with a sledgehammer – just as he would be wasting his time trying to educate a man with cloth ears into why rather than instruction, he ought to be concentrating on encouragement. He decided it might be more productive to ask how he himself got into his present position, and he was not referring to the hole in which he was standing because after meeting

SURVIVING JOE TASKERMAN

Joe Taskerman it had been a fast flowing river in which he'd found himself, counting the ripples as the water had risen up his wellington boots. Where, before he'd known what day it was, and long before he'd realised it didn't matter what day it was, things had gone from bad to worse and he'd found himself up to the eyeballs in crocodiles the likes of which would have made old Dundee himself wish he'd never been born.

'Everyone makes mistakes, but walking into that river of no return was the stupidest thing I've ever done.'

'Arrrgh.' His failure to make much of an impression on the slab reminded him again that it was one thing to identify inadequacy in a potential employer, quite another to imagine this inadequacy gave you an advantage. The feeling of ascendancy that came from the knowledge of greater ability was one of the false prophets of human endeavour. Abilty was merely an attribute, the question was – who decided? The truth was… and there was another thing because no-one knew what the truth was any more. But there again no-one ever did. Not even the logical positivists. Especially not the logical positivists where even the verification principle itself had turned out to be unverifiable.

'Ooosh.' The truth was never having to say you were suffering from Pontius Pilate's dilemma. ('Is this truly the son of Joe Taskerman's father?') Ivan thought it didn't really matter because in any case there was no way of knowing whether the account of Pilate's dilemma was true or not. With any matter of historical accuracy it depended upon who was holding what to be true. Even if you were talking to someone who claimed to have been there at the time. Ivan mused that with the way he sometimes felt it was possible he could have been there at the time…

I was born ten thousand years ago.
There ain't nothing in the world that I don't know.
I saw Peter, Paul and Moses, playing ring around them roses,
And I'll whup the guy who says that that ain't so!

The truth was, the truth was what you'd made it. If you'd

made it today by tomorrow it would have become yesterday, and since everyone knew that tomorrow would never come and yesterday had already been, then it could be said – give or take a trick or two of narrative accident – that there had been no output at all last week. And if there had been no output then there was no experience, and if there was no experience then it could be announced with impunity that commencing next week (in a pyramid near you) five thousand per week would be the truth. It would be the truth, because it would be the only truth possible.

'And if you believe that you'll believe anything,' said Ivan.

'Which in a curious way gives you a faint glimmer of hope, if only because when you find you can't make anywhere near five thousand per week you'll realise there might be someone, somewhere, who is telling the truth.'

'Arrrgh.' He knew that too wasn't strictly true, but it didn't matter because one of the few things he'd come to accept in life was that when someone assured you they were telling the truth the only sensible thing to do was hang on to what you already knew. Especially if you were having your ears bent by the likes of Joe Taskerman. For as everyone learned within a couple of minutes of meeting the squawker from cuckoo land, you would be unlikely to get the truth from him even if he knew what the truth was.

'Are you saying that Joe Taskerman is dishonest?'

'No, I'm saying Joe Taskerman is a puppet with a glove up his arse.' The hammer felt suddenly lighter.

'Ooosh… ring out wild bells. Let the land of the living dead rejoice. Joe Taskerman has spoken and now we know the truth.' Unfortunately the truth was that Joe Taskerman had spoken with only his own interest in mind. The one thing he'd ever been heard to say beyond the subject of five thousand per week was that his grandfather had almost been a passenger on the Titanic, a subject on which he could be relied upon to bore anyone who would listen.

'Almost been a passenger? What kind of a claim to fame is that?'

'Better than having been a passenger who'd made the

departure time,' ventured Ivan, who wasn't at all surprised to hear Joe Taskerman say his grandfather had been a passenger who'd missed the boat, claiming to not having known he was facing an impossible deadline... at least if he'd been half the passenger his grandson had turned out to be.

'Following in your grandfather's footsteps eh Footmouth?' Ivan had suspected he'd come from a long line of bounty hunters who'd always known there was a fortune to be made in manufacturing the truth.

'Arrrgh.' The concrete slab continued to show little evidence it was being assaulted by a hammer.

'Unlike that tragic night to remember which had provided a seabed of evidence,' muttered Ivan, forgetting that was yesterday and a long time ago such that nowadays you could build as many ships as you liked with inadequate bulkheads for the truth was that roll-on roll-off ferries were perfectly safe. 'Until you put them in the water,' scoffed Ivan, 'where even now the breeze of that Taskerman-speaks-the-lookalike-truth blows ghostlike through the channel ports.'

'Ooosh.' He supposed he ought to take comfort from that revelation, for now he knew that evidence was not the truth.

'Whose truth? The truth is, the truth is dead. Long live the truth.'

23

DANCING WITH SILVERY SID

'Arrrgh.' Once more Ivan brought the sledgehammer down upon the concrete slab with little discernable effect. Like talking to Joe Taskerman he might just as well have spent the morning banging his head against a brick wall, because brick wall, concrete slab, what difference did it make? There was little to choose between them, and what was more it had been no different in the steelworks back at the beginning of time.

'Which is another thing you might remember when next you raise your glass to warm the cockles of your heart,' a voice within him cried out in deference to the steelworks. For the bloody steelworks had been full of Joe Taskermans too. No-one in their right mind would want to move the spring mill when you could just as well leave it where it was. As had been said a million years ago... if they were interested in change they should concentrate on making springs for a change. Now there was a novelty.

'For Christ's sake,' Ivan was back in the steelworks. 'Don't use that word around here. Don't even think it. The buggers are hooked on novelty. It's a way of life for them. Unless you keep ahead you won't survive.' Being unsure of what he'd been meant to keep ahead of, Ivan had devoted himself to keeping ahead of anything that might trip him up on the road to it mattered not where so long as there were plenty of windows through which he could fly.

'Ooosh.' Get your kicks in mill sixty-six? No-one would make it to sixty-six with the way they were falling like flies, and those who did wouldn't recognise themselves. They could hardly recognise themselves now. Who are you? Answers in invisible ink on the back of an envelope addressed to somewhere that wasn't anywhere the lords of the dance would have the slightest interest in showing off their steps.

'Arrrgh.' The nodule that resembled Joe Taskerman's left ear refused to budge. 'You've never heard things expressed in quite that way before Footmouth? Well don't worry it isn't going to change your life.'

Far from changing his life, the master of dodgy figures was interested only in changing his position for a higher one in the pyramid. I change therefore I am. Cogito ergo bollocks was his Cartesian message to the thinking arm of the western world and no sign of a Martin Heidegger at the end of his existential rainbow. There was no hope of anyone having time to think once they had fallen under his spell, because as far as he was concerned there had only ever been one way to stand the great enlightenment on its head and that had always been a matter of, I am The One, therefore I have no need to stop and think who I am.

'And we all know what happens when someone believes they can do anything they like,' said a voice from a pulpit he remembered having once stood below. 'There's a danger they might start believing they are God.'

Ivan could only agree. Notwithstanding any impression which may have been created that no one in his neck of the woods believed in God, it wasn't a question of believing in God when you had to answer to the likes of Joe Taskerman. He was God of all he surveyed, and there was little alternative but to believe He meant exactly what He said.

'Who's God? Your God, my God?'

'You called?'

'Now look what you've done. You've set the clockwork mouth in motion again.' Refusing to pick up the cue Ivan turned his thoughts instead to the matter of why he was becoming more despondent with each swing of the hammer. The concrete slab was proving tougher than he'd thought, but sooner or later it would surely have to succumb to the onslaught. The weekend may be slipping away but if he really could convince himself the nodule on the slab resembled Joe Taskerman's left ear then there was still time to make amends. He may have drawn the short straw but he should at least be thankful there had been a straw to draw his luck upon, providing he remembered who owned the straws.

'Remember, remember, the fifth of November, gunpowder, treason and the voice of the only one authorised to speak with a forked tongue around here – for as He says, we keep selling the bloody things don't we, and if we keep selling them then we need to keep making them. This is a market economy after all.'

'Ooosh.' As the hammer reached the top of its arc it occurred to Ivan that perhaps Joe Taskerman was using a different system of calculation to the one he'd been using. He couldn't make the figures add up. But then he never could. He'd hardly progressed beyond counting on his fingers. Well, he'd only been at school for eleven years and there wasn't a lot you could teach anyone in a mere eleven years of moving from one damned desk to another whilst being told not to ask questions because you weren't supposed to talk in class.

'Arrrgh.' He remembered that once upon a time there had been an old steelworker who'd never been to school, and therefore didn't know that he was speaking out of turn. His instinct had told him that asking questions was the way to learn about the world and he could never understand why the world didn't seem to like the questions he asked. But neither did he enjoy being ignored, and so instead of keeping quiet like the cog-in-the-machine he was supposed to be, he'd begun to knock on doors – doors behind which he thought there should have been an answer to some of his questions. Poor old chap's been neither seen nor heard of since. Could he have had something to do with the cause of the impurities in that steel casting lying on the scrapyard waiting for a decent elapse of time before being brought back into production? Did he jump or was he pushed? Discuss with reference to an alternative theory of steelmaking.

'Ooosh.' The exertion was taking its toll as this time the hammer swung on a somewhat lower trajectory.

'Arrrgh.' Again the concrete slab took the force of the blow with little effect. The slab was beginning to feel like the steel casting waiting to be recycled, keeping its head down, intent on survival. The subject of which reminded him of all the efforts put into keeping below the line of fire in the steelworks.

'Ger a move on mate. ther ain't many places left.' It was the big man on the door to the melting shop urinal speaking now. 'Oh aye yer'll be safe enough in 'ere. Yer won't find any big nobs in 'ere, cept in yer magination. Might smell a bit but t'foreman won't come looking for yer in 'ere. That's why ther's on'y a few spaces left, but if we pack ony more in they might get s'picious.'

'Standin room only nah, pass further dahn t'stalls if yer will.' The man of decidedly smaller proportions mustering the men along the stalls would have been a good man to have in a crisis too. Just like the big man on the door he seemed to know what he was doing. 'Christ has ther been an evac'ation or som'ert? Dunkirk's got nowt o' this place. Tak yer turn ther's room dahn ther. Jus'keep yer hands in yer pockets. Ther's a reason for that yer know. These buggers wer trained down at United on packed terraces. Pee in yer pocket as soon as look at yer they would. Gi's a donkey jacket a whole new meanin.'

'Ooosh.' The memory of the camaraderie in the steelworks brought a new vigour to the swing of the hammer.

'O reight, o reight nahr. It's gettin a bit throng in ere. Don't let any more in Tommy, some of em are near to passin aht dahn ere. No passin aht ah said. Tell em to come back when t'buzzer goes. This lot'll goa then, wouldn't miss ther dinner for owt. Can't be caught crappin in ther dinner, if yer see what ah mean. We're all enti'led to a crap. Basic human right i' any civ'lis'tion. But even t'Barb'rians didn't crap in ther dinner.'

'Arrrgh.' Ivan remembered it had been the man behind the sweeping brush in the arc furnace control room who had provided them with their means of survival. You had to maintain an illusion of activity, he'd said. It was the one defence you had against the cretins who thought they were in charge. It wasn't difficult. All you had to do was show that you were going somewhere. It wasn't necessary to have a destination. In fact if you ever found yourself arriving the best thing to do was set off again before someone with stripes on their ambition enquired of you… er, what are you on with at the moment? That was when you had to be at your most inventive. I'm on my way to... wait, that's all you need say, they've stopped listening. You're obviously involved in something quite important.

'Ooosh.' Lost in memories of the steelworks Ivan had almost forgotten the weight of the hammer.

'What a mornin, what a mornin.' It was Harold the lad (a right lad) who was no longer a lad, speaking now. 'Where's me tea, where's that bloody mate o' mine, allus missin when he's needed? What a mornin, if I've moved that desk wunce I've moved it fifteen bloody times and I'll be movin it another fifteen times this aft'noon if I'm not careful. What a performance. Complete waste of a mornin. Oh Christ I've got corned beef, now ain't that typical. I spend all bloody mornin walkin three steps back'ards to nowhere in circles and when I sit down I'm lookin at corned beef. I ask yer, I do I ask yer. Ere, who fancies a... oh belt up and eat the buggers yerself Harold, at least yer won't have to eat em fifteen times nor chase em around in ever decreasin circles… that is if it's not too much trouble Harold. It's too much trouble waitin for y-o-o buggers to make up yer minds I can tell yer. If we leave it here the light isn't right and if we put it over there I won't be able to see the door. If we place it over there the files will be too far away and if we put it over there I shall be too far away from Digby. Hell fire, chuck it out the window then we can all go and piss in the wind and get us own back in more ways than any of us planned.'

'Arrrgh.' Still the slab gave no sign of surrender.

'Ello, ello, what's this? Lunchtime in the steelworks was always worth waiting for. It's cabaret time,' cried Harold the lad. 'It's Silvery, Sid the Prince of ballroom dancin. Ok who's put him up to this? Rehearsing in his dinner? I'll say one thing for him, he's got a bloody nerve has Sid….and now dancin for home counties north-south-east-west or wherever it is you come dancin from Sid-en-ey, we bring you Silvery Sid the cream of your lunchtime entertainment. Workers playtime with a capital P. Come and enjoy the show, if you can stand the excitement. You can feel the tension in the air, will he or won't he complete his routine before I take the corned beef from my sandwich and wrap it around his... slow-slow, quick-quick, slow, now Sid-en-ey is wearing a polo neck sweat shirt and matching blue boiler suit. Of course he has to practice but I'm buggered if I'm goin to hum. I've been hummin all mornin, and what's more I've also been dancin – dancin around the bloody universe with a desk for a partner, and if Digby's friend has his way I shall be doin so again for another three and a half hours this aft'noon. Perhaps I'll start a rumour. Aye, I'll tell them there's been a change o' plan – tell them their office is being moved to Beijing next month and it doesn't matter a toss where they put the bloody desk in the meantime.'

'Ooosh.' Ivan struggled to keep his balance under the increasing weight of the hammer.

'I'm only kiddin Sid-en-ey. Oh God I've got a banana, I daren't think twice 'bout that un... ne'ah mind, only three and a half hours to go. Hey Sid looks knackered doesn't he? Looks as though he mightn't make it. Best not try makin it with her on that job he's doin dahn in't strip mill. Might finish him off for good. Nah there's a thing. Yer won't hear that kind o' talk in't sub-burb-ban drawin rooms of t'home counties wherever it is y-o-o come dancing from Sid-en-ey lad, will yer?'

'Arrrgh.' In retrospect, Ivan wondered what Harold the lad had been thinking of. You could hear that kind of talk in whichever town you cared to mention this side of Joe Taskerman's miserable little birthplace, any reticence in such talk having little effect on the rise of the feminist cause if the chattering of the women in the tool room polishing bay was anything to go by.

'That's if yer can hear anythin dahn there in the toffee nosed sprawl where y-o-o come dancing from Sid-en-ey lad. Yer can hardly hear a thing dahn there fer bloody lawn mowers and hedgetrimmers, and that's in t' barbers.'

'Ooosh.' Ivan put a foot backwards to steady himself

'Come on lads. Time 'surrender us sanity. Time wunce more to put us-sens at mercy o' great decision makers o' world. Heigh ho, heigh ho, it's off to work we go, with a hump a sack on your broken back, heigh ho – heigh ho, heigh ho, heigh ho. You have been watching the history of ballroom dancing part twenty-four, which brought you that star of the bending boards, your very own Silvery Sid. Of course I dun't mean it. I like Sid-en-ey and his dancin just as much as y-o-o twats do. I'm just as big a Jessie as rest o' yer really. I hate me fuckin job that's all. I hate me fuckin job and what's more I hate me fuckin sen fer hatin me fuckin job. I've hated me fuckin sen for whole of me fuckin life for hatin me fuckin job. I can't get away from hatin me fuckin sen for hatin me fuckin job even when I'm on't fuckin job that's how bad things are. Now tell me, how do yer get out of that one with yer bucketful of nine O levels young Ivan lad?'

'Arrrgh.' With the benefit of hindsight Ivan would have told them how you got out of that one if your name was Joe Taskerman. You denied you were in it in the first place. Which was why he could walk around with his eyes closed and still see his way to jump up and down to the tune of anyone with more stripes on their tunic than he had, to the ultimate cost of those who had nothing but their own good fortune to serve by devoting their lives to keeping out of his way. That was what Ahmed with all his knowledge had consistently failed to do. And so Ahmed too had become one more notch on the belt of Footmouth's march to someone else's funeral. Surplus to requirements – redundant, and he being the one who knew more about the chemistry of the plant than Footmouth had ever dreamed of knowing. Still, stood to reason the last thing needed was to pay someone to spend their days looking for something that might be used to reveal the possibility of Joe Taskerman having been wrong.

'Wrong? Who, Joe Taskerman?'

'We have carried out extensive tests and there is nothing to suggest abnormal levels of anything in there, with the exception of too much talking. We have found the concentration to be no more than would be expected and have come to the conclusion that no-one is at risk. The fact that we have taken the trouble to have everyone screened is itself a measure of our concern for your well-being.'

'Well I don't find that very reassuring,' said Ivan,

reminding himself that it mattered little whether he was reassured, because Joe Taskerman was just a blip on the surface. Of more concern was the blip on the logic – the logic of great men and women that enabled a thousand and one Joe Taskerman's to maintain their positions whether they knew what they were doing or not.

'Ooosh.'

24

TAKING A BREATHER

'Arrrgh,' the hammer fell, releasing it's energy on the slab.

'I dread to think what this is doing to your blood pressure,' said Bernard, noticing that a pulsating vein was threatening to break out of Owen's left temple. 'To say nothing about the state of your back.'

This turned out to be a timely remark for the exhaustion finally took its toll leaving Owen unable to raise the hammer above his waist. The journey upwards began, but then stopped, before he suddenly dropped the hammer and jumped backwards like a resigning weightlifter trying to avoid being hit by the falling weights.

'You're quite mad,' said Bernard, concerned the sudden increase in humidity might well be due to Owen, who was sweating so much the ground around him was becoming almost as soggy as that around the burst water main which had flooded the street two and half years ago.

Owen sought the support of the wall beside him and drew in a great gulp of air, conscious the sweat was running into his eyes but not having the strength to raise an arm with which to stem the flow.

'What on earth are you doing?' said Henry.

'He's trying a new approach to watering the garden,' said Bernard.

Owen stared at them for some time before gasping, 'I'm not, not... not building... not building a nuclear shelter.'

('*I don't believe it.*')

'You look as though you're trying to knock one down, said Henry.

'What did you just say you were not doing?' said Bernard scarcely able to believe what he'd heard.

Owen repeated the information that he was not building a

nuclear shelter.

Bernard said that fitted nicely into the overall picture, which needed only the additional information that Henry was not eating a pomegranate and that he himself was not filling out an application for a dog licence.

'You... you don't er... like dogs,' said Owen.

'Which is precisely why I am not filling out an application for a dog licence,' said Bernard, adding there was a whole world of things he was not doing but none of them had anything to do with what Owen was doing at that moment.

'I'm.. .I'm... I'm taking... taking a breather,' spluttered Owen.

'And about time too,' snapped Bernard. 'But taking a breather from what?'

'From....from....from not building....'

'We can all see what you're not doing, said Bernard turning towards Henry for support to find himself confronted by a cursory raising of eyebrows. 'And here is Henry, who having scorned the idea of eating a pomegranate now seems to have fallen asleep on his feet.'

Bernard examined the area of darker ground extending outwards from where Owen was leaning against the wall of the house. He surmised that he must be severely dehydrated by now and decided it was time to say what he thought. A full blown rebuke was no more than Owen deserved, and so taking a deep breath he launched into one of his more fluent expositions with which no-one could fail to be impressed. Delivered in classical form he began with an eloquent introduction in which he set out the nature of the problem, before moving on to the main theme of his argument, the unfolding logic of which led to a natural and powerful conclusion. He made sure there was a clear recommendation and for good measure included a summary before ending the whole performance with a more than pertinent punch line. In the course of his rebuke Bernard was careful to convey a concern for Owen's well-being, in which he underlined the importance of keeping oneself in a reasonable state of physical fitness; drew attention to the influence of one's lifestyle upon one's condition; suggested that Owen should begin to take account of his age; reminded him that he alone was responsible for keeping himself in good shape; and told him to grow up and stop behaving like a thick headed stupid old goat.

'Guess what... what... what I'm not doing now,' said Owen by way of response.

'Listening?' said Bernard.

'Save us from more thoughts about what you're not doing, said Bernard.

'I'm not... not... not having a cup of tea,' said Owen.

'Well that's something upon which we can all agree,' said Bernard, leading the way off around the side of the house from where they emerged a few moments later onto a sunlit lawn.

'That selective weedkiller seems to have worked,' said Owen, admiring the texture of the lawn.

'Why are you talking about weedkiller?' said Bernard, 'whilst we are still waiting for an explanation of what you've been doing all morning.'

Owen suggested that weedkiller was an important component in any effective system of pastoral care, to which Bernard said he was at a loss to see how the use of weedkiller could be conceived as a function of pastoral care other than in a rather narrow materialist sense.

Ivan sat down disconsolately. He knew this was doing nothing to help him relax, and that he would unable to resist embarking upon a treatise of his own.

'Metaphor is a pervasive feature of language,' he declared fearlessly to a collection of songbirds, earthworms and woolly caterpillars, such that even the ubiquitous blackbird was silenced by the imperiousness of his pronouncement.

'A feature providing a dimension in discourse which is the envy of other species.' He wagged a determined finger at the blackbird, prompting the bird to raise its beak in the air and proclaim the territorial ambitions at the core of its own existence.

'You are quite right,' said Ivan gesturing to the bird. 'Those are empty words in the circumstances, and poor old Archie is a living… er that is the memory of poor old Archie is a no-longer-living proof of that.' He coughed roughly as he recalled the finality of the words with which Archie Munroe had come face to face, whilst Joe Taskerman had survived. Clenching his fist at the injustice of it all he leaned over to examine the extent of frost damage on a battle scarred magnolia in the border beside him.

'Many an illlustrious metaphor has been wasted on the deaf,' he said pulling on the blackened shrub. The damaged flower head came away in his hand but the stem was left nodding its head, causing him to contemplate the prospect of applying weedkiller to Joe Taskerman. Shock, horror. Now where could an idea like that have come from? The shorn stem of the magnolia seemed in agreement, but it was to the blackbird he looked accusingly. Only to find the bird had retreated, perhaps in search of less fiercely contested territory. Leaving him to shrug his shoulders and accept that no matter how precocious, a blackbird was an unlikely source of iconoclasm, even in a town garden.

'The condition of the lawn is important,' said Owen. 'Footnotes to Plato are all very well but they don't keep the weeds down.'

'I wish I could say I had the slightest interest in understanding this obsession with weeds,' said Bernard.

'It's quite simple really,' said Owen. 'You have to keep the weeds down otherwise the grass won't grow.'

'Some would say that grass is a weed,' said Bernard, casting an eye over what remained of the old rose bed.

'Not when its in the middle of a lawn,' said Owen.

'Well obviously not when its in the middle of a lawn,' said Bernard.

'Ah, so you're a relativist then,' said Henry mischievously.

'Of course I'm not a relativist,' said Bernard. 'No-one can be a relativist in the real world. You can only be a relativist on a desert island. He suggested that relativism was a tendentious form of naïve idealism, because in order to engage in communication there had to be a stock of agreed definitions and shared knowledge which required a means of discriminating between competing claims. From which it followed that in the case under discussion grass was a

143

weed....except for those situations in which the agreed definition of weed happened to exclude grass.'

'Sounds a pretty relativist position to me,' said Henry.

'That's because you don't understand indexicality,' said Bernard, 'whereby a great deal of what we say and do relies on (bracketed) knowledge.'

'I think I'm a naïve idealist really,' said Owen stopping everyone in their tracks. 'Well I mean, I'm naïve enough to believe you two know what you're talking about, and that doesn't seem very realistic. Therefore I'm clearly not a realist, and if I have understood it correctly realism runs in some way counter to idealism then I must be an idealist, and since we've already established that I'm naïve...'

'Profound,' said Bernard.

'Worthy of the Tractatus,' said Henry, just as Rowena appeared carrying a tray of tea.

'Ah,' sighed Ivan in appreciation of her superb sense of timing.

Rowena set down the tray and enquired as to how the work was progressing. Ivan said it was a slow and exhausting business, and rolled over from his sitting position towards the weather-beaten table in the middle of the lawn, upon which the tray of tea had been placed. Rowena poured herself a cup and was already on her way indoors when she paused to say that lunch would be ready in half an hour.

'I think you're wasting your time,' said Henry, picking up a piece of concrete that had broken away from the edge of the patio.

'You may be right,' said Owen, his eyes following the disappearing figure of Rowena.

Henry tossed the piece of concrete to Bernard, drawing attention to its flintlike qualities. He suggested that if the builders had used the same mix around the other side of the house then Owen would never break it with a sledgehammer.

'I'm still waiting to hear why he wanted to break it in the first place,' said Bernard, examining the specimen.

'I'm not....'

'We know, we know.'

'But it's true.'

'It may be true, but so is the fact that this cup of tea is not being emptied into your lap... at the moment.'

'Well perhaps you should take a look at this,' said Owen, fishing out a soggy roll of paper from his pocket and passing it over to Bernard.

Bernard unrolled the scroll of paper expecting yet another diversion from the matter in hand. Peering at the contents his eyes lit upon the words, nuclear fall-out, whereupon he began to study the paper with a little more interest. It seemed to be a sketch of some sort and turning it first one way and then the other he saw that the sketch depicted some kind of building. The paper was in such a terrible state that some of the details had been obliterated, but along the bottom of the paper he could just make out the words – Civil Defence. He looked at Owen in disbelief, and to his lasting regret heard himself saying – you're not building a nuclear shelter?

'That's what I've been trying to tell you,' said Owen.

Ivan lay on his back staring up at the sky speculating upon the degree to which a particular cloud resembled the health and safety inspector's bacon sandwich. Recalling the size of that sandwich he knew it would be one more thing for which Joe Taskerman would insist Ivan take full responsibility. Not for Joe Taskerman a full report on the working practices involved in the production of the sandwich. Joe Taskerman never waited for a report on anything before attributing responsibility. And what was more, if the health and safety inspector's own report went the way of his previous reports, no-one would be any the wiser as to where the real problem lay. For all Joe Taskerman had ever been prepared to say about any report from a health and safety inspector was that he had no idea why the report had not been made more widely available.

REPORT TO REMAIN UNPUBLISHED - is what anyone reading the headline in the business section of the Sunday newspaper lying unopened on the kitchen table would have seen that it said. The company have decided, the article beneath the headline began, that no useful purpose would be served by publishing the report. It seemed that a spokeswoman (for it was she) had confirmed there were no plans to publish the results of the enquiry. Those who had continued to read the article would have seen that when questioned further the spokeswoman had gone on to suggest that in view of the decision not to publish the report it would be inappropriate for her as spokesperson to say anything further on the matter.

'What I don't understand,' said Henry, 'is why, if you're not building a nuclear shelter, you're showing us the plans for one?'

Owen could contain himself no longer and slapping his thigh with delight, pulled out another soggy roll of paper, tossing this one to Henry.

'I found the plan for a nuclear shelter amongst some old papers the other day,' he nodded to the scroll which Bernard had discarded in disgust. 'What I'm really doing is on there.' He pointed to the new piece of paper which Henry was unable to prevent Bernard from snatching from his hand.

'It says something about a drain,' said Bernard.

'That's right,' said Owen, 'and so as you can see I decided to do it myself.'

'Do what yourself?' said Bernard, still trying to make sense of the detail. 'It says here that it would be five hundred and seventy pounds.'

'Exactly,' said Owen.

'It looked a good deal heavier than that,' said Henry.

'No, no, this is an estimate of the cost of something,' said Bernard. 'Five hundred and seventy pounds for excavating a drain.'

'In order to locate the exact position of the leak and assess the extent of the damage,' said Owen.

'Five hundred and seventy pounds. I see, and so you decided to do it yourself?' said Bernard.

'Brilliant,' said Owen, throwing a fist into the air.

'What are you going to do when you've located the leak?' said Bernard.

'Hold his nose?' said Henry.

'I shall have to decide upon that when I've assessed the

extent of the damage,' said Owen.

'Say... about the middle of next year?' said Henry.

Bernard said that he ought to have let builders undertake the work. They at least would have known what to do when they'd exposed the damaged section, and that in itself might have been worth the cost of the job. Owen wasn't too sure since. The builders estimate didn't include the cost of any corrective work that might be required. Their intention was to submit another estimate when they'd seen the extent of the damage. By doing things this way he could still get them to carry out the repair when he'd exposed the damaged section.

'Don't you find it a little strange they should not have included the cost of repairing the drain?' said Bernard. 'What do you think they expected to find?'

'We shall see,' said Owen, placing his cup on the edge of the patio.

'You don't think that might be where the yellow monster lives do you?' said Henry, dodging the blow aimed at his head by Bernard.

Raising his hands to support his neck as he lay back, Ivan yawned and decided it wouldn't hurt for the exact location of the leak to remain hidden a little while longer. As his eyes began to close his thoughts turned to why Ahmed with all his knowledge had done nothing to seek redress given the appalling way he'd been treated.

The gentle sound of snoring was soon the only thing disturbing the peace of the morning. Apart from a flap of wings from the resentful blackbird, which deciding the sound of snoring was far from gentle, took off in disgust for the top of the pear tree in the garden next door, from where it was treated to a brief suspension of sonorities as the snorer struggled to breathe through partially restricted airways.

25

A FIFTEEN ROUND CONTEST

Clouds were racing across the sky. Ivan wondered why they were in such a hurry. There was surely no cause for them to run away from a morning so beautiful as this. But then he saw the reason for their haste. They were being pursued by a long faced man in a plastic raincoat. The man was wielding a fearful looking whip, which he didn't hesitate to use, lashing out whenever a particular cloud looked as though it might fall behind the pace he was setting. He was screaming and shouting at them but above the noise of the whip Ivan couldn't make out what he was saying. It did seem to be having the desired effect however, for the man had soon cleared the sky of any trace of cloud and without so much as a pause to admire his work had disappeared.

There was a ripple of applause to Ivan's left and he was about to join in when his attention was drawn to a shadow which had fallen across his face. Looking up, he saw that the long faced man who had moments ago been chasing clouds was now standing over him. Not only had the plastic raincoat gone but the man was stripped to the waist revealing through a forest of glistening hair, an array of muscles which he flexed first on one side of his body and then on the other.

The display of muscular strength turned out to be a precursor to more productive action as the man picked up a pneumatic drill and began wielding it against a road that meandered away into the distance. In no time at all he had torn up a strip of tarmac across the entire surface, and he contined with each stride to take up sections of road as though they were made of jelly. Such was the ferocity with which he attacked that Ivan doubted whether there would be any road left. But he needn't have worried for the man's efforts had reached a point at which the vibrations caused him to shake so violently that in the space of what must have been only a few seconds his body became a blur, before suddenly disapearing, leaving the drill to slowly topple over in the middle of the road where it had been so cruelly deserted.

Ivan stared at the space where the man had been standing. Could he really have shaken himself to pieces? Or had he simply become obscured by the cloud of dust sent up by the drill? Before having time to find out Ivan realised that he too had been stripped to the waist and was now in the middle of a boxing ring with a canvas so blood-stained it was difficult to see what the original colour had been. There was no time to worry about the colour of the canvas however, because heading straight for him was the long-faced man with rippling muscles. As he came nearer, Ivan saw that in the middle of his long face he had a terribly flattened nose.

Ducking just in time to avoid a blow which might easily have removed his head, Ivan decided that keeping out of range of this adversary would be the best form of defence. He set off upon a twisting and weaving path around the ring, throwing punches whenever he could catch the man with the flattened nose off guard. None of his punches had any effect, and it was with relief he realised the referee had intervened and was ordering them back to their respective corners. His opponent protested that he hadn't heard the bell, but the referee seemed to be more intent upon telling Ivan to sit down so that he could start the meeting.

Ivan felt it was extremely silly of him to have come into a meeting wearing boxing gloves and made an attempt to hide them by sitting on his hands and trying to look casual. The referee standing on a platform at the front of the hall began to address the meeting.

When he heard the subject of the talk was to be on the matter of survival Ivan thought it might be safe to bring out his hands. To his surprise he saw the gloves had been replaced by a pair of high fidelity speakers, from which the voice of the referee was coming. And as if this were not confusing enough, the voice was suggesting that everyone was a contender in a glorious fifteen round contest.

'Speak for yourself,' Ivan muttered in a tone he would have

sworn was inaudible were it not that several people turned round and told him to be quiet.

Undaunted by his heckler the referee went on to say that everyone had a duty to keep fighting. Raising his guard, he told them fighting was the only way they were going to survive. No matter how many times they were knocked down they must pick themselves up and continue the fight. Ivan was in no mood to listen to such nonsense, and turning off the raving voice in the speakers at the end of his arms, got up and stamped from the hall muttering that he'd never heard so much rubbish in his life.

Expecting to emerge into the street where the air would be cleaner, he was surprised to find himself inside a Victorian swimming pool, and that he was dressed in a bathing costume which came down to his knees. He felt more conspicuous in this outfit than he had when wearing boxing gloves in a public meeting. Seeking to hide his embarrassment he dodged behind a column to find he'd emerged into what seemed to be a ballroom in which the shorts and striped blazer he was wearing looked equally out of place, not least because the dancers in evening dress had now taken a rest and the ballroom was filled with men in morning suits and women in satin dresses. To his consternation he saw that a microphone had been placed in front of him and before he knew what was happening he heard himself speaking to the assembly. He told them it was downright perverse to imagine life bore any resemblance to a fifteen round contest.

Noticing people were beginning to leave he grasped the microphone in both hands and tried to think of something more interesting to say. But the noise created by his departing audience was distracting and when his hesitation was greeted with a cascade of bread rolls, he decided the most sensible course of action was to duck under the table.

Whereupon he found himself in a tunnel facing an enormous slug-like creature hissing menacingly as it advanced towards him. He hoped it wasn't seeking revenge for all the pellets. Whatever its mission there seemed little alternative but to look for an escape to the rear and turning on his heel he started to run. He didn't get far before having to slow down as making progress in the tunnel became more difficult. He surmised he must have been gaining height because he was already out of breath and the headroom in the tunnel became more and more restricted so that he had to lower his head and run in a crouched position. How strange the constructors should have failed to take account of the rising ground and correspondingly inclined the roof of the tunnel.

There was no question of turning back to face the slug-like creature, which judging by the intensity of the hissing seemed to be keeping pace with him. He had to press on, hoping at some point to find a turning out of the tunnel. But no turning appeared, and what was more the pinprick of white light in the distance which was to have been his salvation turned out to be a spotlight shining on another boxing ring.

He wondered what all the fighting was about. The place would be full of bloody noses if they weren't careful. That concern was soon replaced by another as a rushing sound like a train accelerating out of a station came from the darkness behind. His response was to try to run faster but he succeeded only in banging his head on the roof of the tunnel which caused him to stumble. The resulting dizziness deposited him headlong onto the floor of the tunnel where he lay sweating profusely and listening to the thumping of his heart as it tried to leap out of his chest.

Opening his eyes he was just in time to see the blackbird returning to the garden in a swoop that was rather too close for comfort. Grunting dismissively at the bird he closed his eyes again and slowly drifted back into the world of blood-stained boxing rings and ill-constructed tunnels. He recalled that of the many awkward situations from which he'd managed to extricate himself none had been more taxing than the one to which he was now returning... to find that in the land of hissing slugs and accelerating trains any attempt to get a grip on where he was could advance no further than conjecture as to how anyone could survive in a such a place.

Of more concern was the question of how he was going to

find a way out. There was little point in asking for directions. Anyone who could tolerate living in such a place was the last person from whom to seek information of that kind. You might as well ask someone suffering from a loss of memory what they'd been doing immediately before the memory loss occurred. You could count yourself lucky if they'd retained the merest notion of what amounted to a reply to a question let alone know what constituted an appropriate one.

He decided the only sensible thing to do was to take his mother's advice and follow his nose. But his nose betrayed him because he then found himself confronted by yet another boxing ring. This ring had been positioned in an antechamber that had suddenly appeared on his right giving at least some relief from the close confines of the tunnel. It had a strange familiarity too. It surely couldn't be the same ring in which he'd fought earlier. It did appear to have the same referee who he could have sworn gave him a knowing wink. How could that be? Had he been retracing his steps without knowing it? He hadn't been walking backwards and so he must have been going round in circles. The tunnel hadn't given the impression of being circular but nothing was as it seemed, and so he would have to accept that he had less idea of where he was than at any time since he'd left the web of that great spider of a storyteller who'd never done much to help him decide who or where he was.

He sought consolation in the thought that the man with the flattened nose would have equal difficulty finding his way around the place. Obtaining a map would be of little help given the problem of keeping it up to date with the speed of changes that seemed to be occurring all around him. The latest example of which revealed that the antechamber had acquired a false ceiling which for some reason had been covered in bread rolls. He began to worry the place may have been designed to prevent anyone from leaving. That was an unnerving prospect. He couldn't bear to think about what sort of people would inhabit a place with no exits.

As though in response, a voice boomed out so as to leave no doubt in anyone's mind that they were listening to a voice of authority. Ivan recognised a voice of authority when he heard one, and he knew this was a voice of authority from the way the hairs on the back of his neck were standing up. He straightened his collar, stiffened his resolve, and waited for details of evacuation procedures. But no such details were given. The voice turned out to be giving a news update. He had no idea what was said because he stopped listening the moment he realised he was listening to a news bulletin.

The news bulletin ended as abruptly as it had begun, to be replaced by an equally authoritative voice giving an update on a different topic. He wondered why after hours of hissing slugs and thudding gloves, news summaries were being made continually as one authoritative voice after another took to the airwaves. It then occurred to him why there were so many boxing rings. That was the only way of determining whose turn it was to read the next news bulletin. Ivan didn't care whose turn it was. His only thought was the sooner he got out of the place the better. He felt he could have learned more from the blackbird. Perhaps that was what the blackbird had been trying to tell him. And if a blackbird had been the only one in possession of the information he was seeking, then it wasn't surprising so many authoritative voices had been left with nothing to do but give news updates.

Now he'd assured himself there was nothing to be gained from listening to any of the updates he began to feel more at home. Coming from where he did he was well practised in not believing anyone who told him there were no pollutants in the air he breathed, and no residues to worry about in the food he ate. But then he opened his eyes and remembered that even if you were lying on the lawn in your own garden it wouldn't necessarily mean you were more at home.

Blinking in the sunlight he sat up in time to see the blackbird once more take off, evidently having decided the position into which it had ventured was a little too exposed. Picking up a handful of grass Ivan threw this wildly in the direction of the departing bird and uttered a silent curse in the knowledge that so much of what people were told was designed to make them feel grateful for what they already had. He knew there was nothing surprising in that, since the first job of anyone in authority had always been to convince others that the real threats came from elsewhere. With a groan at the extent of such deception he hammered his fist into the lawn.

Feeling the warmth of the sun on the top of his head he lay down again and closing his eyes found himself spinning backwards into a void that could well have been a million miles into space, had it not been for the existence of a false ceiling through which he descended onto the floor of yet another boxing ring, to find himself covered in bread rolls.

26

THE WOMAN IN CORDUROY JODHPURS

'I shall soon be entitled to a Lonsdale belt,' he muttered as he picked himself up to discover he was not after all in a boxing ring, and neither was he still in the underworld. Whether he'd finally been given directions by someone or whether he'd simply wandered out of the tunnel he had no time to consider, because now of more concern was that right in front of him was a steep rock face. He wondered whether he ought to look for a way of scaling the slippery surface but decided that not having a head for heights it would be safer to go back into the tunnel.

A return to the underworld was out of the question however for the entrance to the tunnel seemed to have disappeared having been replaced by a precipice... right behind him. He must be half way up the rock face already. His head swam and he closed his eyes, repeating to himself over and over again that he must not look down. Yet he had to look somewhere, and so opening an eye he saw that far from being half way up a rock face he was in the middle of a wood. Now there was a stroke of luck for even the densest of woods couldn't be as impenetrable as the tunnel had been. There might be a track in the wood and he might even be lucky enough to find it. On the other hand given the state of his luck so far perhaps he would do better to remain where he was. But then he noticed to his left was a prickly hedge beyond which was a ditch. Imagining he saw something move on the other side of the ditch it occurred to him that with movement might come knowledge of how to return to civilisation, and being an incurable optimist he set off in that direction.

The hedge proved to be less of an obstacle than he'd feared, and give or take a few scratches and a bruised shin he was soon standing on the edge of the ditch. The ditch on the

155

other hand was another matter. It must have been all of ten feet deep and the banks were steep, such that one look down was enough for he suddenly lost his balance and fell headlong into it.

The bottom of the ditch was hard and dry and considering himself fortunate to be still in one piece he picked himself up and began to look for a suitable place to climb out. His eye was drawn to the opposite bank where a figure looking remarkably like the referee seemed to be pointing at him and roaring with laughter. Having had more than his fill of referees for one day he turned his back on the figure and began to walk briskly away along the bottom of the ditch.

His initial impression of the ditch being dry turned out to be mistaken, and he found his shoes beginning to sink into the sludge which seemed to be forming at an alarming rate. Walking became more difficult as his shoes were now under the surface. But worse was to come for he then realised his ankles too were being sucked into the sludge so that he could make no progress at all. Each attempt to move forward made him sink in further. He turned to see how far he'd come since falling into the ditch and his heart missed a beat when he saw coming along the ditch and heading straight for him, was an enormous dredger. Realising his hope of survival rested on being able to get out of the ditch, he looked for a place where he could scramble up the bank. He imagined the speed at which sludge was forming might work to his advantage, enabling him to hammer his toes into the bank which surely must be softening too, thus making for the kind of progress you could only dream about if you were climbing an ice wall in crampons.

He began the ascent and was doing well until he made the mistake of looking down and promptly fell back into the ditch. With the dredger advancing rapidly he decided the sensible thing to do would be to close his eyes and with a one-two-three-four-five steps, propel himself up the bank and leap over the rim. With an enormous effort he finally managed to exit the ditch, to find that he'd tumbled head-over-heels into a field of mushrooms in which so much weedkiller must have been applied there wasn't a blade of grass to be seen.

Picking himself up he heard a noise to his left where he saw a woman in corduroy jodhpurs spraying the field from a hose pipe. The woman was walking backwards, applying the hose pipe in a series of arcs intent upon covering as much ground as possible. At the end of each traverse she jerked on the hose and issued a belligerent cry as though dragging a disobedient dog away from prohibited ground.

Ivan waved his arms to attract the woman's attention but her reaction was not what he'd expected, and before having time to take evasive action the woman had pirouetted and turned the hosepipe on him. With a cry of, 'good morning to you too,' he set off across the field, anxious to put as much distance as he could between himself and the deranged woman.

It would have been difficult enough to make progress on a carpet of mushrooms, but it was altogether out of the question now they were acquiring a covering of the thick greasy liquid coming out of the hosepipe. The stuff was a shade of yellow only a few tones lighter than the woman's jodhpurs with a smell uncannily like that of... he had to be mistaken, for even if the field turned out to belong to the tunnel people they surely wouldn't apply the garlic sauce before picking the mushrooms.

'For God's sake,' Ivan yelled over his shoulder realising she was gaining on him.

'What the hell do you think you're doing,' she cried above the sound of her squelching boots.

'I'm not building a nuclear shelter,' he cried inadequately, the information having no effect as she continued to spray the liquid over him until his trousers were in such a state he thought it might be easier if he were to stop and take them off. But taking off his trousers under the gaze of a strange woman was more than he could face, and so he concentrated instead upon trying to stay on his feet. He hadn't the faintest idea of who the woman in corduroy jodhpurs was but there was a hint of something in her voice that perplexed him. Which was to to be his undoing because on turning to take another look, he lost his footing and fell headlong, to find himself slithering along the surface of the mushrooms for what seemed like half a lifetime before the woman was upon him, holding him in a grip of steel that made it difficult for him to get any purchase on the mushrooms. Much as he might have relished the idea of being overpowered by a strong woman, he decided this was not the time, and a desperate struggle followed in which each move he made seemed to tighten the woman's hold on him. Sliding this way and that as the movement of their bodies propelled them across the surface of the mushrooms, Ivan became convinced at one point he'd broken free, to find he was more at her mercy than ever, for now the woman was standing over him with a foot on his chest.

From his trapped position beneath what he now saw was a leather riding boot with a spur in his face, the thought occurred to him that she had a striking resemblance to the Eiffel Tower. Drawing inspiration from the thought of being somewhere else he made a heroic attempt to ascend the external structure. Forcing his chest from beneath her boot he began hauling himself upwards, hand over hand seeking purchase on her jodhpurs, to find himself moments later looking into her eyes. Without a thought for what he was doing he gathered a handful of hair behind her head and forced his mouth down hard upon hers. To his surprise he felt her mouth yield and was aware that the jodhpurs had begun to move against his sodden trousers. He wondered whether he ought to be encouraging her movements, or whether he should be doing everything in his power (admittedly not very much) to resist this madness. But he was in no condition to resist, for having once more tightened her grip on him he realised she was now running her fingers along his spine. Her breathing suddenly became shorter and fiercer and her body stiffened before being racked by a shudder as she threw her head back and with a groan became soft and pliant in his hands.

Being aware he was in a compromising position he looked nervously over his shoulder and was relieved to discover the field was deserted. The hosepipe having become a trickle he thought perhaps he ought to introduce himself to the woman in his arms, but a sharp pain in his groin caused him instead to thrust the woman away from him.

Opening his eyes he found he was lying against the hard edge of the patio where he'd rolled over at an awkward angle, such that a protruding piece of the concrete base was threatening to puncture a delicate part of his anatomy. Now he had all the evidence he needed to confirm the stuff was extremely hard.

'Well, I'm not going to allow a slab of concrete to put me off,' he said aloud, though without the conviction he would have liked as he rolled away from the offending edge of the patio and once more closed his eyes.

27

HERE IS THE NEWS

'What the…' Ivan spluttered, noticing his body had become distinctly shorter. He looked down to discover his legs had become shorter too and he seemed to be walking along without any part of his anatomy being in contact with the ground. He considered how useful that would have been in the field of mushrooms but had second thoughts for if his feet had been no longer able to reach the ground he would have had no way of controlling the direction in which he went.

This latest predicament posed more of a threat than the man with the flattened nose. Wondering how to respond to this new turn of events he decided he must do what came naturally and so he began to whistle as though he hadn't a care in the world.

A voice from behind him said he sounded as though he'd lost his dog and he turned to find he was being confronted by a strikingly dressed media woman with a microphone in her hand.

'Tell me Mr Driver, when did you first realise your dog was missing?' said the woman in an overly serious voice, suggesting she was from a television news channel.

'I don't have a dog.'

'But you were whistling and therefore guilty by association.' The woman had a three hour time slot to fill.

'I will have you know my credentials are impeccable. There are too many dogs in the world already. If you ask me it's the pet food manufacturers who are guilty by association,' said Ivan staring in astonishment as the woman slowly disappeared. He wondered whether it had been something he'd said. Narrowing his eyes he peered into the space where she had been less than a second before. But there was hardly a sign of her now. He reached out and was surprised to feel her hand still holding onto the microphone before she finally vanished without trace. He made a move towards where she'd been standing but it was too late and he succeeded only in falling over again.

Picking himself up and brushing away the dust that had now collected on his wet trousers he was suddenly blinded by the lights of a television studio into which he seemed to have wandered.

'Five seconds.' A voice rang out.

Ivan saw he was in front of camera and shuffling the papers on the desk, found himself, on cue, reading from them.

'Here is the news.' It was unbelievable he could have become so quickly embroiled in such a task.

'Another six hundred fines for speeding offences have been served today, bringing the number of charges this week to five thousand three hundred and forty,' he went straight into the main story. 'The decision to use the missile tracking station in the identification of offenders is being hailed as a huge success.'

'Well it's done little to protect us from anything else,' said a voice from somewhere off to his right, where in the corner of his eye Ivan saw a crowd was gathering in the studio.

'I wonder what will happen to the missiles?' queried a voice in the crowd.

'I expect they'll use them to target non-payers,' someone said.

'There weren't any missiles,' said another, anxious to put the record straight.

'Cut,' a voice full of panic yelled out.

'We can't cut... this is live you pillock,' an answering voice rang out in no less panic.

'Never mind the missiles, it's the tracking that has always worried me,' said a voice from the back of the studio. 'You'd do well not to believe their reassurances about side lobes.'

Ivan began to worry the voices might be going out on air, an unforgivable occurrence on the six o'clock news. For this was indeed the six o'clock news which had been speaking with one voice since the first day of transmission. He stared at the camera as if commanding its attention and sure enough the camera moved in towards him.

'Things are looking up,' said Ivan surprised by the note of authority in his voice.

'I suggest you keep looking down,' said a technician still trying to get the autocue working.

'Figures released today show that as a result of the number of drivers receiving penalties the incidence of serious injuries sustained in traffic accidents has reduced,' he continued, before again being interrupted as a scuffle broke out at the back of the studio. This was more than any newsreader could tolerate and he leapt out of his seat determined to teach these people a lesson. Unfortunately by the time he reached the place where the intruders had been standing they'd made good their escape. But he was not going to give up so easily. He was determined to seek them out and make an example of them.

'The scheme is working,' said Ivan now running along a corridor at the rear of the newsroom. 'As more and more fines are imposed we are seeing a reduction in the seriousness of injuries.'

'You're not suggesting there's a correlation?' said a statistician from beyond an open door.

Ivan was unsure whether the enquiry referred to the attempt to attribute the reduction in injuries to the number of fines or whether the voice was talking about something altogether more important, such as the increasing tendency for interruptions to occur in the six o'clock news.

'I'm afraid there may not even be a connection,' said a passing figure in a station masters uniform.

That was the last straw. No self-respecting newsreader could be expected to continue in such circumstances. It was intolerable. How could any passing figure imagine they knew more than the newsreader did about the lead story. Newsreaders knew more than anyone...

'Except about what they were doing,' said someone with a finger on the pulse.

'Who said that?' snapped the newsreader. It was time to stamp his authority on the situation. That was his job. Being a newsreader was a responsible job – as responsible a job as anyone could wish to aspire. His eye was drawn to a piece of action running on a screen in an open area to his left where a notice told him a training workshop was in progress for those needing to improve the authoritativeness of their delivery no matter how unlikely the story they'd been given to read. In front of the screen were rows of young newsreaders gazing in awe as the action on the screen cut to the figure of a masterful old newsreader of previous times.

'The government have announced that a more efficient method of calculating the number of people out of work is to be introduced. Those wishing to declare they have done no work will be asked to register their claims by logging onto the claimants website. The plans released today show that claimants will have to provide full on-line explanations as to why they are out of work in respect of any hour of any day in which they have done no work... and now I understand we can go straight to that interview with the winning owner of the Siddlecombe Gold Cup we were unable to bring you earlier.'

Ivan opened his mouth but nothing came out.

'You cannot equate a periodic summary of the number of fines imposed to an episodic change in the injuries sustained without a consideration of the intervening variables,' the statistician insisted from along the corridor.

'Look, I can say whatever I want, I'm the newsreader remember,' Ivan managed to blurt out forgetting that he could only say what his editor had authorised him to say. The assurance with which he played his trump card however raised the worrying prospect that he may be in possession of the right qualities after all. And when he began to speak to a camera as it followed him along the street into which he'd emerged, the rantings of the crowd were silenced for a moment in the face of such authority.

'As a result of the penalties imposed there have been indications that drivers are now beginning to reconsider the urgency of their journeys,' he resumed the main story reading from the new set of papers which had been thrust into his hand. 'The speed reduction campaign seems to have captured the imagination of the people,' he enthused, whilst trying to discern what the voice in his earpiece was screaming.

It seemed he was being reminded of recent commitments to make the six o'clock news more relevant to the man and woman in the street and so he turned to a woman and asked her what she thought of the results.

'Oh I think it's wonderful,' she said. 'Why only this morning I crossed this very road… and for the first time in years I was able to reach the other side.'

The newsreader smiled and looking back to camera was suprised to see the cameraman and the entire crew tearing off down the street pursued by a huge dalmation dog, closely followed by the crowd shouting encouragements to the dog.

Finding himself alone at last Ivan began to worry about the high levels of adrenalin pumping through his veins. He wondered why he was pacing around in the middle of the pavement. But then it came to him. There was little wonder he should have become so unsure of himself. The newsreader had been cut off in the middle of the six o'clock news. What was the world coming to? The silence was deafening.

He must pull himself together and pick a direction in which to make a dramatic departure from the scene, taking care to walk away in precisely the opposite direction to the one chosen. But that would have to wait because now his attention was drawn to what looked like an old cabin trunk moving slowly towards him along the pavement. Eyeing the trunk guardedly as it edged its way along the pavement he saw that it was the old wooden one which had been used as a toy box in Timothy's bedroom.

'My God we've been burgled,' he cried, stepping forward to raise the lid of the trunk where he saw something that made him quickly close it again.

Looking nervously around him he raised the lid of the trunk for a second time and gasped when he saw lines of soldiers marching along, their feet protruding through holes in the base of the trunk. He'd always said the trunk would get woodworm if it was left unattended, but this was more than anyone could have foreseen. The soldiers were marching along in silence, causing him to wonder whether he might be losing a last foothold on his sanity. Especially when he saw that the silence was due to the fact that none of the soldiers were wearing boots.

He remembered the line of soldiers he'd seen in… where was it now… he wasn't sure except to say they hadn't really been soldiers. Although they had been marching like soldiers and therefore not surprising they should have been mistaken for soldiers. In a way they had been soldiers. Christian soldiers. They too had been marching along in bare feet, although far from marching in silence they'd been marching to the sound of a drum, and straining every nerve in his body he was able to pick out the sound of a drum, scarcely audible, but exactly in time with the soldiers in the trunk marching along in ranks of three.

He closed the trunk and turned away, straight into the arms of the woman in corduroy jodhpurs who had reappeared. Throwing her arms around his neck the woman began smothering him with kisses. Whispering into his ear that she was on the march too, she had him on the ground in no time and had begun to tear off his clothes, when Ivan heard the statistician, who now seemed to be dressed as a referee, laughing uncontrolably. With an almighty heave he managed to untangle himself from the woman, and just in time too for then he heard the voice of Rowena coming from the end of the street.

'Ivan Ivan, I'm afraid... I'm afraid there's bad news. It's Footmouth... I'm afraid Footmouth has been eaten by his dog.'

Suddenly wide awake Ivan sat up to find that Rowena was calling him in to lunch. He struggled to his feet and slowly dragged himself across the lawn towards the house, where he spent most of Sunday lunchtime in silent debate with Freud as to the best way of explaining to Rowena why he had been so intent upon convincing her that Joe Taskerman didn't have a dog.

28

THE NEXT DAY'S STARTING POINT OF PLAY

ELVIS IS ALIVE, the words screamed out from the parapet. Ivan nodded in agreement, quickly returning his eyes to the road on realising he was veering towards the hard shoulder where a broken down lorry was waiting to collect him.

'And living in a pyramid,' he said in a rejoinder of the kind you were unlikely to find in a part of the country where soccer was king and pyramids were kept under wraps, such that you might think they didn't exist.

'Pyramids are an illusion,' declared the voice of an erstwhile news reader anxious to prevent any more challenges to authority.

'Of course they are,' said Ivan remembering Jean Baudrillard's words on the blurring of illusion and reality.

'I suppose it would be good to see the old firm in action again,' said Bernard, not quite under his breath, still amazed by the report he'd been reading when summoned to get into the car under dire threat it was about to leave without him.

'Which old firm is that?' said Owen.

Ivan cursed his judgement as in overtaking a slow-moving car he ran over more Catseyes than intended. Strange how cat's eyes never seemed to be where you'd thought they were. He'd never heard of anyone having a good word for them in daylight hours. Though strange too that even after dark one set was regarded as being as good as any other. Efficiency deriving little from appearance. As the evidence of any road mender who'd spent a hot day in the sun would confirm – a chip off the corner of one; a scuff along the edge of another; a tear in the rubber here; a smear on the glass there. No-one seemed interested in character anymore. Catseyes could display any peculiarity they liked but no-one would notice so long as it didn't affect their performance. In which respect they were no different to that other equally misunderstood species having the additional benefit of two arms, two legs, and two sets of one-two-three-four-five educated fingers, it being less than necessary for an individual to possess a complete set of any of those in order to stake a claim on species membership.

Although a full set could be quite useful for a would-be fast bowler, Ivan nodded to a passing cyclist.

'Which old firm is he talking about?' Owen appealed to Henry for information.

With a shake of the head Ivan again tried to recall when the characters who were sharing much more than his car had first appeared. Over the years it had become apparent that Owen often said things he didn't mean, which could be irritating, especially to Bernard, but at least Bernard had a deep understanding, and an affection for the game of cricket... as did Henry, and therefore there had been little reason for Ivan to question their values. But he still had no idea why any of them had come in to his life, nor in whose interests it had been for them to stay. He had his suspicions and guessed the psychoanalysts would have something to say about their origins. But rather than colourful tripartite structures ('*good to see you again denial, how've you been?*') he preferred Spinoza's idea of there being many dimensions in the universe to which earthly life forms had no means of access. Indeed many had been the night when the possibility of gaining access to those other dimensions had kept him awake. That is when he hadn't been already engaged in his continuing quest to decipher the defining characteristics of gender... an example of which was the narrator's insistence upon concealing her identity.

('*You are the narrator.*')

'I know.'

'I imagine he's referring to the fact that Dennis Lillee is proposing to make another comeback,' said Henry, imagining that Bernard would have reached the sports pages by the time he'd been called to the car.

'I'm not sure that declaring your intention to play in a charity match constitutes a comeback,' said Bernard. 'But you're right. I was referring to the best old firm the Aussies have produced since Miller and Lindwall.'

'Miller and who?' said Owen.

'What do you mean Miller and who? You'll be telling us next that you don't know who Victor Trumper was,' mocked Bernard returning in exasperation to the newspaper he'd been reading, pondering whether at the time he'd been summoned to the car it might have been better to have been caught in the middle of a paragraph on the Brazilian Grand Prix. But all he heard himself say was, 'Out first ball again I see.'

'Who... Victor Trumper?' said a tight-lipped Owen.

'I expect he's been reading the overnight scorecard from the county championship,' said Henry.

'That's it,' cried Bernard.

'What is?'

'The next day's starting point of play... that was the clue for fifteen across and six down. Get it? The overnight scorecard. These combined clues are always more tricky, well I find them so, though goodness knows why. They're simple enough when you get the hang of them.' Bernard filled in the details of the combined clue that had been preventing completion of the crossword.

'The next day's starting point of play... three, nine and nine... the overnight scorecard.'

'God preserve us,' said Owen.

'At 135 for 6 from 45 overs, He is probably the only one who could have preserved the position England had got themselves into,' muttered Ivan reflecting upon Saturday's defeat by the Duckworth-Lewis method in the rain affected one-day international, disaster having struck before he'd realised that play had resumed – prior to being interrupted again. And yet such was the quaintness of the game which had been so much a part of his life, that far from bemoaning the influence of the weather on the result, he could think only of what prospects there would have been for an England recovery in the days when there had been enough space in the schedules for one day internationals to become two day one-day internationals.

29

A LAND OF GOLDEN OPPORTUNITIES

Driving along the open road, still ruminating on the likelihood of a saviour enacting a recovery in Saturday's one day international had rain not intervened, Ivan remembered how his days in the steelworks had shown that some things were beyond redemption. He recalled a feeling of hopelessness had been one of the reasons why leaving the steelworks had seemed a good idea, and just as well the way things had turned out. You only had to look at what the steelworks had become. Except you couldn't look at what the steelworks had become. It was no longer there. Dismantled. Gone. All evidence of its existence wiped from the valley.

From the beginning Ivan had been one of those who'd been expected to move on. He'd never been told that of course. The only one's who were told to move on were the unfortunates who – as they'd put it – were being invited to move on. Should you not be one of those invited to move on, it was nevertheless assumed you would leave one day, for you wouldn't want to hang around in the steelworks until the day you died. Dying in the steelworks on the other hand, was another matter. As the accident board at the entrance to the steelworks would be quick to confirm.

'Hey no-one told me this was a death trap… who killed cock robin?'

'I,' said the sparrow. 'I did it for the marrow.'

Perhaps Johnny wasn't doing so well after all. Johnny was doing as well as anyone because if they were honest they were all doing somebody, with no such activity having anything to do with Rose Lane.

'That's enough of that. Rose is up to her elbows in this too you know.'

'I know, I know, but we have to laugh at our adversity now and again and you should understand that we're not pointing a finger at Rose. It's ourselves that we're making fun of. But you're right, we ought not to abuse her name like that. We're guilty. Guilty as hell.'

Ivan had realised even then that he ought to have taken a firmer grip on the bigger picture. He ought to have remembered it was a zero sum game they were playing. It was an economic system, in which they were the victims. All you could expect to hear from market forces was look after yourself and let someone else have the rotten apples. Even the Keynesians couldn't get out of that one. John Maynard may have done his best, but as he never quite got around to saying – whilst ever the majority had so little say in things they would have to spend a long time eating rotten apples.

Ivan grimaced when he recalled how he'd been led to believe that eating rotten apples was not for the likes of him. He had a great career ahead of him. In the beginning was the career and the career was good. Ivan had thought his own career was far from good. Until that is he'd been made aware that it wasn't a career he had. It was a job he was employed to do, and he must learn to distinguish between a job and a career. Being one of the lucky ones, he did at least have a job, whereas it seemed a career was more a question of someone else's job. Such as Jimmy's job. He must learn to think in terms of there being an opportunity when Jimmy left. Unfortunately he could see only too well what kind of an opportunity that would be, working his hands to the bone in the hope that one day they would give him Jimmy's job – along with a thousand and one others also waiting for Jimmy's job. Poor old Jimmy he would say, considering that Jimmy was only twenty-eight. It seemed they were meant to regard that as a simple rule of the game in which everyone was dispensible sooner or later.

Ivan had taken the view that in his own case he could be dispensible sooner than he'd originally thought, for as far as the career plans scribbled on the wall of the inner sanctum were concerned everyone was a Jimmy, including (nay especially) those who were called Jane. He overtook a couple of joggers behind whom he'd been crawling until a safe stretch of road appeared.

SURVIVING JOE TASKERMAN

When it was revealed that Jimmy had in fact gone, Ivan discovered they'd already given his job to someone else. Still, he couldn't say he wasn't warned to think about his career and not his job. Although if that was their idea of a career then he was off too, before they gave the job he already had to someone else. If only he could remember where he'd left that bike his mother and the first wicket down had given him for his sixty-fourth birthday. Will you still love me? How could anyone still love him the way things had turned out?

Of course it wasn't really his sixty fourth birthday, no matter he'd spent a good deal of his life wishing that he was sixty-four (with only one green bottle to accidentally fall). On the other hand, judging by the state of its brakes, it could have been the bike that was sixty four – on yer rusty old bike there yer not so young Jimmy Driver – but there again, young, old, it didn't really matter so long as it got you to a place where someone thought you were still employable. It wouldn't lead to improvements in the air you breathed, but it might get you through to retirement, until they changed the retirement age too.

'For goodness sake keep your despondency to yourself. If we all went around shouting our mouths off from the rooftops of long-gone Hollerith buildings there'd be nobody left to read the situations vacant columns, and then where would they be?' No-one wanted to know.

When Ivan had left the security of the steelworks it had taken him less than an hour and a quarter to realise things were not going to get any better. Yet such was the way of things, that with much anticipation he'd reported for duty in the land of golden opportunities, having been unable to sleep for two nights.

'You will be responsible,' they'd said. ('That's what you think,' he'd thought.) 'You will be responsible for ensuring our business continues to grow,' they'd said. ('None of us will grow much on the peanuts you're paying us,' he'd thought.) 'You will be responsible for ensuring we stay within budget,' they'd said. ('You must be joking,' he'd thought, 'you couldn't maintain a caterpillar on a budget like that. Call that a budget?')

'A budget is a statement of operations expressed in financial terms,' they'd said. ('A statement expressed in financial terms by whom,' he'd wanted to say but had decided not to put himself at risk.)

'A budget is a means of silencing anyone stupid enough to accept responsibility for a budget in the first place,' said a disgruntled former employee. 'And if you think that's tautological then you should try running around in circles for fifty years and see what condition you are in to pick up your imitation gold watch at the end of it all.'

Ivan sometimes regretted that an hour and a quarter of having thought he'd made it, was the most he could hope for in his life. Perhaps he should draw comfort from it having taken him only an hour and a quarter to realise how naive he'd been, but for the moment he couldn't bring himself to be thankful for having an anti-climax to look back on in his old age, no matter how many times he'd been told that was something of which Johnny could be proud.

'Oh yes, my word yes, young Ivan must be doing really well Mrs Driver,' the words echoed in his ears.

'And so what do you say to that now that you're no longer so young as you were young Ivan lad? You try not to think about it? And Rowena – how about Rowena now that she's become the one and only Mrs Driver?'

'Rowena is much better at taking things in her stride than I am.'

Everyone knew Rowena was the one with the brains, which was just as well given the questions being put to her. 'Your husband's doing well Mrs Driver?' 'He's doing very nicely thank you… now that he has my back-up, ha-ha, Mrs er… .(what did she say her name was?)'

Yes Rowena was definitely the one with the brains. She certainly had most of the marks. Far from arcane assessment criteria, those were the marks from the chains that were thrown around her when they decided to play their full part in ensuring the continuation of the arm and a leg Building Society into at least one more generation. Marks of resistance? Marks of existence – from hanging onto life by her fingertips whilst walking to the end of the road and back again, and again, with a pram or a pushchair and an old pair of boots that only let water in when it really rained. With all that you had to live for being a rattle and a cry and a wish that you could fly, fly, fly away from the end of the string on Timothy's kite. Timothy. Timothy, keep away from the edge of that... before with a blinding flash you realised it was over and you were left wondering whether it had really happened.

Ivan thought that seemed like only yesterday. But yesterday had been and gone (if you recall) and should you be a member of the human race, the chances were you too would be back in the treadmill that you'd never really left.

'Well it was a life sentence we were talking about,' said a wise old soul with no longer anything to lose. 'And at least they haven't taken your life away from you. What would you do if you were told that your life was about to be taken away from you? Demand a little more from your last hour and a quarter?'

Ivan supposed an hour and a quarter might seem an eternity if you'd just been told you had only an hour left to live. Especially with a man in a pale blue tee shirt and matching trousers waiting to see you. It would take him the best part of an hour to get there. Would he be in any condition to undertake the journey, that was the question? Although it was no use asking a would-be great man like Joe Taskerman for the answer to that one. He wouldn't even know it had been raining.

'Raining? Why do you have to beat about the bush so much?'

'Be thankful you were alert enough to notice I didn't specify what it had been raining. Let's just call it rain for now.' Ivan knew how careful you had to be about putting these things, even when you had the proof.

'What kind of proof do I have? What kind of proof would it take to persuade you to live each hour and a quarter as though it was your last?'

Ivan had been wanting to live just five minutes of his life as though he only had an hour left to live ever since he'd been born, and he still wasn't sure whether that made him an an existentialist. He knew that the proverbial bus was only proverbial if it wasn't coming round the corner at that very moment.

'So just in case it is, I'm taking no chances. Bye, byeeeeee…'

'I haven't really gone. It's just that the sad, sad man from targetland can't hold his concentration for longer than three and a half seconds, and that's something we can put to our advantage. For that my friends, my lovely long lost friends from the university of our own back yards, is where the Empire strikes back.'

30

THE MAN BEHIND THE MASK

From the vantage point of his current position, burning up the road on his way to another cricket match, Ivan's entry into an apprenticeship that would one day lead to a meeting with Joe Taskerman seemed a long time ago. Yet memories being what they were, he knew that was far from the case. Not least because your past was the one thing you could hang on to. The future would never appear, and the present didn't (couldn't) exist. Stay with the here and now the man had said. If only I could, Ivan had thought. Here it is (was) oh dear it's gone already, having been replaced by another. Imagine trying to live at the very point where the present, so recently the future, was on its way to becoming (too late, it's already become) the past. You would do better to forget it, accept your station in life, and live in your head.

'True enough,' thought Ivan as an image of the man with the flattened nose appeared in such sharp focus that it seemed he might be faced with the prospect of once more squaring up to him. But no, the man seemed to be more intent on putting his latest acquisition through its paces as he swung a hammer against the very face of the globe, sending it spinning through space, thereby ensuring there would be at least one more orbit.

Ivan blared on his horn as a car coming towards him overtook an unsteady cyclist, leaving him with no choice but to take evasive action.

'I can just make it,' he cried in derision as he slammed on his brakes and swung the car onto the grass verge. 'Providing this pillock slams his anchors on.'

Whereupon another image imposed itself in the shape of a silk-suited professor peering over a pair of half spectacles that were about to fall off the end of his nose. Seemingly oblivious to the fact that most of his audience were asleep the professor was expounding on a subject with which Ivan was all too familiar.

'Throughout the history of enterprise there has been a most striking correlation between the success of a company and the close defining of responsibility.'

Curtailing an urge to make a rude response, Ivan wondered whether the idea of being in two places at once was beginning to sour. A suggestion came from one of the few still awake in the audience that someone should remind the speaker of which planet he was on. Whereupon, the man with the flattened nose reappeared and proceeded in his own way to oblige, as with one swing of his hammer he brought the silk-suited professor down to what at that very moment he would have been surprised to learn was an exceedingly flat earth. Those members of the audience still awake cheered loudly.

'Yes sir, no sir, three bags full sir.'

He decided it may be time to reconsider the worth of the man with the flattened nose. He could think of one person he would like to see a recipient of the next swing of his hammer.

'Feeling rather glad, to see you oh so mad, whilst scraping out the meat sir, from your golden teeth sir, disgusting thing to eat to give yourself a treat sir.'

Aware that he was again gripping the steering wheel too tightly for the good of his circulation he tried to imagine what it would be like to have a close defining of responsibility that worked.

'A budget is a bird, a little, yellow bird sir... which only goes to show... what a fool I am sir, I really didn't know, your feathered friend was blue sir. But spare a thought for me sir, I couldn't even tell a yellow bird from you sir.'

Driving with only his fingertips on the steering wheel, Ivan told himself that with a lighter touch he might stand a better chance of persuading Joe Taskerman it was in everyone's interest for him to meet the man with the straight-talking hammer.

'That's why the air is blue sir, just like my song of you sir.'

'Whereas what I say to you,' he addressed the flattened remains of the silk-suited professor lying on the raised platform at the front of the hall, 'is one-two buckle my shoe. This is a co-operative venture we're running here. Hands make shoes and shoes transport hands on to the next job waiting to be done, there generally being a tie up in these things somewhere.'

'Yeeoooouueeee…' In his determination to make a difference, the man with the flattened nose fell over himself and disappeared into the abyss – the abyss which Ivan acknowledged was somewhere behind the bridge of his nose and what was left of his hairline.

'The importance of holding people accountable for their areas of responsibility cannot be overestimated,' came a voice from the platform upon which the silk-suited professor had been expounding. But the audience needn't have worried. This was not a case of reincarnation. This was another voice entirely, it being only the tired old theme that was familiar. The realisation of which led to the re-emergence of the man with the hammer who quickly took out the figure behind the further voice too. Then once more he disappeared into the abyss, leaving Ivan to marvel at how much more useful the man was going to be than he'd ever been in a boxing ring.

'From the throat of who sir, that surely can't be true sir, the figures aren't yet due sir, they can't be red if blue… disagree with you sir, that I'd never do sir.'

'I think he had a point you know,' said a voice coming out of the auditorium.

Ivan scanned the faces emerging into the bright sunlight but couldn't make out from whom the latest utterance had come, although he had a fair idea of on whose behalf the words had been spoken. Which reminded him of the way he himself had come face to face with the blithering Joe Taskerman – by not realising on whose behalf the immensely helpful man behind the mask on the third counter from the left at the arm and a leg Building Society (cashier number four please) had been speaking.

31

TURNING THINGS AROUND

'Now that we've been able to get some focus into what we're doing we have a better idea of how things stand. It's been hard for some people to accept the changes, but I suppose that was only to be expected. I can't imagine how they thought an operation like this could function without knowing precisely how much had been made at the end of each week. It had to be one of the first things we did, and in a way it was a pity people were so resistant. Still, some people would never understand that if time was spent considering every alternative then no-one would get as far as having a tea break, let alone failing to notice that some of their people had extended that tea-break to most of the working day. It's amazing what can be achieved when you channel your efforts. We've begun to turn things around – simply by getting our teeth stuck into one thing and seeing it through to the end. We've shown what can be done, and now we can turn our attention towards the rest of the plant. On a prime site such as this where the fixed costs are so high, it's necessary to move a good deal quicker than some of them have ever moved in their lives. The age of the plant is such that most of the initial costs have been written off, but little provision has been made for replacement and that simply cannot be allowed to continue. Not if the plant is to have a future. If we're going to make this place profitable we have to act quickly. The future won't take care of itself. The future has to be planned. And when you are faced with so many problems you have to approach them in a logical order – according to plan. That's the only sensible way to proceed. The trouble is that some people are reluctant to get off their backsides in order to ensure their own survival. Some of them would rather complain about lack of job security than concentrate on doing everything they can to keep themselves in work. Reorganisation never threatened anyone pulling their weight. Flexibility is the only way forward. It's no good thinking about what used to happen. Robotics is the future, but in the meantime the important thing is to decide whether there is to be a future or not. With so much needing to be done the company can't afford to let anyone sit around chewing over their grievances. The company can't carry people. Anyone not prepared to give their all in order to save the plant has to go. I've always thought we could turn this place around. I was convinced of that from the day I first started to put the figures together. To be honest, I've felt pretty glum on occasions about the ability of people to respond to a system of more flexible working. Yet having decided that things were in need of a good shaking up, I was sure there would be some with a little fire in their bellies who could be relied upon to play a part in getting things moving. It's unnerving to look back on how things were done in those days. The place was in such a mess there was little point in launching into the things you would normally do on taking over a plant – looking for bottlenecks, getting a grasp of the downtimes – since we had no reliable figures for the end of each week. We knew only what we were getting out in relation to invoice accounting periods. That wasn't much good for the production runs we were trying to control. In short, we had no idea whether we'd made any money in a particular week or not. People seemed to think it didn't matter so long as we showed a profit each year. It's funny how people can't see the wood for the trees. It isn't difficult when you think about it. Unless you know you are making money every single hour of the day, every day of the week, you have no way of knowing whether you are doing the right things. You can accommodate fluctuations of course – though not unless you have accurate information. We may not have all our information on-line yet, but I must give credit where it's due, because people have seen to it that we know exactly how much goes through the gates each week and now we can begin to do something about that because quite simply it's pathetic.'

32

ONE WAY TRAFFIC

Ivan pulled onto the service station forecourt and came to a stop beside the one available petrol pump.

'Thank goodness there isn't a one day international to interrupt proceedings,' he said thinking of the number of portable radios that otherwise would have been deployed trying to keep up with news of England's fortunes. Stepping out of the car, he removed the petrol filler cap, picked up the unleaded fuel line from the pump console and placed the nozzle into the fuel inlet. Then carefully positioning his feet so as to avoid any blow-back reaching his shoes, he squeezed the handle.

'Hey look at that,' said Owen excitedly.

'I am looking,' said Bernard, blinking at the numbers coming up on the pump dials.

'It's us, said Owen.

'Of course it is,' said Bernard. Petrol pumps have an unfortunate facility for registering the precise amount for which the user is going to have to pay.

'Uh?' Owen saw that Bernard was looking in the wrong direction. 'No, not the fuel console... look... over there.' He directed Bernard's gaze towards the car standing beside the next pump.

'What's the matter with you now?' said Bernard, turning to investigate the source of Owen's excitement.

'Look.'

Bernard saw that Owen was pointing to the red mini facing them.

'We're the ones she's yelling at,' said Owen. 'She's yelling at us.'

Ivan's eyes fell upon the shape of a woman hanging from the passenger window of the car. She was waving her arms about, and was clearly annoyed about something. Sensing it might not be a good idea to let the woman see that he'd noticed her, Ivan averted his eyes and tried to pretend he couldn't hear a word she was saying.

'Selfish inconsiderate oaf.' The high pitched accusation was emitted through a spread-eagled arrangement of teeth that reminded Ivan of an ancient stone circle. Stealing another glance at the woman, he saw the teeth occupied most of her face in much the same way as bindweed occupies a hedge. There were two eyes and a nose in there somewhere but the teeth were definitely in the box seat.

'Can't you read?' screamed the woman.

'What's wrong with her?' said Henry, noticing the commotion being created by the woman. 'Why is she so concerned about standards of literacy?'

Ignoring the outburst from the red mini, Ivan removed the nozzle and returned the fuel line to the pump console. Then turning his back on the woman he replaced the filler cap and set off for the pay point.

'You've come in the wrong way,' cried the woman.

Ivan turned towards where she was pointing, and saw that his own car was facing in the opposite direction to all the other vehicles standing at the pumps, suggesting he'd entered the forecourt in what he might have to concede was an unconventional direction.

'That may be the case,' said Bernard. 'But why get so upset about it?'

'You'd be upset if you had teeth like that,' said Owen.

'Imagine having toothache in even one of those blighters.'

'Toothache is the least of her problems,' said Henry. 'If she carries on spitting at that rate she'll need a saline drip.'

'Ignorant. Plain ignorant some people,' cried the woman as Ivan emerged from the pay point, replacing the card to the pack he kept in the innermost reaches of his wallet.

'People like you shouldn't be allowed to drive.'

With a quick look at the arrows on the tarmac, Ivan adjusted his collar, muttering as though to no-one in particular that anyone could make a mistake.

'That's no excuse,' screamed the woman.

'It was clearly a mistake bumping into you,' said Ivan

walking quickly back to his car unaware of the predictive potential of his remark.

Just then, a dumpy little man appeared, hurrying across the forecourt towards the red mini. Ivan had to curtail an outburst of hilarity when he saw that on top of the rolling mounds of flesh someone had placed a most handsomely sculpted head which had been polished to a high sheen.

'There must have been a monumental cock-up in despatch on the morning this fellow was assigned to a stork for delivery, said Henry.

'It's a clockwork Kojak,' cried Owen, realising that the man had a remarkable resemblance to certain fictional character of former glories… if you could bring yourself to ignore the body below the head.

'He looks as though he could use a good hairpiece,' said Henry.

'Kojak didn't wear a hairpiece,' said Owen.

'There'd be little point in this fellow wearing a hairpiece,' said Bernard.

'You're right,' said Henry, observing the tirade now being directed towards the dumpy little man with the Kojak head as he approached the open window of the red mini. 'Madame Stonehenge obviously eats his hair.'

'Look out he's coming over here,' said Owen.

'You been upsetting my Freda?' It was not the voice of a thousand precinct interrogations, but a voice being more reminiscent of middle England than lower Eastside.

'Who me?' Ivan was hardly able to contain himself.

'Didn't anyone teach you to read?'

'Not at the school I went to,' Ivan continued to hold himself in check, as the finely textured face at the window was obscured for a moment by a floppy hand which seemed to be signalling something. Ivan realised the hand was telling him to wind down the window, and for some reason he decided to comply. Unfortunately the man with the Kojak head had come too close and had he been the illustrious lieutenant he would almost certainly have lost his lollipop. As it was, he merely suffered the indignity of a black smudge as the window traversed along his nose.

'You shouldn't be driving sonny if you can't read,' the man with no hairpiece, but a decidedly blackened nose, continued to admonish Ivan.

Inexplicably, Ivan took out his card holder and waved it in the face of the dumpy little man at the open window with a cry of, 'Fuzzy wuzzy baby.' His attempt to capture the rarified atmosphere of a New York precinct was unconvincing, but no matter, for the man had turned on his heel and was scurrying back to the red mini. Where he tore open the door and jumped in as though suddenly remembering a pressing engagement.

'You'd never have thought he'd get in there, said Owen, anticipating a tight squeeze.

'Or that he would survive for long if he did,' said Henry, noticing that Madame Stonehenge was still in full flow.

The incongruous cargo was nevertheless stowed away and the engine came to life almost before the door had closed. Following which, the red mini lurched forward and hit the front of Ivan's car with a thump. The larger car hardly moved, but the mini bounced back like a ball on a squash court.

'Hell's teeth,' cried Owen.

'You can say that again,' said Bernard.

'Look out, he's going to do it again,' said Henry as the red mini emitted a screeching noise with each attempt to restart the stalled engine.

Ivan leapt out of his car, and having the presence of mind to run around the back of the mini, made for the offside door and wrenched it open.

'What the hell do you think you're doing?' he cried, as in one impressive movement he dragged the kicking figure with the Kojak head out of the car, and deposited him unceremoniously onto the forecourt.

'Did you see that?' said Owen.

'I could hardly have missed it,' said Bernard.

'Or ever have imagined it would be possible?' said Henry.

'You came in the wrong way,' the incongruent figure now looking more like Quilp than Kojak, continued his belligerent theme, heedless of the fact that he was in lying in the dust.

'You should talk,' said Ivan considering the prone figure.

'You were blocking our exit.'

'I'll block more than your exit if you do that again.'

'You should drive with your eyes open.'

'I shall close yours if I have any more of your lip.'

Keeping one eye upon the prone figure, Ivan surveyed the damage. He could see there were no visible marks on the front of his car, the impact having been absorbed by the underside of the front panel. With a further warning of the consequences of any repetition he slowly backed away, this time taking the precaution of going around behind his own car. From where he took another look at the dishevelled figure struggling to his feet in the face of a cascade of lava from the tooth mountain, before pulling open the door, jumping in, and starting the engine.

'That was amazing,' said Owen.

'Extraordinary,' said Bernard.

'And with such style,' said Henry, marvelling at the aplomb with which they'd been extricated from what could have been an ugly situation.

'It's a good job he didn't do anything to upset me,' said Ivan with a chuckle, before suddenly reversing off the forecourt at high speed in the manner of an old Buster Keaton movie being hurriedly re-spooled.

33

PLAY

Ivan clung onto his cap as a gust of wind came racing in from behind, whistling through his deckchair like a train before traversing the boundary and flinging itself in all directions across the wide open spaces of the playing area. The arrival of such a biting wind from an innocently clear blue sky reminded him of how perverse the spring weather could be. His habit of bringing his own deckchair and placing it in the far corner of the ground meant that today he would be more than usually exposed to the elements, and it was already clear as he poured another cup of coffee that he would run out of sandwiches.

'They'll certainly need to warm up today,' said Henry noticing that several of the visiting players had emerged from the pavilion.

'Call that warming up,' scoffed Bernard. 'They have neither a bat nor a ball between them, and look, there's a fellow over there pretending to be a windmill.'

Ivan shuddered when he realised how much like his father Bernard had sounded. It was unerving, and prompted him to question whether there were any similarities between Henry and his mother. He decided rather too quickly there could be no likeness worthy of consideration. He did wonder whether making such a connection might have taken him closer to an understanding of who the hell Owen was, but told himself this was no place to pursue such a line of enquiry and settled back to enjoy the fruits of an idyllic Sunday afternoon.

The strains of the school band coming to the close of their pre-match concert drifted across the ground to blend with the delightful sound of leather upon willow, now that the home side had commenced their own warming up in a more traditional manner than the visitors had done.

Unfortunately, no one had informed the elements this was

185

to be an idyllic Sunday afternoon and the cruel mixture of sun and wind began to take its toll. The umpires emerged from the pavilion wearing sun hats, an unusual enough occurrence for the time of year, but a higher than average reading on the Beaufort scale had led them to take precautions against removal of their hats by attaching black bootlaces, the ends of which were hanging incongruously below their chins.

'Surely, in a cricket pavilion of all places they could have found white bootlaces,' said Bernard.

'Never mind the bootlaces,' said Henry. 'Look at their hands – who would have thought we'd live to see the day when cricket umpires came out wearing gloves?'

'I do hope someone has told them this is the cricket season,' said Bernard.

'And that they should have brought their raincoats too,' said Owen.

'What on earth for? It isn't going to rain,' said Bernard. 'Look at that sky. There isn't a cloud on this side of the Atlantic.'

'It feels as though it might snow,' said Owen, rubbing his hands together in an attempt to return circulation to his fingers.

'Why don't you go and look for cover then... over there,' said Bernard, waving his arm in the direction of the stand on the other side of the ground.

'And let you eat all the sandwiches? Not likely.'

'I think we may be about to start,' said Bernard.

'Good,' said Owen. 'Then put up the umbrella for God's sake. At least it will provide some protection from the wind. That is why we brought it.'

'That isn't why we brought it,' said Bernard. 'We brought the umbrella to protect us from a shower… er, should we be unfortunate enough to…'

'No we didn't,' said Henry. 'We brought the umbrella as an insurance against rain occurring, for in case you hadn't noticed, whenever we bring the umbrella...'

'Oh belt up and give the thing to me,' said Owen, grabbing the umbrella, opening it and placing it across the back of the chair where it might provide at least a little cover from the wind.

'Sshh,' hissed Bernard as the first ball was bowled. 'I can't believe we've lost the toss again. That's five in a row, and this is not a day for having much enthusiasm for fielding.'

'No day ever is,' muttered Ivan. 'And some of us have been fielding for a long time,' a reminder of which prompted the figure with a more malevolent umbrella-over-their-lives to put in an appearance.

'You there, I suggest you field in the gulley.'

'Rightful place I suppose – along with the rats.'

Ivan recalled the extent to which the workforce in the plating shop had been reduced in numbers, leaving just a large enough contingent for Joe Taskerman to piss about before making another batch of them redundant, whilst insisting that unemployment was only a state of mind. Only a state of mind – that was his best one yet. Imagine trying to sell that one to a mortgage lender. Not in a hundred years, and that was a long time to suffer the slings and arrows of anybody's outrageous fortune. On the other hand, Ivan was well aware that some people would sell the performing rights of their own grandmother's funeral if they thought...

'It was a joke Footmouth. Not everything has to end up in new product development. Talk about an enterprise culture, you'll be trying to sell your own bad breath next. Oh for goodness sake. Why can't I keep my big mouth shut? Keeping my mouth shut is a requirement for people in my position is it? Well that must have been located in a needle in a haystack part of my contract I've never read. The only thing I remember being asked to deliver is jam today marmalade tomorrow, and I don't need any section of small print to remind me of how much I would have liked to push one of those broken pencils up your nasty little bogey production plant.'

34

THE DEATH OF JOE TASKERMAN

'Why is the umpire waving his arms about?' said Owen.

'He's signalling a wide,' said Bernard, 'and the scorer seems to have gone to sleep.'

'Well at least someone has the right idea.'

It was apparent from the first ball that the wind was going to cause problems for more than just the spectators, players and umpires. The scorer for one, far from being asleep, was having great difficulty in keeping up with things, the extras coming thick and fast as the bowlers sprayed deliveries in all directions. Unable to maintain much of a grip on the ball they were going to take a little time to settle into a consistent line and length. When they did begin to settle, the batsmen became the ones with the difficulties, finding it impossible to judge how much each delivery would swing through the air or deviate off the pitch. The opening batsmen found themselves playing down the wrong line more times than was good for anyone's confidence, and their problems were not confined to those of line. A couple of balls in the second over kept low, one of them resulting in a tremendous but unsuccessful appeal for lbw, and the other going for four byes when even the wicketkeeper with the benefit of an extra twelve yards couldn't get down quickly enough. Then in the fourth over, a good length ball lifted alarmingly, resulting in an extremely lucky four as it was fended away in desperation.

Such fortuitous disturbing of the scoreboard became the order of the day as the unpredictable movement and inconsistent bounce made the batsman's and the wicketkeeper's jobs very difficult. The batsmen had little alternative but to focus their attention on survival and it was only the actions taken to avoid the risk of injury which resulted in any excitement. The concentration upon not losing wickets resulted in the game becoming rather dour and not one of those stylish free scoring games envisaged by the architects of league cricket. Indeed, the visitors innings might have been terminated a good deal sooner had it not been for problems in the home side's fielding, which resulted in a number of cryptic enquiries from the terraces as to whether an attempt was being made on the record for the highest number of dropped catches in an innings.

'Why don't they get on with it?' Owen shifted restlessly.

'Try to understand something about the psychology of the game,' said Bernard.

'It's the mathematics of the game that bothers me,' said Owen.

'I imagine it's the lack of mathematics that will be bothering the visitors,' said Henry. 'I can't ever remember going to a game at any level where the largest contribution was in the extras column.

A welcome cheer went around the ground as a particularly low delivery got through and clipped the bottom of the off stump.

'Did you see that?' said Bernard. 'It only bounced three and a half inches.'

After standing for a long time in disbelief, the batsman reluctantly commenced what Henry described as the slowest walk back to the pavilion since Roy Fredericks had stepped on his wicket hooking Dennis Lillee for six in the first ever World Cup Final.

'What was so special about that?' said Owen. 'I've never seen anyone move that quickly in all the years I've been dragged along to one game after another in pursuit of a higher threshold of boredom.'

'The trouble with you Philistine...' but Bernard was interrupted as the new batsman who'd come to the wicket proceeded to employ a more attacking strategy by driving his first ball back towards the pavilion. There was a ripple of applause, punctuated by a few ironic cheers.

'There you are,' said Bernard. 'What could be finer than a flowing straight drive piercing the field like a well aimed...'

'The visitors are batting,' Henry reminded him.

'What? Oh, hmm, yes, well, one can still appreciate the finer points of the game.'

'I see what you mean,' said Henry, as a thunderous appeal signalled the end of the new batsman's stay at the wicket, given out lbw to a ball that had kept wickedly low, but which the batsman playing so far across the line would have been unlikely to hit even if the delivery had bounced to a reasonable height.

'That's more like it,' said Mortal. 'We'll soon be on our way at this rate.'

Ivan shivered involuntarily as he took another sandwich and poured out the last of the coffee. Well at least its a good crowd he thought casting his eyes along the terraces. The brilliance of the sun had tempted a lot of people to come to the game, some of them no doubt regretting their failure to anticipate the meanness of the wind.

As he finished off the sandwiches and swallowed the last of the coffee, Ivan was grateful for the shelter provided by the umbrella. But he still felt cold, and decided it was time to deploy the blanket he always brought to cricket matches having being caught out by the unseasonal weather on more than one occasion. Wrapping the blanket around his legs he felt the benefit immediately, and decided to draw further on his array of protective armoury in the shape of the woollen football scarf which he had first contrarily taken to a cricket match as a young man many years ago. He wound it several times around his neck and gave himself up to the confines of the chair. Feeling relieved that he might not after all freeze to death, his concentration began to fade. He became aware of a dull sensation across his forehead and his eyes flickered momentarily before his head fell backwards onto the chair.

Another wicket fell and a voice from somewhere to Ivan's right enquired as to who the next player would be. In response his companion produced a larger than normal scorecard which glinted in the sun as he held it aloft to inform them that the next man in was Count Dracula. The first voice told him not to be silly since Count Dracula didn't play cricket. He only went in for blood sports, and everyone knew that Harold Larwood was now confined to playing his cricket in an after life.

The matter was soon resolved for the new batsman to emerge from the pavilion was clearly not the notorious Count. A voice from the terraces confirmed as much by issuing an irreverent appeal to his deity as it became apparent the new batsman was a former Home Secretary who appeared to be walking on his hands. A further voice cried out it was time somebody did, and a chuckle ran around the ground before the whole crowd fell into a hush at the sight of the phantom ex-Minister slowly walking hand over hand towards the wicket.

A surprised voice from the members stand was heard to exclaim that the former Home Secretary hadn't got a bat. An answering call came that this should present no problem, since he could use his head. That turned out to be a piece of intended frivolity which the originator came to regret, as having reached the middle, the former Home Secretary proceeded to take guard with his forehead (the means of requesting which, the umpire decided in the interests of national security it would be better never to reveal, no matter how much he might one day be offered for his memoirs). Whereupon, with no more than a wave of his legs in the air and a cursory glance around the field, the former Home Secretary prepared to play himself in.

The next half hour was a purist's dream as the new batsman gave a textbook demonstration of forward play, the sweet sound of leather on bone echoing around the ground as the right honourable member met every ball with the middle of his forehead, to the irritation of a number of spectators who were insistent upon the need to score runs. The home captain seemed to be reasonably satisfied with things however since the overs were slipping away nicely. It remained for a few of the more vocal members on the terraces to provide the entertainment. There were several admonitions to the local constabulary to move the batsman on for loitering, but these calls were quickly followed by a voice suggesting he should be left alone for he could not in any circumstances be said to be causing a disturbance – and especially not to the scoreboard.

A voice to Ivan's left provided an amusing diversion from the tedium of the proceedings by speculating upon how, since Harold Larwood had been mentioned, he would have reacted to this situation. Someone suggested Larwood would have bowled at the batsman's legs. This was received with a outbreak of hilarity along the terraces, as members of the otherwise bemused crowd took an opportunity to release some of the tension which had been building whilst having nothing to watch but the former Home Secretary prowling around the batting crease on his hands. Pursuing this theme, a further voice suggested there would be a good deal of merit in Larwood taking that approach, since the former Home Secretary was not wearing pads. Another voice said it would be quite difficult to find pads that would fit legs like his, and went on to query whether it was thought likely the former Home Secretary would be wearing a box. The voice which had first suggested Larwood would bowl at the batsman's legs, said he didn't see how he could be wearing a box with a voice like that. When asked to expand upon this observation, the Larwood strategist said you only had to listen to his call of, 'no,' each ball to realise that it was about an octave lower than anyone could possibly achieve whilst wearing a box.

There was a dull fuzz as the former Home Secretary dealt with a particularly nasty yorker, giving the concept of digging one out of the blockhole a whole new meaning. Yet the furrowed brow was unmarked, the whisps of hair unmoved, as the intrepid batsman once more declined a run with a loud but entirely superfluous call of… 'No.'

Ivan opened his eyes, having been disturbed by a commotion somewhere to his left. Blinking hard in the bright sunlight, he almost tipped over the deck chair in leaning forward to discover that the man who'd been wandering around the boundary all afternoon dressed in an old raincoat and green cricket cap was waving his arms at a beer drinking group on the terraces. There seemed to be a disagreement concerning the merits of the various batsmen who had played on the ground over the years. The man in the old raincoat and green cricket cap was loudly proclaiming the talents of Don

Bradman, whilst the slightly younger members of the beer drinking gallery, some of whom Ivan thought might never have heard of the great Don, were countering with claims extolling the virtues of the somewhat younger though undeniably meritorious, Vivian Richards. In the manner of a television studio debate, there was a lot of emotive banter with not much analysis, and the heady atmosphere was fuelled by the intensity of claim and counter claim as eulogies in support of each candidate flowed with increasing speed. There were alternative cheerings and jeerings as the arguments about runs scored and records broken were put forward. The loudest cheer of all came when one of the members of the gallery bringing replenishments to the throng, momentarily stumbled and upset fifteen pints of beer that had been delicately balanced on a bakers tray. Beer was sprayed in all directions, and the ensuing commotion was such that even the players were distracted from their concentration.

'Your round...' A whimsical voice was suddenly cut off as a cloth cap descended with the speed of a striking cobra.

The man in the old raincoat and green cricket cap cheered loudest of all, and was still shaking with laughter as he resumed his walk around the boundary.

'How many hundreds did Don Bradman score in one day internationals?' A voice rang out with a mixture of pique and coup de grace. Even the square leg umpire enjoyed that one, turning round with a broad grin on his face.

'Aaaarrrggh?' A tremendous appeal rang out, upon which to his lasting good fortune the square leg umpire was not required to adjudicate on whether the ball had carried.

'Another one out,' said Owen with relish.

Yawning wearily, Ivan closed his eyes, before quickly opening them and then closing them again in confusion, momentarily unable to disentangle nightmare from reality as he remembered the former Home Secretary. He wondered if he'd been given out caught off his brow, and whether he would uphold the rule of law of which he was so fond, by walking without waiting for the verdict.

When he opened his eyes again, all he saw was a group of

players standing in a circle waiting for the next batsman to appear. Reassured by this familiar sight he allowed his eyes to close once more, and breathing shallowly, became oblivious to what was happening around him.

His body suddenly stiffened, and his legs began to shudder when he saw that the next batsman to emerge from the pavilion was a far bigger problem than the previous batsman had ever been. For it was none other than Joe Taskerman, striding with his habitual brusque gait, straight towards the striker's end. There was some relief in the fact that at least he wasn't walking on his hands, but then Footmouth didn't need to demonstrate his abilities in that direction. He'd been doing somersaults with reality for years. And he proceeded to do so again, as to Ivan's dismay he turned in just the kind of performance of which he would have loved to believe Joe Taskerman was incapable. Driving and cutting like a master he seemed able to take runs when and wherever he liked, in response to which Ivan could only snarl with a ferocity that had it not been a dream, would have put him in danger of attracting the attention of the strolling policeman who'd been patrolling the ground all afternoon.

But he knew he had to do something. And so he did. Leaping out of his chair, he cleared the boundary rope in a stride and went racing across the outfield towards the square. As he approached the point where the bowler had reached the end of his run up he snatched the ball from his hand and set off towards the delivery crease. With a cry of here's a delivery of a kind you wouldn't want to receive anywhere near five thousand times per week, he despatched the ball straight at the batsman's throat. It caught Joe Taskerman off guard and the only evasive action he could take was to dip his head, though sadly not far enough, for the ball hit him with a resounding crack beside his left ear causing his legs to buckle and his body to collapse in a heap, where he remained very still.

Ivan opened his eyes and took a deep breath. Trying to remember where he was, he suddenly sat bolt upright.

'My God I've killed the bastard,' he said, wondering why it was so dark. He realised the scarf had blown across his face and it took a little while for him to remove the offending mask because he also found that his right arm had gone numb and with his left hand he had to hold on to the umbrella which was in danger of taking off into the wind. When he did remove the scarf, he saw that the players had retreated to the pavilion and the outfield was crawling with small boys engaged in innumerable cricket matches of their own.

'Bugger,' he muttered as he realised the tea interval had arrived and all the coffee and sandwiches had gone. His heart sank at the thought of the queue in the refreshment tent, which resembled a wind tunnel on the calmest of days. And so he resigned himself to staying where he was, remembering that he had one more item of protection which hadn't been used. Taking out the waterproof cape from his rucksack, he pushed one end under the bottom of the blanket and hooked the other over the top of the umbrella.

'Is there anybody in there?' came a voice from his left.

'I shouldn't think so,' said a second voice. 'It looks as though they've all gone home.'

'Well you'd have thought someone would have told the umbrella,' said the first voice amidst laughter.

Ignoring this frivolity, Ivan lifted a corner of the cape and peered at the scoreboard, looking for how many runs were needed for victory with a determination suggesting he might be about to go out there and get them all himself.

35

NATURAL CAUSES

There was still a buzz in the air as the crowd, which was almost as large as it was for county games, moved towards the gates at the front of the ground. The slow scoring contest had produced a tight finish, settled only in the last over. The result meant the home supporters were happy, although celebrations were a little restrained knowing that getting such a small total should have been a lot easier than the struggle it had become. In the end luck had played too great a part, and whilst the statistics would show full points had been obtained without regard to the manner of their attainment, the future might not be so forgiving.

The other great contest that had raged throughout the afternoon, the battle of the elements, had taken its toll too, the sea of red faces slowly edging towards the gates serving to confirm that the sun and the wind had played their parts, for it couldn't all be embarrassment.

In the midst of people trying to exit the ground, Ivan found the chill of the wind a good deal less than it had been on the third man boundary, reminding him that his insistence upon using a deck chair had resulted in an afternoon spent in quite the coldest place in the ground. As he manoeuvred for position on approaching the gates, he realised the deck chair was still something of a liability as it furtively sniffed the coat tails of a less than appreciative man in front of him.

As he edged slowly forwards the chanting of a victory song could be heard on the far side of the ground where the consumption of the terrace revellers continued unabated. They were clearly in no mood to go home, having moved on to a ceremonial opening of the beer cans they'd managed to smuggle in with them, now that the bar had closed.

Meanwhile as the departing spectators began funnelling towards the gates, the jostling for position became more intense. There was a rising tide of annoyance as a few selfish individuals fought to make sharper progress unconcerned that their actions might result in others having to struggle to stay on their feet. Ivan wondered if he might be the only one thankful for having been born before the arrival of the me-first generation, but when a toad-like figure in a black coat almost clambered on the backs of the people in front of him it was clear the toad's antics were a long way from being appreciated by anyone.

'Pack it in,' an irate voice called out.

'Bog off,' cried another.

People began sacrificing their hard won positions in order to get out of the toad's way, and this had the effect of propelling the odious creature down the neck of the funnel. The ensuing instability led to a momentary stagger of the whole throng in which Ivan had his ankle kicked and took the full force of an elbow in his stomach. Momentarily winded, his gasp for breath caused a reflex action of the deck chair, prompting a muttered obscenity from a woman in front of him and an enigmatic smile from a man on his left.

Then suddenly he was out on the street. In time to see the toad in the black coat climbing into a white Jaguar which had been illegally parked outside the ground. As the car sped off it threw a shower of grit over a group of people milling about on the pavement. Ivan could only regret that his behaviour had not attracted a parking ticket.

'Berk,' a voice spitting grit cried out.

Taking a firmer hold of the deck chair, Ivan set off along the road, where once again he was hit by the full force of the wind so that in order to make any headway he had to lean forwards at an angle of almost forty five degrees.

'I must say it's warmer on the move,' said Henry. 'In spite of walking straight into the teeth of the gale.'

'I doubt I shall ever be warm again, thanks to the inadequacies of his lordship over there,' said Owen, gesturing towards the sun now much lower in the sky.

'I don't know what you're complaining about,' said Bernard. 'You've been asleep most of the afternoon.'

Ivan remembered how well the cape had performed earlier,

and stepping into a driveway to take shelter behind a hedge he put down the deck chair, slipped off the rucksack, took out the cape and threaded himself into it. He thought about the umbrella, but decided he would rather not spend the rest of the afternoon paragliding, which he might easily find himself doing in this wind. Instead he opted for an adjustment to the scarf that had been riding upwards ever since vacating his position on the third man boundary, to where it was now doing little other than provide a pathway for the wind to race down his spine into the seat of his underpants. Then he picked up the deck chair and resumed his journey, walking stiffly to minimise the possibility of strangulation as the weight of the rucksack pulled the scarf in tighter against his throat.

'Yeeeoou,' Bernard leapt into the air as a dog ran yelping from the end of a driveway.

'It won't hurt you, it's only the tiniest of things,' said Owen.

'The small ones are sometimes the worst,' said Bernard, giving the irritable creature as wide a berth as possible, causing him to stumble over the kerb where it had been crudely cut back to accommodate a new driveway.

'Idiot,' cried Ivan as a car travelling much too fast came close to leaving a coat of black rubber on the side of his shoes. He added a succession of oaths about Sunday drivers but most of them were lost on the wind.

The pavement became narrower where it ran beside a line of terraced houses and he began to slow down so as to lower the risk of losing his balance. Rather than risking his life crossing the road at the junction ahead he decided to take the turning to his right. If his calculations were correct this would steer him away from the full force of the wind and enable him to breathe more easily.

He wondered why he bothered coming to cricket matches in the early part of the season. He wondered why he always ran out of sandwiches no matter how many he took. He wondered whether the umpires would have taken their gloves off to eat their cream teas. He wondered whether Joe Taskerman was really dead. Probably not, but it was a thought to relish for a little while. He knew that one day it would be necessary to give more than a passing thought to who would take on the job as successor to Joe Taskerman. And he also knew that his own name would not appear on the list, whatever might be in the letter he'd received on Friday and had been determined not to open.

'I may park my car in the top car park, but that doesn't make me a contender,' he blurted out. But his thoughts were overtaken by a counter image in which he was swinging around in Joe Taskerman's chair yelling and pointing his fingers in all directions as though he'd been doing the job for most of his life.

He was unsure whether to feel content that he could do the job with his hands tied behind his back, or pleased he'd never been given the chance. Dreams aside, he realised he was indulging in wishful thinking again because no matter how sound the basis of recent conjectures, no-one had the faintest idea of when Joe Taskerman would move on. In the meantime others would have little alternative but to move on, with the coroner, who might at least have been expected to express an opinion on the cause of Archie's demise, having become reluctant to say anything on the circumstances of anyone moving on. Death by natural causes indeed.

36

AN OPEN VERDICT

'Bullshit.'

37

A QUESTION OF SURVIVAL

'Another sacrifice of the brave and innocent. Why was I born so vulnerable?' cried Ivan, kicking a squashed drinks can away from his path.

'Why were you born at all?' came an echo from a rugby club dance he'd once attended.

'You were born to be King,' said a voice from the ministry of unfair trading.

'Aye, along with all the other contenders aspiring to become Csar of all the ancient Russias once Joe Taskerman's cold-hearted Moscow campaign has run its futile course,' said Ivan. 'Someday your Prince will come, and that's a promise we make to anyone who's unable to recognise an imbalance when they see one.'

In the light of the odds against him, Ivan had been inclined to settle for a place as far away as he could from Joe Taskerman, who may at that very moment be on his way to Moscow, proclaiming victory in the face of defeat, the prospect of Borodino being a subject on which he would not wish to engage in correspondence, leaving those still in one piece to re-cross the river Nieman with nothing to celebrate but their own survival.

'Did you hear that Joanna? I'm a survivor. Your father's doing well. Like hell your father's doing well. Your father's doing time. Speaking of which Joanna, there are times when your father thinks he's turning into a pumpkin. Your father is a pumpkin if he thinks he can outlive Joe Taskerman's reign of terror.' Unless it were to transpire that he'd already outlived him. Again he remembered the thwack on the side of the erstwhile batsman's head.

'Sometimes you don't understand me, Joanna? Sometimes I don't understand myself.' With or without a thwack on the side of the head, he suspected Joe Taskerman would be loath to accept his reign was over even when presented with his own death certificate. He would still be claiming it was a case of mistaken identity as they lowered his coffin into the ground. As for who would be held responsible for the error, well who could you hold responsible in a case of mistaken identity? Anybody you liked. And that was what he would do, he'd blame anybody and everybody, from the radiographer to his own dog.

Ivan still didn't know whether Joe Taskerman had a dog, but no matter because it wouldn't stop him from blaming any old dog that came along. He'd blame his own mother and father. Yes, Joe Taskerman had one each of those, whether he knew who they were or not. He'd blame Archie. Yes he'd blame Archie, who'd made the ultimate sacrifice. He'd blame Ahmed too, and anyone else he'd declared surplus to requirements. He'd blame the health and safety inspector, and the maker of the health and safety inspector's bacon sandwich, but why stop there, he'd blame the bacon sandwich.

'Now I've lost you again have I Joanna? Well as I was saying, I sometimes feel I'm losing myself, and yet sometimes it's all so very clear.'

38

SOMETHING WORTH FIGHTING FOR

Ivan had begun to wonder whether the reason he came to cricket matches on days such as this was for the sole purpose of settling down later in an armchair to enjoy an evening's review of the afternoon's play. Perhaps his reasons for sitting frozen throughout an entire afternoon's cricket match were akin to suffering toothache for too long before seeking treatment, wherein it was more a question of the relief which came afterwards than what was happening at the time. That was after all why every relaxation programme began with muscle contractions as a preliminary to encouraging the most intransigent of those muscles to dissipate the tension they'd been harbouring.

And yet, plausible though it may sound, the answer couldn't lie in that direction, if only because he hadn't been able to fully relax a muscle for as long as he could remember. His present situation being a good example, where he couldn't even keep his fingers still, let alone his mind, as he tried to make the numbers add up by counting the assortment of doors, windows and lamp-posts that went by, one-two-three-four…

'You mean the numbers don't add up?' a frantic voice enquired.

Ivan knew there was little chance of that – lack of foresight having led to the formation of a somewhat different set of calculations to the ones he'd grown accustomed to in the classroom of 4B. In the confines of which even now a schoolroom map of the world's resources was unfurling before his eyes.

'Does anyone know why so much of the map is coloured red?' he remembered the question his teachers had asked.

'To remind us of the blood our father's bled,' he had suggested, for which remark he'd been ejected from the room.

'Ignore me if you must, but it isn't the blood of my fathers that worries me. It's my blood that I'm concerned about. My own knife-in-the-back-it's-still-happening kind of blood. And yours too if only you knew it. Our very own blood. Blood which if we relied upon the likes of you sir, we wouldn't even know we'd shed.' That was what his teachers would have heard had he been blessed with foresight and not been in a corridor talking to a wall.

Seeing the map appear before his eyes again, he realised he was still wandering around rudderless in what his teachers would have insisted was the heart of the old empire. Although the empire they'd had in mind was long gone – the task now being to conceal what had been taken from so many by so few, an attempt to remind them of which might one day lead to his own downfall upon an entirely different battlefield to those upon which the fight for the old empire had been conducted.

'Well, they haven't managed to silence me yet,' he said turning his attention to the more enjoyable task of celebrating the demise of a man who'd been father to a generation of suffering inflicted upon those who wouldn't get a mention on anybody's relief map of a shrinking world.

He reminded himself that if he believed in nothing else on this God forsaken planet, he must believe in himself. Perhaps the referee had been right – there had to be something worth fighting for. Even if it did mean spending your life looking for a way-out of a treadmill to which there was only a way-in. Life had its exits and entrances, but to those claiming a way-in to one of its treadmills could also be used as a way-out, he would say only how surprising that so many people should have failed to register their own passage through any of the one-way clicking turnstiles with which the planet had been littered during the last four hundred years – despite there being no record of the ubiquity of treadmills in any history book that he'd come across. Perhaps it wasn't all that surprising when you considered that to write a history of treadmills you would have to find a way of stepping out of the treadmill you yourself were in, whilst for the eyes of your own Joe Taskerman-or-woman maintaining the pretence you were still in the treadmill. Not forgetting that if you were to draw attention to the means of stepping out, you could expose the whole illusion of the inevitability of treadmills to an examination it would be ill-equipped to survive, leaving an army of would-be charismatic leaders each with a badge on their blouse that no one who wasn't a badge collector took the slightest notice of.

'Oh dear, what on earth would they do then?' queried a voice from the front office.

'Rank order the people in the treadmill according to their importance,' boomed a voice of authority.

'Importance to whom?' said an only half awake onlooker.

'Importance to those on whose behalf the instruction was being given of course. Haven't you been paying attention to any of this?'

Ivan could only remind himself that it was a speeding treadmill they were talking about, where tradition ruled, only Kings and Queens had a history, and no matter how many correctives were published, they became part of the story.

He spat his disgust into the scarf that was threatening to suffocate him, and still struggling against the wind in this less exposed part of the town, returned to the more serious matter of whether the knowledge of his own reluctance to be seen as a candidate to succeed Joe Taskerman might have gone further than he'd thought. He'd managed to avoid an expression of his distaste for the prospect, but whether or not they considered him to be a viable candidate they were bound to try and flush him out. Where he would have no alternative but to decline, the chances of his own demise becoming greater. The bastards. That was how they always got you in the end. And he didn't need a letter lying unopened on a desk to remind him of that.

39

WITH DUE AND PROPER REGARD

The magistrate cleared her throat and began summing up. This was, she said, an unusual case. There were some important principles at stake. It was the duty of the bench to ensure that not only was the law upheld but that it was seen to be upheld. Due regard had to be given to the circumstances of the case. In particular, the condition of the defendant at the time of the offence had to be taken into account. The defendant had been under a lot of pressure. That may have been a mitigating factor, and certainly, said the magistrate, it was difficult to comprehend how a person with the defendant's background could find himself before the bench today. In view of this, the bench had been gratified to hear of the horror and remorse which had been expressed so vividly by the defendant towards his actions. On the other hand, the bench had to bear in mind their responsibility towards the owners of property, and in this respect it was important that the serious nature of the offence be considered. The court had to ensure that offences of this nature were dealt with severely, thereby providing an example to others who might be tempted to transgress in this way. The defendant's position in society was an important one, and in that regard the court was obliged to examine the possibility of mitigating circumstances, but the court also had a duty to act in a manner such as to underline the standards expected of people in those positions. The magistrate stopped for a moment whilst the clerk of the court leaned over to whisper something in her ear. The magistrate nodded, cleared her throat and went on.

'Notwithstanding the difficulties of weighing the evidence….the evidence concerning the motives of defendants who are accused of committing offences of this nature, the bench feels that an overriding concern must be…

must be, that the court is seen to have exercised... is seen to have exercised due and proper regard for procedure in its deliberations as to the particular circumstances... the particular circumstances in which the transgression took place... and in the light of these deliberations, the court has decided that before passing sentence, further evidence should be sought with regard to the precise nature of the circumstances, and the defendant's state of mind...'

40

EQUAL BURDENS

'Ivan,' a voice rang out as the son of the first wicket down reached the point where the new shopping mall joined the main thoroughfare.

On turning he saw the struggling figure of Rowena coming towards him with two bulging bags and a statuette under each arm.

'Good Heavens,' he said. 'Where on earth are you going with those?'

'Here, take one of these for a minute,' said Rowena without regard for how he could possibly do that when his hands were already full.

The tall figure of Rowena was the same height as her husband when she wasn't wearing her heels, so that people often said what an impressive couple they made. An impressive couple was not what they were making at the moment. They were making a terrible mess of things as they tried to divide the baggage more evenly between the two of them. Items went backwards and forwards with the speed of luggage tumbling into an airport arrivals hall as umbrellas were exchanged for bags, bags were exchanged for deck chairs, and deck chairs were exchanged for statuettes.

'Heaven protect us from our ancestors,' said Ivan as the exchanges continued unabated.

When time-out was called, Rowena found she had one statuette, one umbrella, one deck chair, and one less hand than was required for such an arrangement. Ivan was in difficulty too, and a further exchange took place, as a result of which he found himself with one bag, one statuette and one deck chair – an equally cumbersome combination which needed more hands than he possessed. Until they did the sensible thing and resorted to higher mathematics. One plus one multiplied by two, equals... well four, it being quite simple providing you expressed the problem in terms of hands rather than objects, the realisation of which took longer than either of them might have wished. The concept of pairing is a sophisticated means of dealing with large numbers, and sure enough having hit upon the idea it provided an ingenious solution, once they'd identified those items which could be paired together.

The redistribution produced a more satisfactory arrangement until a failure to consider the possibility of hands not taking kindly to mathematical solutions came into the equation, since hands get tired, empirical evidence of this being provided by the testing almost to destruction of one of the statuettes.

'Ivan!'

'Sorry, Sorry, I er, sorry...'

'Put them in your rucksack.' Rowena solved the problem with an inspired piece of lateral thinking.

Ivan wrapped the statuettes in the blanket and stowed them away. That left a total of four items for four hands, and although there would be no spare capacity for the wiping of noses nor fending off marauding insects, at least Joe Taskerman would have been proud of their optimisation of resources.

'Phew.' Ivan was now struggling with the weight of the rucksack. 'This is heavy. What are they made of, plutonium?'

But Rowena was already striding away, leaving him more than a little resentful as to why they collected so many things other people were throwing away.

'What on earth have you got in here?' he cried, referring to the bag in his right hand.

'Wool,' Rowena called over her shoulder.

'Wool?' said Ivan trying to close the gap which had opened up between them. 'Did you say wool? Then might I suggest that next time you arrange to have it taken off the sheep before bringing it home.'

'And needles.'

'You can say that again.'

'I've brought all the needles my aunt can no longer use. Her fingers aren't what they used to be. I think they're in that bag, the needles that is, together with my handbag... hey you have the one with my handbag, you'd better give that one to me.'

'I don't think so,' said Ivan intent upon avoiding any further adjustment to the delicate balance that had been struck.

'I think the skirt I've been making for Joanna is in that one too.

'And no doubt your tapestry.'

'That's right, oh, and the macrame my aunt has been unable to finish.'

'Together with half the contents of the Victoria and Albert museum.'

'How was the game?' Rowena smiled sweetly.

'Terrible, I ran out of sandwiches.'

'Oh no.'

'Oh yes, and I'm bloody starving... here, hold on a minute, I can't keep up with you.'

'I thought you said you were starving.'

'I did, but I wasn't planning on having a heart attack before eating.'

Rowena was unsympathetic. She believed that vigorous exercise was the way to a healthy body and having a healthy body was the first step towards having a healthy mind. Living with whom she did, she knew there was a need for a healthy mind. But it wasn't the imaginary meanderings of her husband that was bothering her now. Throughout the week, no matter how much she'd tried, she'd been unable to prevent images of the insufferable cretin of a Joe Taskerman in her own life from invading her thoughts.

Again she recalled the circumstances that had led to her being issued with a formal written warning. It had been infuriating, and she'd had to restrain herself from sweeping the stuff from the loathsome creature's desk onto the floor when her explanations had not been considered, being met instead by a defence of what had not been in contention, thereby preventing any review of the appropriateness of her actions from taking place.

Although she'd been in danger of allowing her anger to show, she'd known instinctively that would only make matters worse. A feature of working for a living which had taken her husband most of his life to still not have learned. Rather than responding with an immediate outburst at the unjust way she'd been treated, she'd been careful to ensure that her anger was dissipated by an occasional act of resistance, expressed here and there in the days after receiving the warning. Most of these actions went unnoticed, but each one gave her the satisfaction of knowing there would never be enough time for even the most authoritarian of armchair know-it-alls to poke their fingers into everything. Unlike Ivan, she knew there was little point in driving yourself to distraction with expectations of justice. A policy of opportunistic attrition was far more rewarding. A few minutes (when no-one was looking) taken here; a job sheet (but only a minor one) not completed there; an order (but only one that couldn't be delivered) not recorded here; an email (but only a less than urgent one) not answered there.

If only she'd been able to handle her annoyance with her husband in the same way. It was obvious to anyone with an IQ above five that the food chain had been contaminated to an extent that was probably irretrievable. Yet it took someone with Ivan's ingenuity to raise the problem to the level of a Greek tragedy – despite being in a Chinese restaurant at the time. And of course he wouldn't dream of entering a restaurant unless he knew the owners; their staff; their families; their bank manager; their voting habits; what sort of cars they drove, and anything else he could convince himself was relevant. Rowena sometimes worried it would be only a matter of time before he insisted on taking an environmental health laboratory around with him. The routine examinations of food on his plate had become embarrassing. What did he expect to find? Most of the risks you faced when eating out would have been encountered long before the arrival of food on your plate. As for determining the extent of breeding bacteria by an inspection of what had been placed in front of you, you might as well be looking for a Higgs Bosun without a Hadron Collider. Food contamination of that kind wouldn't be visible. Not even if you were a fly. Especially not if you were a fly. Rowena knew Ivan was not a fly. She might have said he was a bit of an old moth, were it not that the bright lights held little attraction for him no matter how much he insisted they did.

(*'Who is this Rowena? Do I know her?'*)

'Get a move on there young Ivan lad,' called Rowena seeing how far he was falling behind.

'Who, me?'

'Yes you with the worried frown and the cares of the world on your shoulders.'

'Worried frown? Cares of the world? Narrgh, I'm not the worrying kind.' His chuckle was shortlived, because in an effort to keep up with Rowena he stumbled over a sunken section of pavement and began cursing whichever of the former Home Secretary's right honourable friends had been responsible for ensuring that local authorities no longer had the funding to carry out repairs.

'You could tear your hands to ribbons on these,' he snarled recalling the earlier antics of the former Minister.

'You misunderstand the former Minister's position my friend. He began walking on his hands in order to confuse the opposition. And now he's addicted. He can't give it up.'

'I would have thought walking with his head close to the ground would have put him in a better position to monitor the requirements for pavement repairs.' Ivan was careful to step over a badly eroded section.

'Pavement repairs? I'm afraid we don't go in for that kind of thing anymore.'

Ivan shook his head, reminding himself that if you were to swallow everything you heard you might come to the conclusion that the condition of the nation, let alone the roads and footpaths, were no longer the responsibility of the Government.

'Along with everything else if I've learned anything on this planet,' he muttered as he contemplated the pointlessness of registering a complaint.

41

PORTRAITS ON THE WALL

When asked whether he'd decided who should be awarded the prize, the man in the grey suit had no hesitation in pointing to the tall boy in the black blazer. The boy showed no emotion when he saw the finger pointing towards him. He might almost have been expecting the finger to single him out. The man in the grey suit had known there was something about the young fellow, something which had told him this particular boy had a great future ahead of him. The ability to identify potential in others was why he himself was so good at his job...

One had been brought up in a family that had taught one the importance of knowing where one stood. After prep one had gone on to the family school, and here of course one had excelled as had one's father and grandfather before one. Those had been wonderful days. One could see one's grandfather now, patting one's head whilst pointing around the family portraits on the wall. It had seemed that one's grandfather had been showing one the very position in which one would one day hang a portrait of oneself. And of course upon leaving school, one's college had been an excellent foundation upon which to build one's career, there having never been any doubt that one would go into one's family business. It had been understood for as long as one could remember. And then, when one had become familiar with the business one would take up one's seat on the board.

In his speech to the assembly, the man in the grey suit emphasised the importance of a good education. A good education was a firm foundation for what followed, and it was icumbent upon everyone to make the best of their opportunities. People also had to know they would be rewarded for their efforts, for only by rewarding people would they be assured that prosperity was just around the corner.

One had always known what had to be done, and that one was going to be the one to do it, there having never been any question that one's future was clear. It was the vision one's father had passed on that would be responsible for why one would always get on well with one's people. One had been brought up to treat others in the way one would wish to be treated oneself. Why there should be a need to see things in any other way one couldn't imagine.

42

A REALLY CLEVER TRICK

Ivan shambled along behind Rowena, wondering why she didn't understand that the downward trend in the quality of television programmes required a rather more indignant response than one of remembering where the off-switch was. Why else did she imagine so many people were unaware of how distorted things had become. A preoccupation with celebrity would never provide anyone with what they needed to know.

'I thought you said they were necessary illusions,' said a mischievous voice in his ear.

'I was being ironic.'

That was the problem with exclusion, Ivan thought. Minority decisions were quicker but you had to remember frustration often spoke louder than words, so that some of the advantages of speed would be lost through low commitment.

'No wonder I'm disaffected,' said a reluctant voter.

'That's enough of that kind of talk, we don't want to alarm the public do we?' said a representative of the hanging-onto-what-we-know-brigade.

'The public? Yes, that's you and me folks. Though far be it from me to lance the boil of apathy with thoughts of having any responsibility for that. Just think of it this way when next you go to meet your long lost uncle from a flight that's been anywhere near a country with an endemic population. It's your disembarking uncle as well as the growing of his food they're spraying with insecticide now.'

'You don't expect anyone to believe that do you?'

'Of course not.'

'Here is the news. The Government says...'

'Oh, the government speaks does it?' Ivan tightened his fingers around the bag he was carrying. 'A really clever trick that. Perhaps you would be good enough to explain to us the means by which a Government can speak. In case it has escaped your attention, only people can speak. The onus may be upon you to disguise your sources but I sometimes wonder if they taught you anything at that hand in hand backscratchers school you went to. Now where did I put that bloody key fob?' he hissed through clenched teeth as he fumbled with his unstable load, determined not to set down a single item until the car boot was open.

'What's that in your mouth dear?' Rowena drew attention to the fact that he'd placed the key fob in his mouth in preparation for this very moment.

'Huh?' Ivan had no recollection of having done so.

'Well you did say you were hungry.'

'No I said I was bloody starving,' Ivan spat through the key fob, taking careful aim and allowing it to fall from his mouth towards the one half of his hand which had a finger available to press the unlock button.

43

MISUNDERSTANDINGS

Ivan and Rowena were thankful their daughter had been brought up to understand the relationship between food and metabolic rates of recovery, and that she'd taken the precaution of preparing dinner for about fifteen people. Which the five of them proceeded to devour in less time than was sensible for anyone's digestion.

The dutiful parents would have liked to visit their daughter and family more often, but something always conspired to prevent that. For one thing Rowena would have liked to play a part in supporting Joanna's return to work, but it seemed the demands of her own job had been designed specifically to preclude that. Like many of their generation who felt they had to work hard for a living in order to stay afloat, Ivan and Rowena were guilty of trying to pack too much into their lives. They had been taught to do so from an early age, the discovery of there being no Father Christmas having paled in the face of their realisation there were only twenty four hours in a day. And no matter how many times they were reminded each week flying by contained seven of those twenty-four hour days, it never seemed to work out that way. They sometimes wondered how they'd ever found time to have a social life. How they'd managed to organise all those dinner parties. Yet for years those evenings had been the way of having a few hours in which to forget how difficult things had become. Then someone had suggested smoking a joint, and that had been the end of dinner parties, leaving Ivan and Rowena with little energy for anything that didn't come under the heading of work.

The infrequency of their visits to Joanna and her family meant there was a lot of catching up to do. There had been incessant chattering throughout the meal, so there were almost as many sore heads as there were distended stomachs when Rowena rose from her chair and motioned Ivan to remove himself to the lounge.

Ivan was uneasy about leaving Joanna and her mother to clear away the remains of the meal, but decided his abhorrence of inequality did not preclude him from occasionally being excused domestic duties. Telling himself no one could make every decision on the basis of their deeply held beliefs, he went through to the lounge and settled into the most comfortable armchair. And when he was handed a glass of vintage port by his splendid son-in-law Robert, he made a resolution to step up the frequency of their visits.

He took a sip of the port and slapped his thigh in a gesture of well-being, the likes of which had been recently all too rare. And when he placed his glass down carefully so as to enable his one and only granddaughter to climb upon his knee, a warm feeling ran through his veins. So good did this feel that for one moment, one brief shining moment, he began to doubt the existence of the problems which had been occupying him all week. Perhaps that was it. The problems were a figment of his imagination. There could not be a problem big enough to inhabit the same planetary system as a glass of vintage port with your granddaughter sitting on your knee.

But then he was reminded that the results of the screening were getting closer and they would not be a figment of anyone's imagination. The terrifying prospect of what they may be told had been on the minds of everyone, and now there were only three days to go. The problem was about to get personal. But more than that, the consequences for the future of the plant were plain for anyone to see. Providing they were looking of course, for you had at least to be looking to see what was taking place under your nose.

It caused Ivan no little pain to suspect Joanna and Robert may have joined the silent majority with their eyes open to so little of what was going on around them. Like ships on the tide he thought, as he lowered his knees sufficiently to tip his granddaughter onto the floor had she not been clinging to him with all her might. Neither Joanna nor Robert seemed aware of the consequences of their innocence. No wonder he was disappointed with Joanna, for whilst an element of myopia might have been permissible in the case of a son-in-law, nothing would bring him to accept that defect in his own daughter.

Thank goodness Robert was one of those referred to in grandiose state of the nation surveys as being employed in an executive and professional category. Ivan had never been able to remember the details of what Robert did, but had seen no reason to create awkwardness by repeatedly seeking clarification. In Ivan's experience the jobs of many people were like that – full of details you couldn't remember, but so long as they were seen to be doing exactly what was required by those who mattered, no-one caring a damn. The important thing to be thankful for was that Robert did have a job, no questions asked.

'Well, there might be an odd question or too. Just in passing you understand.' The absence of answers to which, meant Ivan had to acknowledge that Robert might well be one of those claiming to be paid for what they knew rather than for what they did – the giveaway being that Robert had never been known to complain about a target or deadline set by anyone. The only thing Ivan had ever heard Robert complain about was Joanna's tendency to commit to more than she could possibly achieve. Strange in retrospect how Robert had turned out to be what Joanna had needed at that point in her life. From the outset, Robert had been able to deflate the most outrageous of her ideas, never once creating the kind of backlash with which Ivan and Rowena had become familiar.

It seemed meeting Robert had triggered a sudden and unexpected transformation, such that after they were married it had been Joanna herself who had initiated detailed spending guidelines for each rolling period of five years. What was more, she'd never once strayed outside of those guidelines, suggesting it had been a missing sense of direction rather than lack of financial acumen that had led Ivan to predict their daughter would one day fall into a pit of debt and insolvency.

Rowena had merely felt pleased to see how wide of the mark her husband's predictions had been, the more so since it had always been she who'd ensured their own financial stability, Ivan's thoughts generally having been elsewhere.

Upon leaving school, Joanna had gone on to read combined studies at the same university as her brother had done before her. Despite her lack of enthusiasm for the routines of serious study, she'd succeeded in achieving that most damning of faint praises – a quite respectable degree. Ivan could never understand how she'd managed to do so given her apparent devotion to clubbing and partying to the neglect of her studies. He could only assume there had been a decline in standards since the days when he'd dragged his flat-bottomed feet three nights per week to what had then been a mere College of Technology. Of course there had been a decline in standards. It just wasn't in most people's interests to draw attenion to that. If nothing else, incessant interventions and demands for more instrumental outcomes had more or less ensured there would be a decline in standards.

Given those lower standards coupled with a lack of parental trust, Joanna had developed the habit of dismissing Ivan and Rowena's concerns as essential misunderstandings of those brought up in a previous era. She'd repeatedly told them not to worry, without once seeing this too was a misunderstanding, since she of all people should have known that worrying was natural to Ivan and Rowena. It was what they did.

For one thing Ivan had worried his daughter would have difficulty in finding a job upon completion of her degree and when Joanna had accepted a position in a pet foods company that had been very nearly the last straw. It had been useless for Joanna to argue the product was less important than was the fact that she was learning the rudiments of merchandising fast moving consummables. Her father had been simply horrified that his daughter should be involved in a company whose main contribution had been to increase the dog population. It had been Rowena who'd worked most hard to prevent a complete breakdown of relations at that point in their lives, although she too had been taken by surprise at the rapidity of Joanna's transformation. It was as though she'd stepped through a hole in the continuum and turned into the daughter Rowena had always wanted but had thought she would never have.

Joanna had become obsessed with the idea of settling down and had developed a focus and commitment that made it difficult to believe there had ever been an intention to do otherwise. Such that Rowena had decided to welcome Robert and accept him into the family with open arms without posing a single question, at least to her daughter, of how such a marriage could possibly work.

44

A WEDDING ON THE UHRUMGHALI PLAIN

'Tell me a story Grandpa.' The heart melting picture of innocence on his knee turned her face towards her grandfather. 'Tell me a story... a story, with lots and lots of am-in-als.'

'Am-in-als, my dear?' said Ivan with a laugh.

'Yes, like the doggy island, Grandpa.'

Ivan raised an eyebrow at the memory of the doggy Island having no wish to provoke a rebuke of the kind he'd received at the end of that story. Come to think of it, neither had he much appetite for being regarded as a specialist in am-in-al stories, and yet he could see it wouldn't be easy, for the demands from the bright eyed treasure on his knee would continue until he had to accept there was little alternative but to give in to one of the highest forms of flattery known to grandfathers.

He took a deep breath and launched himself dutifully into a new story.

'This is the story, he began to the obvious delight of the wide-eyed listener.

'This is the story... the story of a wedding.'

'Oooh, a wedding.'

'Yes a wedding,' said Ivan. 'This is the story of a wedding. And a very special wedding it is too, because this story takes us into the heart of the great Uhrumghali plain deep in the continent of Africa, where we shall discover two of the finest creatures that ever lived beside the Khumbhoto river that meanders its way across the Uhrumghali plain.

'Mmmmm.' the listener wriggled into a more comfortable position.

'This is the story of that wonderful day upon which Helena, the most beautiful hippopotamus in the river, married Ryan the most handsome rhinoceros on the plain.'

Ivan paused for a moment to take another sip of the port beside him, and Robert, himself finding a certain fascination in the unfolding narrative, came round to replenish the glass of the storyteller.

'It was only to be expected that on a day such as this the animals would come from all corners of the plain,' Ivan went on. 'But such was the interest that they came in numbers far in excess of anyone's expectations.' Ivan cocked an eye towards his granddaughter causing her to giggle with delight.

'As you might imagine, they were determined to make the most of such an occasion, for there had been some lean times in recent years what with the drought and the illegal hunters.' The storyteller was beginning to settle into his stride.

'Yet in spite of the joy which an occasion such as this brought to the plain, there were some amongst the gathered herds, as is sometimes the case at the most ordinary of weddings,' – he cast a sidelong glance towards the other listener to his story – 'who felt the bringing together of this couple was perhaps a little too, well shall we say, a little too unusual for it to last.' Ivan lowered his eyes towards the tiny figure hanging onto his every word.

'A sense of unease was not altogether surprising, because of course hippopotamuses normally marry hippopotamuses and rhinoceroses normally marry rhin... Ivan laughed as he saw the eyes of his granddaughter staring into his own from a distance of only a few inches.

'Osserfooses,' screamed Molly.

'That's right,' said Ivan.

'There's a wedding mummy, cried Molly as Joanna appeared on her way to return a handful of dinner plates to the cupboard in the dining room.

'Oh that's nice dear. Who's getting married?'

'It's a, a, a ippy-flotter-moos, and a, a, a iner-osser-foos.'

'Helena looked magnificent,' laughed the doting grandfather. 'She had a new outfit of pale green moss with a garland of bright yellow liverwort, whilst Ryan... why Ryan had a fresh coat of newly rolled sand.'

Joanna flashed a worried glance first towards Ivan's glass and then towards Robert, but Robert, crouching beside the telephone as though expecting it to ring at any moment failed to register the warning signs, being too engrossed in the unfolding story.

'And there in all their glory, side by side, the couple made a wondrous sight.' Ivan gestured so as to suggest the couple might be standing in the fireplace beside them.

'Oooh,' sighed Molly.

'The ceremony was a simple affair as was the custom in those parts. The oldest elephant in the herd wrapped his trunk around their enormous necks and holding them very tightly, pronounced them rhino and wife.'

Robert stroked the side of his nose with his forefinger, and in an attempt to prevent a broad grin from breaking across his face pressed his thumb hard into the soft part of his lower jaw.

'Most of the wedding guests were entranced by the sight of the newly weds, and even those with doubts about the wisdom of such a marriage were caught up in the excitement. A python wrapped himself playfully around a hyena…'

'Ooooh… is he going to squeeze and squeeze him, Grandpa?'

'And a crocodile raised his eyes to a precocious looking monkey perched above him, murmuring what a marvellous picture he thought the happy couple made, and expressing his hope that one day… yes one day… one day in the not too distant future, the monkey too would get married and have lots of little ones.'

'Yeeeiou,' cried the listener on his knee with mounting excitement. 'Is he going to eat them Grandpa?'

Ivan paused, afraid he may have strayed beyond the boundaries of plausibility. He wondered whether even the surreal had its limits, but decided probably not, since nothing would ever be surreal if it did.

'The happy couple stood beaming at each other, whilst in the time honoured tradition of the Uhrumghali plain everyone began to shower them with sand and water.'

'Urrgh, Grandpa what a mess,' the wide-eyed listener took her own precautions, bobbing her head down into the storyteller's midriff with little thought for his digestion. Ivan winced but went on gallantly.

'They began to walk amongst their guests, Helena in the river and Ryan on the bank beside her. Presently they came upon a resplendent looking termite hill, which for many generations in the Uhrumghali have served as... he deliberately counted them out on his fingers... one-two-three-four-five tier wedding cakes.'

'Oooh. Can we have some?' cried Molly.

'At which point Geraldo, the elder of the assembled giraffes, dipped his long neck into the river and standing up to his full height proposed a toast to the newly weds.'

'The am-in-als are wedding Nana,' cried the excited voice on Ivan's knee conveying the subject of the story if not the details, as she noticed the presence of Rowena at the doorway.

'Are they dear?' said Rowena with a sense of foreboding.

'And then the main celebrations began,' said the storyteller. 'Geraldo raised his neck in the air and the sweetest of music was heard with almost every animal playing their part, from the trumpeting of a herd of elephants to the wailing of a pack of hyenas.'

'Pra-raa. Pra-raa,' cried Molly, conducting the imaginary orchestra.

'It was evident that the band of all the animals were in fine form,' said Ivan, 'and some of the animals began to dance. Soon the whole area was a mass of gyrating bodies. It became difficult to tell one animal from another as the python tightened his grip on the hyena, the crocodile reached up towards the monkey, a leopard sank his teeth into the back of an impala, and a lion brought an unsuspecting zebra to the floor.'

'Eeeeeeek,' the wide-eyed listener screamed.

'Ivan!' cried Rowena.

'Bedtime dear,' said Joanna whisking Molly away, giving her grandfather barely time to bid her goodnight.

'Ouch,' said Robert, hitting his elbow on the corner of the chair as he turned to close up the drinks cabinet, having noticed that Ivan's glass was once more empty and that Rowena was glaring at him.

45

SMALL TALK

Joanna was upstairs settling down Molly, whilst Rowena was finishing off in the kitchen. Ivan was left listening to Robert talking to an extent neither of them could remember him doing before. He talked about the increasing problems of safety and insecurity in the world, and about the inability of Western Nations to see the global implications of that. He talked about how climate change too was not being taken seriously enough. He talked about the state of the housing market and the burden of currency fluctuations on the economy. He talked about the deteriorating state of the rail network and about the escalating costs of maintaining the motorways. And he talked about whether tolls would soon have to be applied more widely. He talked about the objections that had been raised to the monstrous development being proposed at the end of the street. He talked about the plans he had for the last fifteen feet at the bottom of the garden. And he talked about the state of the decorations in the corner of the lounge where the wallpaper had begun to peel away from the wall. Then he too fell silent. After what seemed like an age, he rose and left the room saying he was going to check upon the position of the thermostat on the boiler.

Ivan stared at the wall, his mind racing backwards and forwards from considerations about whether Joe Taskerman's days might be numbered to thoughts about what would happen if Joe Taskerman were to go. In the midst of which Rowena came back into the room and he began to anticipate the rebuke that would now follow. But Rowena said nothing and her expression gave little away. He suspected her silence was meant to convey more than words could. His eyes fastened on a mark on the ceiling and with a sigh of relief he gave thanks for the deep understanding they had of each other. They had come to the conclusion long ago that language was inadequate for describing what they had. Only trust could do that, and perhaps trust was itself a kind of language. The language of silence. Knowing that they understood and could rely on each other no matter what the circumstances, had been immensely reassuring. They had a sense of permanence and it had enabled them to withstand the severest censures of each other without fear of jeapordising their understanding and trust... so far.

Joanna reappeared, to announce that Molly had at last fallen asleep. Robert too came back into the lounge and the four of them sat around engaging in tense idle gossip, until Rowena adjudged the matter of their departure could be raised without attracting too many references to the infrequency of their visits.

46

ON THE OTHER SIDE OF THE WORLD

'You should have known better than that,' said Rowena adjusting the position of the driving seat for the journey home.

'Yes dear,' Ivan braced himself.

'There is no meandering river that wends its way across the Uhrumghali plain,' Rowena pressed the start button on the electronic ignition and gently released the steering lock.

'Huh?' Ivan thought his ears must be deceiving him.

'And what's more, if I'm not mistaken, liverwort would be unlikely to thrive in what for most of the year amounts to little more than a desert.' She depressed the clutch and engaged first gear, ignoring the message sent by the rev counter in response to the too enthusiastic placing of her foot on the gas pedal.

Ivan looked up in surprise when he realised Rowena was not about to embark upon a thoroughly deserved lecture concerning the inveterate recklessness of the ancestral male species towards its third generation. He could hardly believe his luck, but feeling he had to take advantage of any break that came his way, he settled into the passenger seat rubbing his hands and looking forward to the warmth that would soon flow from the heater, as through the nearside wing mirror he saw the chill of the evening confirmed in the intense white of the exhaust fumes.

The car pulled away smoothly, accelerating into the darkness, making way for a restored image of his granddaughter still gurgling happily upon his knee. The image prompted him to wonder what the children of their son Timothy and his wife Rebecca would have been like had circumstances been different. Failing to get very far in that conjecture, he closed his eyes and instead tried to imagine what Timothy himself would be doing at this very moment, where assuming that bank holidays were celebrated on the other side of the world too, he would probably be thinking about getting up, a prospect which in his current state Ivan found distinctly unappealing.

Timothy was three years older than Joanna and his parents had sometimes worried their concerns about how much time he'd wasted at university had conditioned their response to the subsequent behaviour of Joanna. Unfair that may have been, but understandable, since in his parent's eyes most of Timothy's time at university had been spent on a playing field of one kind or another, not all of them in daylight hours. Timothy's explanation had been that there had been a lot of catching up to do and there was some truth in that, Ivan having protected him throughout his childhood from any possibility of exposure to the feelings of miserable inadequacy of the kind he himself had felt. This had left Timothy without a clear sense of his potential, which was unfortunate because he had more natural talent than his father had ever had.

Despite his sporting activities, Timothy too had done sufficiently well to enable him to embark on a successful career, in his case one that was simply referred to as something in the world of finance, the precise details of which in the interests of his own sanity, Timothy had been anxious to spare his father. Ivan sometimes wondered if Timothy had gone into the world of finance in a rather bigger way than he'd first thought, given the speed at which his son progressed in the acquisition of what passed for the trappings of success in the modern world. Taking articles was one thing, but Ivan sometimes feared Timothy might have been trained to do that literally. He had complained there were far too many unanswered questions in Timothy's life. Rowena had said that such questions were only unanswered if you were determined to keep asking them. To which Ivan had said she was beginning to sound like Joe Taskerman. Whereupon Rowena had pointed to the similarities in Ivan's own behaviour to those he complained about in Joe Taskerman, leaving him with little alternative but to launch into a tirade on the sordidness of the human condition.

Following which he had thrown a cup at Timothy who'd been standing at the window grinning at the explosive exchange taking place.

In being careful to ensure adequate distance was kept between his own affairs and any possibility of influence from his parents, Timothy had felt he was behaving no differently to the way his father would have behaved in similar circumstances. Successful though he may have been in keeping his father at arms length, Timothy was at a loss to understand why his mother too seemed to have little interest in his affairs. He was more than a little surprised when his announcement that he and Rebecca were going to live in Australia was received as though he'd been merely informing them of an intention to move to a house in a nearby street.

His parent's recollections of that occasion were different. The news had come at the end of a day of heated arguments with Joanna, and by the time they'd realised the enormity of what Timothy had been trying to tell them, it was too late. There had been little left but for two bewildered listeners to express their doubts and regrets, along with a resentment at being treated as though they were old fuddy-duddies, a description they had always been anxious to deny, especially to anyone having the nerve to tell them that was what they'd become.

Ivan and Rowena seldom discussed the absence of grandchildren in the Australian branch of the family, preferring instead to regard the condition as a temporary one. Rowena occasionally found herself wishing she was in Australia, but dismissed such thoughts with promises that one day she would go there. In response Ivan had gone so far as to plan a trip to coincide with an England cricket tour. Until Rowena had pointed out that it would take more than an emigre accountant, no matter whose son nor how much of a financial conjurer he was, to raise the money needed for the itinerary Ivan had planned. And so it was thanks to the pioneering work of the infamous Kerry Packer (who Rowena maintained would himself have had difficulty in raising enough money to fund the trip Ivan had in mind) which led to television highlights being the nearest Ivan or Rowena ever got to joining a cricket tour of Australia.

Rowena had sought consolation by writing frequent letters to Timothy and Rebecca, always being careful to avoid conveying the full extent of her disappointment at the infrequency of replies to those letters. Until an email had been received informing them of the irretrievable breakdown of their son and daughter-in-law's marriage.

The news had not come as a complete surprise. On his most recent visit home, Timothy had interrogated his parents with a barrage of strange though in retrospect portentous questions. He had wanted to know how his parents could be sure they were not subconsciously distancing themselves from each other in order to protect their inner selves. How they knew they were not simply putting up with their imperfections and disappointments in order to avoid admissions of failure. Rowena had been at pains to avoid reference to Timothy's own marriage, and had confined herself to saying that she and Ivan knew because it had been the sheer magic of waking to renew their love each day which had kept them together. They had learned the art of compromise and had ensured any sacrifices that had to be made were shared equally between them. Rowena had seen that Timothy had been unconvinced, his response being to raise an eyebrow and pour himself another drink.

On receiving the news that Timothy and Rebecca had decided to separate, Rowena had castigated herself for her reaction. Not so much from a fear that she may have played a part in their deteriorating relations, but from the unforgivable thought that the separation had given rise to a possibility she might now acquire another grandchild from the acquisition of a new daughter-in-law. What an offensive reaction, she'd cried. How could anyone be so loathsome?

Recriminations had come thick and fast and had proceeded more or less continuously from the moment of her first response to the point where she had reminded herself that self denigration was no basis for reparation. She'd sought to console herself by transferring her attention to being grateful her husband had continued to overlook the one aspect of the

Australian adventure about which she'd expected him to become intolerable – namely the move of his once and future son to the land of the arch enemy.

Fortunately, the green cricket cap might have been a symbol of pastoral care, and Sir Donald been nothing more than Walt Disney's duck, for all the connections Ivan made. Unlike his father, who would have made the connection immediately. If not a disconnection – with Timothy. In the eyes of Ivan's father the very idea of wearing a green cricket cap would have been enough to excommunicate him, grandson or not. Perhaps it was as well the old man didn't live to see what he might well have referred to as Timothy's transportation. It wasn't so much that Ivan's father hated the old enemy. On the contrary, being a good sportsman, he'd always been one of the first to have a drink with them at the end of a day's hostilities on the county circuit. But to actually become one of the buggers – that would have been quite another matter.

47

FOLLOWING THE AUDIT TRAIL

'I think I must have fallen asleep at the cricket this afternoon,' said Ivan rubbing his eyes.

'Surprise me,' said Rowena.

'I dreamed that I'd killed Joe Taskerman.'

'Are you sure it was a dream,' Rowena was not in the least surprised.

'Oh it was a dream all right. And yet there may also be a ring of truth in it.'

'Really,' said Rowena wondering what on earth he was talking about.

'Yes, I'm afraid it may turn out that I've helped to see him off.'

Ivan mused over the events of the previous week. What a day to put in an appearance. Three days before a holiday weekend. What a perverse sense of timing.

'Bloody auditors.'

(*'They weren't auditors.'*)

Whether or not they had been auditors, Ivan had been witness to them behaving like auditors. They'd asked the same kinds of questions, looked at things with the same kind of eye for pedantic detail. And just like bloody auditors, they'd been intent on pursuing the most trivial of expenditure imbalances. Imagine thinking he would be able to remember how many birthdays there had been last month. That wasn't the kind of information anyone carried around in their head, and what if they hadn't accounted for the last penny they'd spent? There was a job to be done and a little celebratory birthday cake out of petty cash never did anyone any harm. On the contrary, attending to that kind of thing could do nothing but good. They should have been concentrating on figures that really would have given them a hint of something worth getting their teeth into.

The interest shown as to which schedule despatch note related to which itemed invoice was a little nearer the mark. Perhaps at that point they'd begun to suspect they may be onto something. One of them was even sniffing. Although there was nothing unusual in that. Auditors were always sniffing around something. No auditor worth their salt had ever gone away from a job without thinking they'd got a sniff of something. Following the audit trail? Well, he could have told them they were on the right track if they wanted to get the smell of something putrid in their nostrils. But why should he have told them that? They were the bloody auditors. Why should he have to do their job as well as everyone elses?

With scarcely a thought for why he was once more allowing the miserable world of Joe Taskerman to invade his weekend, he was back in the middle of the previous week, where he still had doubts as to whether they were auditors *('they were not')*. And yet if they weren't auditors, then what were they doing? And there again if they were auditors, why did they ask so many questions about production capacity? Why would an auditor be interested in that kind of thing? Historical information was supposed to be what auditors were looking for. Ego trip fantasies involving five thousand in any operating period in which Joe Taskerman had a hand on the tiller were no places for auditors to be… unless- unless… unless they were masquerading as auditors but were in fact checking on Joe Taskerman. They could have been investigating the would-be maestro himself. They could have been scrutinising his figures. Or seeking further evidence on the question of whether the plant was affecting people's health. Although... although, no one outside the plant was supposed to know about that… unless... unless....unless they'd been sent by the devious bastard himself. He was capable of that kind of trick. My God, he was too.

'Tell the buggers nothing. Tell them nothing I say. Tell them nothing, doubled in spades, hearts, clubs, diamonds, on your bike and down the Champs Elysees. Tell them nothing, squared, cubed, raised to the number of buns in a basket before stacking them in multiples of five thousand. Tell them nothing, tell them nothing I say, tell them nothing… unless-unless… unless they'd been working for a newspaper and were looking for a good story, in which case, tell them everything and I do mean everything. Ladies and gentlemen of the press, put those trumpets to your ears and listen to what we have been trying to tell the world for years. This place is killing us, including yourselves if you stay here long enough.'

But of course they couldn't have been from a newspaper either. They'd put far too many detailed questions to have been from a newspaper. It hadn't been anything like a story they'd been looking for. They'd been looking for something a good deal more than a story. They'd been looking for someone to hang something on. Well they were not not going to hang this one on Ivan K Driver. Until he knew who they were they would get nothing from him. Perhaps it was time to confuse the bastards more than they'd ever been confused before.

'Yeah, give them a taste of the crap we have to put up with.'

'Don't be ridiculous… though wait a minute, you may have a point. I ought not to be so dismissive. We surely ought to try and flush them out if they are from the sewers of Footmouth's bloody mind games… right, listen, look, now, it's like this you see. As they come off the line we have to decide where to stack them. It's perfectly simple, we stack them over here or over there or sometimes we stack them over here or occasionally over there, oh not forgetting that if there's a specific order requirement for them then we stack them over here except that if they're for despatch today then we'd stack them over there unless they have to go for polishing in which case we'd stack them over here but if that isn't the case and they aren't for immediate despatch then we'd stack them over there, providing that is they've been allocated to the stock inventory and are not part of a special call-off order and assuming that they've been double checked for finish and that they're all of the same type and in the correct sequence… you're finding this hard to follow? Well it's not too difficult. It just takes a little time. Talking of which, I'm reminded that a little time is all I have to give you.

I do have other things to do. I can't stand around answering your questions so you can run along and tell Joe Taskerman what good little girls and boys you are.'

Then one of them had unexpectedly let slip they weren't working for Joe Taskerman. Ivan hadn't been convinced. They may have been trying to throw him off the scent. Although if they weren't working for Joe Taskerman, then who the hell were they working for? When pressed to reveal their origins they'd said it was all in the letter. He remembered the letter he'd left unopened on his desk. Could that have been only two days ago? But that couldn't have been the letter they'd been referring to if only because he didn't receive that letter until Friday. Now he too was becoming confused, because of course they could have known the contents of the letter before he'd received it. Especially if they'd written the letter, which they may well have done if they were acting on behalf of those who had appointed Joe Taskerman. But it seemed they'd been referring to an earlier letter – a letter that he'd received and read several times without it telling him anything. Would he have believed it if it had? Did anyone believe everything in the letters they received? You needed only to have been brought up with the picture of an oxo cube on the side of a double decker bus to know how much you could believe what you'd read with your own eyes.

Ivan eased the tension on the seatbelt where it was cutting into his neck.

'The auditors…'

(*'They weren't aud…'*)

'I know I know.'

Whoever the visitors were, they had wanted him to give them a straight answer. Ha. There was no such thing as a straight answer to the kind of questions they were asking.

'I've got a better idea. Why not ask Joe Taskerman? He's unlikely to give you a straight answer either, but he's an artist at dreaming up crooked little questions and so you might feel more at home with him. That's our problem too. We're stuck with him whether we like it or not. Oh we're stuck with you too are we? Up to our necks in stinging nettles, eh?' He moved his arm from the central armrest where it had nudged against Rowena's elbow.

They'd asked Ivan why he seemed to relish making things more difficult. If they'd wanted a serious answer to that question they should have tried dancing to the tune of a moronic little weasel with an army greatcoat for a brain. They should have rolled up their sleeves and tried it for themselves. A few more hands around the place might have been useful. Although on second thoughts, it was brains not hands that were needed, and better if they'd rolled their sleeves down and gone and pissed in the corner of somebody elses porcelain factory.

They should also have known it was no good asking him where Joe Taskerman was. He seldom had any idea of where Joe Taskerman was. He was generally too busy being delighted that Joe Taskerman wasn't poking his nose into something or other that was working perfectly well before he'd arrived on the scene.

He rejoiced in the thought that they must be onto his made-up figures. Why else would they want such precise information as to his whereabouts every minute of the working day? Could they really be onto him?

'I wonder if they've finally caught up with the bastard?' he said aloud.

'I thought you said you'd killed him,' said Rowena.

'In a way, yes,' he said running the tips of his fingers across his brow. 'Isn't this a lovely day. Joe Taskerman may have finally met his Waterloo, riding on his rocking horse with his own troops in full cry with the enemy.'

'Isn't he supposed to be the enemy,' said an only slightly startled Rowena.

'Friend or foe, he can't be sure, because that's what comes to people like you Footmouth. Just when you need allies, up pops a sniper from your own front lines and shoots your balls off from behind you. An accident of course, and all he could tell the court martial (oh there'd be a court martial if he was involved) was that he was looking the other way. Dreaming of a place to store his next five thousand.'

A warm glow spread through Ivan's limbs as he began to

think about life without Joe Taskerman.

'It was just as Harold the lad had intoned in the days of blue overalls and economic miracles… heigh ho, heigh ho, it's off to work we go…'

But then he realised it didn't matter whether Joe Taskerman was on his way or not, because there would soon be another Joe Taskerman to take his place. The myth of great men and women had to be sustained no matter how discredited it may have become. And there he is, a brand new bright and shiny, full of smiles for one and all, Joe Taskerman.

'Hey look, it's that Ivan bloke.'

'Oh no it bloody isn't mate.' A cold shiver went down his spine when he remembered that from next Wednesday he may not be spending much time with them in any capacity.

'Why are we stopping?' said Ivan as Rowena pulled the car off the road and came to a halt in a deserted lay-by. Without knowing quite how, he found himself in the back seat of the car on top of Rowena who was behaving like a renegade from a wild office party with no time to lose. A surge of excitement swept through his veins as he succumbed to the demands of the urgently murmuring body beneath him. No sooner had he located her than Rowena, moving like quicksilver let out a cry, followed by another as her body arched and her hands tore at the clothes on his back. As a result of which he too was racked by an explosion which shook his whole body from the point where his head had come up against the handle of the nearside door to where his feet were desperately seeking purchase against the window of the offside door.

Afterwards they resumed the journey in an exhausted but sensational silence which neither of them wanted to break. When they went to bed that night they lay for a long time holding on to each other, the silence still unbroken, feeling secure and warm in the aftermath of the waves that had washed over them. In the morning there would be an unspoken acknowledgement that even though such heights were less frequent nowadays, the intensity of their intimacy was another reason why they had stayed together, and they were both elated and saddened by that.

MONDAY
48

THE TROUBLE WITH PYRAMIDS

Ivan lay beneath the duvet with his eyes closed, contemplating the vast pools of knowledge held by people who'd been doing their jobs for years.

'Experience is one of the most promising of untapped resources,' said a voice from an open wardrobe.

Though largely ignored, thought Ivan, such that intimidation and bullying were more often the way of things.

'The call to appoint more would-be great men and women is yet another example of providing an answer before knowing what the question is,' said the voice from the wardrobe.

Ivan agreed. Strong leadership had a history of making things worse. Harnessing the distribution of knowledge and expertise took time. Whereas the heavy hand of control was looking for quick results, enabling the would-be great men and women to claim they'd made a difference. And being great men and women, on matters of responsibility they were the ones who decided.

In respect of his own situation, Ivan wondered who would be next to sit in the swivel chair. For even if they'd seen the last of Joe Taskerman, there would be no shortage of candidates lining up for a turn in the chair. That was the trouble with pyramids. The principle was simple enough, but few had understood how it worked... judging by the numbers of would-be great men and women who were out of their depth. Yet having been appointed to a position they were ill-equipped to fill, what were they to do? They could take flight but that would do little to enhance their career paths. Better to stay where they were and simplify matters to a point where it became possible to survive. It wasn't necessary to be near the top of a pyramid in order to simplify anything – a position above someone else was all that was required. The difficulties could then be passed downwards. To the point where they could be passed no further. Following which it became a matter of preventing anyone from noticing. Subjecting a pyramid to that kind of transparancy would run the risk of a structural collapse, which was unthinkable and far more sensible to gather a supporting cast of such magnitude that the pyramid held itself up.

Ivan sighed, wondering whether there was any hope left in the world. He decided there was, for the dawn of a new day still held the promise that when he opened his eyes and raised himself from the bed he would find the wraps had been taken off, the stage had been set, the overture had been played, the curtain was up, and the day was already well into the first act.

Anticipating as much before opening his eyes he felt an urge to leap from the bed throw open the windows and burst into song. It was as though something or somebody was telling him this was just the kind of morning to be encouraged. There was to be no lying in wait for the day to begin. On a day such as this you had an uncanny feeling that your feet – your flat yet nimble feet – would hit the stage running without any question as to how it could possibly be Monday morning already.

Yet Monday morning it was, and a bank holiday too, meaning it was raining, and had he followed his inclination to throw open the windows he would have had to quickly close them again.

There were consolations however. In addition to there being no requirement for him to spend another day staring at numbers on a screen, the rain would prevent him from proceeding with the excavation work. Celebrations were to be short-lived however, as he discovered when he went out onto the landing where he stubbed his toe on an ill-seated floorboard, drawing attention to the fact that it was the carpet rather than the curtain that was up, the curtains, at least those on the landing having been taken down. He went into the bathroom cursing the foresight which had told him that two fine days in a row were an unlikely prospect, and that it would be as well to make preparations for painting the hall, stairs and landing should the weather prevent any further progress being made on the blocked drain.

'Why don't you finish one job before moving on to another?' said Bernard, approaching the spot in the hall where less than an hour later Owen was moving down the doorframe with a loaded paintbrush.

'Because it's raining,' said Owen, being pleased to be making the best use of his time, as the brush deposited a layer of white undercoat along the edge of the doorframe where it met the sandstone emulsion of the wall.

'I had noticed,' said Bernard taking care to retreat a couple of paces.

'Well you always were perceptive,' said Owen, sharpening his concentration by imagining he was edging forwards in a clear inside lane ever conscious of the distance between the kerb and the traffic at a standstill in the lane to his right.

'The possibility that you might get wet didn't seem to bother you yesterday morning,' said Bernard.

'It wasn't raining yesterday morning.' Owen was more concerned with the need for precision in the movement of his arm.

'It may not have been raining,' said Bernard, 'but the shirt you were wearing was far from dry.'

'That was because I was too hot,' said Owen.

'I seem to recall you complaining that you were too cold,' said Bernard.

'That was in the afternoon,' said Owen. 'In the morning I was too hot, and as you know, hot, cold, wet, dry, these things are always relative to what you're doing at the time.'

Ivan ran his free hand around the inside of his collar and told himself if there was one thing he couldn't stand, it was being too hot. Even now his temperature was rising when he remembered it was Monday already, and that the weekend had done little to quell the burning fires which had raised his temperature in the first place. He could only grimace at the thought of why people sought holiday destinations with temperatures hotter than those in which they'd been working themselves into an unfathomable lather for most of the year. Some places of work were hotter than others – melting shops, rolling mills, television newsrooms. Perhaps that was a way out of his predicament. If he were to make enough of a nuisance of himself, Joe Taskerman might be persuaded to recommend him for a job in a television newsroom. He'd had more than his fill of newsreading but it was tantamount to an invitation for the pratt to do precisely that.

'That's what he needs,' cried the voice of Joe Taskerman. 'Give him a real deadline to work to. That might knock some sense into him.'

'It's true, this could be right up your street you know,' intoned the woman from the television news channel who had appeared again. 'I take it that you have settled on a street, and you're not one of those awful politicians who are so worried they might give the game away that they can't remember their own addresses.'

Ivan was only too happy to supply them with his address. All his address would tell them was where he slept. It wouldn't tell them where he lived. He smiled, knowing he'd spent too much of his life keeping one step ahead of a succession of Joe Taskermans to be fooled by that one.

'You live in a dream world,' said the voice of a producer trying to tie up the loose ends of another contract.

Ivan cleared his throat as the fumes from the paint began to penetrate the delicate membranes at the back of his throat. That was what people had been telling him for years. Along with, don't be so negative. Yet the auditors, *('they...')* if auditors they had been, had realised he wasn't being negative. They'd finally understood that his reluctance to answer their questions had shown he was as aware as anyone that wages could only be paid out of profits made, and not from a fantasy world of wishful thinking.

'If we all sat around congratulating ourselves on being able to pay our wages we'd still be looking for a way to replace horse-drawn traffic,' said an entrepreneur launching another product no-one needed.

'Tell that to the horse,' said Ivan.

'Horses can't talk,' said the entrepreneur.

'And I'm supposed to be the one who has no imagination?'

'Why talk to someone who can't answer you back?' said the entrepreneur.

'Look what happens to anyone who does,' said Ivan. 'For one thing they needn't apply for a job on a television channel with a license to broadcast on this planet.'

'Places and positions please,' the voice of a harried floor manager rang out.

THE WOMAN FROM A TELEVISION NEWS CHANNEL   How long have I got?

THE WOMAN IN CORDUROY JODHPURS   As long as you need my dear.

A MAN IN A QUEUE AT THE ARM AND A LEG BUILDING SOCIETY   I could be dead by then.

THE MAN WITH A KOJAK HEAD   Listen sonny, we could all be dead by then.

A MAN PUSHING A SUPERMARKET TROLLEY   Gangway.

OWEN   Lunatic.

BERNARD   Why are you talking to him like that? The poor man was only...

OWEN   I was talking to Footmouth.

HENRY   You're wasting your time, he never listens to anyone.

AN INNOCENT BYSTANDER   Then why do you put up with him?

THE MAN IN A QUEUE AT THE ARM AND A LEG BUILDING SOCIETY   I have a mortgage.

A MAN CARRYING FIFTEEN PINTS OF BEER ON A BAKER'S TRAY   Here, can you take these?

JOE TASKERMAN   I take orders only from my superiors.

A MARXIST HISTORIAN   That's the trouble with pyramids.

THE WOMAN FROM A TELEVISION NEWS CHANNEL   If I can take you back to the optimism you exhibited upon joining the company Mr Tasket...

JOE TASKERMAN   I was convinced that we could turn this place around.

THE RADIOGRAPHER   I wouldn't be too sure about that if I were you sir.

THE WOMAN IN CORDUROY JODHPURS   Leave him alone. I do like a man who can turn things around.

JOE TASKERMAN   Press on regardless.

THE SQUARE LEG UMPIRE   The ball didn't carry.

'Damn,' cried Ivan as the paintbrush deviated from line, reminding him that he of all people should have known not to respond to the tired old charge that he was being negative whenever he raised a question to which there may not be an answer.

49

A COMPLICATED QUESTION

Ivan cursed the ancient Pharaohs, ancestors of Joe Taskerman, whose ideas had spread from the vale of milk and honey and led to the concentrating five thousand years of history into a single working week. And yet who could deny that the invention of pyramids had been brilliant in its simplicity – no matter that the invention had occurred in other civilisations too, Asian, Incan, and no matter that some of those civilisations should have fallen into decline. That was where your inability to see the potential of your inventions got you.

'Or were they perhaps wiser than we'd thought?' said a philosopher still contemplating the identities of the three characters who were sharing much more than Ivan's car. 'Could they have known all along that the invention of pyramids would make the process of becoming civilised more difficult?'

'Who knows,' said Ivan. 'But it's served well enough as a blueprint for the sadistic neo-Pharaohs of the modern world. Imagine a structure deriving from an ancient civilisation becoming the way the age of uncertainty itself was sustained, secure in its own perpetuity no matter how illusory that may be.'

Illusory or not, one thing of which you could be sure was that you must not stand still in any pyramid run by a neo Pharaoh answering to the name of Joe Taskerman. Otherwise you ran the risk of being trampled in the rush to prove who was the best candidate in line for the next offering from the palm of his hand. Leaving you to sink further down the pyramid. To the point where you fell right out of the bottom wondering why you'd ever scorned the idea of upward mobility. Until you remembered that every would-be great man and woman's climb to fame provided you with evidence that higher altitudes had their problems too. The paintbrush continued on its slow determined journey with Ivan monitoring every inch gained. That was why you had to be careful when climbing ladders. Ladders were best ignored. Assuming that you hadn't got one resting on your foot at the time. The more important lesson was that you learned to recognise the snakes.

'Er ahem, it's all very well for you to reduce everything to the level of a boardgame,' said the voice of an optimistic candidate trying to remain reasonable in the light of the odds against his, hers, or anyone else's application for promotion being successful. 'But what concerns me is why, er ahem, in God's name I should keep going in the hope that one day, er ahem, I will be promoted, when it needs only a modicum of discernment to realise, er ahem, that there won't be enough room up there for all of us?'

'Well don't go around shouting your mouth off on that score,' said Ivan, mindful of the work that was going on to prevent that kind of question from being asked. 'Your transgression may not put the whole pyramid at risk, but you have to remember they can throw you and your entire stock of paper clips and elastic bands into the street anytime they like, and I do mean literally.'

'They wouldn't, er ahem, do that. Would they?' said the optimistic candidate.

'Don't put it to the test that's all.'

'If I have understood you correctly then,' said Bernard. 'You are suggesting that yesterday morning's weather would have been more appropriate for the afternoon, with the cooler weather on the third man boundary occurring in the morning.'

'You don't need to be a meteorologist to work that out,' said Owen.

'You do have to be a little more elevated in the scheme of things to exercise that kind of influence though,' said Henry.

Pausing for a moment to reload the brush, Ivan mopped his brow with his free arm. Again he wondered what the ancient Pharaohs would say if they could see the havoc wrought upon the world by their unthinking madness.

'Don't be stupid Dad. They knew exactly what they were doing. Their own pyramids were tombs remember. Some of which are still lined with treasure.'

He recalled that this was a feature of pyramids which his own daughter had been quick to point out, it not being the first time she'd been able to put her finger on the pulse.

'You're right Joanna. They did. But that was yesterday, and the only treasure to be found in the kinds of pyramids we inhabit nowadays is that which is kept well out of sight. Joanna are you listening to your wise old father? Just take a look around you. Everywhere you look, another pyramid and no sign of treasure. Luckily for the Pharaohs of the modern world it isn't necessary to have any treasure in order to sustain a treasure hunt. And that's just as well, because a pot of gold is the last thing you're likely to find in a pyramid in which any Joe Taskerman has had a say. But they do want you to remember that pyramids are tombs. Without a fear of being buried alive you might unearth something they'd rather you didn't know. Such as a realisation they were making promises they couldn't keep.'

Tired of the incessant interruptions the consultant radiologist to whom the results had been referred, shook her head as she examined the evidence in front of her.

How extraordinary to think that when Joe Taskerman had agreed to the screening process people had begun to wonder whether he might have a streak of humanity in him after all. That kind of thinking had been short-lived however, because Joe Taskerman had soon been bobbing to and fro like a gander with an egg up its arse (no wonder he walked so stiffly) making sure that no-one had much time to pause for a thought of what the place was doing to them.

'Now then you lot, enough of this chattering. Your job is to get on with what you're being paid to do. How many times do I have to spell it out for you?'

'Spell it out? Hasn't he realised that no-one does that any more? Doesn't he know everyone has a spell-check nowadays? Has no-one told him about the wonders of new technology? That might be something we can put to our advantage. Get those spurs working (not you Rowena, ouch) come on run, run like the wind, yes the wind, it's not just your supper you're running your legs off for in this pyramid. The reward structure of a pyramid is only temporary as far as any one of us is concerned. Those who climb higher may breathe cleaner air for a time, but when they fall… lets just say that everyone is a sitting target down here, and whilst it's true that shit doesn't float (unless you're a vegetarian) remember when that stuff hits the fan it goes absolutely everywhere.'

Ivan had often been told that he was obsessed with pyramids, and that they were nothing but a figment of his imagination. What his critics had failed to see was the shadow cast over their lives by the pyramid they themselves were in. A shadow of such proportions that it was sometimes difficult to believe it belonged to the same pyramid. Shadows were supposed to be a reflection of their origins, but a more important job for the shadow of a pyramid was to provide a picture of how distorted things had become, remembering that reflections were often disturbed by troubled waters.

'My God, we're trapped in a pyramid which can't even cast a decent shadow,' said a woman who'd been a sitting target for most of her life, not having realised that the point of a pyramid concealing the shape of its shadow was to maintain the illusion of ascendancy. She would have done better to put her trust in the shadow which would have informed her of the competition for places, the opportunities for any individual being decidedly limited. Figment of Ivan's imagination or not, the only ones who could ever be in the majority in a pyramid were the downtrodden.

'Why don't you just answer the question? Why are you painting that doorframe?' said Bernard.

'That's a complicated question,' said Owen.

'No it isn't,' said Bernard. 'It's a perfectly simple question. Why you are painting that doorframe? Get it? W-h-y, a-r-e, y-o-u, p-a-i-n-t-i-n-g, t-h-a-t, d-o-o-r-f-r-a-m-e? You see? When you take it slowly it's not difficult even for a numbskull like you.'

'You may speak as slowly as you wish,' said Owen, 'but it remains the case that I'm not at all sure how to begin to answer the question.'

Ivan loaded the brush once more and holding it at arm's length carefully folded his legs beneath him in order to lower himself into a position from where he could reach the bottom of the doorframe.

'He merely asked why you were painting that doorframe,' said Henry.

'So he did,' said Owen. 'But I'm sure you'll agree that questions which appear on the surface to be quite straightforward often turn out not to be so, and therefore the first thing to do with any question is to establish the sense in which it is being asked.' He was determined not to deposit any paint on the floorboards as the brush approached the end of its downward traverse.

'Perhaps the sense in which it is being asked derives from wanting to know why you are painting the doorframe this morning,' said Henry.

'Ah, said Owen. So you feel the question refers to why I am painting the doorframe this morning.'

'You see, he is capable of getting there in the end,' said Bernard.

'As distinct,' continued Owen, 'from yesterday morning.'

'Yesterday morning you were swinging a sledgehammer against a lump of concrete,' said Bernard.

'Ah, you remember.'

'And therefore yesterday morning does not come into it.'

'I see,' said Owen, 'and so you are suggesting that the fourth dimension is not after all at the heart of the matter.'

'The heart of the matter is why you are painting that bloody doorframe,' spat Bernard in exasperation.

'Really,' said Owen. 'So you feel the question refers to the condition of the object rather than to the temporal position of the subject?'

'The question refers to the fact that you are not sitting in a deck chair with your feet up,' said Bernard.

'Isn't it a little wet for that?' said Henry, stepping back out of range of Bernard's arm for a moment.

'I was speaking idiomatically,' said Bernard glaring at Henry as he pointed accusingly at Owen's paintbrush. 'The significance being that if it was too wet to continue excavating the drain then he had a perfectly sound reason for putting his feet up for the rest of the day.'

Ivan paused for a moment and rotating his neck in an attempt to ease the stiffness he found himself wondering whether it was possible there could have been an ancient King Taskerman.

'Good grief,' cried a voice from the audience of the silk suited professor who had reappeared. 'An ancient King Taskerman, king of all the con-men.

'Don't forget the women,' cried a voice from the back of the hall.

'Women are not con-men,' said the woman from the television news channel. 'Women are not in a position to be con-men... or women. Women do not exist.'

'Speak for yourself,' said the woman in the corduroy jodhpurs.

Evidently Ivan was unaware of the extent to which the paint fumes were taking their toll as he loaded the brush once more.

'For God's sake. What sort of a woman are you?' said the woman from the television news channel. 'If women had not existed it would still have been necessary for men to have invented a means of excluding them.'

'But wouldn't that mean the end of the species,' said a confused voice from the front row.

'Of course it would, that's the point, you fool.' The woman from the television news channel was losing her patience.

'It's a point I seem to have missed,' said the silk suited professor.

'As only a man could,' said the woman from the television news channel.

'But I'm not a man,' said the silk suited professor revealing a feature of her identity which no-one had suspected.

'We all have to be men when it comes to making progress in this world,' said the woman from the television news channel, provoking the silk suited professor to point to a number of subjugated assumptions in that claim.

Ivan carefully applied the loaded brush to the doorframe.

'I think we should address ourselves to those subjugated assumptions.' (A philosopher on the late show).

'I'd rather address myself to his subjugated needs my love.' (Undoubtedly the woman in corduroy jodhpurs).

'Subjugated assumptions are often a reflection of underlying anxieties. (A voice sounding uncannily like that of Joe Taskerman, were it not for the erudition and therefore probably a philosopher on the late show again).

'You don't know what you're talking about.' (An unidentified voice that could have been Bernard, had he not been occupied in keeping clear of the paintbrush in Owen's hand).

'There's far too much talking if you ask me.' (Had to be Footmouth).

'Who's in charge of this pyramid.' (Her Majesty's chief inspector of pyramids.)

'Er, that will be me sir.' (A descendent of King Tutankhamen).

'He who considers more deeply knows that whatever his acts and judgements may be, he's always wrong.' (The ghost of Friedrich Nietzsche).

'Are you proposing to change your defence.' (The deliberating magistrate).

'It all depends on the position you take,' (A defending advocate.)

'Position, position and position.' (A chorus of candidates for a post in the shadow of a pyramid.)

50

A WALK IN THE PARK

'You had to hand it to them, they'd got the whole thing off to a fine art,' thought Ivan wiping away a splash of paint from the corner of his eye. 'You had only to turn your back for a second and they'd built another pyramid. They were probably building five thousand pyramids per week by now, and to think when they began, it took more than five thousand weeks to build a pyramid.'

'I was wondering about that,' said a descendent of an ancient Pharaoh. 'If it's taken us five thousand years to get to a position where we can make five thousand per week that represents a lot of investment capital, perhaps we should consider increasing our prices.'

'Did someone say we ought to put up our prices? Now that is a good idea. Shame it's taken us five thousand years to realise the value of what we have. Just think where we might have been if we'd had a reliable data base.'

'Oh come on, there's never been a data base which lasted five minutes, never mind five... how long did you say it took to build the first pyramid? Five thousand weeks? Why that's close on a hundred years. Have these figures been audited?'

Ivan dipped his brush into the paint can, still unclear about why it come to pass that so much had grown and developed from structures of ancient times... such that your position in life depended largely on whether you'd been dealt a good hand of cards – a good hand of cards being essential if you were not to be up against it from the start. Although contrary to what you were told, the law of averages would do little to ensure you received your fair share of good cards. You would do better to remember whose interests were being served by the dealers of those cards.

It could have been a case of lightheadedness from the pungent effect of the paint in his nostrils, or it could have been a case of hysteria of the kind which is apt to surface during periods of prolonged exhaustion. Or perhaps it was something else entirely which gave rise to the impression of the doorframe he was painting having acquired a resemblance to a proscenium arch. Whatever the reason, and with scarcely a thought for who might be listening beyond a thousand household mites in the room behind the door, Ivan launched into what could easily have been mistaken for the most important speech of his life.

'I come not to disturb you from your thoughts,' he made an impressive entry such that every echo that had ever breathed life into the hallway found itself at full stretch. 'I come only to remind you...'

'Get on with it,' said a voice in the front row.

'Out with it my boy,' said the magistrate.

'Forget the speeches Dad,' said his one and only daughter.

'Quit the talking laddie,' said the voice of Joe Taskerman.

Ivan made a gesture with the paintbrush, which had it not been for the stickiness of the handle would have danced right out of his hand. Applying the loaded brush to the doorframe he decided it would be a good deal safer to revert to the more familiar form of discourse in the shape of a complete conversation with himself – beginning with a reminder that no matter how miserable a hand you'd been dealt, there were other ways of acquiring a good hand of cards.

He was relieved to have found a way of getting things off his chest without running the risk of sending the whole can of paint cascading across the hall. But then he found himself providing his own interruption in the form of a question as to why so many modern day Pharaohs had failed to appreciate the limitatons of the pyramids they'd built, whereby people would be forced into trying any means they could to improve the hands they'd been dealt.

Reloading the brush as he approached the bottom of the doorframe he paused for a moment to admire the progress he'd made, which allowed a voice from inside his head to ask why indeed it wasn't forseen that this would lead to the stealing of cards, which in turn would lead to more violent means of acquiring better hands. He stubbed the end of the brush into the crack between the doorframe and skirting board. With the paint ever higher in his nostrils he responded with a reminder that it was after all the ancient principle of market forces that were at work.

'I'm afraid it's true,' he began to speak aloud again. 'And because there has never been a way of escaping those market forces, it should have been evident enough that things were only going to get worse when the modern day Paraohs tried to limit the amount of theft taking place. Since there were so few other ways for citizens to improve their hands, the modern day Pharaohs had to accept increasing levels of violence in their pyramids.

'No-one would condone that kind of behaviour,' said a man collecting a payment on a pay-day loan.

'But they did, and they have... and because the modern day Pharaohs too have understood only their own positions in the pyramids they've built, attempts to re-establish their control has led to violence to the spirit too... to the point where threat and intimidation have become common currencies.'

Ivan wiped the brush handle where the paint had begun to congeal.

'I told you a common currency would be disastrous,' said another politician on a campaign trail.

'But of course modern day Pharaohs have never been unduly concerned, since they've always had a ready supply of new card players coming forward,' Ivan continued.

'They should have known that couldn't last,' said a harassed looking official Ivan remembered having once met in an employment exchange.

'It could not,' said Ivan, determined not to be upstaged by an overworked civil servant, struggling with another requirement to produce dubious figures. 'For just as in ancient times, no one forsaw that a great plague would sweep across the lands, in which many people would perish, leading to a shortage of fit and trained card players. Which would put modern day Pharaohs at the mercy of their enemies, the same old market forces.' Loading his brush once more, Ivan began painting the skirting board from the point where it met the bottom of the doorfame.

'Unfortunately, the response of modern day Pharaohs has been to take ever more draconian action to control what they believe is theirs to control. And these modern day Pharaohs have grown so accustomed to believing in their right to control, that they've often failed to understand the motives of those in their command. This misunderstanding has often brought their underlings into direct conflict with their Pharaohs, the great men and women of the modern age. So disruptive has this become that the invisible real masters of fortune have introduced the practice of social regicide, in which a Pharaoh too can be removed and replaced with another.

'That's th' idea,' boomed the voice of Foghorn. 'Priv'tise regicide. That'll show em.'

'The Pharaoh is dead, long live the Pharaoh,' cried a man running across a platform in his underpants.

Ivan held onto the brush for all he was worth knowing that he was perilously close to flinging it the entire length of the hall.

'I suppose it's a question of aesthetics,' said Owen.

'What is?' said Bernard.

'The reason why I'm painting…'

'If you were interested in aesthetics, then you might have paid a little more attention to preparation before you started painting. Just look at the state of this,' said Bernard, running his hand in front of the brush along an unpainted part of the skirting board. 'Why didn't you get someone in to do it?'

'There's a brush,' said Owen, nodding towards a tired looking specimen lying beside the can of paint.

'No, no, I mean a professional, er that is, I mean er, of course I don't mean a firm, naturally I don't mean an actual firm.' Bernard remembered the estimate for excavating the drain. 'I mean an amateur, that is an amateur professional, you know, a painter who works for a firm but who does jobs.'

'You're surely not asking Owen to support the black economy?' said Henry.

'An amateur professional eh?' said Owen. 'I don't think I've come across that one before. Although I suppose in a way I am myself what might be called a professional amateur.'

Owen recalled how much decorating he'd done recently.

Ivan moved the paintbrush into his other hand to allow a flexing of the wrist of his painting hand, which brought such relief that he decided to put the brush down for a moment. Raising himself to his full height he inhaled slowly and then suddenly collapsed his shoulders to expel the air from his lungs. He felt the blood surge into his head and closing his eyes leaned into the wall. He realised he was in danger of falling asleep but was unable to force his eyes open. He was overtaken by a strange impression that he was in a park leaning against a tree. Whereupon his arms fell by his side and he slowly slid down the tree, coming to rest on the floor having narrowly missed the wet portion of skirting board where it met the doorframe.

He looked around, feeling uneasy, but not knowing why. Until it dawned on him that the park he had wandered into was not the kind of park he would have chosen. This was an industrial park.

'Yeeoouuee, the park is full of bloody pyramids,' he cried as his body stiffened, causing his head to bang on the tree which had now become a concrete pillar against which he was leaning.

'They don't look like pyramids,' said a startled bystander.

'They may not look like pyramids, but don't let their disguises fool you.' Ivan hauled himself to his feet to get a better view, where he saw a group of modern day Pharaohs in the midst of a dream… a dream that would not come true, and could not come true, because dreams were not reality, and as everyone who had ever lived and worked in a pyramid knew, reality was not the truth.

'Look at that,' a voice called out in awe at the sight of a group of bowed headed Pharaohs in conference. 'Aren't they impressive?'

Grinding his teeth, Ivan stood up, turned his back on the scene and set off along the road, unable to find anything positive to say about a gathering of modern day Pharaohs planning how to spend the spoils of another five thousand per week, having no regard for the misery that would be created in the reaching of that target.

SURVIVING JOE TASKERMAN

He stopped when he was confronted by a single storey building made entirely of concrete. It seemed inconceivable, but the place had no windows. It was a monstrosity that would not have been out of place in a film on the horrors of Hades. Yet was it not the kind of thing you might expect in a would-be great man or woman's nightmare? The hiring of one misanthropic architect rebelling against the profligate wasting of energy and that was the end of natural light as you'd known it. He was appalled at the thought of anyone spending their lives in a building such as that. The only people deserving of buildings like that were those gritty determined Pharaohs who ruled over such places, forever priding themselves on how down to earth they were, whilst digging themselves further into the sand which they had failed to notice was shifting beneath their feet.

Further along the road Ivan noticed there was a much taller building. Unlike the concrete of the previous building this one had been designed to proclaim its existence in glass. Held together on a minimalist steel framework, it had so many windows that it was possible to look up into the sky from almost any part of the building. This place would no doubt be home to a breed of lofty Pharaohs, who unlike the down-to-earth types in the single storey building were inclined to look upwards more than was good for them. Their heads would be so far into the clouds that they could only see what was above them. And their aspirations would continue to rise long after disappearing into a cloud of hot air deriving entirely from their own futility.

On the other side of the road, Ivan saw there was a much older building on which some of the roofing sheets had begun to lift. He knew instinctively that despite the attraction of the taller building with so many windows through which he could fly, this one would be more to his liking. It would be ruled over by a nervous group of Pharaohs who were forever blinking and looking over their shoulders. They would be so engaged in covering their tracks they would fail to see what was happening in front of them. But in a strange twist of fate, that would be their salvation. These were the ones who would never become inhabiters of the down-to-earth, nor head-in-the-clouds worlds of their counterparts in the newer concrete and glass buildings. Not for them the gritty determination that would ensure they never missed an opportunity. Not for them the etherial aspirations that would help them to see where they hoped to be in one-two-three-four-five years time. They were the lucky ones. Their inadequacies would ensure their survival, because they would never over-reach themselves. They had stumbled upon the means of success and would still be here next year, blinking and looking over their shoulders knowing that the real threats came always from behind.

Ivan opened his eyes, wondering why he was lying on the floor. Then remembering where he was, he hauled himself into a sitting position, reloaded the paintbrush, and resumed his painting of the skirting board. But his efforts were interrupted when the brush suddenly jumped out of his hand in response to a deafening noise coming from upstairs.

'Ah, so you have got decorators in after all?' said Bernard already on his way up the stairs. 'I'd forgotten how many of those employed in the painting and decorating industry are deaf.'

'Why restrict yourself to the painting and decorating industry?' said Henry, following Bernard up the stairs.

Owen, picked up the brush and placed it on the paint can.

Crossing the landing, Ivan opened the door to the small bedroom. Peering inside, he was relieved to find the noise had ceased. Though only to be replaced by a voice extolling the virtues of the next item to be played. More riveting, was the sight of the listener to all this noise. A decorator indeed. He had to stop himself from laughing aloud as his eyes fell on a boiler-suited figure delicately balanced on a stool, applying a coat of paint to the coving. This was no time to disturb the concentration of someone whose tongue was darting backwards and forwards like that of a basking salamander, and so he closed the door and retraced his steps to the hall, where he picked up the paintbrush and once more loaded it with paint.

'Did you see that woman in there dressed as a decorator,' said Owen? 'That was Rowena you know.'

'How could you tell?' said Henry.

'I'd know that tongue anywhere,' said Owen.

'You mean the one with which she was giving herself a bath?'

'She wasn't the only one being given a bath,' said Bernard. 'I've never seen so much paint on a boiler suit... er, why are you painting those wires?'

'Because I don't want them to become a focal point,' said Owen, giving a straight answer for once. 'I'm painting them so that the eye will be deceived into thinking they're part of the skirting board.'

'The way things are going you won't need wires on your skirting board,' said Bernard. 'Turning your back on technological breakthroughs may have been possible in the past, but now I'm afraid the game is up. The last thing we needed was for the whole thing to go digital. I don't know how many more useless channels the satellite companies will launch. And with wi-fi on a roll I expect there'll be a thousand television channels before we know where we are. In fact it's become easier to create new channels than it is to make programmes. There will soon be as many channels as there are viewers.

'But think of the choices that will give us,' said Owen.

'Just imagine, everyone having their own channel.'

'With fifteen minutes being all the time it would take to die of boredom,' said Henry.

'Am I getting lunch love... or are you?' the voice of a paint splattered figure rang down the stairs leaving Ivan in little doubt as to who was getting lunch.

'I will,' he replied.

'We need to get a move on if we're going to get there before dark.'

'Yes dear.'

'Choice did you say?' said Bernard, grabbing Owen's brush and thrusting it into a jar of cold water.

'That's the kind of choice that led to Wittgenstein becoming a gardener,' said Henry.

'Aye,' said Owen, striding off into the kitchen. 'And look at the price of cabbages now.'

51

SECURING THE FUTURE

Ivan and Rowena trudged along the path that ran around the side of the hill. The rain had stopped but the clouds remained dark and heavy, harbouring the threat of more rain, or possibly snow, thought Ivan with a shiver. Taking an optimistic view he decided a covering of snow would have its consolations, the intensity of the rain having done nothing to soften the hard compacted ground of the track now conceding little to their advancing feet.

As they gained height the chill of the wind made breathing more difficult, and the contemplation of snow led Ivan to wonder what else might be in store. The weekend had already treated them to a wide selection from nature's Spring catalogue with periods of dry and occasionally quite warm weather amongst the wet and bitterly cold weather, to say nothing of this year's piece-de-resistance in the shape of an attempt to offer them both hot and cold at the same time. There had been some really quite windy weather too, of which they currently had a good example, but there had also been some calm periods such as the couple of hours at the mere on Saturday afternoon notwithstanding the storms which had elsewhere interrupted play in the second of the one-day internationals. He found nothing surprising in any of that, for had it not been ordained that the purpose of bank holidays was to concentrate the elements? Unquestionably they'd been concentrating during this weekend. There would be a dramatic improvement tomorrow of course but that too was only to be expected.

It occurred to him it was nearly tomorrow already and that being a bank holiday this particular Monday would turn itself into Tuesday quicker than most, bringing Wednesday a little closer whilst seeming so far away as ever. Perhaps the weather was already anticipating the end of the bank holiday, the cessation of the rain having at least allowed a start to be made in the third of the one-day internationals with a better prospect of achieving a result without resorting to mathematical formula than had been the case in Saturday's interrupted game in the second of those internationals.

Rowena was a couple of strides in front of Ivan where she was taking the full force of the wind, feeling it her duty to do so, this expedition having been her idea. She pushed her hands deeper into the patch pockets which hung on the sides of her coat like great shopping bags and tried to feel more cheerful now the only evidence of the morning's rain was a few droplets hanging on the tufts of grass alongside the path. She lowered her head against a gust of wind which did its best to set free the remaining raindrops, before flying off, laughing and singing across the moor.

They stopped for a moment to check on how far they'd come but found it difficult to stand still in the buffeting wind. They were now close to the highest point on the ridge and going on again over the final rise, felt a surge of anticipation as the cottage came into view.

The location of the cottage was quite stunning and fully justifed the decision to approach on foot from the scenic side rather than driving up from the main road. Ivan had one of those moments of foresight to which his species are prone. He felt with a surety he had seldom known, that he would end his days here. Then remembering the news he might receive on Wednesday, as quickly as it had arrived the feeling had gone and he was telling himself not to be ridiculous since his days may be about to end sooner than he'd hoped. Yet the image had been a commanding one. In that moment he'd been presented with a picture of his own funeral. The incidence of funerals in his thoughts was getting worrying and yet on this occasion he had seen his coffin, his own coffin, being slowly brought out from the house. And the strange thing was he hadn't been at all disturbed by that. In fact he'd felt a sense of relief that at last he was being shown that there would be a little while yet before it all ended. There had been nothing morbid about the scene, and he hadn't been afraid. Until he'd begun to worry about why he hadn't been terrified out of his skin at the sight of men in morning suits carrying his coffin.

Rowena in the meantime had been more concerned with the question of whether the building in front of them would remain standing long enough for anyone to have much of a future in it. Never having yearned for knowledge of what the future had in store she was thankful that God had been busy elsewhere.

'Though certainly not busy on a building site anywhere near this grid reference,' she muttered, deciding that the second law of thermodynamics must have been the only thing not busy elsewhere when this place had been built since the whole building was a demonstration of entropic decay. She was afraid it might crumble before her eyes as with every stride it became obvious that the building must have predated the discovery of the load bearing properties of vertical members in structures. The cottage seemed to lean in all directions. It was difficult to believe anything had ever been vertical including the builders who were responsible for having built it, always assuming the place had been built and that the materials hadn't been left to sort themselves out with natural settlement in a kind of early tentative style of building.

Ivan also found that the nearer he came to the cottage the more his attention was drawn to the appalling condition of the place; the missing slates; the crumbling mortar; the broken gutters; the peeling paint; the crack which ran around the base of the chimney. He stopped for a moment and caught his breath in the wind, coughing as the crisp air reached parts of his lungs not normally exposed to such freshness. Delicately patting his chest, he cursed that he should have wasted what little was left of the weekend struggling up a windswept hillside to be confronted by this. Contrary to his initial reaction, a chill went through him at the prospect of spending the rest of his days here and the chill became a flood of panic when he remembered the consultant radiologist may already have advised the man in the pale blue teeshirt and matching trousers how many more days his patient could expect.

On which subject, it ocurred to him that by dwelling on the possibility of the plating plant having damaged his lungs, he'd forgotten how his life had taken him into the path of so many other people's cigarettes. Although he did have the consolation of having been brought up in a free society. He coughed again, this time more productively, watching aghast as the warm damp results issued forth to be irretrievably lost on the wind.

His eyes followed the line of the crack he'd spotted from where it began a couple of feet above ground level to where it stopped half way up the chimney. He wondered whether the crack could be filled or whether the entire gable would have to be rebuilt. Things like that would have to be checked by an engineer, as would the footings, since the way in which the property leaned gave rise to a suggestion that the foundations, assuming there were any, might be on the move. If that was to be the case then a more substantial rebuilding programme would be required, a full structural survey being the only way to reveal the extent of problems of that nature.

Rowena began compiling her own list of things needing attention, beginning with the state of the window by the front door. She pulled off a strip of paint that had lifted where the rain had seeped underneath the putty leaving it cracked and loose, meaning it would have to be redone. Providing that the frame itself didn't need replacing. It was beginning to seem like a crazy idea. It was time to admit she'd been wrong and go home.

With a step backwards to give a wider perspective, she told herself not to be put off so easily. Because apart from bringing in electricity and water, then all that would be required, give or take a little renovation here and there, would be a painting of the outside – once the inside of the cottage had been attended to with a bathroom, a kitchen and a central heating system. She supposed that would have to be oil. Or bottled gas. Or would that be another decision upon which they would be unable to agree?

Leaving Ivan to further inspect the crack on the gable, Rowena decided to take a look at the rear of the cottage hoping things might not be so bad where the structure had been sheltered from the prevailing wind.

Ivan stood there wondering if it would be possible to allow the splendour of the setting to outweigh the awful condition of the property.

'This is a nice place,' said Bernard.

'Yes… is it really for sale?' said Owen.

'I believe so,' said Bernard.

'Though not as a going concern,' said Henry.

Anticipating the work that would be required to make the place habitable, Ivan thought it was going to be a concern to whoever decided to buy it.

'There'll be a lot of painting to do here,' said Owen. 'But at least there won't be a blocked drain to excavate.'

'I don't suppose there are any drains,' said Henry. 'In which case there might be more excavation work required than you think.

'You're right,' said Owen. 'I suspect a good deal more than a sledgehammer will be needed on the rock of this hillside – a stick of gelignite might be a good start.'

'Gelignite?' said Henry. 'This place would collapse if it got a whiff of gelignite. It looks as though it might fall down if you spoke to it harshly.'

You mean like the house that Jack built?' said Owen.

I was thinking more of the house that Jerry built,' said Henry.

Ivan began to wonder whether the condition of the place might after all be sufficient to dampen Rowena's enthusiasm for the idea of acquiring a smaller property. Preparing for your old age may be a sensible thing to do, but this place could make you old before your time, no matter how much you were looking forward to the day when you no longer had to go through the routine of turning up to add another golden eightieth to your occupational pension, should you be fortunate enough to have one. But then he remembered he may not be concerned with matters of that nature for much longer. There was at least one man who may have something to say about his chances of realising any pension he might have accrued. And even if he should be told he was in the best of health, his hopes of drawing that pension could be derailed by any number of possibilities. For one thing there would be little consolation in the knowledge you were on higher ground when you became surrounded by a salt water lake created by the last of the melting icecaps. To say nothing of the escape of radiation from the flooded nuclear power stations you'd built too close to the sea. So much for securing your future. You could forget any hopes of there being much of a future. There might not be a cottage on a hill on the planet with much of a future once that happened.

52

SOMETHING TO LOOK FORWARD TO

'It's going to need a lot of work to prevent this place from falling down never mind get it ready for occupation,' said Rowena anticipating Ivan's reaction as she peeled off a another strip of paint from the window beside which they were standing.

'It is a nice place though,' said Ivan contrarily, as he turned the estate agent's key in the lock on the weather-beaten door. 'Come into the parlour,' he chuckled as he entered the stone porch that clung to the front of the property. The porch was so tiny there was hardly room for two people, and when Rowena joined him she had difficulty in closing the outer door behind her.

Ivan imagined they were in the air lock of a spaceship – or he thought perhaps a decontamination chamber would have been more to the point when he noticed that his left shoe had picked up some of the soft covering from where the sheep sought shelter from the wind on stormy nights. He stamped his feet and scraped the side of his shoe on the step before opening the inner door.

The character of the interior was no different to that of the porch, as Ivan found to his cost when his foot tripped on the edge of a badly seated slab in the stone floor sending him sprawling, arms and legs in the air. Rowena bit her lip as a resemblance to one of the upended woodlice amongst which he'd fallen occurred to her.

Ivan picked himself up, cursing the audacity of the stone slab as he tried in vain to sustain the delicate shell surrounding his mounting disquiet about what they were doing.

'We must be crazy. Absolutely crazy. Completely out of our minds.' He turned on Rowena as though she was wholly responsible. 'We have half the garden excavated trying to locate a cracked drain. We're in the middle of decorating the hall and the small bedroom, and what do we do? I'll tell you what we do?'

'I'm sure you will dear,' said Rowena.

'We come out here on a day suitable only for classic films and rugby internationals in an armchair by the fireside with tea and dark fruitcake. It's typical of us. Here we are, climbing one of the highest peaks in the western Himalayas, spending the afternoon wandering around Annapurna cottage, and with a view to what? With a view to creating yet more work – sufficient to occupy every weekend from now until the second coming.

'It looks as though this place could have been built around the time of the first coming,' said Rowena trying to decipher a hieroglyphic she'd discovered on one of the stone walls.

'More likely the middle of the ice age?' said Ivan.

'It does have character though.'

'So had Quasimodo.'

'And as you yourself said, it is a nice place.'

'Oh it's a nice place all right. It's a pity someone had to go and ruin it by putting this bloody eyesore on it.'

'I imagine there'll be a good view from up here,' said Rowena venturing onto the staircase twisting its way upwards from the corner of the room.

'I wouldn't go up there if I were you,' said Ivan. 'Put your trust in that,' he waved an arm towards the landing at the top of the staircase, 'and you might find yourself having a not quite so good view of down here. In fact you could easily end up in the cellar.'

'I didn't know there was a cellar,' Rowena's voice drifted from above as she reached the top of the stairs.

'You'd probably create one if you fell from there.'

'But it's a stone floor,' said Rowena.

'Don't remind me,' said Ivan massaging his hip as he cast his eyes around the inside of the cottage. He'd noticed there was a black-leaded fireplace and a stone sink. On looking closer he saw there was also a mysterious looking pipe coming out from the wall above the sink, which could mean that counter to his first thought there might be running water, had it not been that the only place in which water was likely to run in this cottage was through the hole in the roof.

Turning towards the fireplace his eyes fell upon a door he hadn't noticed before. Treading carefully he pushed the door and shivered as it creaked open with the seasoned expertise of one that had spent its life in a Hitchcock movie. Feeling that he too had spent most of his life in a movie, he put his hands over his ears and shook his head as though trying to rid himself of some terrible nasal congestion. When just as suddenly he let go, the release of pressure made him feel light-headed for a moment and he had to put a hand on the door to prevent himself from falling over.

He told himself not to become downhearted. This particular cottage was merely one example of the many properties on the market, and Rowena was right, they would need to lower their outgoings when they retired. Retirement at least was something to look forward to, next Wednesday permitting, because then for the first time in his life he'd be able to stand and stare at trains full of occupants on their way to line the pockets of some Joe Taskerman or other. He would need to concern himself no longer with doing what was required by someone who had no idea of what was required. He would be one of those passing his time on the embankment waving with as many or as few of his one-two-three-four-five fingers as he liked.

He must keep reminding himself retirement was something to look forward to, and that it wouldn't be the end of his life. Frightening people with that kind of nonsense was all part of how so many would-be great men and women maintained their positions. Far from being finished he would be only just beginning. Notwithstanding what he might be told on Wednesday he'd never felt better. Perhaps a whole new career would open up to him.

'Excuse me sir, we are thinking of injecting new life into the six o'clock news and we think you might be a suitable candidate.'

'I don't think so. We've been through that one and decided it's the kind of career I could do without... unless you're going to start presenting alternative perspectives in the six o'clock news?' Ivan leant into the wall beside the door, which also had peeling paint reminding him again of how much painting he'd done already.

'Oh nothing so contentious. It's just that we've become concerned that some of our viewers are left not knowing what to make of our stories, and so we're going to provide a little more background to the items.

Fearing a lot of his retirement would be spent decorating, Ivan wondered whether there would be enough paint to finish painting the hall.

'You mean you're going to start putting news items into their historical context?' He supposed it was more than likely another can of paint would be required.

'Not exactly their historical context. Our viewers would soon switch off if we did that. No, no, we're going to, how shall I put it, actually I'm not sure I should be telling you this. The point of the exercise is that no-one is meant to notice but since it seems you may be going to play a part in our plans, I don't suppose it will do any harm. We're going to introduce laughter by way of a pre-recorded soundtrack.'

'You're going to introduce canned laughter into the six o'clock news? You can't do that. What am I saying? You can do anything you f***ing well like with the six o'clock news.' It seemed that even a residual smell of the morning's paint in his nostrils was enough to make his head spin.

'Careful now, remember you have signed a confidentiality clause.'

'Oh no I haven't. And as for keeping this to myself, I'm sick of being reminded I have to stay on message if I don't want to be held up as an example of the treason being committed in our midst. As I have been trying to tell anyone who will listen, that's the trouble with pyramids. If I have to keep my mouth shut, that's not treason, that's tyranny.

53

MAKING A DIFFERENCE

For a long time he stood looking at the range on offer. He wondered how he would ever bring himself to decide. The choice was bewildering and he found himself unable to put forward a hand to touch a single one of them. There were so many colours, so many patterns, so many styles, so many fabrics (cotton rich, easy iron, cotton polyester, polyester cotton, viscose). He told himself to make his mind up and got as far as taking his hand from his pocket before returning it as his attention was drawn to a smart number with red stripes visible in the corner of his eye. That was more interesting, but what would it look like with a Paisley tie? He hadn't the faintest idea. But neither had he time to stand around all afternoon trying to imagine how it would look. Pick it up and go. That's what he must do. But he stayed exactly where he was. Outside it was threatening to rain. Half an hour ago he'd been walking along the street in the sunshine his whole body breezing towards the point where he now stood unable to move. 'Buy your own ****ing shirts,' she'd said. He couldn't be sure of the precise adjective but it hadn't sounded like anything he'd come across before and he'd been around a bit in his time. 'I will,' he'd replied without having any idea of what he was saying. And here he was. And there they were. Pink ones, blue ones, striped ones, checked ones, plain ones, green ones, grey ones, long sleeved, short sleeved, red ones, beige ones, loose fit, regular fit – no difficulty there of course, he'd always had regular fit. Hadn't he? Yellow ones, brown ones, white-collar, without-collar, single-cuffs, double-cuffs, small, medium, large, fifteen, sixteen (please ask to be measured if you are unsure of your size) grey ones, black ones, should he take one or two. He didn't know. And yet he was the one who could always decide what to do. Sorting out the information flow had been the best thing he'd ever done. Things could now be put on a better footing, with output controlled through a call-off system according to throughput requirements enabling them to programme the feed-time more accurately. He was surprised how busy the store was this afternoon. He wondered what all these people were doing. They surely couldn't all need shirts as urgently as he did himself. He drew himself up to his full height when he found himself sandwiched between a large woman on his right trying to reach the pure cotton regular fits and a long haired youth on his left contemplating a double pack. A double pack? Perhaps he should go for a double pack. He must get out of this place. But he couldn't leave empty handed, and so white, large, regular, easy iron, yes easy iron, that would do the trick, one, two, or maybe three, yes three (it's very hot in here) three it is then... three shifts, of course... then we could reduce the headcount whilst announcing an expansion... rid ourselves of complaints about pollution then... phew, fresh air at last.

'What? Here, take your hands off me. Who do you think you are? What do you mean you're a...? Who me? Do you know who I am?'

54

A LAPSE IN PROCEDURE

Realising he was again in danger of falling asleep on his feet, Ivan peered beyond the door he'd opened in the hope of finding something to distract him from concerns about the condition he was in. It was difficult to understand how anyone could be so tired. And towards the end of a long weekend too. Could it be that the tiredness was a symptom of something more serious… about which he might be told on Wednesday? And yet there couldn't be anything wrong with him. He wasn't in any pain. Who was he kidding?

He was ready to believe it might be preferable to remain where he was forever, peering through an open door into the pantry which had now been revealed, when right on cue a voice he knew only too well cut in.

'Now then what's going on here?'

'Oh dear I think we've been spotted.'

'No we're all right he hasn't noticed us. He's making one of his periodic radar sweeps, looking to see what he can pick up. We have cause to be jumpy but there is no reason to reveal ourselves… yet.' Ivan wondered how many defects in a property could be revealed in one afternoon.

'No reason to reveal yourselves?' queried the square leg umpire. 'How long are you proposing to take between innings? Ten minutes is all the time you're allowed, if you remember.'

'Sometimes I can't remember how to tie up my own shoelaces,' said a tense voice padding up at the back of the pavilion.

The woman from the television news channel looked over the top of her spectacles, but before she had time to realise, she'd been replaced by the woman in corduroy jodhpurs who was interested in asking only one question. It was an important question but unfortunately in the middle of asking it, the defendant suddenly leapt up from where he'd been sitting and threw himself upon her. The woman in corduroy jodhpurs went backwards over the chair, legs in the air, dragging the defendant with her.

To everyone's surprise the defendant turned out to be none other than Joe Taskerman, who having been unable to stop himself from taking advantage of the situation, lay clinging to the woman sobbing uncontrollably. Unconfirmed reports would later say that it took four constables and a sergeant to console him. From the left, number off, one-two-three-four…

The magistrate was determined not to let the defendant's state of mind influence her, but when she passed sentence the whole court gasped.

'Is that all?'

'Is that all? It was only a moments loss of concentration.'

'But they've set him free.'

'You didn't expect them to clap him in irons did you?'

'No, but I would have thought at the very least they'd have given him, you know, something which might have jeopardised his reputation.'

'Reputation? The only reputation he has is for being out of his depth. You couldn't expect them to hold that against him.'

One thing held to be in his favour had been the circumstantial nature of the evidence. Furthermore, the case against him had not been aided by the advice given by an intense sounding psychiatrist whom the court had consulted as to the defendant's soundness of mind.

The journalists in the press gallery were afraid they hadn't been left with much of a story, and were intent on pursuing the psychiatrist, who had fortunately by then forgotten who was supposed to be questioning whom.

'If you are er, asking me to say er, whether this is a case of er, where did I er put my notes, then I er, have to say that er there is er, nothing to suggest that the er patient, er that is, er the defendant, was aware of, er his actions, until asked to, er explain his purchase, er that is er, his neglect to purchase.'

The clerk of the court was unsure why further evidence was being taken in a case in which sentence had already been passed, and enquired whether the reporters were questioning the verdict of the court.

'No, but we are,' cried a chorus from the public gallery.

'Silence in court,' proclaimed the magistrate jumping up with a start afraid she may have fallen asleep.

A voice in the crowd coming out of the court still couldn't believe he'd managed to get away with it. A fine would have been better than nothing but they hadn't even given him that. This prompted someone to enquire as to whether he might have known the magistrate or something.

'Or something,' thought Ivan… unsure what a magistrate was doing falling asleep in a pantry.

'Where the hell did you come from?' said Bernard leaping in the air at the sight of Owen emerging from behind the door.

'Good evening sir,' said Owen, ostentatiously placing a white handkerchief over his arm. 'Would you like red or white this evening?'

'White I should think judging by the colour of his face,' said Henry, appearing from behind Owen.

'For Goodness sake stop it the pair of you,' said Bernard. 'This place gives me the creeps.'

'Really?' said Henry. 'But you were the one who said it was a nice place.'

'I was referring to its location. Just look at that view, said Bernard, waving an arm towards the window. 'We ought to get someone to paint it.'

'Paint it?' Owen looked at Bernard in dismay. 'Did you say paint it?'

Ivan prodded the estate agent's key into a hole in the edge of the door causing consternation to the hindquarters of a snoozing woodworm.

'If you ask me this place needs a good deal more than paint,' said Owen.

'You know that isn't what I meant. I was talking about someone committing it to canvas,' said Bernard.

'Oh you mean paint it?' said Henry. 'It's no use telling him. He can't paint.

'I seldom do anything else,' said Owen.

274

'I wasn't thinking of asking Owen to paint it,' said Bernard.

'That's a relief,' said Owen.

'What I had in mind was an established landscape painter, someone who might enjoy capturing the spirit of the place.

'Spirit of the place? You think the place might be haunted?' said Owen, looking cautiously over his shoulder.

'I can picture it now,' said Bernard. 'A vista of moorland landscape, with the cottage as a focal point conveying an essential feeling of...'

'Heath Robinson?' said Henry.

'Heath who?' said Owen.

'Heathcliffe?' ventured Henry alternatively.

'You're right,' laughed Owen. 'This place does have a feeling of Wuthering Heights about it.'

'This is a long way from being a place of historical fiction,' said Bernard.

'I wouldn't be too sure of that,' said Henry, noticing that the crack on the outside of the cottage was also visible on the inside. 'It looks as though Emily Bronte may still have a presence here.'

'I thought Emily Bronte was dead,' said Owen.

'Emily Bronte will never die... which I suspect is more than you can say for this place,' said Henry as a piece of masonry dislodged itself from the ceiling and fell, narrowly missing Bernard.

55

THE BEAST IN THE BUSHES

By the end of the afternoon Ivan and Rowena's dream of a cottage in the country had become thoroughly tarnished, although they had not admitted that to one another. For the moment they were happy to concentrate on getting the circulation back into their veins knowing they were a little clearer about the difficulties they were facing, such that neither of them need feel the afternoon had been entirely wasted.

They had decided to cheer themselves up with a meal in the country hotel by the lake which they'd noticed on the way up to the cottage. The menu in the a la carte restaurant had looked promising and they'd ordered with much anticipation. The first course had arrived in surprisingly quick time, an occurrence that would have given rise to a multitude of questions concerning its origins had Ivan not by then become engrossed in a review of the afternoon's work.

'We could do with some estimates,' said Rowena loading a portion of Provencal pate onto a piece of toast and placing it on the front of her tongue.

'You think it's worth considering then?' Ivan picked up the empty butter plate wondering how anyone could imagine that four pats of butter were enough for two people. He looked around as though expecting butter to materialise from the atmosphere, an eventuality not out of the question given the humidity of the place, much of which derived from the location of the restaurant on a balcony overlooking the swimming pool. In principle this may have been an excellent idea but in practice the arrangement had created a reverse, not to say perverse, ventilation effect, resulting in the restaurant being too hot and the pool being too cold.

'That rather depends on what it's going to cost to renovate,' said Rowena.

'True, but we ought to be sure it's the kind of thing we're looking for before asking people to go up there and run tape measures over it.' Ivan abandoned his pursuit of more butter and concentrated on the wine.

'On the other hand,' said Rowena. 'We can't afford to delay too long or we might lose the opportunity.'

'I can't imagine that being much of a problem,' said Ivan, balancing the butter plate on the neck of the now empty wine bottle in the hope of attracting someone's attention. 'There can't be many people who would contemplate taking on a place like that. It would have to be someone with so much money it was of no consequence how much they spent. In which case it wouldn't matter how quickly we made up our minds because they would outbid us whatever we offered.'

'I was thinking,' said Rowena. 'If it needs someone with a lot of money then why are we considering it?'

'Are we considering it?'

They continued to consider it nevertheless, albeit in a way that had he been more sober and less exhausted, Ivan would have been loath to acknowledge it had a striking resemblance to Joe Taskerman's propensity for seeking evidence in support of what had already been decided.

Fortunately he came to his senses, and through the haze of hunger and alcohol seriously began to question the principle of what they were trying to do. Could it be they were falling for the simplest trick in the book and about to become victims of the biggest property hoax in the western world? Of course they were. Wasn't that the means by which the beast in the bushes got its breakfast? Gulp, another couple of dreamers walking into a trap with their eyes closed. Gulp gulp, another pair of brain-dead optimists trying to get themselves into a better position. When would these people realise that progress was an illusion? When it was far too late no doubt because it wasn't until you'd committed yourself to getting out of the rut you were in that you realised you were digging yourself in deeper.

Ivan had long thought the idea of winning was a dubious concept. Keeping one step ahead of the competition may be possible on an uninhabited island, but on this particular island you could only do that if there were eight days in a week. Once you'd realised there were eight days in a week you would at least have a chance of surviving in a world run by people whose one interest in life was in parading the gold stripes on their ambitions, and yes, it was indeed the poor old eighth day of the week he was thinking of using now because that might be a way out. He could work eight days per week as easily as anyone with the possible exception of those who hadn't realised they were doing so already. But why would anyone want to spend eight days per week striving to get themselves into a position where they would have to… well in the interim, pay for the privilege of owning two houses. Both of which he recalled with a shudder would be mortgaged. In which case their hope of realising some of their capital by disposing of their present house would have put them at the mercy of the housing market, making them about as superior as a fairy on a Christmas tree, because when it came down to it hope might be the only thing they would have left.

His optimism having deserted him for a moment, Ivan began to think he might be fighting a losing battle, not least with himself. He wondered what else he could do. He was unlikely to ever convince himself he and Rowena were forging ahead when nothing was more certain than that one day life would find a way of catching up with them. Even if it meant introducing conscription for old age pensioners, the thought of which brought a smile to his face.

He told himself not to be loose with his tongue. He was in danger of giving them ideas. Even the most ridiculous of suggestions had a history of becoming government policy. Imagine the years of experience in an army of pensioners in spite of a good number of them having realised it would be in their own interests to deny most of what their experience had taught them. Just think how expendable they would be. There would be no need to worry about casualties in that army. Most of them would be casualties before anyone got around to issuing them with uniforms.

'Stand in line there you orrible old… d-don't know what a line is sir, I'll show you what a line is sir. By the left, number off, one-two-three… at the double, up two three down two three… you there, what the devil do you think you're doing?'

For an awful moment Ivan thought he was the one the sergeant major was glaring at.

'Who sir, me sir, you want me to tell you what I'm doing… how the hell should I know? You don't want me to tell you anything of the sort? You have been trained as well as I have to know that such questions are best avoided. I have no idea what I'm doing.'

The empty butter plate balanced on the neck of the wine bottle had still not attracted the attention of a waiter.

'Hey watch your elbows Grandma (no discrimination in the pensioners' army). You're not in the playground now,' cried a voice reminding everyone that being careful with your elbows was essential when you became a member of the pensioners' army, there being rarely enough elbow room in that kind of line. You could piss and fart as much as you liked so long as you didn't flail your elbows, because standing right next to you was another paid-up member of the pensioners' army looking only for their rightful dues.

'Rightful dues?' said the sergeant major. 'I'll tell you what rightful dues you have. You have a right to stand in line, and that's all you have. Up-two-three down-two-three. Looking for a good standard of living in your retirement? Think you've earned it? A word in your shell-like crinkly my friend. All that you've earned is the right to receive what we can afford to give you. Where do you think we'd be if we paid everyone what they thought they were worth… squad-squad-squad, squad will move to the right in threes.'

Ivan looked out of the window across the surface of the water to the fells on the opposite side of the lake from where the crags reached upwards into the darkening sky. The dramatic scenery had an uplifting effect on him, though to his consternation the uplifting occurred in more ways than one as the impact of the wine on the Provencal pate, to say nothing of the prior intake of whisky, caused an embarrassing eruption.

He was horrified that he should be the victim of such a fate and tried to make himself invisible by sinking into his seat. He sank rather too quickly however, and the back of his head hit the top of the chair making him jump up sharply so that he banged his knees against the table causing the butter plate to fly off the neck of the wine bottle. He tried to catch the newly launched missile but was too late. It had already come to rest in that area of no-mans land inhabited by shark finned waiters intent upon bringing any trespasser to heel before so much as leaving their chairs. He decided it would be reckless to attempt to retrieve the marooned plate. It would be much safer to pretend to be somewhere else and so with a sweep of his eyes he soared across the lake and took up a position on the summit of the tallest crag. But then he remembered his vertigo and hurriedly relocated to the foot of the fells at the edge of the lake. Which seemed to help until he realised he was pouring wine up his nose and that his glass was now empty too.

He returned his eyes to the dining room, and to the plate still lying where it had fallen, but in trying to reach out and return the plate he succeeded only in engendering nausea. He wondered whether there might be more to fear than he'd thought from the man in the pale blue tee shirt and matching trousers since the slightest thing seemed to make him feel sick nowadays. Well he would soon know because Wednesday was now only two days away. Only two days. He preferred it when it was almost a week away. He swallowed hard in an effort to prevent things from getting out of hand, but his throat felt constricted and so he tried to distract himself by concentrating upon the precise point at which his centre of gravity lay. This proved to be beyond him too for there seemed to be a large weight located on the top of his head where it ought not to have been.

He was sweating profusely and put his mind to the simple task of trying to sit still in his chair. But his eyes were drawn back to the plate and he had to force them to look elsewhere on this occasion getting no further than the panes of the window. One-two-three-four-five, he counted the panes. One-two-three-four-five, he compared that with his fingers. Thankfully the architect had been numerate. One-two-three-four-five, he counted the panes again. Then he counted the mullions between the panes which were perfectly aligned except there were only four because five panes required only four mullions, not counting the sides. That was the real world for you, least help when you most needed it, and so he began counting tables instead, one-two-three-four, four, four… typical, the dining room was full of tables but there were only four tables in view and he dare not turn around. Only four, four, four, y-e-s, plate-five. He heaved a sigh of relief at the resolution as his eyes were again drawn to the butter plate still lying where it had fallen. He looked to Rowena for inspiration.

'Leave it,' she said with a shrug, conveying little understanding of the weight of responsibility that lay on the shoulders of an inveterate butter plate thrower.

He decided that the cultivation of an air of innocence was his only hope.

'Leave what? Which butter plate is that my dear? You'd like a little more butter would you? Perhaps we should go to a restaurant with waiter service.'

He ventured to steal a glance at the sea of faces staring at him from behind and to his surprise found he was not the centre of attention. All eyes were not directed towards him. They were focused upon the far corner of the dining room where in front of the doors which led to the kitchens he was just in time to observe the final stages of an act in which a waiter carrying four rib-eye steaks and a sherry trifle had attempted a forward somersault with two reverse turns and a backward flip, counting only those which Ivan had seen. It was impressive stuff and had it not been for the vertical entry onto the carpet no-one would have known the performance had gone terribly wrong. Ivan was relieved to see the butter plate had not been responsible so that he too could enjoy the spectacle and play his part in the ensuing hysteria which continued long after the initial impact had subsided.

In the aftermath of this debacle, Ivan and Rowena's main courses arrived and the butter plate was finally flicked away by a waiter with the nonchalance of a soccer player conceding a corner. Rowena divided up the accompanying vegetables and began removing them from her plate with the speed of a starving gannet. She devoured the meal almost without tasting it as she furiously planned the renovation of the cottage; a door here; a window there; a kitchen here; a bathroom there; a new internal wall would be required, but think of the cost. Back to the drawing board. Forget the wall, the living area could double as a kitchen and we could put the sink in the corner and the cooker there.

Ivan too had become engrossed in a new design for the layout of the cottage. His own plans were only marginally more restrained than Rowena's, although he became considerably more depressed when he also ran over in his mind the work outstanding in their present house; continue excavating the drain; repair the damage; replace the concrete; fill in the hole; reinstate the ground; cover with tarmac; complete the decorating in the hall and the small bedroom; lay the new floor in the kitchen; board up the chimney in the lounge; a thousand and one things to do in the garden; oh and not forgetting snooker. There would have to be allowances made for the odd game of snooker. He would be lucky if he ever got another game of snooker in his life.

'Coffee will be served in the lounge sir,' the waiter announced as he saw Ivan sprinkle a spoonful of sugar over his remaining peas.

Ivan wondered why the waiter wasn't offering them a pudding. 'Hey I say, yes you, oh forget it, I've probably eaten too much already. Coffee in the lounge? That's right, keep the punters moving.'

Ivan decided there was a more pressing matter to attend to before coffee, and leaving the restaurant, went down the stairs and along the walkway beside the pool towards the place Henry had been heard to refer to as that of which we cannot speak. The pool was deserted at this time of night and so he swung away through the reception area towards the door displaying a caricature of a bear in trousers, thinking of Owen's oft added, wherein we cannot remain silent.

Emerging from the tiled emporium Ivan looked confused as he searched for a sign that would indicate the direction of the lounge.

'That's a relief,' sighed Owen, 'I was ready for that.'

'For God's sake don't answer him,' said Bernard.

'I didn't know he'd asked a question,' said Henry.

'There doesn't need to have been a question for some damn fool to provide an answer,' said Bernard, seemingly oblivious to his own part in such affairs. 'It matters not whether anybody knows what the question was – here is the answer. The world is awash with answers to questions that haven't been asked.'

'What's he complaining about now?' said Owen.

'Why are you asking me?' said Henry.

'And that's another thing,' said Bernard. 'Why do we always ask someone else to answer our questions? Why do we find it so difficult to direct our enquiries to the person concerned?'

'My question was rhetorical,' said Henry, 'since I knew full well why he was asking me what you were talking about.'

'Whereas my question was redundant,' said Owen, 'because I already knew he wouldn't have the faintest idea of what you were talking about.'

Again Ivan tried to remember when he'd last enjoyed a little time to himself. He sometimes felt the only occasions on which he could find any peace and quiet were those involving physical danger. None of the characters who were sharing much more than his car would be of any use to him in the kind of fracas you feared might be awaiting you in a dark street at night. They could be a million miles away for all the good they would be to him then.

'Look out.'

'****Arrgh.'

'Did you see that?'

'Oooph.'

'See what?'

56

A POCKETFUL OF STARDUST

Ivan found Rowena in the lounge, where having annexed two of the largest armchairs in the room, they sprawled, watching their coffee go cold in stupefied silence.

Raising himself in the chair so as to relieve the pressure on his back, Ivan looked at Rowena with a renewed appreciation of the strength of their union. He knew that having such unquestioned love and support had enabled him to survive some of the worst excesses of a world in which reducing the margins by which you had failed to achieve unrealistic targets was held to be a measure of progress. But his thoughts were interrupted, as a group of American tourists came into the room.

'I laughed so much at you guys I gave myself a Goddam indi-go-gestion,' a voice from the mid-west explained to one of his fellow travellers.

'Yeah, yeah. I cain't ever remember having had trifle served with ma' steak 'afore,' drawled a voice from somewhat to the south of that.'

'Heh heh. Ha ha,' cackled a chorus of tourists.

The group shuffled around each other like travellers indeed from another world not knowing what to do or where to go next, having become so used to standing around in hotel lobbies and airport departure halls they were unable to move without further instruction. The entrance to the lounge was becoming congested and Ivan considered taking on armchair traffic duties but thought better of it.

'Well now, where do we go tomorrow?' said a Boston lady in a silk blouse, unamused at the banter prompted by the unexpected cabaret in the dining room.

'You've only just got here,' said Ivan not quite to himself.

'Chicken and ice cream on the sidewalk?' suggested the southern voice.

'Heh heh. Ha ha,' the chorus echoed.

The Boston lady in the silk blouse looked down her nose and turned her back upon the proceedings. Noticing the Boston lady's disapproval, an urbane New Yorker in an aubergine jumpsuit, cut in.

'Tomorrow? Why tomorrow lady, tomorrow we go all the way to bonny Scotland.'

'I wonder what Scotland has done to deserve that?' muttered Ivan.

There were exclamations of approval from the chorus and given this encouragement the southern drawl again took up the story.

'We stop for lunch at a place just over the state line, where we can see all o' that purrty tartan cloth. Yes sir, that purrty purrty cloth, made into those son-of-a-gun skirts that're so fine even their men folks wear 'em.'

Ivan forced his hands to retain their grip on the arms of the chair.

'That's ma' boy,' cried a woman in checkerboard trousers.

'If that ain't so?' whistled her partner in a lurid green dress.

'And then...' The speaker with the southern drawl was distracted from his role of assumed courier as four young women came into the lounge talking animatedly. 'And then... why hello there school teachers of America,' he greeted the four women. 'Ta-ra, ra-ra-ra, ra-ra-ra.' The patriotic anthem rang out across the room as the voice of the south stood to attention and conducted an imaginary orchestra. The teachers laughed politely and hurried past him to the far end of the lounge.

'We're going to Scotland tomorrow,' said the aubergine jump suit.

'Why wait until tomorrow,' said Ivan.

'So are we,' one of the teachers replied over her shoulder.

'Yeah,' sang out the woman in the checkerboard trousers.

'Sure thing,' said her partner in the lurid green dress.

To everyone's relief the crowd in the doorway began to disperse, leaving just a drone from the four teachers at the end of the lounge. Ivan closed his eyes and as his head sank onto his chest the murmuring of the teachers gradually faded.

He was aware of a rumbling noise outside the hotel and getting up to investigate saw that an enormous truck had been driven onto the forecourt. The trailer attached to the cab seemed to possess more wheels than he could count, although he did try... one-two-three, but decided to forget it when he saw the reason for all the wheels. The trailer was transporting a huge metal structure the size of which he would have thought impossible had he not been familiar with methods of slowing down traffic on motorways. Meanwhile a team of men were feeding pipes along the roadway and into the lake at various points. As soon as the pipes had been laid they began to bolt them to the underside of the metal structure, following which one of the men held his hand in the air and with a screech and a roar the machine burst into life.

The noise was unbearable and Ivan put his hands over his ears staring in disbelief when he saw that the effect of all this activity had caused a lowering in the level of the lake. No sooner had this been accomplished than a further team arrived and began planting trees in ground which only a few moments before had been submerged. The lake was now much smaller and the scene was further transformed when a fleet of excavators moved in and began to demolish the crags on the other side of the lake.

Turning from the window, Ivan saw there was a good deal of activity going on inside the hotel too. The place seemed to be brimming with painters and decorators. His first thought was this must be their annual convention, but that was an unlikely explanation because upon arrival each one of them stripped off and got straight down to work. They were followed by upholsterers, carpet layers, and furniture removers, and they too began to work with a precision which could only have been achieved by familiarity with a detailed plan, the enactment of which continued throughout the night such that when breakfast arrived another day of the Grand Tour could begin in a new location with the minimum of inconvenience to the travellers.

'Come on,' said Rowena shaking Ivan awake.

'Huh?'

'Let's go.'

'Oh yes let's,' mumbled Ivan, not knowing where he was but happy it was time to be somewhere else. He pulled himself from the chair and set off across the lounge in pursuit of Rowena, unsure of why the question of whether or not Joe Taskerman had a dog was still troubling him.

'I'm beginning to wonder whether I ought to have told the story myself. The trouble is I'm not... well you know what I'm not. She's seen to that. I thought I'd found someone I could trust. My own omniscient narrator. And what happens? She starts inventing things. Things that didn't happen. Why would she do that? What did she imagine gave her the right to ignore so much of what I'd told her? I know we agreed to change names and allow an element of poetic license but now I'm not sure whose story this is. Joe Taskerman's? I don't think so. It isn't the story of anybody I know. She says that's the nature of storytelling. Illustrative but unreliable. Well if this is an example, I can tell you that's one thing she's said that is true. Storytelling is indeed unreliable. Narratives are not always persuasive... and especially not to those with first hand knowledge of events drawn upon. For one thing I'm still not sure whether Joe Taskerman has a dog and I guess neither is she, but... oh look out here comes Rowena again.'

'There's an extraordinary amount of traffic about. Makes you wonder where they're all going,' said Rowena pulling out onto the main road.

Ivan saw she was struggling to maintain forward vision against the approaching headlights. He resolved to take his turn with the driving more often and as his head spun he consoled himself with the thought that it would be a relief from trying to do most of the drinking for them both.

He closed his eyes but the oncoming headlights continued to flicker across his face like a set of dancing figures on a screen. And what a set of dancing figures on a screen. A projection of his times unfurled. That was the weekend that was. The time had gone so quickly and yet so slowly that it might have been a few seconds or a whole lifetime. Well at least it had been a carbon free weekend, although perhaps not entirely since he'd been breathing all weekend sometimes heavily, and that meant a lot of carbon dioxide had been produced. He wondered whether that was a contribution he would have to off-set. It would probably depend on who was telling the story.

A voice within told him that the weekend hadn't quite ended because the remaining minutes of the day were still part of the weekend. Were it not for knowing that every week which followed a weekend started as soon as you began to think about it, and he acknowledged he'd begun to think about it. The odd conjecture had begun to occur. It was pointless to deny that. It was almost tomorrow already. Let the voice of Joe Taskerman rain down upon their ears once more.

He wondered how a belief in the sovereignty of weekends had been sustained when everyone who'd had to work for a living knew that work often invaded leisure time and thoughts of being somewhere else frequently occupied the hours of work. Had that not been so, then how would he have survived when things had become more or less intolerable? Being able to think of holidays with Rowena had enabled him to get through some of the toughest times he'd known. Without similar recourses to the more important things in life, how would anyone survive?

He supposed that by any standards it must have been a good weekend for there to have been at least a few moments when the existence of Joe Taskerman had completely slipped his mind. Only for him to put in an appearance in an unlikely situation before being removed for ever, the would-be great man being no longer so great. Except his demise had occurred in a dream, and being a dream, then what a waste of time the weekend had been. He might as well have gone to South East Asia. He might as well have gone to the moon. Although on second thoughts maybe not, because with his luck he'd probably have bumped into Joe Taskerman, dead or alive, looking for another pocketful of stardust to add to his collection of unlikely possibilities.

As the car sped homewards towards the hundred and one jobs awaiting his attention, it occurred to Ivan there would be those who would say that by concentrating upon survival rather than striving to improve his relationship with Joe Taskerman he'd been complicit in his own mistreatment. He could only think that such people had never felt (or noticed) the hand of conditioning on their shoulders. Never experienced (or recognised) the pains of exclusion. Never understood (or accepted) that escape was an illusion. Never realised it was the charge of victim complicity that had enabled the would-be great men and women to thrive.

He decided these conjectures and refutations would have to wait for another day. For now it would be better to congratulate himself on those moments when he had all but forgotten about Joe Taskerman. The one question remaining on that subject being whether the man who believed he was better than Don Bradman or Vivian Richards would survive the imminent report of a team who had initially been mistaken for auditors. Well there was something to keep them all interested for another ten minutes in the morning, or maybe fifteen for those holding on to a folorn hope that beyond the forthcoming report a whole world of Joe Taskerman's would be exposed.

As for those who'd spent most of their lives in the plating shop, a radiographer may already have decided how many of them were about to be exposed in ways they would rather not anticipate. Ivan tried to tell himself there was nothing new in that. He himself had been dogged for years by a nagging voice telling him that his suffering would soon be over, enabling him to start the process of redemption.

'Redemption? We were under the impression you didn't believe in an after life,' said an evangelist to whom he'd regretted having opened a door so many years ago.

And with a flash of headlights on the windscreen another door opened upon the question of what he'd been doing for the last few days. Perhaps it had after all been a great weekend. The myth of great men and women had been defused, if only in his head. And now even the evangelist too could be put in his place, for in retrospect you could always come up with a better reply than the one you'd thought of at the time.

'I can't imagine there being an after life worth a second

thought if it required a belief in its existence for it to survive,' he said aloud causing Rowena to momentarily take her eyes from the road. The insight may have startled Rowena but it was wasted on the evangelist, whose life's work was being subjected to a raised finger from an altogether different square leg umpire having adjudged that he'd been well out of his ground.

'Which after life is that?' said Rowena. 'I seem to recall you saying you hadn't even been baptised. You're not trying to claim falling in the river was a case of total immersion qualifying you for one of those Christian fundamentalist groups, are you?'

'God forbid,' said Ivan.

'Oh please. We've always known you were an anal retentive, but you could at least spare us the blasphemy,' muttered the evangelist before passing through the pavilion gates.

'There is nothing blasphemous in what I have to say,' Ivan smiled knowingly. 'It's neither your God nor any one else's God I'm talking about. You should have realised by now that in an effort to protect ourselves from the delusions of would-be great men and women, a worrying number of whom seem to think they are God, some of us on this side of the fence have also learned to speak with our tongues in our cheeks. We have in our time distorted as much communication as anyone. You can be assured that we too often mean precisely the opposite of what we say, such that when we tell you to keep your head up you should understand it's keeping your head down that will ensure your survival, even if that does cause us to engage in a little obfuscation.'

Rowena pulled the car onto the drive and Ivan slipped out to open the garage door. The cold air struck him and he told himself it would be more than a little chilly returning to Annapurna cottage at this time of night. What a terrible state the place had been in, and yet...

Later, congratulating himself on having remembered his phone would need charging, he stood in front of the bathroom mirror trying to imagine living on a hillside in the middle of nowhere. He decided he'd be better occupied in trying to decide whether or not to shave in order to save time in the morning. With a yawn he came to the conclusion that the only thing you could do with this hour of the day was to call it a day. Before a glance at his watch confirmed it was now time to call it another day. He coughed roughly at the thought of what lay in wait for him and of how little chance there was of preventing Wednesday from following Tuesday.

And so it had all come down to this. For the first time in his life he might have to admit he was afraid. He looked into the mirror and saw that the pair of eyes peering at him were almost closed.

'Of course I'm afraid. I'm bloody terrified,' he exclaimed.

'Who are you talking to love?' Rowena's voice drifted through from the bedroom.

'Anyone who's listening,' said Ivan as his chin fell onto his chest where it stayed for what seemed like a whole weekend before he suddenly raised his head, blew a raspberry at the face in the mirror, switched off the light, and crossed the landing to the bedroom.

'I was talking to someone who there will never be enough time for either you or I to ever really get to know,' he said stepping out of his trousers, thankful to be sure of something at last.